PRAISE FOR

“A grippi
from the … aut, liter-
ate prose … ne in the
far reache … Be aware
that, in th … hould be
trusted.” —Margaret Coel, author of *Blood Memory*

“Like the best of all crime fiction, *The Shadow Walker* is as much about the place (Mongolia) as the plot, which makes it an exceptional read . . . In the land of Genghis Khan we’re introduced to a fascinating new protagonist named Nergui . . . An exotic mystery by a writer to watch.”

—C. J. Box, author of *Blue Heaven* and *Blood Trail*

“Nail-biting . . . It’s a complex book, but compulsive reading, and the descriptions of Mongolia are richly enjoyable. I look forward to another bloodthirsty visit with Nergui as my guide.”

—*The Independent* (London)

“A sense of place has always been an important ingredient in crime fiction, with the descent into a different culture, time, or environment key to establishing foreboding or atmosphere. This debut . . . chooses its locale well, a previously uncharted crime destination: Mongolia. Walters ably brings his uncommon setting to teeming life. A worthy new series in the making.” —*The Guardian* (UK)

“An intriguing police procedural, with a formidable sleuth . . . It’s Nergui who is firmly in charge, assisted by his young protégé, Doripalam, as they slowly unravel a complex mystery. It’s a promising debut.” —*The Sunday Telegraph* (London)

continued . . .

"Walters's debut novel is a real page-turner, fast paced and masterfully written. If *The Shadow Walker* is a preview of what Walters is capable of, I look forward to his next book. The character, Inspector Nergui, is refreshingly unique and complex. Walters manages to plot a story that will keep the reader guessing till the end with a beautiful climax. I can't wait to see what he does next."

—*Crimespree Magazine*

"*The Shadow Walker* has a discerning sense of place and Walters has used this to great extent; he has brought this rather unusual location to teeming life with all its secrets. From the Mongolian capital, Ulan Baatar, to the vast Gobi Desert, the reader certainly gets a feel for the area. As a debut novel, this is no slouch. Edgy, tense, and a dark twisty tale, this is an impressive first novel. Walters shows why places like Mongolia are still suffering from their past and finding it hard to cope with their future as well. A highly entertaining police procedural that is certain to gain its own following."

—*Shots*

"Walters has produced a crime debut that evokes modern Mongolia with vividness and flair—from the steaming vents of Ulan Baatar to surreal tourist resorts in the Gobi Desert . . . A robust and entertaining first novel."

—*The Age* (Melbourne)

"A very well-written first novel with a most unusual location . . . Well worth reading, especially for its insights into an almost unknown country."

—*Tangled Web UK*

Titles by Michael Walters

THE SHADOW WALKER

THE ADVERSARY

THE ADVERSARY

MICHAEL WALTERS

BERKLEY PRIME CRIME, NEW YORK

THE BERKLEY PUBLISHING GROUP
Published by the Penguin Group
Penguin Group (USA) Inc.
375 Hudson Street, New York, New York 10014, USA
Penguin Group (Canada), 90 Eglinton Avenue East, Suite 700, Toronto, Ontario M4P 2Y3, Canada
(a division of Pearson Penguin Canada Inc.)
Penguin Books Ltd., 80 Strand, London WC2R 0RL, England
Penguin Group Ireland, 25 St. Stephen's Green, Dublin 2, Ireland (a division of Penguin Books Ltd.)
Penguin Group (Australia), 250 Camberwell Road, Camberwell, Victoria 3124, Australia
(a division of Pearson Australia Group Pty. Ltd.)
Penguin Books India Pvt. Ltd., 11 Community Centre, Panchsheel Park, New Delhi—110 017, India
Penguin Group (NZ), 67 Apollo Drive, Rosedale, North Shore 0632, New Zealand
(a division of Pearson New Zealand Ltd.)
Penguin Books (South Africa) (Pty.) Ltd., 24 Sturdee Avenue, Rosebank, Johannesburg 2196,
South Africa

Penguin Books Ltd., Registered Offices: 80 Strand, London WC2R 0RL, England

Cover illustration by Richard Tuschman.
Cover design by Rita Frangie.
Interior text design by Kristin del Rosario.

PRINTING HISTORY
Quercus hardcover edition / November 2007
Quercus mass-market edition / March 2008
Berkley Prime Crime trade paperback edition / March 2009

Library of Congress Cataloging-in-Publication Data

Walters, Mike, 1960–
The adversary / Michael Walters.—Berkley Prime Crime trade pbk. ed.
p. cm.
ISBN 978-0-425-22596-7 (trade pbk.)
1. Organized crime—Mongolia—Fiction. 2. Police—Mongolia—Fiction. 3. Missing persons—Investigation—Fiction. 4. Nomads—Mongolia—Fiction. 5. Mongolia—Fiction. I. Title.

PR6123.A474A63 2009
823'.92—dc22 2008063200

PRINTED IN THE UNITED STATES OF AMERICA

10 9 8 7 6 5 4 3 2 1

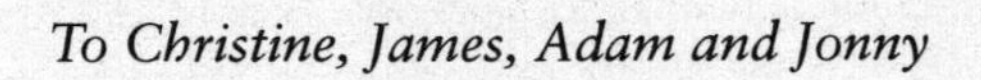

To Christine, James, Adam and Jonny

They are out on the steppe, miles from home. Miles from anywhere.

It is late afternoon, early spring. The immense sky is clear, just a few wisps of cloud against the rich blue. Everything—even the snow tipped mountains that surround them—is dwarfed by comparison.

The sun is already low, and the mountains are casting vast shadows across the green plain. Behind them, the distant hazy sprawl of the city is still drenched in bright sunlight, windows and towers blinking as they speed towards their destination.

He has been told to keep his head down. But it is difficult not to look around. He has never been this far from the city, never seen such openness, such unfilled space. He has lived on the steppe and the mountains were the boundaries of his world, but he had no idea that, after driving for mile after mile, they would still remain so distant and unreachable.

He looks back at the endless strip of dirt road behind, gazing through the wake of dust at the old car that follows their gleaming truck.

He looks forward along the same road, wondering how far it will be before they reach their goal. And he looks out as they pass an occasional camp, grazing goats and cattle, old men on horseback who watch their passing without evident interest.

There are four of them in the Jeep. He sits in the rear with the boss. The boss's eyes are closed as though he is sleeping, but he suspects the boss is awake, listening to the aimless conversation of the two in the front. He has never seen the boss sleeping, though clearly he must. He finds himself nodding from the motion of the truck but tries to keep awake by guessing how far they have to go.

On their return, there will be five of them in the truck, so it will be more crowded. He imagines the boss will sit in the front then.

At some point he falls asleep. When he opens his eyes, the sun has almost set and the truck is slowing. It seems they have reached their destination, though when he looks out of the window this place looks no different from the endless miles of empty grassland they have already passed.

The truck pulls to a halt, and the boss instantly opens his eyes. The driver twists in his seat to look back at him. The boss says nothing but nods faintly. This is the place.

Behind them, the car draws to a stop. The boss opens his door, and they all climb out and stand around the truck, as the car driver manoeuvres his vehicle around them. He stops, finally, thirty or forty metres away. They watch as the driver climbs out, opens the rear door and pulls out two metal petrol cans.

The sun has nearly set now, just a brilliant red sliver visible over the mountains. The mountaintops and the western sky glow crimson, and the remaining sky is a deep mauve, the first stars beginning to emerge.

In the far distance, the city is a tiny bundle of smoky light. But otherwise, the steppe seems deserted.

In the dim light, they watch in silence as the car driver systematically pours petrol across the roof of the old car. The rear door is still open, and he leans inside to pour more of the liquid across the rear seat. When both cans are empty, he throws them back inside the car. Then, as if making a final adjustment, he unscrews the cap of the car's petrol tank.

He pauses and looks across at the boss who gives his usual almost imperceptible nod. It is not clear whether it will be visible to the car driver in the twilight, but it seems that he has received the signal. He begins slowly to walk backwards away from the car, watching where the spreading pool of petrol has begun to seep across the grass. He pauses and pulls something from his pocket. He makes a sharp movement with his hand, and then he tosses a glowing object on to the damp ground at his feet.

He pauses, momentarily, to ensure that the discarded match has ignited the petrol. Then he begins to walk, much more rapidly, to where the rest of them are standing.

He nods to the boss with a faint smile, and then they all turn to look back at the car. It is almost dark, the clear sky laden with stars, and the spreading wall of flame is dazzling in the gloom. They watch as it sweeps unstoppably across the body of the car.

Without a word, the boss turns and climbs into the passenger seat of the Jeep. The rest follow, three of them squeezing into the rear seat, and then they pull away, turning back on to the road towards the city.

The young man looks back through the rear window. The car is burning, a meaningless beacon on the vast empty plain. He watches as it diminishes behind them. The glare expands briefly as the petrol tank ignites and the car explodes. And then it is disappearing once more, soon little more than a tiny earthbound echo of the star-filled night.

And, as the Jeep pounds back along the dirt track towards the city, he is still unsure whether it was only his imagination, or whether he really could hear, in those moments before the fire caught hold, the pounding of fists and the crying of a panic-filled voice from inside the spreading wall of flame.

ONE

The court room faced east, its large windows looking out across the city and the blank expanse of Sukh Bataar Square. At mid morning, early in the year, the low sun streamed across the pale wooden benches, silhouetting the figures of the room's few inhabitants.

Judge Radnaa leaned forward, momentarily dazzled by the sunlight, blinking impatiently. "So you are saying we cannot proceed?" she said. She could barely make out the features of the man facing her, could not read his expression.

"It is complicated," he said. "We need more time."

Judge Radnaa looked across at the panel lined up on the bench beside her. Two other, less experienced judges, and three citizens' representatives. The maximum possible representation, reflecting the seriousness of this case. Behind them—as if to remind them of the gravity of their responsibilities—the courtroom wall was adorned with the striking red and yellow geometries of the national flag.

"We have already been sitting for two weeks," she said. "And, before that, we spent a long time in preparation. You assured us that the prosecution case was comprehensive."

"As I say, it is complicated," the man said. "There have been developments."

"But you are not prepared to enlighten us as to the nature of these developments?"

"It is—"

"Complicated. Yes, Mr. Tsengel, I think we have grasped that. I understand that you are relatively new to your role in the State Prosecutor's office. It may surprise you to learn that the law is frequently complicated."

"Yes, but—"

"I do not think this is acceptable, Mr. Tsengel. We have already invested very substantially in this case. We have listened to the evidence that the State Prosecutor's Office has so far presented. This is clearly a very important case with many ramifications—"

"Well, that's exactly—"

"And yet, now, two weeks into the case, you are seeking a significant adjournment because of—developments. And yet you are unwilling to share with us the nature or significance of these developments. That is, I think, an accurate summary of the situation?"

"Yes, but, well, it is—"

"I think we understand very well what it is, Mr. Tsengel. I think we should perhaps now seek Mr. Nyamsuren's views on this topic."

Tsengel opened his mouth as if to intervene, but remained silent. He was a short, rather awkward young man, who looked uncomfortable in his cheap, Western-style suit. He shifted from one foot to the other, as though keen to make his escape from the judge's presence.

Judge Radnaa looked across at the two other men who had been sitting at a desk in the middle of the room, whispering incessantly to one another during the previous discussion. She gestured to one of the two men, a tall slim figure in a black suit of considerably better quality than Tsengel's. He rose slightly, acknowledging her gesture.

"Mr. Nyamsuren," she said. "Will you join us for a moment?"

Nyamsuren exchanged a glance with the other man, a heavily built middle-aged man with a shaved head, and then rose to approach the bench, a quizzical expression on his face. "There is a problem?"

"So it would seem," Judge Radnaa said. "The State Prosecutor's Office is seeking an adjournment."

Nyamsuren raised his eyebrows. "Really?" He looked across at Tsengel, smiling vaguely. Tsengel stared down at the floor. "There is some difficulty, Mr. Tsengel? Mr. Muunokhoi has already been substantially inconvenienced. I presume we are not talking about a long delay?"

Tsengel looked up, his face pale. "Well, it's difficult to say. I mean—"

Nyamsuren turned to stare at Tsengel, as though in astonishment. "I am sure this is some simple misunderstanding, Mr. Tsengel. The State Prosecutor's Office is always very thorough. And my client has cooperated fully with the authorities at every stage. I cannot see what further developments might have occurred at this point."

Tsengel coughed, looking between Nyamsuren and the judge. Behind them, the other judges and the citizens' representatives had been watching the discussion with close attention. "Well, yes, but the situation is very—" He caught the judge's eye and coughed again. "The situation is very difficult. You will appreciate that I am in an awkward position . . ." He trailed off, as if unsure what to say next.

"You place us all in an awkward position, Mr. Tsengel. I think Mr. Nyamsuren would be entirely within his right to object very strongly to your proposal."

"With respect," Nyamsuren said, his glance moving from the judge back to Tsengel, "I am still not entirely clear what Mr. Tsengel's proposal actually is."

"Mr. Tsengel?" The judge gestured pleasantly towards the young man.

Tsengel shifted awkwardly. "Well, we're seeking an adjournment of the trial. While we resolve the issues that have arisen."

Nyamsuren smiled without any evident humour. "I see. And how long an adjournment are you seeking?"

"Well, I can't exactly—"

Nyamsuren laughed. "I must confess, I had not previously been aware that the State Prosecutor's Office possessed a sense of humour."

"I'm sorry, I don't—"

"Mr. Tsengel, Mr. Muunokhoi has been continually harassed by the police and by the State Prosecutor's Office for many years. Statements have been made about my client's business activities which verge on the libellous. He has been accused of trafficking everything from heroin to, I believe, uranium. And yet, not only has my client never been prosecuted, until now no charges have ever been brought against him. Six months ago, for reasons best known to themselves, the police decided that they had amassed sufficient evidence to justify my client's arrest on various charges including—" He glanced down at his notes, as though the precise charges were a matter of indifference to him. "Including charges of, ah, underpayment of import duties. Since then, he has been subject to the most stringent bail conditions, severely curtailing his ability to conduct his legitimate business. And now, when my client finally has the opportunity to demonstrate his innocence, you come forward to seek an indefinite adjournment on the grounds of some—difficulties which you are apparently unable to share with us. I can conclude only that this is an elaborate joke."

Tsengel looked miserably at the judge, as though pleading with her to take pity on him. "With respect, the core charges relate to illegal imports. Rather more serious than the underpayment of duties—"

"Yes, of course," Judge Radnaa said. She raised her eyebrows inquiringly towards Nyamsuren. "I take it that you are not prepared to accede to Mr. Tsengel's request?"

Nyamsuren smiled. "I think you can take it that that is our position," he said.

She turned to Tsengel. "And you are not in a position to present the State Prosecutor's evidence?"

Tsengel hesitated, as though trying to come up with an alternative answer. "As we speak, no," he said, finally.

She nodded slowly, and then looked back at her colleagues. "We will need a brief adjournment to consult," she said, "but as I see it we have only two routes available to us." She paused. "First, we can continue the trial on the basis of whatever evidence you can present. I take it that this would not be your preferred option?"

Tsengel blinked and nodded faintly.

"Or," she went on, "since Mr. Nyamsuren is, quite reasonably, not prepared to agree to an indefinite delay, we can perhaps agree to a short adjournment while the Prosecutor's Office considers its position. Perhaps until tomorrow morning?"

"It is not your fault. You need to realise that." Nergui was sitting in Doripalam's office, leaning back in his chair, his ankles resting neatly on the corner of the desk. Doripalam thought that he had never seen him looking quite so relaxed. He only wished that he could share Nergui's composure.

"It's a mess," Doripalam said. "The whole thing's a mess."

Nergui shrugged. "We know that. But nobody's blaming you."

Doripalam leaned forward across the desk. While they had been talking, Nergui noticed, Doripalam had been doodling aimlessly on the lined pad in front of him, large spirals, starting at the outside and working down to a tiny enclosed point in the centre. "Maybe you're not blaming me," Doripalam said. "Because you know what this place is like. But others will be."

"Of course. There will always be ignorant people looking for scapegoats. But this is not your fault."

"It's my responsibility."

Nergui carefully dropped his feet from the desk to the floor and leaned forward. As always, his clothing was an apparently unstudied blend of the conventional and the eccentric—a dark, well-cut business suit, offset by a lemon shirt and a louder-than-usual tie in varying shades of yellow. His socks, Doripalam had noticed as Nergui had balanced his ankles on the desk, had apparently been selected to match the shirt.

"And what form should your responsibility take?" Nergui said. His dark features were as expressionless as ever and his tone was casual, but Doripalam felt obliged to take the question seriously.

"I don't know," he said. "But if it's thought that I'm not up to the job, then I shouldn't be in it."

"So you would resign?"

"If it came to it, well, yes, I suppose I would."

"Then I suppose I would have to ensure that your resignation was not accepted." Nergui smiled. "If it came to it. But I think we can assume that it will not. Not over this, anyway."

Doripalam pushed back his chair. "But it's a mess, though, isn't it? After all this time. After all the effort we've put in. We nearly had Muunokhoi. And now the whole bloody thing's down the pan."

Nergui shrugged. "We have to be philosophical. You are sure there's no chance of salvaging it?"

"Some of the evidence we've got holds up. So it's not quite dead, but it's as good as. It's all tainted by the fake stuff, so nobody's going to take the case seriously. We tried to buy ourselves some time, see if we could make more of the evidence we've still got, but they weren't having it."

"No, well, that is not so surprising."

Doripalam smiled for the first time. "No, but at least we forced those smug bastards in the Prosecutor's office to do some work. Though I imagine that's the last satisfaction we'll get in that direction."

Nergui nodded slowly. "They are looking for an enquiry, you know?"

Doripalam rose and walked across to the window. It was a cold clear spring day, the sky a brilliant cloudless blue beyond the clutter of grey buildings. The view from his office was not impressive—the back of a disused office block, most of its windows smashed. Between the two buildings, there was an abandoned yard, filled with the detritus of the failed business—an old desk, some office chairs, even a broken filing cabinet. Somewhere beyond all this, he thought, there was the open steppe, the mountains, the miles of emptiness. "I didn't know," he said, "but I presumed they would." He laughed faintly. "They behave as if they're the ones who've put in all the work. Perhaps we should institute an enquiry into all the times they've messed up our evidence."

"We could have only so many enquiries," Nergui said. "But, no, I don't think we can avoid it this time. There will be too many questions." He paused. "I have put my own name forward."

Doripalam turned from the window. "You have?"

Nergui shrugged. "Why not? I understand the operations of this place better than anyone. Of course, if you are uncomfortable—"

Doripalam shook his head. "No, of course not. But wouldn't they see a conflict of interest?"

"If I were to chair the enquiry? I don't see why."

Doripalam leaned back against the window, his thin figure silhouetted against the daylight. "Well, for a start, you appointed me."

"But I am clear," Nergui said. "This is not an enquiry into you or your performance. There is no suggestion that you were even aware of what was happening."

"I know that," Doripalam said, "and I hope you know it too. But I'm sure that others will be only too keen to think the worst."

"There are always such people," Nergui said, apparently with genuine regret. "But I think the situation here is straightforward. I know what you inherited here—not least, because I was the one who bequeathed it to you. And the Minister knows all this. He knows that the civil police force was a shambles from the start—the ones the military didn't want, the detritus who couldn't find a better government job. He knows how much we've done to develop some professionalism—"

"Or at least some competence," Doripalam added softly.

"As you say. He also knows how much we have done to change things, you and I. And how unpopular we have made ourselves in the process."

"Very gratifying," Doripalam said, with only a mild edge of irony. "The Minister's good opinion does of course mean a great deal to me. But I'm not sure I see the relevance."

"The Minister is no fool. He knows the problems you are facing. An enquiry is necessary, but he does not wish to make your life any more difficult."

"So he wants a whitewash?"

"On the contrary, he wants a thorough and rigorous enquiry into all the circumstances behind this case. He wants transparency and openness. He wants, I suppose, an appropriate apportionment of accountability and blame." As Nergui mouthed the ministerial vocabulary, it was impossible to tell whether there was any undertone of satire. "He wants to ensure that you have the resources to resolve the situation."

Doripalam nodded. "And the Minister wants all this? He is taking such a personal interest in the case?"

"He is aware of it. I speak on his behalf, you understand," Nergui said. "Perhaps, from time to time, I paraphrase."

Doripalam shook his head. "You cunning old bastard," he said.

"So I'm fired?"

Doripalam shook his head. "It is not within my power to fire you, even if I wished to. You know that."

He's playing games, Doripalam thought. Why does he continue to play games, even now? "But of course you are suspended from duty," he added. "On full pay. Pending the outcome of the enquiry."

"So I will be fired? In due course. Pending the outcome of the enquiry."

Doripalam sighed gently. An apology would have been nice, he thought. Some kind of recognition of the inconvenience, the embarrassment, that Tunjin had put them all through. Not to mention the implications of Muunokhoi potentially being out on the streets again, more untouchable than ever. Doripalam had intended to approach this interview in a spirit of equanimity and fairness, but he found himself losing his temper. "You do realise what you've done, of course? I mean, you do understand the implications of your actions?" He was talking to Tunjin as if he was some sort of imbecile, rather than an officer with thirty or so more years' experience than his own. But he found it hard to regret either his tone or his words.

Tunjin leaned back in the seat facing Doripalam's desk. He looked considerably more relaxed than Doripalam himself. "I'm sure I do. But you may care to remind me. Sir." Tunjin presumably assumed that his long career was already over, and was behaving accordingly. Or, more likely, he well understood the impact of this kind of behaviour on Doripalam, particularly when exhibited by junior but more experienced officers.

"Do you know how long we have been trying to get to this point?" Doripalam asked, almost instantly regretting the question.

"For many years," Tunjin said. "Since well before your time. Sir."

Doripalam nodded slowly, trying hard to control his anger. "I am sure you can tell me precisely how long, Tunjin. I am told it is at least fifteen years."

"I think it's longer. Sir."

"Well, I am sure you are right. So—how long? Eighteen, twenty years. Perhaps longer—" Doripalam held up his hand, sensing that Tunjin was about to provide the relevant information. "And, now, when we get so close, this happens. No. I am sorry. I underestimate your contribution. *You* make this happen." He paused. "And so, after whatever it is—nineteen, twenty years—we are back where we started. Which in my view is precisely nowhere."

Tunjin, gratifyingly, seemed rather taken aback by Doripalam's short speech. "With respect, sir—" Doripalam was pleased to note that, for the moment, neither of the latter words sounded entirely ironic. This, he supposed, was progress. He decided to press on. "No," he added, as if after some thought. "I am wrong. We are somewhere. We are deeply in the shit. The criminal world sees us as a laughing stock. The Prosecution Service believes that we are considerably worse than useless. The Ministry believes that we are either corrupt or inept, or more likely both." He paused, but not long enough to allow Tunjin to interrupt. "I find it difficult to see any positive aspects to this position. And there's only one person responsible for our predicament."

Tunjin was, he noted, finally beginning to lose his temper. Doripalam was unsure whether this was desirable, but, given his own current state of mind, it was at least moderately satisfying. "With respect, sir," Tunjin repeated, with the ironic note now reinstated, "given that we had, in effect, made no progress in the last two decades, I thought my actions were justified. The evidence we had wouldn't have stood up on its own. I thought it was worth the risk."

For the first time, Doripalam's anger and irritation were overtaken by something close to astonishment. He sat back in his chair and stared at the figure sitting opposite him. Tunjin was a mess—physically and, it was beginning to seem, perhaps mentally as well. He was a short, fat, shapeless figure of a man, completely bald, who stared back at Doripalam over a stack of badly shaven chins. He was wearing a cheap black suit, worn shiny at the elbows and knees. The jacket and trousers were dotted, at disturbingly frequent intervals, with what were presumably stains of spilled food.

"Worth the risk?" Doripalam repeated finally. He was finding it difficult to come up with any coherent response. Tunjin sat watching him, playing with a badly chewed ballpoint pen, apparently unconcerned.

Doripalam shook his head, trying to find an appropriate form of words. "This is what I find so extraordinary," he said. "This will no doubt sound patronising, but you're one of the best—the most experienced—policemen we have in this team. We have problems—you know the problems we have. I have little respect for some of your colleagues, and doubtless they have little respect for me. But in your case—"

Tunjin had placed the end of the pen in his mouth, and was proceeding to mutilate it still further. After a moment he withdrew it, gazed thoughtfully at the dogeared tip, and then inserted it carefully in his ear. Doripalam watched the process as though hypnotised.

After a pause, he tried again. "We have not always seen eye to eye," he said. "I have often found your approach cavalier, lacking in discipline." Tunjin had proceeded to prod his inner ear methodically with the pen, and Doripalam was finding it increasingly difficult to sustain his train of thought. "But I saw that you achieved results. I recognised—I thought I recognised—your integrity, your honesty, compared with some of your colleagues." He hesitated, increasingly convinced that he was wasting his time. Tunjin's manoeuvres with the pen were an almost literal demonstration of his deafness to Doripalam's words.

"It had not occurred to me," he said, finally, "that you might be guilty of this kind of act. Of falsifying evidence."

Tunjin withdrew the pen from his ear and peered at whatever he had managed to extract. Finally, he looked up at Doripalam and shrugged. "I am a police officer," he said. "I just do what I can."

Doripalam stared at him in bewilderment. "But can't you see," he said, "that, even if you had succeeded, this kind of behaviour, this kind of manipulation of justice, is just not acceptable for a police officer? Especially for a police officer."

Tunjin shrugged again and inserted the chewed end of the pen back in his mouth. "So," he said, "it is clear. In due course, and no doubt after due procedure, I am fired."

"So—we are now in session." Judge Radnaa looked closely at Tsengel, who was sitting hunched behind the pale wooden desk. "Are you now able to clarify the situation, Mr. Tsengel?"

Tsengel shifted awkwardly and then climbed slowly to his feet. "Yes, madam. At least, insofar—" He paused, as though words had deserted him.

"Mr. Tsengel?" Judge Radnaa looked around the almost empty courtroom. Trials were normally open to the public, and even the most mundane case usually attracted at least a few idle visitors with time on their hands. A trial of this nature would normally have attracted queues of sightseers, not to mention the full representation of the press. But it had been clear right from the start that this was in no sense a normal trial, and the Ministry had insisted on a closed courtroom on the grounds of protecting its intelligence sources. The defence team, perhaps recognising that their case would, if anything, be strengthened by this anonymity, had raised no objections.

Tsengel seemed to gather his wits. "Insofar as I can," he concluded. "I have consulted with my superiors," he said. "Our position remains the same. We have run into some difficulties with our evidence. We would ideally like to seek an adjournment to see if these can be resolved."

"And are you now able to specify the proposed length of this adjournment?"

Tsengel hesitated, and then glanced across at Nyamsuren, who was sitting, apparently relaxed, next to the accused. "Well, we do not believe that we are able to resolve our difficulties unless we obtain a substantial adjournment. A matter of weeks, at least."

Judge Radnaa nodded slowly and then glanced over at Nyamsuren. "I take it that your client's position has not changed in respect of such an adjournment?" she said.

Nyamsuren nodded and rose languidly to his feet. "I am sure you appreciate our position, madam." He glanced back at his client, who was still staring fixedly at the table, his shaven head bowed forward.

"Indeed." She looked back at Tsengel. "And on this occasion I can only agree that the defence counsel's position is entirely reasonable. I can see that you have some difficulties, Mr. Tsengel, though I confess I am at a loss to understand precisely what they might be. But I think that the defence also has the right to assume that, particularly in a trial of this nature, the State Prosecutor's Office will be fully prepared before the case reaches court."

Tsengel looked as if a literal burden had been dropped onto his shoulders. He nodded, miserably. "I understand," he said. "My instructions are that, if it should not prove possible to obtain the kind of adjournment we are seeking, the State Prosecutor's Office wishes to confirm that it has no further evidence to offer. In short, there is no case to answer."

Judge Radnaa stared at him for a moment. "In formal terms," she said, "the trial has commenced. I do not believe, therefore, that we are in a position simply to dismiss the case."

Nyamsuren rose. "If you will permit me, madam?" he said. "My client has been charged with an extremely serious offence, as well as being the victim of a continuous stream of unsubstantiated innuendo. In the interests of my client's reputation, I think it is essential that the verdict is reached on the basis of the evidence that has been presented—"

"Or, to be precise, not presented," Judge Radnaa said.

"As you say, madam. But I believe that, given the seriousness of the charge, a clear verdict is needed in order to remove any doubts about Mr. Muunokhoi's position."

"I can only agree with you, Mr. Nyamsuren." The judge looked across at her colleagues and the citizen's representatives. "We will withdraw and consider our verdict, though I imagine it will not take us long." She paused. "In the circumstances, I presume that the defence has no further evidence to offer?"

Nyamsuren glanced over at Tsengel, who was now sitting

staring blankly at the floor. "We had of course prepared a thorough defence. However, in the absence of a prosecution case, I think this is now superfluous."

"As you say, Mr. Nyamsuren. Very well. We will consider our verdict and then reconvene in—" She glanced at the clock on the far wall of the courtroom. Its convex glass face, she noticed, perfectly enclosed the reflected image of the Mongolian flag that dominated the wall behind the bench. "Well, I do not think we will require more than thirty minutes."

She rose and strode purposefully out of the room, followed by the team of junior judges and citizens' representatives. The door closed behind them, and the courtroom was silent. Tsengel still stared at the floor, avoiding Nyamsuren's eyes.

Nyamsuren was smiling. He nodded at the two silent policemen who had been stationed on each side of the courtroom door throughout the trial. "I think your escort duties are almost finished, boys," he said.

The two policemen made no response, but looked pointedly back past Nyamsuren. Nyamsuren looked over his shoulder. For the first time, his client had ceased staring down at the desk and had raised his head. Beneath his bald head, his eyes were dark and staring, now fixed on the two officers who stiffened, fingers resting on their rifles. There was no evident humour or warmth in his blank eyes but, like Nyamsuren, he was now smiling.

TWO

She should have gone with the others, taken the chance when there was still time.

But she had been afraid to leave, worried that her departure would reveal too much. After all, a mother would never leave her child, would not willingly return to the steppe with her son's fate still unknown. She had made that clear to the policeman. She had said: "I won't leave. I won't move on. Not till I know where he is. What's happened to him."

The policeman had nodded, jotted down some words in his notebook. She suspected that he was not really interested, that he would never look again at the sentences he was scribbling down. He was going through the motions, trying to make her believe that they were taking this seriously.

"We don't know that anything has happened to him," he had pointed out, in a tone that was presumably intended to be reassuring, but which sounded merely dismissive.

She didn't blame him. He thought she was just another anxious old woman. Probably his own mother was the same. No doubt she fussed about the life he was living, about the risks he was facing as a police officer, about what his future might hold.

"I know," she said. "I know that something's happened to him."

The policeman looked up at her, apparently surprised by the quiet certainty of her tone. "But you've told us everything you know?" he said. "You have no other information?" There was a mocking edge to his voice. He didn't care about any of this. He didn't care what she felt.

She stared back at him for a moment, as if she were about to say something. Then she shook her head. "No. I've told you everything I can."

It was true, she thought. She had told him everything she could. Not everything she knew. But everything she was able to say.

She had no idea who to trust. She certainly had no reason to trust this smiling, insincere young man. Outside her immediate family, she had no reason to trust anyone. All she could do was try to bring it all out into the open, make it public, arouse as much noise as she could.

And hope that this would be enough to stop him.

After the policeman had gone, she had sat hunched on the small stool at the entrance to her *ger,* staring out across the empty grassland. Behind her she could hear the soft movements of the horses, the clattering of equipment, the desolate cry of a baby.

Her family was preparing to move on. She would not be travelling with them. Not yet. Some of them had offered to stay with her, but she had said no, fully aware that they were also afraid. Afraid for her, afraid for her son. But, mostly, afraid for themselves.

They knew he would come.

The rest of the family struck camp a week later, packing up their tents and equipment with the characteristic efficiency of the nomad. When the horses and trucks were loaded, her brother had come back to speak with her.

"How long?"

"As long as it takes," she said.

"We will come back for you. When we're settled. As soon as we've found somewhere suitable. It will only be a few days."

"As long as it takes," she repeated.

She had watched them go, feeling as if her heart was being torn from her body. A mother does not willingly leave her child.

She had not even been able to say what she felt. Had not trusted her emotions. But, also, had not trusted that somehow, in this vast empty plain, they might not be observed.

It had been a long time before the last black specks of the convoy had vanished into the pale haze of the horizon. Afterwards, she had returned to her *ger,* boiled water for tea, and sat down on her stool, nothing now to do but wait.

He would come. She was sure of that. Soon, he would come.

That night, she lay awake, listening to the faint sounds of the spring breezes rustling through the tent-frame, the occasional distant sound of a bird or a barking dog. She imagined him out there, perhaps already approaching, perhaps close at hand.

She imagined meeting him again.

The next morning, when her mobile rang, she was almost certain it would be him. She was sitting outside the *ger,* her husband's old heavyweight *del* slung over her shoulders against the early chill.

She answered hesitantly, wondering what she would say.

But it was not him. It was the police, again. A different policeman, more senior than the one who had visited before. No, they had nothing more to report. But, yes, he would like to meet her, hear her story for himself.

She agreed to a time later in the week, not taking in what the emollient voice was saying. She did not fool herself that the call had any significance. It was the publicity, she thought. In that sense, at least, her plan was working. She was getting her story out there. She was getting it noticed.

Perhaps that would help to keep him away. Or perhaps it would bring him sooner. She was no longer sure which she preferred.

He came the next day. When he appeared, it was hardly a surprise to her and she realised that she had forgotten to be afraid.

He was alone. She had somehow imagined him arriving with an entourage, the centre of everyone's attention, because that was how she remembered him.

But of course he was alone. He parked his truck carefully, yards away from the remaining cluster of *gers,* and walked slowly across the scrubby grassland to where she was sitting. The morning sun was behind him, and he was little more than a silhouette, but she fancied she could see the empty depths of his eyes.

She remained seated almost until he reached her. Then she rose and slowly made her way into the tent, feeling his presence close behind her.

The discussion went as she had expected. He did not stop to question what she might or might not know. He did not bother with explanations. He did not attempt to bargain or cajole. He simply told her what he wanted and waited calmly for her to agree.

When she refused, for a moment he looked almost surprised. Then he repeated his request, quietly, in the same polite tone. The sense of threat was palpable.

She refused again. And then she told him what she knew,

or what she thought she knew. She told him what she had, and what she would do with it.

She did not know what reaction she expected. Perhaps she had hoped that he would simply turn on his heel and walk away. Perhaps.

But when the first blow came, she knew she had been waiting for it. She tensed just for a moment as his fist struck her cheek, and then she staggered against the wall of the tent. His second blow struck her in the chest, and she fell back, her head hitting the solid wood of the tent frame.

She was semiconscious, aware of an absurd disappointment that she should have succumbed so easily. She felt his foot slamming hard into her back. She thrust herself against the side of the *ger,* knowing now that at least this—all of this—would soon be over.

But then he was leaning over her, and she saw his eyes, blank and expressionless as he pulled a cigarette lighter from his pocket.

And she realised that it was all only just beginning.

"It's a new one. Really moves when you put your foot down."

Doripalam didn't doubt it. He eased himself further down into the backseat of the Daihatsu 4x4, and tried to relax. This was something of a challenge when being driven by an over-enthusiastic young officer with a habit both of driving too quickly and—perhaps a greater immediate concern—of slowing insufficiently on the tighter bends.

"See that," Luvsan said, twisting the wheel. "Holds the road beautifully."

"So far," Doripalam agreed, feeling the dirt road slide beneath them. "Though I am not sure how long the fates will be on your side." That would be all he needed at the moment, he thought. A brand new vehicle written off by an idiotic young officer. Particularly if he succeeded in writing off his commanding officer at the same time. Though some might see that as a bonus.

Once again, Doripalam wondered quite why it was he had decided to take on this trip. The case had received some coverage in the press, for reasons he knew all too well, but he could hardly pretend that it was a major priority. The truth was that there was almost certainly nothing to it. Nothing that the police could deal with, at any rate.

Partly, it was about the public profile of the department, he supposed a necessary but tiresome part of his job. Given the coverage that this story had received in the media, he needed to be seen to be taking some action, however much he might think it to be a waste of time. If questions were asked in the Great Hural, as they conceivably might, he could at least demonstrate his personal commitment to the case.

But, if he was honest, there was only one reason he was out here today, speeding north into the shadow of the mountains when he should have been firmly seated behind his battered desk. He was avoiding Nergui. He was avoiding his former boss, his mentor, who was making yet another return visit to what inevitably still felt like his home turf. Not that he could avoid Nergui forever, or even for very long. But by the time Doripalam returned to headquarters, later that day, Nergui should at least have completed the round of ritualised greetings and glad-handing. Doripalam knew Nergui well enough to recognise that he would neither welcome nor be fooled by such ceremony. After all, most of those who were acclaiming Nergui's return had previously been only too glad to see the back of him—and for much the same reasons that they now resented Doripalam. But he knew they wouldn't hesitate to use Nergui's arrival as yet another stick to beat their current boss.

So, all in all, this was a pretty cowardly excursion, and would probably end up producing precisely the opposite effect from that Doripalam had intended. On the other hand, it would give Nergui the chance to get himself installed without further interference. And it would perhaps give Doripalam the chance to prepare himself for—well, for whatever it was that Nergui was up to. He was still unclear about precisely what that might be. And, knowing Nergui's ways, that continued to disturb him.

They had left the city well behind them now, and were heading north towards the mountains. It was another beautiful spring day, the sky a deep clear blue, the grassland lush and fertile at the start of the new year. Luvsan religiously consulted the truck's state-of-the-art GPS navigation system as they sped away from the city, but it was hardly necessary. The single hard-packed road stretched endlessly in front of them, and the landscape around them appeared deserted, mile after mile of rolling steppe.

"That's the place," Luvsan said, unexpectedly. He gestured ahead of them, momentarily taking both hands off the wheel. The truck jerked and swerved slightly, until Luvsan calmly tweaked back the wheel with his left hand. "See that," he said. "Handles like a dream."

Doripalam sat back in the seat, breathing hard, wondering quite what kind of dreams Luvsan was used to. But he could see the encampment now—a small scattering of the traditional round tents, the *gers,* still some distance away across the empty grassland. It did not appear to be a particularly large camp, just five or six tents. Quite probably most of the group had already moved on, seeking new pastures for their animals now that the spring was here. If so, he thought, it was not surprising that the mother had decided to stay on here. He wondered how long she might have to wait.

As they drew parallel with the camp, Luvsan twisted the wheel with obvious enthusiasm, and pulled off the dirt road towards the cluster of tents. Doripalam relaxed, resigning himself to the bumps and bruises that would result from driving at speed across this rough terrain. He knew from experience how much this empty landscape could distort one's sense of distance, but even so he was surprised by how long it took them to draw close to the camp. Finally, though, they drew up by the *gers,* Luvsan hitting the brakes more abruptly than necessary so that the truck skidded slightly on the hard earth.

"You're sure this is the right place?" Doripalam said. The camp looked deserted, though he knew that the nomads would never abandon their *gers* as they moved to new pastures.

Luvsan twisted in his seat and gave Doripalam a look that bordered on the pitying. "Of course it's the right place," he said. "I was up here about ten days ago, when we first interviewed the mother." He paused, looking back out through the windscreen. "There were more tents then, though. Some of them must have moved on."

"It's spring," Doripalam said.

"They've not left much, though," Luvsan said. "I don't see any animals."

He was right, Doripalam thought. One would normally expect to see grazing sheep or goats, as well as the tethered horses used for transport. And it was unusual to find a camp of this kind which wasn't jealously guarded by at least one oversized dog, running out to greet any passing truck. But here there was nothing. No animals, no sign of life at all. Not even one of the ubiquitous motorbikes that were increasingly becoming the preferred mode of desert transport. Just the small cluster of *gers,* a tiny island of human construction in the middle of the vast natural landscape.

"Maybe the rest haven't moved far. Probably Mrs. Tuya is waiting for us, and then she will join them." Doripalam had arranged this visit a few days previously, speaking to Mrs. Tuya on a surprisingly clear mobile phone line.

"And how's she planning to travel?" Luvsan said.

Doripalam shrugged. "I presume the rest will return to collect her."

Luvsan looked sceptically at him. Doripalam shook his head. "Okay, you tell me."

But Luvsan was right again. Doripalam's suggested narrative didn't make much sense. Mrs. Tuya travelled with her family, a tightly knit community. It was conceivable that some might travel ahead to seek out the more fertile areas, but it was unlikely that they would leave her alone to deal with the police. Especially given her state of mind, and everything she had been through over the preceding two weeks. This was supposed to be a routine meeting, but for the first time Doripalam felt a stirring of unease.

He slowly opened his door and climbed out into the cool morning air. The summer was some way off, but it would be warm later, he thought. Apart from the whisper of the wind through the sparse grass, there was almost complete silence. Behind the *gers,* the steppe stretched out until it merged with the darker green of the snow-tipped mountains.

"It's eerie," Luvsan said from behind him. "The silence."

"Not something you often encounter in your own company, I imagine," Doripalam said, but the jibe was halfhearted. "What state was Mrs. Tuya in when you interviewed her?" he asked finally.

"She seemed okay," Luvsan said. "I mean, worried, as you'd expect, but relatively calm in the circumstances."

Doripalam nodded. He wondered just what "relatively calm" might mean, given these particular circumstances. A missing teenage son. Disappeared on his first significant journey away from the family. A puzzling final phone call which indicated that he had found a new job. And then nothing.

"I read the transcript of the interview," Doripalam said. "She seemed calm enough but she wasn't giving much away as far as I could see."

"She answered the questions fully enough," Luvsan said. "But you're right. There was something closed about her."

"You think she was hiding something?"

Luvsan shrugged. "I'd guess not. But it's hard to be sure. People behave strangely when they're worried. And I think she holds us partly to blame for not making more progress."

"She might be right," Doripalam said. "That's certainly what the press think. But it's hard to make much progress when we don't even know for sure that a crime's been committed."

"You think he might have just taken off on his own?"

"He's a teenage boy," Doripalam said. "I don't think it's beyond the bounds of possibility, do you?"

There was still no sign of life or movement from the *gers*. Doripalam realised that both of them had been stringing out the conversation in the vague hope that someone might emerge from one of the tents, relieving them of the necessity of entering the *gers* themselves.

"It doesn't look as if there's going to be a welcoming committee," he said, finally. "I think we'll need to take a look for ourselves."

Luvsan nodded and then, in an unexpectedly loud voice, called out: "Hold the dog!"

It was the traditional greeting, called as one approached a *ger* as a visitor. Doripalam had always found it mildly absurd, and here—with no sign of life, canine or otherwise—it sound ridiculous. There was no response, so he walked slowly forward and pulled open the door to the leading *ger*.

He blinked, peering into the darkness. He ducked and stepped into the tent, moving slowly to allow his eyes to become accustomed to the gloom. Luvsan followed a few steps behind.

The *ger* appeared to be deserted. There were a few pieces of furniture in there—some brightly coloured chests, a cupboard, a low table with a white cloth thrown across it. Opposite the door, there was a single bed covered with a garish tapestry.

"No one here?" Luvsan said, stating the obvious.

"Doesn't seem so," Doripalam said. "The place is very tidy. Doesn't look as if anyone left here in a hurry."

"But it looks as if they did leave," Luvsan said, stepping past Doripalam into the gloomy interior of the tent. "Not much sign of life." He pulled open one of the brightly painted cabinets. Inside, the shelves, lined with old newspapers, were empty.

Doripalam turned and stepped back out into the bright sunshine, blinking from the glare. There was a stiff breeze now, whipping through the scrubby grasslands, and Doripalam realised that, despite the brilliance of the morning sun, he was feeling cold.

He walked across to the neighbouring *ger* and, without bothering to call a greeting, he pulled open the door. As his eyes grew accustomed to the darkness, he saw that this tent was as empty as the first. Again, it was tidy, still furnished with garish cupboards and tables. But there was no sign of habitation.

"Just the same?" Luvsan said from behind him.

"Exactly the same. Tidy but deserted."

"How long do you think they've been gone?"

Doripalam shrugged. "No way of knowing. I spoke to Mrs. Tuya—when? Four days ago."

"And there was no sign that she was planning to leave?"

"Of course not," Doripalam said, with a touch of impatience. "She didn't say much, but my impression was that she was planning to stick around as long as it took. Until she had some news." He walked farther into the empty *ger,* and pulled open more cupboard doors. All had been emptied, and no trace of any recent inhabitation had been left. "And why would they clear everything but not pack up the *gers?* Nomads don't leave their *gers* behind."

"Not through choice," Luvsan agreed.

The two men stepped back out into the sunshine, Doripalam carefully pulling the door of the *ger* closed behind him.

"We'd better check the rest," he said. "Just in case." There were three more *gers,* standing some metres back from the first two. "You take that one, and I'll look at these two."

Luvsan nodded and stepped across, to the *ger* that Doripalam had indicated. Doripalam himself turned and pulled open the door of the next tent.

Even before he had fully opened the door he knew that this one was different. The smell was not strong and was quickly whipped away by the breeze, but, to a policeman of Doripalam's experience, it was unmistakable. He reached into his pocket and, for the first time, pulled out a flashlight. He suspected that he would want to spend as little time as possible inside the tent.

He switched on the flashlight and stepped forward cautiously into the darkness, holding the torch out before him. Once inside the tent, the smell instantly grew stronger, almost unbearable. In the sunshine, the interior of the tent was growing warm, and he could hear an incessant buzz of flies.

As his sight cleared, he moved the torch-beam carefully around the interior. At first, it looked much like the previous two—tidy, apparently deserted, no sign of life.

And then the light finally fell across the sight he had been anticipating. There was no sign of life here, either, at least not human life, but the life had, he thought, departed relatively recently.

The body was lying sprawled against the side of the tent, its limbs spread out across the earth. The head was set at an odd angle. Doripalam moved the torch to light up the body and saw, with a shock, that the throat had been brutally cut.

He forced himself to move closer, scarcely breathing, trying not to inhale the rich scent of human decay. It was the body of a middle-aged woman—probably late forties, through it was difficult to be sure as the face lolled unpleasantly away from him. She was dressed in a traditional dark brown *del,* the heavy robe bunched tightly around her twisted figure. A pair of highly polished black boots protruded from beneath the robe. It looked as if she had been attacked and then fallen back against the wall of the tent.

But there was something more, something odder. Reluctantly, Doripalam reached out and moved the body slightly. Its arms were trapped underneath the trunk, twisted awkwardly. As Doripalam succeeded in raising the body slightly, he saw that the figure's arms were tied, knotted with strong plastic twine at the wrists. The arms themselves were bare, the thick felt of the *del* apparently ripped away. Along the length of each arm, he could see an ugly tapestry of what looked to be bruises and inflamed burn marks.

Doripalam heard footsteps behind him, and allowed the body to fall back to the hard earth. He turned to see Luvsan standing in the doorway, silhouetted against the sunlight. He moved the torch light to shine full on the dead woman's face.

"Mrs. Tuya?" he said.

Luvsan moved forward and stood behind him, all his previous energy and enthusiasm apparently sapped. "I think so," he said, finally.

"Anything in the other *gers?*" Doripalam said.

"Nothing like this. More or less like the first ones. Deserted. Cleared out. All the cabinets empty."

Doripalam moved the flashlight around the interior. He realised that his initial impression had not been entirely accurate. Although this *ger* was tidy and sparsely furnished, it had not been cleared like the others. There was some crockery neatly stacked on a cabinet on the far side of the room, and one of the larger cupboards stood half open to reveal some clothes inside. In front of the cupboard there was a large metal chest, its lid thrown back, with a further pile of clothes and other household items—a kettle, some saucepans, a few cheap-looking ornaments—stacked inside.

"It looks as if Mrs. Tuya was preparing to leave as well," Doripalam said. Luvsan nodded, his mouth clamped firmly shut. His face was pale, and it looked as if he might be sick at any moment.

Doripalam nodded and then turned to lead the younger man back out into the daylight and fresh air. Once outside, he took a deep breath, relishing the cool of the morning breeze, the clean air smelling only of the broad empty grassland and the mountains. Luvsan followed close behind, and then slumped down on to the bare earth, breathing heavily.

"And it looks," Doripalam said at last, completing his earlier observation, "as if someone was very keen that she shouldn't go."

THREE

For a moment he thought there was someone in the outer office. He froze, his hands still deep in the drawer of the filing cabinet, mentally rehearsing the excuses he had prepared. All the good reasons why he should be here, searching through the records at this time of night.

He looked cautiously behind him and realised that the sound was nothing more than his mobile phone vibrating on the wooden desk. He had been half-expecting the call, of course. That was why he had left the phone out there. He hadn't dared switch on the ring-tone, in case there should be someone else left in the building. But he couldn't risk missing the call when it came. There was no room for sloppiness. He knew only too well the price that others had paid for missing their cues.

He picked up the phone and glanced at the screen. No calling number. He had no doubt that the call would be untraceable, if anyone should be inclined to try.

He thumbed the phone on. "Yes?"

As always, there was no preamble. "Everything is under control." It was a statement, not a question.

He swallowed, his mouth suddenly dry. "Yes. I've got it all in hand. Don't worry." He immediately regretted the unnecessary reassurance. The phone was silent, and he thought for a second that the caller had hung up. "I've got it all in hand," he repeated, his voice cracking slightly.

Finally, the caller spoke again. "There's one loose end."

"Not here," he said. He was aware that his voice was sounding overeager, but he could do nothing to prevent it. "I've checked and double-checked everything—"

The caller gave no acknowledgement of his words. "You need to finish tidying up."

"Everything—" He stopped, understanding what the caller was saying. "He's no threat now," he said. "He's been suspended. His career's finished—"

"I want you to tidy everything up."

"But wouldn't it be riskier—?" He was about to bite back the words, knowing how dangerous it would be even to ask the question. Then he realised that, in any case, there was no point in continuing. The phone was dead. The caller had already hung up.

He straightened up, suddenly realising how tense his body had been during the call, how tightly his hand had clutched the phone.

That was it, then. Tidy everything up.

He bent over and finished running through the files in the cabinet, though his mind was no longer focused on the task. He dropped the last of the folders back into the drawer, careful to ensure that his gloved fingers left no marks, that there was no trace that anything had been disturbed.

Tidy everything up.

It was not a surprise. But he had hoped that the task would be allocated elsewhere. This was all too close to home.

Which, of course, was precisely why he had been chosen. He knew well enough by now how this all worked. How quickly he had become implicated. How few options had been left for him.

He carefully slid the drawer of the cabinet shut, and then twisted the combination lock back to where it had been when he had entered the room forty minutes earlier.

He stood for a moment and looked around him, satisfying himself that he had left no sign that anyone had been in here. Then he quickly stepped across the room, gently pulled open the door, and left Doripalam's office.

"Have you been avoiding me?"

Doripalam looked up from the mass of files spread out across his desktop. Nergui was standing in the doorway, his shoulder resting casually against the framework. From somewhere behind him, the sun was shining and his heavily built body was visible only in silhouette.

"Why should you think that? I've been busy." Doripalam gestured towards the papers in front of him.

"So I hear. Especially after yesterday."

"Especially after yesterday," Doripalam agreed. "All we needed at the moment."

"Killers rarely exercise any consideration," Nergui said. "What's the story?"

Doripalam hesitated. He had found himself increasingly reluctant to discuss current cases with Nergui. He was aware how quickly in these informal discussions they tended to revert to their former roles—Nergui the experienced chief, himself as the eager deputy lapping up the older man's wisdom and advice. It wasn't deliberate on Nergui's part, he thought, and Doripalam always tried hard to resist the tendency, but their old relationship was too deeply ingrained. And, whatever his motives, it was clear that Nergui still couldn't fully tear himself away from this place.

"I've no idea," Doripalam said at last. "There's not much to go on yet. We're waiting for the full pathologist's report. But she was clearly murdered—her throat was cut. Probably been dead for at least twenty-four hours. Maybe more. The body had been tied up—the wrists were still tied and there were rope marks around the ankles. And she had been subjected to—well, torture seems the most accurate word. The body was covered in bruises and burns—probably from a cigarette. At the moment, that's about all we have."

"It sounds plenty. What about the rest of the family?"

"We're trying to track them down," Doripalam said, finding himself drawn into the conversation despite his best intentions. "It looks as if some of them must have moved on after we first interviewed Mrs. Tuya, but we don't know where they are or why they abandoned some of the *gers*."

"But some *gers* seemed to have moved on?"

"Apparently. The officer I was with, Luvsan, had been up there to conduct the original interview. Reckons there were eight or nine tents then—probably more than twenty people in the camp. When we went back, there were just five tents."

"And all deserted?"

"All deserted and cleared out, apart from the one where we found the body. Mrs. Tuya was clearly in the process of leaving—there was a half-packed case. We found one or two other personal items in the other tents, but only the kind of thing that might have been left behind accidentally."

"So why not pack up the *gers* as well?"

Doripalam shrugged. "Who knows? Maybe they left in a hurry, if one of them was responsible for Mrs. Tuya's death. Or, if they weren't responsible, maybe they were afraid of whoever was."

"Doesn't take long to dismantle a *ger,* though, if you know what you're doing."

"Maybe long enough, if you're really afraid."

As they had talked, Nergui had sat himself down in front of Doripalam's desk. He was, Doripalam noted, carrying a box file labelled "SCT Enquiry" which he placed unselfconsciously down on the corner of the desk. Doripalam wondered if he was supposed to ask about the file, but he decided to delay that for a while. All things considered, at the moment he felt more comfortable discussing the murder case.

Nergui leaned back in the chair, lifting the front legs off the ground. He looked the same as ever, Doripalam thought, and it was difficult to gauge whether he was going native in the Ministry. Doripalam had not honestly expected him to stay in that role for very long. Particularly after the incidents with the Englishman. And yet here he was, more than a year on, apparently settled into his role as the Minister's bagman, supposedly dealing with issues of national concern but—as far as Doripalam could judge—spending most of his time processing files in his small but well-appointed office on the third floor of the Ministry. Except, of course, that he wasn't there at the moment. At the moment, he was sitting in Doripalam's office, once again sticking his nose into the business of the Serious Crime Team and engaged in—well, who knew what?

As always, Nergui's dark-skinned face gave nothing away. He gazed impassively at Doripalam as though he had been following every twist of the younger man's train of thought. "Do you think it's connected with the son?" he said, after the silence had become uncomfortably prolonged.

"Again, who knows?" Doripalam said. "Until now, I hadn't been taking the son's disappearance particularly seriously."

"But you thought it was worth going up to talk to her yourself?"

Doripalam shrugged, still uneasily aware that he had, for whatever motive, timed the visit to Mrs. Tuya to coincide with Nergui's return. He had no doubt that Nergui had noted the fact. "That was a PR thing, mainly," he said. "You saw the kind of coverage she'd received in the press. Another example of precisely what we didn't need at the moment."

"She had a relative on *Ardiin Erkh,* I understand?" This was one of the privately owned national daily newspapers that had appeared with the arrival of democracy in the country.

Doripalam nodded. "A cousin. Assistant editor or some such. That was how she got the original coverage. Then all the others jumped on the bandwagon."

"Widow of military hero loses son. Police have no leads. That kind of thing."

"Precisely that kind of thing. Except that the implication was 'police can't be bothered.' "

"Because you didn't take it seriously?"

"Well, we didn't particularly, to be honest. The boy, Gavaa, was nineteen. He'd moved to the city to take up a clerical job in one of the state departments. A large well-built boy who apparently took after his soldier father. Bright and self-sufficient. And, by all accounts, not on particularly good terms with his mother. Nothing there that made you think of him as a natural victim."

"You thought he'd just taken the opportunity to leave home properly?"

"Pretty much so. All the signs were that he'd settled into the city pretty quickly and pretty successfully. He had a good circle of friends. For a young man without commitments, he was fairly well-paid. He was renting a flat near the centre, just a few hundred metres from Sukh Bataar Square. All in all, a fairly cosy lifestyle."

"But you couldn't track him down?"

"Well, no, that was the mystery. That and the circumstances of his disappearance, such as they were."

Doripalam was becoming aware that, once again, the two of them had indeed slipped back into their old familiar pattern of dialogue—Nergui asking questions, prompting Doripalam to think harder, underpinned by the same old desire to please and impress the older man. This was not, he thought, appropriate behaviour for the chief of the Serious Crimes Team. On the other hand, he was forced to acknowledge that, on the basis of previous experience, it might enable him to come up with some answers, or at least some new questions.

"I read that he got himself a new job?" Nergui said. Doripalam wondered precisely where Nergui had read this. Admittedly, the story had been well covered in the press, thanks to Mrs. Tuya's cousin. But Doripalam was also aware that Nergui could gain access to pretty much any internal police information if he chose.

"We don't know for sure," Doripalam said. "He phoned his mother a couple of weeks before the time we think he vanished—though we don't have an exact date for that, or even know for sure that he really has disappeared. He told her he was leaving the Ministry, that he had a new opportunity in front of him which was too good to refuse."

"But he didn't tell her what it was?"

"No, in fact, she said that he seemed very secretive. Kept hinting that there was more he could tell her but that he had to keep it confidential. That kind of thing."

"Not a Government job," Nergui said. It was not a question.

Doripalam smiled faintly. "Well, I imagine you would know. But, yes, we did check that, because we couldn't think what kind of role might have any requirement for confidentiality."

"If not a Government role, that suggests something more dubious," Nergui said.

"Maybe. That is, if we take what the mother said at face

value. By that time, she seemed keen to stir up as much trouble as possible. I wasn't directly involved, but I read all the transcripts of the interviews and I couldn't decide whether or not she was exaggerating what Gavaa had said. Making it sound more mysterious than maybe it was."

"But he still vanished?" Nergui ran his fingers slowly through his thick black hair.

"Well, in the sense that we don't know where he is, yes. But his disappearance doesn't seem to have been particularly sudden. He'd given his landlord a month's notice on the flat, so was clearly expecting to move. He'd also given notice in his job, telling them that he'd found something that paid better, though he didn't say what. But he left both the job and the flat a couple of weeks earlier than expected. The landlord came to drop in some mail one day and found the place deserted."

"Like the *gers?*" Nergui said.

"Well, yes, I suppose so. It was a furnished flat, and, from what the landlord said, I don't think Gavaa had many personal belongings in any case. Just some clothes, a few books and pictures. They'd all been stripped away, but I imagine they would have fitted into a small suitcase. The landlord was surprised he hadn't said goodbye, as they'd got on fairly well, but just assumed Gavaa had decided to move early for some reason. When we spoke to him, he seemed to think the whole thing was just a fuss about nothing."

"What about the friends? If Gavaa had just moved to a new flat or a new job, surely they'd know where he was?" Nergui crossed his legs and rested one ankle delicately across his other knee. His socks, Doripalam noted, were pale blue today, matching the shirt and tie beneath his standard dark grey suit. Doripalam wondered vaguely how many colour combinations Nergui had in his wardrobe.

"You'd have thought so, wouldn't you?" Doripalam said.

"That's the only bit of the story that doesn't hang together, where the mother's concerns were understandable. He'd been out drinking with a group of the friends the night before he vanished—pleasant evening, no indication of anything unusual, no sign that he wasn't intending to go to work in his civil service role the next day. But he never turned up at work. Like the landlord, his employers just assumed that he'd decided or been required to take up his new job earlier than expected. They were a bit annoyed, but people often don't work out their notice, so they weren't surprised."

"And the friends?" Nergui prompted.

Doripalam shook his head. "We've spoken to all of those who were with him the night before he vanished, plus a few others who were known to be acquainted with him. They all claim they've not seen him since. I don't know whether they're telling the truth. Again, I wasn't directly involved, but I get the impression from the interview transcripts that maybe some of them were a little surprised to find themselves on the end of a police investigation."

"You think they might have been lying?"

"Well, not all them. It's hard to imagine that they'd all have managed to stick to a consistent story. But I suppose it's possible that some of them are not telling us everything."

Nergui frowned. "But why would they bother keeping it quiet if they knew where he was? You don't think they're responsible for his disappearance?"

"I think it's more likely that, if he has just decided to make himself scarce for some reason, one or two of them might know where he's gone to."

"Presumably we put some pressure on them in the interviews?"

Doripalam nodded, noting the "we." "Of course. All the usual stuff. We told them that withholding information from the police is potentially a very serious offence—impeding the course of justice and all that. We also told them that this had the potential to become a murder investigation—which is certainly the direction that his mother was pushing us, even without a body. But looking at the transcripts, I don't think they were all that impressed."

"That's the trouble with the youth of today," Nergui said. "No respect."

Doripalam smiled. "I think the trouble with the youth of today is that they're generally a bit too smart for their own good. And for ours. If any of them did have any information, they didn't see any reason to share it with us, and nothing we could say was going to influence that."

"In my day," Nergui said, "you could have thrown them in jail until they decided to cooperate."

"In your day, Nergui, I'm sure you could have done much worse than that if you'd chosen to," Doripalam said. "But things have changed."

"Oh, I know," Nergui said. "But don't expect me to like it."

"Anyway, that's where we are with it. Until now, I'd assumed that Mrs. Tuya was overreacting, that Gavaa had simply taken this as an opportunity to leave home properly, cut all the ties, that kind of thing. I thought he'd pop up again in his own time."

"And maybe he will," Nergui said, though with an ominous note in his voice. "What about the relationship with the mother? What do we know about that?"

"Well, let's say it was strained," Doripalam said. "Not entirely clear why. The father was a soldier. Fought as part of our force alongside the Russians in Afghanistan."

"And that's where he was killed?" Nergui said.

Doripalam leaned back in his chair and looked at the older man. Nergui gazed back at him impassively, his bright blue eyes revealing nothing of his thoughts. Doripalam had the uneasy sense, as he so often did with Nergui, that he was somehow being played with—possibly to his own benefit, but played with nonetheless. How much did Nergui really know about all this? "Yes," Doripalam said, finally, "killed by a sniper, supposedly. Gavaa would have been little more than a baby at the time, so would hardly have remembered his father. But he grew up with—at least according to his mother—a rather idealised version of what his father had been like. He idolised him. The military allowed them to stay on in army accommodation after the father's death so Gavaa was brought up in army houses, in sight of the parade ground. Saw his father as part of the great Mongolian martial tradition. Wanted to follow in his footsteps."

"But he didn't?"

"That was part of the problem. His mother didn't want him to follow in his father's footsteps—perhaps understandably, given what happened to the father. So she blocked and discouraged him. Then, when he was old enough, he went off without her consent and tried to join. And ironically enough he failed the medical. Suffered badly from asthma. So they wouldn't have him anyway. And that of course only made things worse. No doubt his mother couldn't conceal her relief."

"Complicated things, children," Nergui observed. "I've generally managed to steer clear of them."

"I imagine this wasn't helped by the fact that Gavaa was faced every day with the sight of a world he couldn't be part of. So, as soon as he could, he took the opportunity to get out there and find himself a job in the city."

"How did the mother end up out on the steppes?"

"She came from a family of herdsmen. After it became clear that Gavaa wasn't going to return to the family home, she decided to return to her own family. Gavaa had already been in the city for six or seven months then, and it looks as if there wasn't much contact between them."

"Is it possible that he was responsible for his mother's death?"

Doripalam nodded. "I can see that your razor sharp mind hasn't been blunted by your time in the Ministry," he said, smiling faintly. "Yes. We're also looking at that possibility."

"In any case, perhaps the news of his mother's death will bring him out into the open," Nergui said.

"Perhaps. It will certainly receive enough coverage. I am sure that Mrs. Tuya's cousin will see to that."

"It's always good to have friends in high places," Nergui said. He half rose, as though about to leave, then paused, holding out the box file. "Speaking of which, you haven't asked me about the enquiry. I assume you're interested in its progress."

Doripalam smiled. "Of course. But I knew that if I didn't ask, you wouldn't be able to resist telling me about it anyway."

Nergui sat down again, nodding slowly. It was impossible to tell from his smoothly carved features whether or not he was amused. "You are right," he said. "Young people today are much too smart for their own good."

FOUR

The apartment was a mess, there was no doubt about that. In fact, looking round it, he had to admit that that would be a polite description. The room was—there was no way of avoiding this conclusion—squalid. There were dirty plates and dishes piled in corners, gathering mould and perhaps worse. There was a large pile of unread newspapers, stacked unsteadily on the seat of the worn sofa. There was a bog-like pile of apparently unwashed clothes, outerwear and underwear, squashed haphazardly against the filthy sink. There were arrays of glasses and cups, most half filled with vodka or other spirits, lined up across the table, chairs and floors. Several empty bottles lay under the table.

And, most of all, right in the middle of this panorama of filth, there was him. Spread-eagled, barely sentient, probably smelling worse than the rest of this mess put together.

How the hell had this happened?

He sat up slowly—he was incapable of moving with any greater acceleration—and looked slowly around him. He could scarcely believe what he was seeing. Admittedly, he had never been the tidiest of men. Some might say, he reluctantly acknowledged to himself, that he was one of the least tidy. But he had never found himself living in a state like this.

And, at least for the moment, he still couldn't quite remember how he had reached this point.

He had, he realised, a severe headache, pounding at the rear of his skull. His throat was parched, and tasted as if he might have tried to chew some of the discarded clothing before his collapse. As he stared at the stacked rows of empty and half empty glasses, the source of his condition became clearer. He was fortunate only that much of the contributory liquor remained unconsumed.

He pulled himself very cautiously to his feet, blinking as the sunlight from the uncurtained window caught his eyes. The cheap clock was still there above the sink, he noticed, its crimson plastic as gaudy as ever. Ten past eight. He assumed that was morning, though at this time of the year it could still be light at eight in the evening. In any case, he had no idea how long he had been unconscious.

He dragged himself across to the sink, found a relatively clean-looking glass, rinsed it out and filled it with water from the tap. He drank the water down in one, then refilled the glass and emptied that one in the same fashion. He repeated the process a third and then a fourth time. By that point, he felt slightly more human, though now nausea was beginning to replace thirst as the dominant sensation in his body.

As he moved away from the sink, he caught sight of himself momentarily in the full-length mirror he kept propped behind the main door of the flat. The mirror had been his wife's, and he couldn't for the life of him think why she had decided to leave it with him. Possibly only to maximise the unpleasantness of moments like this.

There was no way round it. He looked an even worse mess than the rest of the flat. He was dressed in a filthy cotton vest, stained with sweat under the arms and spilled food down the chest and stomach. Below that, he was wearing a pair of sagging old boxer shorts which were in a state some way beyond rational description. And he was even wearing a pair of socks with matching large holes through which each of his big toes protruded.

But all of that was relatively reassuring compared with his face. He looked like death. No, he looked like death in an advanced stage of decomposition. He had never seen any living person, let alone himself, looking quite as awful as this. In fact, over the years he had seen one or two corpses that might have been in a healthier state.

He was unshaven. That went without saying. Three or four days' growth at least. His pendulous stomach served only to emphasise the filthiness of his yellowing vest. And his hair looked as if it had been dipped liberally in some deeply unpleasant viscous substance—possibly oil, or possibly something sweeter to attract the lice which he suspected were breeding enthusiastically somewhere in there—and then held in a wind-tunnel for a considerable length of time. It was, he reflected, quite possible that this was exactly, or at least approximately, what had happened.

He couldn't remember last night. That wasn't unusual. What concerned him more was that he couldn't remember any of the preceding ones either. He poured himself another glass of water, and then slumped down on the threadbare sofa, carefully moving a mould-encrusted plate out of the way first.

So what did he remember?

Well, he remembered being suspended, that was for sure. Now, how the hell had that happened?

Partly, he'd just had enough. He put up with this crap, year in, year out, throughout his whole career, and he'd thought it was about time he did something about it. It wasn't as if he didn't take his job seriously. That was the main problem. He took it all a bit too seriously. That was why he was in the mess he was. He looked again round the devastation of the flat. One hell of a mess.

So he'd tried to get smart. But smartness wasn't his thing. Granted, he could call on some low cunning when he needed to, and he'd thought that would be enough to get him through. But he should never have tried to get smart. Not where Muunokhoi was concerned. That had been a big mistake.

The thought of Muunokhoi made him uneasy. He wasn't clear, even now, quite how much Muunokhoi knew. The word was that Muunokhoi knew everything, and on the whole Tunjin was inclined to believe that. He'd certainly managed to unravel Tunjin's idiotic plan quickly enough, though Tunjin had no idea quite how. It was obvious that Muunokhoi had sources on the inside, though Tunjin had thought he'd got all that covered. But they'd clearly worked out what was going on, and it surely wouldn't take them long to finger Tunjin as the perpetrator.

His suspension hadn't exactly been publicised—he was supposedly on sick leave—but he couldn't believe that it wasn't already common knowledge. And if Muunokhoi was getting the right information, it wouldn't take long for him to put two and two together.

And in the middle of all that Tunjin had taken the opportunity to render himself comatose for—well, who knew exactly how long? No, smart definitely wasn't his thing.

For a moment, panic almost overwhelmed him. If Muunokhoi was after him, he was finished. There was no question about that. He knew more than enough about what Muunokhoi could do to people who crossed him. He'd seen plenty of evidence of that, which is why he'd taken the steps he had. But all he'd done was make things worse, and put himself in the firing line.

He breathed deeply and forced himself to relax. That was the one thing you could say about blind panic. It could take the edge off even a hangover like this. Suddenly a pounding headache and churning guts seemed a relatively small price to pay for staying alive.

Okay, so he wasn't smart. But he was cunning and streetwise. He knew this city, and he knew more than enough about the lowlifes who frequented it. He ought to be capable of staying one step ahead of Muunokhoi, at least for a while.

But for how long? That was the question. He couldn't keep hiding forever. And he knew enough about Muunokhoi to recognise that he was a patient man. Ruthless. Unforgiving. Implacable. Vengeful. All of those. But nonetheless patient. Unlike Tunjin, he wasn't the kind of man who would rush into some half-formed scheme without a clue how it was going to end up. He would take as much time as it needed. Tunjin might make himself safe today, tomorrow, maybe a year or more from now. But at some point, probably when he was finally beginning to relax again, Muunokhoi would be there.

And that, of course, was assuming that Tunjin managed to keep himself at least moderately sober. He shivered at the thought of just how vulnerable he'd been over the last few days, no doubt stumbling from bar to bar and then back here to knock back more dregs of vodka from all these scattered bottles. All things considered, it was surprising that he'd woken up at all.

Tunjin staggered up from the sofa, trying to force himself to think clearly. It was possible, of course, that he was simply below Muunokhoi's radar. Why would a big wheel like Muunokhoi concern himself with an insignificant mite like Tunjin?

But then he knew the answer to that well enough. Muunokhoi would bother with Tunjin because he was the only person who had ever come close to putting him behind bars.

Tunjin looked around the flat. Maybe Muunokhoi's people had already been here. Frankly, they might have ransacked the whole place and it wouldn't look very different. Though maybe the smell would have been sufficient to discourage them. Taking care to avoid the scattered plates and bottles, Tunjin stumbled through into the bedroom. It was in a marginally better state than the larger living room, in that there were no plates of half-eaten food and only a single empty vodka bottle lying by the bed. The bed itself was disturbed, though he had no recollection of using it on the preceding nights. But then he had no clear recollection of sleeping anywhere else either.

He moved slowly into the bedroom, shaking his head to try to clear his thoughts, swallowing the panic that was once again beginning to well up in his stomach. And then he stopped, and for a moment the fear overwhelmed him.

There was something lying in the centre of the unmade bed. A grey cardboard file, bound with an elastic band. A file he recognised. A file he had last seen sitting, apparently unregarded, on the Chief's desk.

The case file relating to Muunokhoi.

He walked forward slowly and reached out to touch the file, as though suspecting that it was a hallucination. Stranger things had happened, he imagined, after the consumption of this much alcohol. But there was no question that it was real.

Had he somehow contrived to bring it home with him? Maybe sometime over the last few days, his drunken logic had somehow led him back to police headquarters with the aim of stealing the evidence. Though it was difficult to imagine that anyone would have let him in, and he couldn't believe that he had been in a state to enter without being spotted.

Maybe he'd somehow picked it up on the day of the interview with the Chief. Picked it up off the Chief's desk, without either of them registering the fact. It didn't seem very likely.

Or maybe someone else had stolen the file on his behalf and brought it here as—well, as what? As a warning? To incriminate him in some way?

He leaned over and carefully picked up the file, a wave of nausea sweeping over him as he did so. He pulled off the elastic band and opened the file, rifling through the stack of papers inside.

They were exactly as he recalled them. Including those notes and documents that he had either forged himself or had had painstakingly prepared by one of his contacts, a former fraudster, who had worked for nothing other than a few mild blackmail threats. Tunjin wondered, in passing, whether Muunokhoi might have expressed any interest in the person who had actually carried out this skilled work.

But Tunjin's more immediate concern was his own wellbeing. The papers in the file were almost as he had seen them last. But not quite. There was one small, but highly significant, difference. Slipped into the front of the file, on top of the pile of documents, was something new, something which Tunjin was sure had not been there when he had last seen the file.

It was a photograph. A high quality photograph, apparently taken in a photographer's studio, with the subject carefully posed. If the subject of the photograph had been, say, an actor or a singer, this might have been the shot selected for sending out, over the artiste's signature, to fans. There was no need for a signature here, though, since Tunjin recognised the subject only too well. It was Muunokhoi. His eyes were empty, but his mouth, as always, seemed to be smiling.

* * *

"I'm here to report a crime. Or a potential crime, I'm not sure. Is this the correct place?"

Sangajav, sitting uncomfortably at the reception desk, looked up confusedly. He had been working painstakingly through a series of statistics that Doripalam had requested and now he had lost his place. "I'm sorry?"

The woman before him presented an impressive figure. Probably around forty, he thought, with a severe haircut and features that were striking rather than conventionally attractive but still with a very decent figure. Very fashionable clothes, too, he noticed—an expensive-looking dark business suit, probably imported from the West somewhere. Sangajav had little aptitude for mathematics, but, at least in his own mind, he was highly experienced when it came to appraising women.

"Is this the right place to report a crime?"

Sangajav carefully gathered up his papers and looked up at her. "Well, no, not really. I think you want the police station."

"Isn't this the police station?"

Sangajav shook his head, as though dealing with a very elementary error. "No, this is police *headquarters*."

"And you're not a police station as well?"

"Well, no. This is mainly administration, and some specialist units—"

"But you are the police?"

"Yes, we are, but—"

"So why can't I report a crime here?"

"It's just that—well, you have to go to the police station."

"But since I'm here, can't you deal with it anyway?"

"That's not really the way—"

"But why not? If you're the police and I want to report a crime, why can't I do so?"

Sangajav sighed. Why did this sort of thing always happen when he was around? This wasn't even really supposed to be a reception. The building wasn't strictly open to the public, so the desk was really just here for greeting official visitors. But visitors were so few that there was little point in employing a permanent receptionist, so the informal procedure was that one of the officers rostered for administrative duties would sit here just in case anyone turned up. As far as Sangajav could judge, this only ever happened on his watch and it was always people like this.

"It just doesn't work like that," he explained patiently. "We're not an operational police station. That's on the other side of the square. As I say, we're mainly admin people here, and one or two specialist units like the Serious Crimes Team—"

"The Serious Crimes Team," she interrupted. There was a faint hint of a smile around her mouth. "Well, what if I wanted to report a *serious* crime? Could I do that here?"

Sangajav was beginning to suspect that, despite her impressive appearance, the woman was deeply insane. He wasn't sure quite how to respond. "Do you want to report a serious crime?" he asked.

"I'm not sure," she said. "What constitutes a serious crime?"

Sangajav shook his head, despairingly. His only thought now was how he might get rid of this woman. It didn't seem appropriate simply to throw her out. "It's difficult to say," he said at last. "Perhaps if you tell me what the crime is, I can tell you whether it's serious. But you'll still have to report it at the police station."

She nodded as though carefully absorbing this information. "What about a threat of physical violence?" she said. "Would you consider that serious?"

"We might," he said. "It would depend on the circumstances."

She nodded again. "What if the purpose of the threat was to intimidate a member of the judiciary?"

"A member of the judiciary?"

"Yes," she said. "A judge. A judge who generally deals with major criminal trials. That is, what you might call 'serious crimes.'" She stared fixedly at Sangajav, and it was impossible to be sure whether she was being ironic.

"I think that might count," Sangajav said. "If that were the case."

"It's the case," she said, slowly. "I'm a judge. And I've been threatened. It may just be nonsense. But it may not."

Sangajav still wasn't entirely sure about her sanity. But if what she was saying was true, then it probably merited taking seriously. The Chief probably wouldn't thank him if he turned away a senior judge from the door. And, at the very least, it would give him a legitimate reason to fob her off on to someone more senior. "I think I probably need to get someone to talk to you," he said at last.

She paused, as if some thought had struck her. "You said the Serious Crimes Team was here? It's just that I think I know the Chief."

"Doripalam?"

There had been a look in her eye which Sangajav—experienced as he was in the appraisal of women—couldn't quite read. But as he spoke, the look vanished with the suddenness of a light being extinguished. "Doripalam?" she said. "No, I don't know him. I was thinking of someone else."

"Perhaps his predecessor," Sangajav said, intrigued despite himself. "Doripalam's not been in the job all that long. His predecessor was a man called Nergui."

The same look, or something very close to it, reappeared in her expression. "Nergui," she said. "Yes. It was Nergui I knew." She hesitated. "We had some dealings—oh, years ago. He has—moved on?" She asked the last question hesitantly, as though concerned about the possible nature of Sangajav's response.

"Promoted," Sangajav said, bluntly. "To the Ministry of Security."

She nodded. "That's good," she said. "Though hardly surprising, I guess. I'm sorry not to have been able to meet him, though."

Sangajav had begun to see a way in which he might extricate himself from this increasingly insane conversation. She had expressed a desire to see Nergui, and that was good enough for Sangajav. "Well, actually, you probably can," he said. "He's here at the moment, as it happens, carrying out some assignment." Like most of the team, Sangajav was as yet unclear precisely why it was that Nergui had reappeared, though experience suggested that the impact of his return was unlikely to be straightforward or comfortable. "I can try to track him down for you, if you like."

She smiled fully for the first time, and Sangajav was forced to revise his original judgement. She was indeed a striking woman, but she was also, he realised, actually very beautiful.

"I would like that," she said. "I would like that very much."

FIVE

"I still don't understand what exactly it is you're up to, Nergui. But I do know that I don't feel very comfortable about it."

They were sitting in Nergui's temporary office. It was much smaller than Doripalam's, tucked away somewhere at the end of the corridor. When he had first received the request from the Ministry to provide some temporary accommodation for Nergui, Doripalam had been tempted to find him a broom cupboard, if only on the accurate grounds that they were already severely pressed for space. In the end, by reorganising some of the administrative staff, they had managed to vacate this room, which was an improvement on the proposed broom cupboard in that it at least had a window. In fact, it had a window which, unlike those in Doripalam's office, actually had a partial view, sandwiched between two adjoining office buildings, out over Sukh Bataar Square.

Doripalam was currently standing staring out at this view, trying to avoid catching Nergui's eye. He was getting better at standing up to him. At least now he felt comfortable saying what he thought. But he still felt faintly patronised, as though Nergui were patiently tolerating his comments rather than paying them any serious attention.

"I've explained," Nergui said. "I'm conducting the enquiry as instituted by the Minister. You know that we have to go through this."

Doripalam was watching the traffic swirling slowly around the square in the chilly morning sunshine. There was the usual procession of battered old Soviet cars and buses, belching thick fumes. The square was thick with clouds of pigeons, scattering for breadcrumbs thrown by a small group of schoolchildren passing on the far side. It was still early, and there were relatively few pedestrians other than a few suited figures heading into the government and commercial offices in the streets around the square. "I know *I* have to go through it," he said. "But I'm still not clear why you have to."

Nergui shrugged. "I thought we'd been through this," he said. "I know the team well. I understand all the pressures you have to face. I've no axes to grind—"

Doripalam turned, shaking his head fiercely. "No axes to grind? Come off it, Nergui, this is your show from start to finish. It's nothing to do with the Minister, except that his signature has somehow appeared on the bottom of the terms of reference. What was it he thought he was signing?"

Nergui smiled. He was, as always, leaning back in his chair, his ankles resting on the corner of the desk. How did he always manage to look so relaxed these days? Perhaps after all the life of a pen pusher had turned out to suit him. "I think you're getting much too cynical," he said. "It must be the job that's getting to you."

Doripalam sat himself slowly down in the chair opposite Nergui, trying to control his exasperation. "Okay," he said. "Tell me again, very slowly, what it is you're trying to do here."

"It's really very simple," Nergui said. "We have had something of a political embarrassment. We know it wasn't your fault, and I know exactly the problems that you've been facing. They were problems I faced when I was in the role, and I never succeeded in resolving them. We've both made some progress, but we both know there's a long way to go."

"You mean corruption?"

Nergui nodded. "We all know that the civilian police was made up initially of every deadbeat that they wanted to kick out of the militia. We took people who could barely string a sentence together and then stuck them in positions of real power. And then we seemed surprised when that power became corrupted almost overnight."

"There are some decent people in the team," Doripalam said.

"I'm not denying it," Nergui said. "Especially among those we recruited later—as the present company amply demonstrates—though even there we were hampered by the poor wages we could offer. Who wants to come and risk their life in the police force when you can earn twice as much working in a shop?"

"I suppose I did."

Nergui nodded. "I suppose you did. And one day I'll have to make a serious attempt to find out why." He smiled faintly. "But you're the exception, along with one or two others. There's a hell of a lot of them out there who really just aren't up to it. The worst ones are corrupt—not seriously so, for the most part, but taking the odd quiet backhander just to turn a blind eye. The ones who aren't corrupt are just incompetent—they don't understand what the job is or why it matters. They don't follow the procedures. They lose us virtually every case we manage to get to court. And the few who aren't corrupt or inept are just lazy. They can't be bothered with the job."

"That doesn't say a lot for my leadership."

"Oh, come off it, you've only been in the job five minutes, and I know you've made some real progress. How long was I in the job? What does it say about my leadership?"

Doripalam knew better than to try to answer that one. "Okay, so where does that get us?"

"It gets us to a point where maybe we have an opportunity to begin to put things right."

"I'm not sure I follow."

"Doripalam, when I was in the job, I pushed and pushed for more resources to get this place sorted out. I managed to get some, but never anything like enough. I imagine you've been doing the same, and I've certainly tried to use whatever influence I've got to support you."

"Well, I'm sure I'm very grateful," Doripalam said. He intended to sound ironic, but was conscious that he merely ended up sounding petulant.

"But no one's interested. There's a flurry of excitement when something really serious happens—like our murders last year—but that kind of thing is generally too embarrassing so all they want to do is sweep it under the carpet."

"As they did very effectively in that case, as I recall."

"Indeed. They're politicians. Their job is to avoid embarrassment. And unfortunately they tend to see a team like this, not as a force for social good, but simply as a source of potential embarrassment."

"And you think we're a source for social good?" he asked.

"Of course I do. You know me. I'm a patriot, for all my cynicism. I want what's best for this country. I think, in a thousand small ways, we're under siege. We're under siege from the West, from the East. And, potentially, we've already been infiltrated. Our defences are already being undermined."

"Sounds a little over-dramatic to me." From the corner of his eye, Doripalam could see the pedestrians strolling across Sukh Bataar Square on their way into work. There was a man, dressed in a grey business suit, sipping American-style coffee from a paper cup as he made his leisurely way past the large statue of the revolutionary hero towards the government offices. Close by, a couple of teenage girls, dressed in T-shirts with Western designer labels emblazoned across the front, had stopped to chat before going their separate ways. This did not look like a country under siege. On the other hand, young as he was, it did not look much like the country Doripalam had grown up in.

Nergui shrugged. "Maybe I spend too much time with politicians. Too much rhetoric. But I think it's true. We expend all our time and energy on the big political questions—our relations with China, with Russia, with the West—while I grow increasingly afraid that it's the smaller crimes, the smaller corruptions that are undermining the stability of the state."

"The state's always been corrupt," Doripalam pointed out.

"Maybe. But, whatever we thought of the old system, things were under control. Now I'm not sure they are. Profit drives everything, and it's slipping away from us. I'm not sure anybody cares enough to fight back."

"Except you?" Doripalam was unsure whether he intended his question to sound mocking or sincere.

Nergui smiled. "I'm just a civil servant. Just doing my job. But I do want to have the resources to do it properly."

"So what does this have to do with the enquiry?"

"We've suffered yet another political embarrassment. The Minister's ridden out the storm, as he always seems to, but the opposition has made serious capital out of it."

Doripalam nodded. "The Minister made that very clear to me. Kept assuring me that it wasn't my fault, but it wasn't clear who else's fault it might have been."

"Certainly not his. But the point is that, for once, they couldn't brush this under the carpet. Which, by a very entertaining irony, was largely the Minister's own fault."

"Because he extracted such political kudos from the fact that we were bringing Muunokhoi to trial in the first place?"

"Precisely so. If I recall correctly, I did warn him that this might not be the wisest move, but he can be an impetuous fellow where political advantage is concerned."

"Even if the case hadn't fallen apart quite so spectacularly, the Minister's comments might have been prejudicial to a fair trial," Doripalam pointed out. "I wasn't exactly pleased about that, though in the circumstances it didn't seem appropriate to bring it up afterwards."

"I understand that Muunokhoi's lawyers were planning to argue precisely along those lines," Nergui said. As always, it was not entirely clear how he had come by this particular piece of information. "But the question was entirely academic, as things turned out."

"And so now we—by which I mean you—have to investigate how Tunjin was allowed to get us into this mess? I'm not sure I quite see how that's likely to help us. I certainly don't see how it's going to help *me*."

"I'm just being opportunistic," Nergui said. "The Minister has to be seen to be doing something if only to cover his own back. He wants a short sharp review that will result in a few suitable rolling heads."

"With my name high on the list?"

"Of course not. The Minister can be impetuous, but he's no fool. He knows—not least because I've repeatedly told him so—that you're the best asset he's got in this force. He's not going to risk losing you over something like this. But, in any case, that's not the way this thing is going to go."

"Why not?"

"Because the Minister has made what might turn out to be—in terms of short term political expediency—one tiny error. He agreed to let me run the enquiry."

"Which means?"

"Which means we do it properly. You and me. We take this as an opportunity really to get to grips with the problems in this team. We can root out the real problems—the real corruption. We make as many heads roll as we need to, knowing that the Minister has to back us up."

"Why does he have to? He's never been keen on raising his head above the battlements before."

"Because having announced the enquiry—which he did with as much fanfare as when he announced Muunokhoi's arrest—he can't then be seen not to support it just because the outcome turns out to be rather more radical than he might have expected."

Doripalam shook his head. He was beginning to suspect that Nergui had been with the politicians too long. "Are you sure about this?"

Nergui shrugged. "Not at all. I'll probably be whipped off the enquiry and find myself facing a sudden early retirement. But I think it's worth a shot, don't you?"

He's bored, Doripalam thought, suddenly. That's what this is about. He's bored witless in that comfortable office of his, shuffling his paperwork. All that talk about the nation under siege—well, that was probably sincere, knowing Nergui's distinctive form of patriotism. But it wasn't what was really driving Nergui. What was really driving him was the need to stir the pot again, to get things moving. To raise some sort of hell.

Doripalam smiled. "As long as it's you facing the early retirement and not me. Yes, maybe it's worth a shot."

* * *

Nergui sat silently at the desk, listening to Doripalam's footsteps receding down the corridor. He supposed that it might have been possible to have found him a temporary office that was smaller and even more isolated than this one, but probably only by utilising a broom cupboard. Not that he could blame Doripalam. On the whole, Nergui thought that the younger man was taking it all rather well. Nergui was behaving like the very worst kind of manager. The kind who gets kicked upstairs and then just can't tear himself away from the job he's supposed to have left behind. Just can't believe that anyone could do it as well as him.

Was that it? Nergui hoped not. He had enormous respect for Doripalam—he thought Doripalam handled the day-to-day aspects of this job better than he had, if only because he seemed to have infinitely more patience with all the nonsense involved. No, it was the job he couldn't leave behind. And not just because he liked the pace and the excitement of it, compared with the cerebral challenges of his Ministry role. But also because he thought it mattered. It was important. It was what held the fabric of this increasingly fragile society together.

All the rhetoric he'd trotted out to Doripalam—well, of course it was overblown. How else did you get the Minister to take any notice of this kind of thing? But, nonetheless, it had been sincere. As he saw the growing influx of drugs dealing, mindless violence, not-so-petty theft—the slow but sure seepage of influence from the wider world—he did begin to think that maybe the battle was already lost. All those grand ideological battle-cries—equality, freedom, democracy—and yet it was this mundane criminality, the underbelly of capitalism, that would end up on top of the pile.

So here he was again, dabbling in things that he should have left far behind. If he'd been in Doripalam's shoes, he'd probably have told them precisely where to stick their enquiry. But that was why Doripalam was good in this role. Because he only fought the battles that mattered. Because, much as he might resent Nergui's repeated intrusions, he also recognised that the older man's experience and knowledge could be useful. Maybe, in the end, it was Doripalam who was exploiting Nergui. At least, Nergui hoped that was the case.

His musing was interrupted by the telephone on the desk in front of him. The sound was startling. Nergui didn't think that anyone yet had this contact number. The Minister would call him on his mobile—probably several times a day once he realised that Nergui wasn't immediately on hand to respond to whatever minor crises were brewing—as would any of his Ministry colleagues. Nergui liked the mobile, partly because he could switch it off when he chose.

He cautiously picked up the receiver. "Nergui?"

"Sir. I'm sorry to disturb you. I have a visitor down at the reception. She's here to report a crime—a threat of physical assault."

Nergui shook his head, wondering, if the call had been transferred to the wrong extension. "I'm sorry," he said. "I think you want someone else."

"No, sir. I'm sorry, but she was keen to speak to you."

"To me? Why should she want to talk to me? Just send her over to the police station."

"Well, yes, sir, that's what I told her. But she says she knows you. She's a judge."

"A *judge*?" The dialogue seemed to be drifting into the realms of the surreal. Nergui had become acquainted with a number of judges in the course of his professional life, but he couldn't think of any who might actively seek him out for the purposes of reporting a crime.

"Yes, sir. She says she's been threatened."

Nergui leaned back in his chair. Through the window, between the angles of the surrounding buildings, he could see a rectangle of pure blue sky. "Threatened?"

"Yes, sir."

It sounded like some kind of lunatic. Someone claiming she was a judge, that she'd been threatened, that she knew Nergui. How did she even know he was here? He sighed gently. "And what's your name, son?"

There was a pause at the other end of the line. "Sangajav, sir."

"Well, Sangajav, I suppose you'd better bring her up. But I hope you're not wasting my time."

There was a second, longer pause. "I'm sorry, sir, but she does claim she knows you."

"Bring her up." Nergui slowly replaced the receiver. He pulled himself upright and walked across to the window. The partial view over the square was not particularly impressive, but at least it was possible to see some real life out there. At the nearest corner of the square there was a cluster of older men, all dressed in traditional robes and sashes, chatting and smoking. Nergui wondered vaguely who they were, and why they were gathered in this way. Beyond there, there was another knot of humanity—this time a group of Japanese tourists, endlessly rearranging themselves to take photograph after photograph of each other standing in front of the government buildings, Sukh Bataar's statue, the post office building.

There was a soft knock at the office door behind him. Nergui turned as the door opened, and Sangajav, a short, colourless figure with his head bowed deferentially, ushered in an attractive dark-haired women in a grey, formal-looking suit. "Sir," he said. "Ms. Radnaa."

She was gazing at Nergui with an amused expression on her face. "It *is* you," she said. "I hadn't quite believed it."

For a second, Nergui stared at her. He half registered that, somewhere behind her, Sangajav had managed to make a discreet and hurried exit and was closing the door gently behind him. "Sarangarel," he said, finally.

She smiled. "Well, I am relieved. For a moment there, I genuinely thought that you didn't remember me."

He shook his head, still trying to reconcile all the information that he had received in the preceding minutes. "I nearly didn't. It's been a long time," he said, aware of how inane his words sounded. Strange, he thought, how shock propels us back into conventionalities. "Ten years."

"Twelve, I think," she said.

He nodded slowly, gesturing her to take a seat. He lowered himself into the seat behind the desk, still staring at the self-possessed woman in front of him. "How did you know I was here?"

"I'm glad to see that your ego hasn't diminished over the years," she said. "I didn't know you were here. I just came to report a crime."

"You should have gone to the police station."

"So I was told by the helpful young man who brought me up here. But I'm glad I didn't."

"Yes," Nergui said, after perhaps slightly too long a pause. "I'm glad you didn't."

"That sounded almost sincere," she laughed.

Nergui shrugged. "No, really, it's good to see you. A bit of a shock, though."

"I can imagine."

"You look very different," he said. "Still terrific, though."

"You know, you keep pausing in the wrong places and for just a moment too long."

Nergui laughed. "But you haven't changed, have you? Whereas I think my hearing must be going, because I thought I heard young Sangajav say that you were a judge."

"That's right. I'm a judge. Trying criminal cases. I'm surprised we haven't run across one another."

He stared at her for a moment, as though trying to make sense of a particularly obscure joke. "You really are?" He shook his head. "You always did have a sense of humour."

"I always did," she said. "But I'm deadly serious about this. And I'm good at it."

"I don't doubt it. You'd be good at anything you put your mind to. But why the judiciary?"

"Well, I think I'd got to know the ways of the law quite well, don't you? Somehow it seemed a natural move."

"Not to me," he said. "And you've not encountered any—problems?"

"As a result of my past, you mean? Why should I? It's not as if I was the criminal. I couldn't help who I was married to. I didn't even know."

There was a sense that she was protesting too much. But that wasn't so surprising, Nergui thought. She'd no doubt had to rehearse these arguments pretty frequently over the years. He couldn't believe that her past hadn't at some point returned to haunt her.

"Of course not," he agreed. "But people can be unforgiving."

She shrugged. "I can't pretend it's been easy. After—well, after it all happened, I didn't know what to do. I was completely lost. There was a point when I thought that maybe you and I . . ." She trailed off, as though suddenly conscious that she might have said too much.

Nergui was watching her intently, his dark face giving nothing away. That had been part of it, she realised. She had never known for sure what he was thinking, could never get quite as close to him as she had needed.

"There was a point when I might have thought the same," he said, surprising her.

She looked up at him, smiling. "It's probably just as well then that neither of us knew what the other was thinking," she said.

"Just as well," he agreed. "But what happened to you? I thought about trying to keep in contact afterwards, but it didn't seem appropriate."

No, she thought, it wouldn't have. And very probably he was right. It wouldn't have been appropriate. "I floundered for a while. There was nobody. Things could have turned out very badly, I think, if I hadn't got a grip of myself."

It was difficult now to imagine her having anything less than a very firm grip on herself, Nergui thought. But he knew that hadn't always been the case.

"I managed to get myself a job. Ironically, with the legal firm who'd handled the case—"

Nergui nodded. He recalled the lawyer who had acted for Sarangarel's husband and could imagine that his motives for offering her a job after her husband's death might not have been entirely altruistic. But the lawyer would also have been smart enough to recognise that, whatever else he might or might not get from the arrangement, he would at least get a very capable employee.

"I started doing clerical work. I did well, got myself promoted, and eventually they offered me the chance to take a law degree with the aim of moving into a professional role in the firm."

"Which I've no doubt you undertook with consummate ease," Nergui said.

"I'm not sure I'd say that," she said. "But I did it, worked as a criminal lawyer for several years and then got the chance to apply for the judiciary. One of the benefits of a burgeoning democracy—it does create a whole new set of employment opportunities. Did you know that over half our judges are women?"

"It just confirms what I've always assumed about female judgement," Nergui said. "Considerably more reliable than the male equivalent."

"And women tend to be less patronising, as well," she said.

Nergui smiled. "But, as you say, it is ironic. That you should have ended up passing judgement over—"

"People like my late husband? Well, I suppose you don't need to delve too deeply into the psychology of that."

"In my experience," Nergui said, "it never pays to delve too deeply into the psychology of anything."

"And what about you, Nergui?" she said. "I followed your progress for a few years—I suppose I could claim it was a professional interest, as a criminal lawyer. I thought I might bump into you when I was trying the Muunokhoi case. That was one of yours, wasn't it?"

He looked up at her sharply, a glint of suspicion evident in his eyes for the first time. "You tried the Muunokhoi case?"

"Well, insofar as it was tried. If it was one of yours, it wasn't your finest hour."

"It wasn't one of mine," he said. "Not directly. I'd already moved on by then. But it's why I'm back here now. And, no, it wasn't our finest hour."

"What went wrong?" she said. "I've never seen the State Prosecutor's Office look so rattled. Normally they're the ones rattling everyone else."

Nergui absently straightened the pile of files on the desk, acutely conscious that the entire Muunokhoi case history was spread out on the polished surface between them. "Are you sure you're here entirely by chance?" he said. "One hell of a coincidence."

She sat back and gazed at him coolly, a faint smile on her lips. "You really don't trust anyone, do you, Nergui? I suppose I should have remembered that. You're always careful to ensure that no one else is a step ahead of you."

"I'm not worried when people are a step ahead of me," he said. "It's when they're a step behind me that I start worrying what they're up to. I've been caught from behind just once or twice too often. Literally and figuratively."

She laughed. "But, no, I am here entirely by coincidence. And only because I went to the wrong place." She paused. "But I suppose that wasn't entirely accidental. I came here because I'd been interviewed here so often. I'd assumed this was the station."

"There's no question that what your husband was involved in were serious crimes," Nergui said. "That's why you came here. But—okay, I won't be suspicious—why are you here? What is all this about threats?"

"I don't honestly know. It may well be nothing. It started not long after the Muunokhoi case, actually. Somebody had got hold of my private phone number and I got three or four calls—"

"Threatening?"

She shrugged. "Not really. Not at first. Just nothing. But with a sense that there was somebody still there, that the line was open."

"Everybody gets these automated marketing calls these days. Even here. We live in a global economy. Or it could just be someone's mobile playing up. The signals are always poor outside the city."

"I don't think it's someone I know. The number is always concealed."

"Marketing calls, then. These predictive dialling machines. The operators can't keep up with them."

"Of course it could have been. But then more recently I've

had some that do seem more threatening. Always late at night. A voice—sounding metallic, as if it's been disguised or treated in some way—repeating a name. My husband's name."

Nergui stared at her. "Anything else?"

"Nothing. Just that, over and over. Till I put the phone down. Sometimes even then the line isn't cut, so if I pick it up again the voice is still there, still repeating." She paused. "Those are the most unnerving times. When I think I'll never stop it—that it'll just keep on and on like that."

"Does it sound like a recording?"

"It might be. I don't know. Maybe yes. That would explain why it sounds so relentless."

"And is there anything explicitly threatening?"

"No. Just that. That's why I've been so reluctant to do anything about it."

"There must be a procedure for you to follow," Nergui said. "As a judge, I mean. If you receive threats."

"I'm sure there is," she said. "But I felt foolish invoking something like that unless there was a good reason. And I'm not sure there is."

"But you were willing to come and talk to the police?" Nergui's blue eyes were watching her intently, and for a moment she realised what it would feel like to be on the wrong end of one of his interrogations.

"I suppose . . ." She hesitated. "Well, I suppose that's why I came here, though it wasn't particularly conscious. On the whole, I'd been treated well here, in the circumstances. Not least by you. So I thought maybe someone here would listen to me. Just talk it through. See if I'm being ridiculous."

"Which is what we're doing," Nergui said. He wondered how accidental her appearance here had really been. She had never struck him, even when she was in the middle of those dark days a decade before, as someone who would engage in a fool's errand. She had thought that Nergui was still in charge here. Maybe she had come intending to have precisely this kind of discussion.

"And do you think I'm being ridiculous?"

"No, of course not. If anything, I think you're probably being too relaxed about the whole thing. It sounds as if this is something specifically designed to unsettle you. It's obviously someone who knows about your background. How widely known would that be?"

"I don't know. I've not lied about it, but I don't particularly go out of my way to publicise it either. But, no, it wouldn't be widely known."

"And I think we can reasonably assume that it's someone trying to put pressure on you in your judicial role."

"But not very effectively?"

"Not so far, no. But it's already moved up a gear from the original silent calls, so we can probably assume that they may become more threatening."

"I'm glad I came to you for an objective opinion rather than comfort," she said.

"I'm much better on the former."

"So I recall. But, yes, I suppose you're right. I should report it."

"Report it as you need to with the judiciary. I imagine they need it on the record in case there are any subsequent questions about your impartiality."

She looked up at him with a slightly startled expression. "Impartiality? Yes, well, I see what you mean. It's stupid of me. I should have thought of all this."

Nergui watched her carefully. As he recalled, she was anything but stupid, or even absentminded. It was difficult to believe that she hadn't really thought through all this before turning up, unannounced and unexpected, at the door of police headquarters. "You're probably feeling anxious about it all—maybe more than you realise. After all, just hearing that name after all these years will have stirred up a lot that you probably thought was long buried."

She nodded, as though this idea was also new to her. Nergui thought back to her earlier comment about being patronised. He suspected that she might be someone who tolerated being patronised if this allowed her also to be underestimated.

"I can deal with the police side of it," he said, wondering even as he spoke whether this was entirely wise. "We can do some checking on the calls. We might be able to track down the calling number, though I wouldn't be too hopeful on that front. Might be a good idea if we give you some protection too."

She smiled. "Is that really necessary, do you think?"

He shrugged. "I don't want to alarm you unnecessarily. Chances are that this is just some half-baked idiot who's trying to cause a bit of trouble. Maybe someone with a grudge against you. Someone you sent down, maybe?"

"Well, of course, that's possible. But do you think there's any real danger?"

"I doubt it, to be honest. These people usually just like to stir things up. Those who want to do harm will generally just go ahead and do it. But you can never be sure."

"I bow to your superior knowledge," she said. "I hope you're right."

"So do I," he said. He paused. "It's been good to see you again, Sarangarel."

She nodded. "It must be fate," she said. "I came to the wrong place, and you weren't supposed to be here. Though you never did explain what it is that you are doing here." She looked around the tiny, sparsely furnished office. "And this hardly looks like the head man's room."

"It isn't," he said. "I'm not the head man here. Not anymore.

And, to be honest, I'm not even entirely sure what it is that I'm doing here."

"That's not like you, Nergui," she said. "You usually knew exactly what you were doing."

"I did, didn't I?" he said. His blue eyes were unblinking. "And, if I remember rightly, so did you."

SIX

Tunjin was slumped on the bed, looking as though someone had just struck him a hefty blow in the stomach.

He looked again at the open file, the picture of Muunokhoi staring back up at him with its empty smile. If this meant what he thought it did, then he could expect far worse than a blow in the stomach in the near future.

He tried to find some other interpretation, some other explanation for the presence of this photograph. Perhaps it had been in the file all along, an aid to identifying Muunokhoi. There were, after all, no official police mug shots of Muunokhoi—not until his recent arrest, at any rate. The arrest for which Tunjin had been responsible.

But he knew that this picture had not been in the file. He had been through the file dozens of times, collating the genuine evidence, checking the confected material, searching for inconsistencies, searching for anything that would reveal the forgeries. He had been convinced that it had all been perfect, foolproof.

But Muunokhoi had seen through it. And now the only fool here was Tunjin.

And, in any case, even if the photograph had been there all along, this didn't explain how the file came to be here, in Tunjin's flat. He had been over and over this in his mind in the preceding few minutes. Okay, he remembered little or nothing of the past few nights, but that itself indicated that he had not been in a condition to start stealing files from police headquarters. There was no question—this file had been stolen and placed here by someone in a far more coherent state of mind than Tunjin.

He needed a drink. He really needed a drink. He thought back to the numerous nearly empty vodka bottles in the other room. There was still plenty of booze left. More than enough.

It was tempting. Simply to slip back into oblivion. Just lie there and wait for whatever might happen. Except, of course, that nothing would. He would die of alcohol poisoning before Muunokhoi would do anything to him while he was unconscious. Muunokhoi liked his victims to know precisely what was happening to them and why. Not someone with a great tolerance of ambiguity, Muunokhoi.

Tunjin shook his head. No, for once, the answer wasn't to hide himself away in drink. He shuddered at the thought that, sometime over the last day or two, probably while he lay in a drunken stupor, someone had entered the flat, probably stepped over his comatose body, and placed this file on his bed. That was a fairly powerful incentive to eschewing the booze, at least for a while.

So how close were they? Were they nearby, just waiting for him to wake up, so they could finish things off?

He had to be careful. Fortunately, with the brilliance of the sunshine outside, he had had no need to switch on the lights and the curtains were already drawn back. No one watching from the outside would have seen any movement so far.

Unless they were listening for the judder of the plumbing as he had turned on the tap to get himself some water.

No, he was being paranoid. The plumbing in this place was so ancient that there was no way of tracing any noise back to any individual flat. But the principle could well be right. They could be waiting for some sign of life. Maybe waiting for him to leave the flat so they could pick him up and take him to some more suitable place. But if that was the case, why hadn't they just snatched him while he was unconscious? They could have taken him where they liked and then waited for him to wake up.

Because they were playing with him. That was why they'd left the file here. That was why they were letting him wait. Because they knew what he'd be thinking. They knew what he'd be thinking about. They knew—because it was now here in front of him—that he'd read Muunokhoi's file.

And that was it. He knew—and they knew he knew—what Muunokhoi was capable of. He couldn't just sit here and wait for it.

He pulled himself to his feet and stumbled over to the window, standing carefully to one side so that he wouldn't be seen from outside. He blinked at the sunlight, noting from the position of the sun that it really was still morning.

The bedroom window gave a view of the main street below. It was certainly nothing impressive. Depressing Soviet-style apartment blocks—just like this one—lined both sides of the street, preventing the sun from penetrating except in the very middle of the day. The occasional puttering car went by, mostly clapped out old Ladas, the only kind of vehicle that could be afforded by the people who lived in these endless anonymous blocks. Tunjin peered out, his eyes flicking across the grey-stained concrete.

There was a figure standing, motionless, a hundred or so metres up the street.

Tunjin pulled back, hoping that no movement had been visible. The figure had been casually dressed—some sort of sweatshirt and loose trousers, a shaved head, cigarette in hand. But watching, definitely watching.

Tunjin shook his head hard, trying to clear the confusion that was gathering there. He needed to think clearly. He needed to concentrate. He needed—he needed a drink, but, no, that was the last thing he needed.

What he really needed was to get out of there.

He looked down at his stained clothes. He couldn't go far dressed like this. He needed to plan this carefully, as carefully as a severely hungover man could.

He moved away from the window, and stepped back over to the built-in closet on the adjoining wall. He slid back the door and looked inside, his expectations very low. To his mild surprise, there were a couple of clean T-shirts hanging up, and at least one pair of the large, elastic trousers that were the only kind suited to his gut. The presence of these clothes was, he suspected, nothing more than proof that he had actually been wearing his current ones for several days.

He quickly pulled off his T-shirt and trousers and tossed them casually into a corner, where they joined several others. After a pause, he pulled off his enormous Y-fronts and threw them in the same direction. There was a pile of apparently clean underwear on the floor of the closet.

He pulled on the new Y-fronts, then quickly donned the new black T-shirt and trousers. Both were perhaps slightly too small and stretched across his fat body, but—he thought, as he caught sight of himself in the mirror—it was a definite improvement on his previous appearance. He thrust his feet into his only pair of boots, kicking off some of the dried mud, and then grabbed his anorak from behind the bedroom door.

Right, he thought, ready for action. The only question now was what he ought to do.

He walked slowly back through into the living room, taking care not to approach the windows. He reached the front door, carefully turned the catch and silently pulled open the door. This was make or break, he thought. If they were watching out in the corridor, this was the end. But he'd bargained on the fact that they wouldn't have left anyone inside the building. Too conspicuous, he thought. Some of his busybody neighbours would have challenged any intruder within moments.

The corridor appeared deserted. He glanced back at the clock. Eight-forty now. Most of his neighbours would have gone off to work, other than the older ones who tended not to stir from their flats till later in the day. He put the door on the latch, and then stepped quietly out into the corridor.

Nothing.

He walked, as silently as he could manage—and surprisingly so for one of his bulk—towards the head of the staircase that led down to the lobby. Tunjin's flat was on the first floor, so from the top steps he could peer down into the entrance to the apartment block. It was a depressing hallway—a mix of discarded debris from previous tenants, a couple of stacked bicycles, and piles of uncollected mail and newspapers. But it was, at least, apparently unoccupied.

Tunjin made his way slowly down the stairs, trying to ensure that his movement was not visible to any external observer. The main doors to the apartment block contained large glass panels, but the glass was sufficiently filthy and the interior of the lobby sufficiently gloomy that no movement was likely to be visible from outside.

Tunjin moved forward slowly, reaching down as he passed to pick up two items from the pile of discarded items that littered the lobby. The first was an old broom, apparently thrown away because the head was worn out. The second was an old pencil stub. Improvisation was always his strong point.

He stepped slowly across the lobby, still keeping back from the door to ensure that there was no risk of his being seen from outside. Through the grimy glass, he could see the shaven-headed figure he had spotted from the bedroom. There didn't appear to be any other observers that he could see, although it was possible that there was another at the opposite end of the street, out of Tunjin's sight. The man was looking bored, pulling on another cigarette and shuffling his feet. Tunjin waited until he had turned his back, sheltering from the breeze to light another cigarette, then he stepped forward swiftly and jammed the broom handle firmly into the pull handles on the doors, preventing them from being opened from the outside. Then, crouching down so that he was still invisible from outside, he locked the doors with his own set of keys and then forced the pencil stub hard into the lock, breaking off the end to ensure that the lock was solidly jammed.

He felt a little guilty about this. He was undoubtedly going to inconvenience the other residents of the block, and he just hoped that there would be no other, more serious consequences—in common with many of the Soviet-era apartment blocks, this unit had no other escape route in case of fire.

But given that he was unsure when Muunokhoi might decide that he had exercised enough patience, or even when the boredom of the man outside might precipitate him to take some unsanctioned action, Tunjin thought it was prudent to try to buy himself a little extra time. It would be possible to break the glass in the doors, of course, but the glass would be toughened and the act of breaking it would be conspicuous even in this relatively deserted thoroughfare. And there was no other route into the building, other than that which Tunjin was planning to adopt as his exit route, and this, he hoped, would not be immediately obvious to an outsider.

He slipped back from the doors, and then began to climb

the stairs as rapidly as his considerable bulk would allow. The worst symptoms of his hangover seemed to have receded now, though he couldn't claim that he felt well, either physically or emotionally.

He passed his own floor, and carried on climbing past the second and third floors, wheezing heavily by now, his breath coming in short spurts. There were definitely times when he thought that a healthier lifestyle might be recommended.

Finally, he dragged himself up the last flight of stairs on to the fourth floor. There were no flats up here, only a couple of storage and utility rooms, mostly filled with junk. His objective lay in the far corner of one of the cluttered rooms—a skylight in the ceiling with a pull down ladder fixed beneath it.

He forced his way through the clutter, pushing aside a rusting twintub washing machine and a couple of broken chairs, until he was standing directly underneath the skylight. As he passed, he reached down to pick up an old screwdriver that had been left on top of the washing machine. Pausing to regain some of his breath, he reached up and pulled on the ladder. It was stiff and a little rusty, but, as he tugged, it eventually juddered down.

Tunjin looked at it carefully, and then looked down at his own bulk. The ladder should be capable of holding his weight, he thought, though he was glad that he wouldn't have to rely on it for too long. He took a deep breath and then slowly began to climb up the rungs. The metal frame of the ladder creaked ominously, but seemed to be holding.

He reached the skylight, pulled on the handle and began to force it upwards. For a moment, he thought that it would fail to open, but eventually, with a little shaking and pushing, it gave. Tunjin climbed the remainder of the ladder and, gasping for breath, he pulled himself up and onto the roof of the apartment block.

He lay for some minutes, feeling nauseous, his breath coming in painful gasps. He really wasn't cut out for this kind of thing. Not anymore, at any rate.

The bright sunlight and fresh air hit him almost as strongly as his breathlessness and the aftereffects of his hangover. He rolled over onto his back and lay, still gasping, his eyes closed, the brilliance of the sun crimson through his closed eyelids. Thankfully, the sun was still relatively low and the air still chilly, the breeze riffling gently through his sweat-soaked T-shirt.

Finally, he recovered his breath and rolled over to shut the skylight firmly behind him. He looked around to see if there was anything on the flat roof he could use to jam the skylight, in the hope of buying himself a little more time, but there was nothing.

He sat up and looked around. The rooftop was little more than an empty stretch of grey asphalt. A line of identical apartment blocks stretched off down the street, with a similar row opposite.

He had been up here on a couple of previous occasions, with the aim of getting an idea of the layout. The rooftop gave an attractive view of the city. In the distance, he could see the large buildings that dominated the centre—the Post Office, the Parliament house, the Palace of Culture. He could see the pink and black monolith of the Chinghis Khaan Hotel, the wide green spaces of Nairamdal Park, and the Naadam Stadium. In the distance, he could make out the haze and black tangle of buildings that denoted the industrial areas, and the long silver sheen of the railway line. And beyond all that, the wide open green of the steppes and the distant mountains.

He had grown up in this city, known it all his life and—in all honesty—had never thought much of it. But now, just at this moment, it looked genuinely beautiful. But that might, he supposed, have something to do with the fact that he really might not be enjoying the sight of it for very much longer.

He pulled himself slowly to his feet and walked unsteadily across to the edge of the roof above the main street. He lowered himself and peered cautiously down. The shaven-headed man was still there, but was now talking on a mobile phone. There was no obvious sense of urgency in his manner, so Tunjin assumed that his own departure had not yet been noticed.

He pulled back and began to make his way slowly across the rooftop. His aim ought to be to put as much space between himself and Muunokhoi as possible. Or, perhaps more accurately, to give himself the opportunity to try to get a step or two ahead of Muunokhoi. He could perhaps simply flee the city—head off to another town, maybe down into the Gobi. Surely it must be possible to find somewhere where Muunokhoi couldn't track him down.

And it wasn't as if he had much of a future ahead of him here. He had been deliberately provocative in his meeting with Doripalam, but he assumed that the outcome would be the same—his current suspension would be followed by dismissal. Someone's head was going to have to roll for what had happened, and Tunjin was the only candidate. If he was lucky, he might get to hold on to part of his pension. But he didn't have too many grounds for assuming that he would be lucky. He had been on borrowed time anyway, he knew that, given his drinking and the general state of his health, which was why he'd started all this in the first place.

He'd reached the end of his own apartment block. The rooftop continued on the next block, with a space of about half a metre between them. He peered down—the gap between the two buildings stretched four floors to the ground below. Typical Soviet design, he thought. It would have been too simple and too efficient to have built one large apartment block. Probably building them as separate units created enough additional work to help someone hit their production target.

There was no option but to jump the gap. It wasn't far, and for most people it would have presented no problem. Tunjin had a good head for heights, but his general obesity, not to mention his still mildly spinning head, meant that this was likely to be a challenge. He held his breath for a moment, teetering as close to the gap as he dared. Then, trying not to close his eyes, he leapt across.

He fell flat on his face on the other side, his fingers scraping at the asphalt, his knees and chest stinging from the impact. His feet, he was aware, were still sticking out over the gap. But he seemed to have made it over.

He looked ahead of him. There were two more similar gaps he would have to cross before reaching the final block. And then he would be faced with the problem of how to get down again. But he hoped he had that one sorted.

He continued steadily along the rooftop, until he reached the next block. Then—and this time he did close his eyes—he threw himself forward. Again, he landed roughly but safely. Maybe he was fitter than he thought. He rolled over, pausing to recover his breath. At least this exertion meant that, for the moment, he could postpone thinking further about what the future might hold.

He was dragging himself to his feet again when he heard the sound of some kind of commotion behind and below him. He slowly moved towards the edge of the roof and peered down at the street below, trying to see what was happening without risking being seen himself.

There was no doubt that the disturbance, whatever it was, was happening outside his own block. There was a shouting and a banging. The shaven-headed man, he noticed, was no longer standing in the same position, but had moved into the middle of the street, apparently looking at what was going on.

Tunjin moved himself forward, trying to get a better view, but conscious that—with his equilibrium still disturbed—it would not be wise to lean too far forward. But he could see enough. There were a couple of figures standing outside the door of his block, banging on the glass doors and shouting. Tunjin couldn't recognise them from this distance, but he assumed that they were fellow residents of the block who had discovered that the front door was both locked and firmly jammed.

Perhaps, on reflection, his attempt to buy himself some extra time had not been a wise one. If Muunokhoi's people had tried to make a move straight away, it would have certainly given him an additional respite while they forced their way into the building. As it was, the barring of the door had probably simply highlighted to the shaven-headed man that there might be some sort of problem. Tunjin could see that the man was already drawing closer to the door, and that he was engaged in some sort of dialogue with the locked-out residents.

Tunjin was contemplating his next action when he saw the man gesture furiously to the residents, waving his arms to signal them to move aside. Then—when they had presumably obeyed his instruction—he raised his arm and the sound of a gunshot echoed down the empty street, followed an instant later by the sound of shattering glass.

Tunjin needed no more prompting. He rolled over and staggered to his feet, thinking that, perhaps for the first time in years, he really did have an incentive to lose some weight. He began to jog, as fast as his bulk would allow, towards the next rooftop, this time by some miracle managing to stay on his feet as he threw himself over the gap.

He knew that the end block was identical to his own, and his original plan had been to use the screwdriver to lever open the skylight. In retrospect, he thought, perhaps this whole scheme would have benefited from a little more thinking through. And now time was definitely not on his side.

He reached the skylight and pulled out the screwdriver, slipping its blade into the gap along the edge of the framework. He pushed it down, but the frame showed no sign of giving. He looked across at the rusted hinges of the window, aware that the screwdriver was already bending under his weight.

Finally, he pulled it out and slammed the blade down into the centre of the glass, which shattered explosively beneath him. He pulled his hand back just in time, avoiding being badly cut. Then he lifted his foot and began to slam down hard on the remaining glass, rapidly clearing the edge of the frame until he felt it would be safe to drop through.

He looked down into the empty gap. There was a ladder, as in his own block, but this one looked to be badly broken. He reached and tried to lower it, but couldn't move it at all. Finally, he looked behind him and, clutching hard on the edges of the frame, dropped through the gaping hole.

There was a battered kitchen table, now only half a metre or so below his dangling feet. He scrabbled for a moment, then dropped, trying to land safely on the polished wooden table-top.

His feet hit the table and skidded so that he slipped sideways, his fingers desperately clutching for some kind of purchase. His stomach landed heavily on the table surface and then, just when he thought he had landed safely, he heard the sound of cracking wood as one of the table legs shattered beneath his weight. The table tipped sideways, and Tunjin toppled off to one side, landing heavily among a pile of empty paint-pots, as the table fell across him.

For a moment there was silence, and Tunjin lay breathing heavily, convinced that every bone in his body was broken. It took him a few moments to realise that this probably wasn't the case, and that he appeared to have survived the fall with no more serious consequences than some bruising.

He pulled himself into a sitting position, pushing the table away from him, trying to manoeuvre his body away from the scattered pile of paint tins. For a moment, he felt relief. He was alive. He had—at least for the moment—escaped.

Then his relief vanished, to be replaced by a gut-wrenching fear. He choked, feeling waves of nausea sweeping over him, as though all the symptoms of his hangover, having been suppressed during his traverse of the rooftops, were now returning in redoubled form.

The two barrels of a shotgun were inches from his face, pointing unwaveringly at his forehead.

From behind them, a quiet voice said: "I do hope you're going to clean all this up."

SEVEN

"But you know what he's up to. It's what he's always up to. Undermining you."

Doripalam shook his head, trying to close his eyes. The sight of his wife pacing up and down the room always made his head ache. "I don't think that's it," he said. "I don't think that's really ever been it. But certainly not this time." He had a small glass of vodka in his hands, chilled from the fridge, and he wanted just to enjoy it, but Solongo, as so often, seemed to have other plans.

"You're just too trusting, that's your trouble. That's always been your trouble. You let people walk all over you."

He knew she meant well. She always meant well. That was part of the problem. Of course, she was concerned for her own interests—who wasn't? But, deep down, he was convinced that this wasn't simply selfishness, that she really did care about his own interests as well. But then, he reflected, maybe he was just too trusting.

"Why should he want to undermine me? He appointed me into the job."

"He wouldn't have appointed anyone into the job if he could have helped it, you know that. He'd have been in the job himself. For life."

"But now he isn't in it. He's in a much bigger job. So why should he care about me?"

"Because you're in the job that he used to do—that he still wants to do—and you're handling it far better than he ever could."

This was rare. Solongo was generally reluctant to make positive comments about her husband, even when criticising her favourite hate figure—his former boss, Nergui. Maybe this was some sort of positive sign.

He opened his eyes and took a cautious sip of the vodka. "Well, I'm flattered that you should think so," he said, trying his hardest not to sound sarcastic.

"Well, it's obvious," she said. "You're no fool, Doripalam, even if you quite often act like one. You can do your job very capably. Nergui's going to feel threatened."

Doripalam found it difficult to envisage Nergui feeling threatened even by physical violence, let alone by the possibility that some youngster might possibly upstage him. "But even if that's true," he said, "it doesn't explain what he's up to at the moment. Why he's been so keen to lead this enquiry."

"Are you sure he's not going to offer you up as a sacrificial lamb?" Solongo said. She finally sat down and picked up her own glass of vodka, watching him carefully. "I mean, I know he'd made all these positive noises. But this case with—what's his name? The gangster?"

"Muunokhoi."

"Yes, Muunokhoi. Well, this case would give Nergui all the ammunition he needs if he wants to get rid of you."

"And replace me how? There's no one else who could do the job. No one who would want it, anyway."

She shrugged. "I don't know. Maybe Nergui would bring it back under his own empire again. I'm sure he's arrogant enough to think he could do both jobs without breaking a sweat."

"You're just paranoid," he said.

But maybe she was right to be. Doripalam looked around the living room in which they were sitting. A decent-sized room in a decent-sized apartment in one of the better areas of the city. A large leather sofa, thick crimson pile carpets, expensive rugs and a scattering of tasteful ornaments and paintings. It really wasn't too bad. He'd progressed much further in his life and career than he had ever really believed possible, even if it wasn't yet quite as far as Solongo would have preferred. His father—a factory worker under the old regime—wouldn't have believed that his son would ever be living in a palatial residence like this.

So maybe Solongo was right. Perhaps the Muunokhoi case could be the one that stripped him of all this. It had happened on his watch. And arguably he should have been more observant. After the event, he had heard countless rumours about Tunjin. Tunjin's instability since he had split with his wife. Tunjin's insubordination. Tunjin's drinking. Especially Tunjin's drinking. He had obviously kept it well under control during work time, since Doripalam had never seen any signs of it. But it was now clear that, outside working hours, Tunjin was drinking heavily—that he was regularly found semi-comatose in various of the more unsavoury bars around the city. Doripalam suspected that a number of Tunjin's colleagues had covered up for him over the years, getting him home when perhaps, in other circumstances, he would have found himself in a prison cell for the night.

So, yes, perhaps it was reasonable that his neck should be on the block over this. But he still couldn't believe that Nergui would be the one to raise the axe.

He sat back in the crimson leather armchair, sipping on his vodka. "Anyway, I still think there's more to it than that. This isn't about me. It's about Nergui in some way—"

"It's always about Nergui," Solongo said. She stretched out her legs, smiling at her husband and shaking her head. She really was a remarkably elegant woman, Doripalam thought, wondering yet again how it was that he'd come to be married to her. She was most definitely out of his league, not just in terms of her beauty but also in terms of her social status. Her father had been a senior party officer under the old regime—one of the small elite who had prospered under the yoke of communism. Doripalam had met him only a few times before his death, and he had never been quite sure what the old man's role had actually been, which was probably ominous enough in itself. But there was no doubt that it had been accompanied by significant wealth and power, most of which he had apparently managed to hang on to even after the arrival of democracy.

He also wondered, in his more suspicious moments, whether the old man had, somewhere in his working life, stumbled up against Nergui. That, he thought, might explain Solongo's antagonism.

"You're far too naïve," she said, breaking into his thoughts. "You assume that everyone's as well-intentioned and altruistic as you are." She gazed at him, with an expression that might have been affectionate, but which was also oddly reminiscent of a young girl's attitude towards her favourite pet or doll.

"Whereas you know differently," he said.

He swallowed the last of his vodka and moved to pour himself another, gesturing with the bottle towards Solongo. She held up her nearly full glass and shook her head. "And you drink too much," she said.

Maybe that was true, too. Doripalam had certainly become conscious of an increase in his alcohol consumption over the last few months, particularly as the Muunokhoi case had collapsed. It was still just a few glasses in the evening, but it had increasingly become a welcome retreat from the pressures of the day. He thought again about Tunjin, and wondered at what point Tunjin's own drinking had tipped over from social relaxation into something much darker and more dangerous. Would Doripalam ever recognise that point if he were to approach it himself?

"So what do you think Nergui's up to?" he said, refilling his glass and slumping back down by her side. "Other than undermining me. I mean, Nergui's right. There was always going to have to be an enquiry about the Muunokhoi case. The Minister's already taken too much flak in Parliament. He's got to demonstrate that he's doing something."

"But why does Nergui have to run it?" Solongo said. "Surely he's the last person who should be involved."

"That's what I said," Doripalam countered, defensively. "I thought there'd be a conflict of interest. But Nergui didn't seem very bothered about that. He obviously wants to use this for his own ends, which seem to be about cleaning up the team once and for all. But I've no idea quite how he thinks he's going to do that."

"And do you have any idea what all this might do to you?"

Doripalam took a deep swallow of the vodka. "I'm just hoping that Nergui will protect me more than anyone else might care to do."

She shook her head slowly, smiling at him. "I think it's rather sweet that you're so trusting," she said. "I just hope that you're right."

While he waited, Nergui thumbed for the fourth or fifth time through the ring-bound notebook in which he'd jotted down all his thoughts on the Muunokhoi case. He'd spent most of the day sitting in that cramped office working his way through the various relevant files—the case file itself, files relating to various other past cases that he thought might potentially be relevant, Tunjin's personal file, personal files relating to a number of other officers, even Doripalam's own personal file.

The last of these was not stored within police headquarters, in recognition of Doripalam's seniority, but held in the Ministry itself. Strictly speaking, it was accessible only by Doripalam's own line manager within the police hierarchy. But Nergui had quickly discovered that, in the face of his own assumed proximity to the Minister, very few Ministry doors remained closed for very long. Even so, he felt mildly guilty that he had taken advantage of his unofficial authority in this particular case. He told himself that his motives were good, but had also made every effort to ensure that no trace of the file would be found within police headquarters. At the end of the day, he had taken the file back to his own apartment and locked it safely away in his well-concealed strongbox. He would return it to the Ministry in the morning, still unsure whether he had made an error in removing it in the first place.

And now, thirty minutes later, he was sitting among the bright décor of Millie's Café in the Center Hotel, sipping a coffee and wondering if he was about to commit another error.

He looked around him. It would have been difficult to imagine, even five years ago, that places like this would have appeared in the city. Nergui still felt that there was something unpalatable about the existence of such outlets alongside the poverty and deprivation that continued to dominate large parts of the country. It was only a few winters ago that there were people literally dying on the steppes—caught between the natural rigours of the harshest weather in memory and the man-made pressures of the new free market economy. And yet now here were throngs of well-dressed, prosperous people, locals and westerners alike, sipping freshly squeezed orange juice and fancy coffees to the burbling sounds of American pop music.

Nergui had spent enough time in the West to be used to this kind of thing, though he never understood why the Americans deluded themselves that they could make coffee. Here, though, he could get the Italian-style coffee he liked. He sipped slowly on his espresso and continued to leaf through the notebook.

It was telling him nothing new, but he had not expected that it would. He was at the stage—which he recalled well from his days as a more conventional investigating officer—when the priority was simply to ensure that he knew the facts as well as he could. He always felt that it was critical that he should be able to piece together all aspects of each case thoroughly in his mind. In this way, if he subsequently stumbled upon some new piece of information, some anomaly, he could isolate it immediately. He had a good memory, but it was far from photographic. Nevertheless, if he worked hard he could embed detail in his mind sufficiently comprehensively that he would know instantly if something didn't fit. It was a useful skill particularly in more complicated cases when key details could easily be overlooked simply because it was assumed that they had already been addressed.

In this case, though, he still wasn't sure quite how much he was investigating, quite how far this went. The immediate concern, of course, was Tunjin's falsification of evidence. There was no real doubt there, though it was far from obvious to Nergui how it had been exposed in the first place. The forged documents were not particularly sophisticated, but they would probably have passed muster with the Prosecutor's Office if someone hadn't started raising questions internally. But where those questions had first arisen, no one seemed sure.

Lacking any other sense of direction, Nergui had worked his

way through the piles of individual staff files for the officers. The majority, including Tunjin's, yielded little that was unexpected. He had asked for the files relating to other cases that had been dropped or abandoned, but had been told that the numbers were so large that it would be easier for Nergui to visit the archives for himself. He had done so, and had spent part of an afternoon ploughing disconsolately through page after page of uninformative paperwork. Somewhere in here might be the single thread that would start everything unravelling, but it would take weeks of work to uncover it.

In the end, with no other way forward, he had returned to the bulging pile of files, dating back nearly two decades, that related to Muunokhoi. The content here was at least moderately interesting. Muunokhoi was a figure well-known to the police in Ulan Baatar, just as, for different reasons, he was familiar to most of the adult population of the country. The files, in accordance with Muunokhoi's status, comprised an odd mix of formal case documentation and endless newspaper clippings.

When had he first encountered Muunokhoi? He had been aware of the name for a long time—nearly twenty years. He had heard the rumours along with everyone else. From time to time, and more frequently as the years went by, he had had reasons to investigate Muunokhoi's activities. But they had finally come face-to-face a decade before.

They had brought him in, initially only as a potential witness, in connection with the torching of a garment warehouse on the south side of the city—a massive blaze that spread into surrounding buildings and resulted in three deaths and the evacuation of a neighbouring residential block. There was little doubt that the cause was arson, and the first assumption was that it was a straightforward case of insurance fraud. But the owner of the warehouse, initially the primary suspect, had been quick to point the finger at Muunokhoi's people. "We find them importing shoddy versions of our goods—pirated copies—selling them for a fraction of the price. But that is not enough for them. They have to destroy my business, destroy my property, even kill my staff. I know who they are—"

Given that the apparent victim's business was already in trouble as a result of this new competition, it was equally likely that he had himself arranged for the warehouse to be torched. But it had provided Nergui with an opportunity to bring Muunokhoi in for questioning.

Muunokhoi had still been a young man—thirty-two years old according to the files, although Nergui had suspected that this was a conservative figure. But he was already on his way to becoming a legend.

Nergui still remembered his first impressions. A slim, good-looking young man, at ease with himself, exuding a self-confidence that bordered on arrogance. He had been sitting in the interview room, apparently untroubled, one leg slung over the side of the metal chair. It was a room designed to intimidate, but somehow Muunokhoi managed to dominate it.

"You wish to speak with me?" he said, in the manner of one granting an exclusive interview.

Nergui had lowered himself into the chair opposite. "We wish you to provide a witness statement, yes."

"Only too happy to be of assistance. I admire the work you people do."

"We're very grateful," Nergui said. He raised his eyes and stared unblinkingly at the young man. "I'm sure the sentiment is reciprocated."

"I'm sure it is. So what can I tell you?"

Nergui ran through the circumstances of the case, as far as he was able to reveal them. He was aware that there was little here of substance. They had no evidence, other than the warehouse owner's accusations, to link Muunokhoi to the fire. Even if

Muunokhoi had been involved, Nergui had little doubt that any connection would have been remote and well-concealed. They were going through the motions, making sure that every stone had been upturned. And, Nergui hoped, recording just one tiny theoretical strike against Muunokhoi's apparently untainted record. Perhaps one day they might accumulate enough strikes to count for something.

Muunokhoi had laughed, as Nergui had known he would. "This is what you've dragged me in here for?"

Nergui shrugged. "It's our job. We have to investigate every possibility."

Muunokhoi had nodded, apparently earnestly. "Of course. I understand that. You have to eliminate witnesses." Something about his tone suggested that this was, perhaps, a familiar concept.

"As you say. Of course, we would like to eliminate you." Nergui's gaze was unwavering.

Muunokhoi nodded. "I can provide an alibi."

"I'm sure you can," Nergui said. "That is not really the issue. I think there is no suggestion that you started this blaze yourself. The question is whether you might have had an interest in it being started."

Muunokhoi nodded, a smile playing about his thin lips, as though he were unsure how seriously to take this. "I understand," he said. "Of course that must be a consideration. This was a competitor."

Nergui had nodded, knowing at that point that there was no likelihood of taking this any further. Muunokhoi had already covered all the angles. Even if he had been involved, there would be no way of proving it.

And so it had turned out with every case where Muunokhoi was a potential suspect. At every stage, he was polite, charming, cooperative, occasionally showing just the expected level of irritation as he was called in yet again. But there had been a gleam in his eye that suggested he treated it all as little more than a game. A game he was winning hands down.

Nergui had studied Muunokhoi's history—the kernel of the files that, now, twenty years on, he had in front of him—hoping to find some clue, some chink in Muunokhoi's apparently impenetrable armour. But there was nothing. A first class degree in engineering. An early career as a civil servant in the Ministry of Fuel and Energy, working on the administration of gas supplies from domestic and Soviet Union sources. A rapid progression, leading to a key middle-ranking role in the early 1990s as the USSR disintegrated and democracy made its first impact in Mongolia.

As the state authorities were privatised, Muunokhoi had positioned himself as a Director and major shareholder of one of the newly privatised gas companies. The company had been sold to Russian investors, netting Muunokhoi and his fellow shareholders a substantial profit. It was difficult to imagine that this had occurred without some shady dealing, but the turning of blind eyes had been a characteristic of those early free-market days. It was only when the money finally ran out that anyone thought to ask where it might have gone.

By the time the economy ran into trouble in the mid 1990s, he had established himself in a number of key monopoly positions. Money was scarce, but Muunokhoi was often the only game in town—particularly when it came to energy trading—and could command whatever price he liked. During the harsh winters of the late 1990s, it was probable that Muunokhoi was indirectly responsible for much suffering and some deaths. Nergui did not imagine that Muunokhoi would have lost much sleep as a result.

At the same time, Muunokhoi was a public figure, on the

verge of celebrity. He was part of the glitzy new social scene of the city, an extremely eligible bachelor regularly photographed with an attractive woman by his side. He made frequent appearances in the privately owned scandal sheets, though in practice there was little scandalous about his lifestyle. Or, at any rate, no evidence of the types of scandal likely to be of interest to the popular newspapers. He had a string of supposed girlfriends, but no serious relationships. He was polite to journalists, and friendly and personable with anyone he had dealings with.

But there were claims that Muunokhoi's legitimate trading was only the tip of a much less palatable iceberg. Muunokhoi was an astute businessman, but the size of his wealth did not seem commensurate with the nature and scope of his business. It seemed likely that his visible trading activities were paralleled by other, more covert transactions. There were countless rumours—drugs-, arms-, even people-smuggling.

Nergui consulted endlessly with tax and customs officers to shed some further light on the disparity between Muunokhoi's legitimate business activities and his apparent wealth. But all he had received for his trouble was a repeated shrugging of the shoulders and an increasingly obfuscatory set of technical explanations. Yes, there were inconsistencies, but investigations had uncovered no substantive evidence of wrongdoing. "It's not impossible," one said. "He's a smart businessman. He knows the dodges. People like him don't pay tax anyway, not really, not these days. They're too busy creating wealth for the rest of us. It doesn't mean they're criminals."

Nevertheless, the Serious Crimes Team built up a substantial dossier on Muunokhoi. Much was hearsay—more of those tiny, unsubstantiated strikes against his record. Once or twice, Nergui thought they might be getting close. There was a recurrent suggestion that Muunokhoi's people had gained access to caches of weapons intended for the Mongolian army or diverted from the Soviet army during the chaotic final months of the old USSR. The police and security services had made a few arrests, picking up shipments on Mongolia's extensive borders with Tomsk; Tyumeny, and Irkutsk, and even managing, in a few cases, to infiltrate the gangs operating in the dark mountains and forests to the north, identifying arms shipments due for exchange with consignments of heroin from Afghanistan.

This was the area that most interested Nergui. Mongolia had no major drug problem—certainly not compared with parts of the former Soviet Union—but the availability and abuse of hard drugs was increasing. Alcohol remained the drug of choice, but there was growing use of heroin, amphetamines, prescription psychotropic drugs, morphine and other substances. The proportions of serious users were small, but the problem would escalate rapidly if serious commercial interests became involved. Nergui could see that such interests, combined with the relative youth of the population—two-thirds under thirty—and high levels of unemployment and economic deprivation, presented a volatile combination. The prospect that Muunokhoi might be involved was not comforting.

But the evidence never quite held up. Whichever side of the law they might respectively be on, Muunokhoi and the traffickers were in the same business—moving goods and materials across national borders. It was hardly surprising if, from time to time, they should encounter—and even do business with—the same people. It was frustrating but, to Nergui, hardly surprising. He knew enough about Muunokhoi to know that the man made few mistakes. He had a well-paid entourage around him whose role, in large part, was to ensure that their boss's tracks were well covered. He was unlikely to be caught out unless someone got things badly wrong.

In the end, Nergui had scaled down the enquiry, knowing that this covert digging was unlikely to yield any real results. But he kept the files open and encouraged his team to keep their ears to the ground. Because, while Nergui knew that Muunokhoi would have covered all the bases, he also knew enough about humankind to know that, someone—somewhere, sometime, somehow—would eventually make that mistake. And Nergui wanted to ensure that, when it finally did happen, he would not be too far away.

His musing, spurred by his aimless flicking through the notepad, was interrupted by the sight of Sarangarel easing her way through the crowded café towards his table. Nergui glanced at his watch. He had lost track of the time, and she was late, though by only a few minutes. She looked, he had to acknowledge, stunning. Even if he had not been waiting for her, he would have been struck by her extraordinary presence among the chattering crowds. It was not just her physical appearance—though that was certainly striking enough, with dominant features, her long flowing black hair, and the sense of an unconventional beauty. It was also her manner—calm, untroubled, but with a visible sense of purpose. She was going somewhere—figuratively as well as literally—and there was little that would stand in her way.

That, Nergui supposed, was how he remembered her originally, though it had been less obvious in those days. Then it had been her late husband, Gansukh, who was going somewhere. And the place he was going, it seemed all too clear, was prison. That was why her appearance at this moment felt more than coincidential. Because Gansukh, or so Nergui had believed at the time, had been the man who had finally made the mistake.

EIGHT

"Don't move," the voice said.

Tunjin had no intention of arguing with the instruction. The twin barrels of the gun moved slowly down from his forehead towards his chest. The figure behind them, no more than a silhouette against the light from the open door, leaned forward and Tunjin felt a hand slowly patting his pockets, moving down his body to check whether he was armed. It was hardly a professional search, but it seemed thorough enough. Finally, the figure seemed satisfied and pulled back, gesturing brusquely with the gun. "Stand up."

Tunjin staggered slowly to his feet, clutching on to the toppled table. His feet stumbled on one of the paint-pots, which clattered off somewhere behind. He still could not make out the face of the man in front of him.

The figure waved the gun vaguely up towards the skylight. "Quite an entrance," he said.

Tunjin shrugged, feeling the bruises around his back and legs. "It wasn't quite how I intended it," he admitted.

The man with the gun stepped aside and gestured Tunjin to walk in front of him. "You're either the most incompetent burglar I've ever encountered, or this is something else."

"This is something else," Tunjin agreed. He was beginning to relax slightly now. He had initially assumed that this person was one of Muunokhoi's people who had somehow managed to predict his intended escape route. But that didn't seem to be the case. Maybe this was nothing more than a resident who had—reasonably enough—reacted aggressively to the sight of an eighteen stone man falling unexpectedly through his rooftop.

The man nodded, as though this explained everything. "Downstairs," he said. "We can talk there."

Tunjin made his way slowly down the staircase to the third floor. This block was virtually identical to his own, even down to the colour of the cheap paint on the walls. The view from the landing windows was different, though, looking out beyond the end of the street to one of the *ger* camps that clustered on the outskirts of the city. Tunjin could see the rows of round grey tents, billows of smoke issuing from their central chimneys, whipped away by the strong breeze. There was a man tending a goat, and beyond that—and much more interesting to Tunjin—a row of old but apparently serviceable motorbikes.

"This way," the man said, waving Tunjin forward towards the door at the foot of the stairs. Still holding the shotgun firmly, he pushed open the door and led Tunjin inside.

The apartment was similar in size to Tunjin's own, although considerably tidier. It was, Tunjin thought, like stepping into a *ger*. There was the usual mix of brightly painted cabinets, rich embroidered rugs and tapestries stretched across the walls and floors, and, by the far wall, a single camp bed. There were two hard backed chairs against the wall, and the man gestured Tunjin to sit in one of them. He spun the other round and sat on it, with his gun resting on the chair back, pointing steadily at Tunjin.

"Now," the man said, "why don't you tell me what this is all about?"

Tunjin was beginning to recover both his breath and his presence of mind. He could feel the wooden chair creaking slightly under his weight, and he hoped that he wouldn't soon be responsible for the destruction of yet another piece of furniture.

He reached into his pocket and pulled out his identity card. "I'm a police officer," he said, waving the card in front of the man's face. The man calmly held Tunjin's wrist and surveyed the card carefully. After a moment, he nodded, apparently satisfied, and lowered the gun slightly, though still leaving it resting on his knees.

He was, Tunjin now realised, a relatively old man—probably mid-seventies. He was dressed in traditional costume, the brown thick felt *del* wrapped around his frail-looking body, heavy brown boots sticking out beneath. He was gazing at Tunjin through untroubled grey eyes, his thinning white hair combed back from his forehead.

The old man nodded slowly. Finally, with a sudden movement, he held out his hand. "Agypar," he said.

It took Tunjin a moment to realise that this was the old man's name. He shook the man's hand and said, pointing to himself, "Tunjin."

"It is good to see more officers on patrol," Agypar said. "But there is no need for you to patrol our rooftops."

Tunjin smiled obligingly. "It's a long story," he said. "I am being pursued."

"Pursued?" Agypar said. "On the rooftop?"

"Well, no. But that was why I was on the rooftop. I live in one of the blocks farther down the road. There are intruders. So I escaped on to the roof."

Agypar nodded as though this was perfectly conventional behaviour. "These intruders," he said. "They are pursuing you because you are a policeman?"

Tunjin nodded. "More or less, yes," he said. "As I say, it's a long story. Let's just say that I have made some enemies."

"I heard the gunshot," Agypar said. "That was them, yes?"

"I think so," Tunjin said. "To be honest, I didn't stay to check."

"You will wish to be leaving shortly," Agypar said.

"Very shortly," Tunjin said. "I don't know how much time I've got. They'll have realised by now that I'm not there, but I don't know how long it will take them to work out where I've gone."

Agypar nodded, taking in this information. "And they will be watching the street, I imagine."

"I imagine," Tunjin agreed. In all honesty, he hadn't really thought this part through, but Agypar was almost certainly right. By now, they would have stationed someone out on the street, surely, as they tried to understand how Tunjin had disappeared and where he might have gone to. They might also, he realised, have stationed someone at the rear of the blocks in order to cut off his escape in that direction. All in all, his prospects were beginning to look considerably less positive. Agypar might, he supposed, be willing to lend his shotgun, but it was difficult to see that much else was in his favour.

"These are bad people?" Agypar said.

"These are very bad people," Tunjin said. "As bad as they come, I think."

"You are unable to contact your police colleagues? Surely it must be possible to summon some backup?" He spoke the words as though an expert in matters of police procedure. Everyone watched the television shows, Tunjin thought. The problem was that life was more complicated.

But Agypar did have a point. Tunjin realised, with a mild shock, that he had almost ceased to think of himself as a policeman. It was as if a thirty year career could just melt away overnight. Suddenly, he was just another civilian. Though even a civilian was entitled to help from the police.

But he knew he would not be calling them. In reality—and this was another shock—he realised that he did not believe that the police could help. At best, they could get him out of his current predicament, and maybe, assuming that they believed his story, they could provide him with some sort of protection. But the truth was that Tunjin did not know who he could trust. There was no doubt that Muunokhoi had unravelled what was going on very quickly, despite all Tunjin's best efforts to cover his tracks. That suggested that he had inside information. If Tunjin were to call the police now, there was no knowing just who might take the call.

"I don't think that's an option," Tunjin said.

Agypar regarded him silently for a moment, then nodded. "Out here," he said, "none of us trusts the police. We have seen them do too many bad things to ordinary people. And we remember the old days."

"We all remember the old days," Tunjin said. "Things have changed. But not necessarily always for the better."

Agypar nodded. "So," he said finally, "you need to get away from here. You will need some help."

Tunjin stretched out his bulk, feeling the chair again creaking beneath him. He wondered yet again quite how he'd got into this. When Doripalam had interviewed him, he had been deliberately blasé, as if this had been an entirely natural thing for a policeman to attempt as he neared the end of his career. But even if, like Tunjin, you had a suspicion that your career was spiralling out of control already, this had still been an insane move. Not just career suicide, but probably the literal version as well.

He heaved himself slowly up from the chair, conscious of how time was passing. Quite probably he was already too late. His half-baked escape plan was already falling apart. "I definitely need help," he said. "The question is where do I find it?"

Agypar smiled and reached past Tunjin to one of the ornately decorated cupboards. He pulled open the cabinet at the bottom and dragged out a canvas shoulder bag. "Take this," he said.

Tunjin looked quizzically at Agypar, then unfastened the top of the bag and peered inside. He reached in and pulled out a handgun, well-polished and in apparently good condition. Below that, nestled in the bottom of the bag, there were several rounds of ammunition.

Tunjin looked back at Agypar, who was sitting, rocking slightly on his chair, looking very pleased with himself. "What is this?" Tunjin said.

"What does it look like? Don't worry. It's in good condition and it's loaded. Don't forget to take the safety catch off if you want to use it."

"But where—?"

Agypar shrugged. "I'm an old soldier," he said. "We all kept a few souvenirs. This was one of mine. I've looked after it. You never know when it might come in useful."

Tunjin opened his mouth to say something, but could think of nothing sensible to say. "Thank you," he said, finally.

"Now," Agypar said, "we've got to get you out of this place."

It was likely that, by now, the main road at the front was being carefully watched, and it was probable that similar observation was being carried out at the rear. "Is there another way out of here?" Tunjin asked.

Agypar nodded, looking as if he'd been waiting for Tunjin to ask precisely this question. "There's one other way," he said. "Come with me."

Agypar led them out of the room, the shotgun still wedged firmly under his arm. They walked down three more flights of stairs, Tunjin peering cautiously through the landing windows to see if he could see any movement outside. The *ger* camp showed little signs of life, other than the herd of goats munching placidly through a pile of grass and leaves. As they reached the bottom of the final flight of stairs, Tunjin paused to listen, trying to discern any sounds of disturbance from the street outside. He could hear nothing, but that provided only the mildest of comfort. Maybe someone was already waiting for him out there.

The lobby itself was deserted. It was less cluttered and in a better state of repair than that in Tunjin's block, but displayed the same mix of pale wood veneer and beige painted walls. Tunjin began to move nervously towards the glass panelled front doors, but Agypar held up his hand. "No, this way," he said.

He turned back behind the stairway. Set into the wall under the stairs was a door with a combination security lock. Agypar adeptly entered a sequence of numbers and then slowly pushed open the door. Beyond, Tunjin could make out a further flight of stairs heading down into a basement.

Agypar reached behind the doorframe and pressed a light switch. There was only a single, low-wattage bulb hanging halfway down the stairs, but it was sufficient to allow a safe passage. Agypar gestured Tunjin in front of him, and the two of them began to make their way down, Agypar carefully closing the door behind them.

"The rubbish bins are down here," Agypar explained. "I think the layout of this block is a little different from the others."

It was certainly different from Tunjin's block, which had concrete floors at ground level and no basement. Tunjin was aware that the land fell away behind the rows of apartment blocks, so he assumed that while the ground floor of this block was at street level at the front, there was room for an additional lower storey at the rear.

At the bottom of the stairs, there was a further door. Tunjin pushed it slowly open and peered into the gloom beyond. It was, as he had expected, a utility room—there were a couple of large-scale sinks, a workbench with some evidence of recent use, a scattering of household furniture and appliances in varying states of repair, and what appeared to be part of a motorbike. At the far end of the room there were two pale rectangles where daylight shone faintly through two grimy windows.

Agypar moved to stand beside Tunjin and gestured down the length of the room. "The door there," he said, "it has a security lock on the outside, but you can open it from in here. It comes out into the camp, so it's not immediately visible from the road or the back of the apartments."

He led Tunjin through the dimly lit maze of junk towards the door. "I will not turn on the lights in here," he said. "We do not want to risk giving any prior warning. We need to gain as much time as we can." It was clear that he was enjoying the experience. This was, Tunjin supposed, the closest he had come to combat since retiring from the army. Tunjin wondered whether he had had a civilian job, or whether, like so many discarded from the army as the Soviet Union imploded, he had found himself without any job or prospects. At least, unlike many others, he had not found himself on the streets.

As they approached the windows, Agypar paused, raising his hand to stop Tunjin moving farther forward. The windows were grimy and dust stained, and had clearly not been cleaned for many years. Combined with the bright sunshine, this meant that their movements were unlikely to be visible to any external observer.

Agypar pointed through the window. "There," he said, "you see the row of motorcycles." It was the same row that Tunjin had observed from the landing windows earlier—a line of aged but apparently serviceable machines. "The one on the far left, the black one. That is mine." He reached into his pocket and produced a single ignition key. "Do you know how to ride a motorcycle?"

Tunjin glanced down at his overweight body. "I used to," he said. "I was a real enthusiast when I was younger. Used to ride out on to the steppes. But I haven't done it for a long while. I guess you don't forget, but I don't know that my body's got as good a memory as I have."

Agypar smiled. "I don't think you forget," he said. "I still ride it from time to time. But not much now. So take it. It will start perfectly, first time. It always does."

"Are you sure? I mean, it's—"

"You need help," Agypar said. "I am in a position to provide it. That is all. Basic hospitality. And I am sure when you return here, you will return the bike."

"Well, yes, of course," Tunjin said. "But I don't know when that will be. Or even if it will be. I don't know how far I'll get."

"If you don't get far," Agypar laughed, "I will come and collect the motorbike for myself."

"Okay. Well, thanks. Thank you very much."

"So," Agypar said, reverting to his military manner, "you open the door. You run, as far as you can—" He glanced down at Tunjin's body, tacitly acknowledging that this was unlikely to be particularly quickly. "Get the bike and get the hell out of here. Do you want me to cover you?"

"Cover me?"

Agypar waved the shotgun in front of him. "Cover you."

"No," Tunjin said. "You've done more than enough for me. You mustn't do anything to put yourself in danger." He wondered whether the old man really understood what he was potentially involved in here.

Agypar shrugged. "A pity," he said. "I was always good at providing cover."

"Thanks, anyway," Tunjin said. "For everything." He had little time to waste, he realised. There was no telling where Muunokhoi's people were by now, no telling how much—or how little—time he might have.

"Okay," he said, breathlessly, and, twisting the handle of the security lock, he stepped out into the cool sunlight.

The *ger* camp seemed deserted, although there was still smoke rising from one or two of the tents themselves. Off to his left, a flock of chickens in an enclosure was burbling gently, scratching in the dust. Somewhere in the distance, he could hear the faint hum of traffic, the shouts of children.

He looked right towards the main street, but there was no sign of life. To his left, behind the apartment blocks, the land fell gently away into waste ground. Beyond that, there were the remains of some industrial buildings, now unused and collapsing, their roofs open to the sky.

Tunjin took a deep breath and began to jog as quickly as his bulk would permit. The motorcycles were perhaps a hundred metres away, no more. He clutched the key firmly in his hand and pounded on, his breath already coming in gasps.

He was perhaps twenty-five metres from the bikes when he heard a shout behind him. For a moment he almost paused, tempted to look back in case Agypar was trying to attract his attention. But there would be time enough for that when he reached the bike.

There was another shout behind him and then the sound of a bullet shot. He tensed, poised for the potential impact, but nothing happened. He pounded on. Ten yards. Five yards. The sweat poured from his body. Finally, he grabbed the motorbike handlebars, and pulled the machine towards him. Gasping, he lifted his leg over the seat, slumped down and looked for the ignition, forcing the key into the lock. It turned and, just as Agypar had predicted, the engine fired immediately.

Finally, the machine throbbing beneath him, Tunjin looked back the way he had come. There was a figure running towards him, brandishing a handgun, shouting. Still probably fifty metres away.

Tunjin hesitated a moment, wondering whether to try to flee and risk being shot in the back, or to drive straight at the shouting figure. He was beginning to rev the engine with the intention of doing the latter when a second gunshot echoed around the buildings. The man paused, as though surprised, and then fell forward, clutching his knee, his shouts transformed into screams of pain.

Tunjin looked back behind the man to where Agypar was standing in the doorway of the basement, the shotgun in his hand. Tunjin was too far away to see his face, but he suspected that Agypar was smiling at the accuracy of his shot.

There was no time to ponder the implications of what he had just witnessed. He twisted the bike handlebars, and then—initially unsteadily as his large body grew accustomed to balancing on the narrow seat, but then with growing confidence—he accelerated the motorbike across the waste-ground, down between the walls of the broken down factories, and then out towards the open steppe.

The bike was a smart 1950s British Vincent, which must have been lovingly maintained by the old man. For a brief second, before rationality caught up with him, he almost enjoyed the sensation of power and speed as he pulled out of the dark alleys into the brilliant sunlight beyond. This machine would need looking after, he thought, until he could get it back.

But that, of course, was to assume that he ever could, or that Agypar would be there to receive him. In truth, the future looked bleak. He could scarcely look after himself, let alone the bike. He had no idea where he was heading, or what he was going to do once he got there. Behind him was a ruthless gangster who would, he was sure, now stop at nothing to catch up with him. And, in shooting the man chasing him, Agypar had very probably signed his own death warrant.

It was a mess. It was the biggest mess that Tunjin, never the most fastidious of individuals, had been caught up in. And, this time, he really couldn't see how he was going to extricate himself.

NINE

"They were here. Not so long ago," Doripalam said. "Look, you can see the marks in the grass left by the tents."

Luvsan was leaning back against the bonnet of the Daihatsu, smoking a cigarette. "I feel like the Lone Ranger," he said. Luvsan prided himself on his knowledge of Western popular culture.

Doripalam raised an eyebrow. "Which would make me Tonto, I suppose."

"Certainly not, Kemo Sabe," Luvsan said. "I'm the sidekick here."

Doripalam stared at him for a moment. There were times when Luvsan's youthful exuberance bordered on the insolent. "And you're the one with the tracking skills," he said, gesturing towards the satellite navigation equipment in the front of the truck. "I'm trusting you know where we are."

"More or less," Luvsan said, in a voice that implied that he was above considerations of geographical precision.

"More rather than less, I hope," Doripalam said. "All I know is that we're miles from anywhere."

This was probably another waste of time, he thought, but there was a risk that everything was slowly spiralling out of his control and he wanted to try to get some purchase on it before it was too late. It wasn't just the Muunokhoi case and everything that went with that. There'd also been the missing youth, Gavaa, a case that had seemed trivial but nevertheless brought them unexpected flak from the press. And then there was the murder of Gavaa's mother, which had come from nowhere and, so far, seemed to be leading them pretty much to the same destination.

Fortunately, for all their previous criticisms of the handling of the Gavaa disappearance, the press seemed more interested in the mystery of his mother's murder than in throwing more mud at the police. For the moment, anyway. Doripalam didn't delude himself that this was anything more than a respite. The truth was that for now the murder story—middle-aged woman found brutally slain in a *ger,* son missing, nomad family apparently moved on—was extraordinary enough in its own right. It didn't need the added spice of routine police-bashing. But as soon as interest in the story began to wane, the press would once again begin to ask how the police had allowed this to happen, why they weren't doing more to solve the crime, whether they could guarantee the safety of other citizens, and—well, any other hook they could find to spin the story out for a few more issues.

His team had been working relentlessly over the last few days—the usual grind of detailed police-work, driven by the ever-present knowledge that, without some rapid breakthrough, the case was increasingly likely to slip through their hands. Doripalam had overseen all the key activities—setting up a response team close to the crime-scene, allocating the familiar round of essential duties, holding daily briefing meetings with the core team, fending off the gaggle of news and TV reporters. It was all straightforward stuff, the usual well-rehearsed routine. The kind of activity he could handle without thinking. And that was the trouble. He wasn't thinking. Not directly about the murder, anyway. His thoughts kept drifting elsewhere, pulled away from the task at hand, drawn inexorably by the sense that the true story was elsewhere, that there was some link he was failing to grasp.

But the routines of the investigation went on. The first task had been to try to track down Mrs. Tuya's missing family. It was still not clear whether their departure was linked to her murder—although the abandonment of the *gers* suggested so—or whether they had already moved on when the killing occurred. Either way, the family of nomads had so far proved surprisingly elusive.

In practice, tracking down nomads was never entirely straightforward, particularly if they did not want to be found. These days, many travellers carried shortwave radios, and there were established procedures for sending and receiving messages through the state radio channels. Some even carried satellite phones, although the cost of these was prohibitive to most. The majority of nomads were now registered within a given region for voting and social security purposes, and some would make regular trips into the local towns to collect benefits or for other purposes. Again, there were standard arrangements for leaving messages through these channels. And, finally, of course, the police and other local services had their own networks within particular regions and could often establish, relatively quickly, the location of a particular individual or group.

Establishing contact with a nomad might be a slow process, but it was usually successful. The message would be picked up by someone locally and, through whatever tortuous means, would eventually make its way to the intended recipient.

In this case, the police had taken all the steps they could to get the message out. The story had been well covered in the press and on the television and radio, and the police had issued an appeal for the family to contact them. They had sent out similar messages through the police and social security networks in the north of the county, with the assumption that, before too long, someone would have identified the party of herdsmen.

But, for several days, there was very little response. There was the usual scattering of crank calls, a few that were well-intentioned but contained no information of substance, and one or two that appeared promising but where the apparent trail very quickly vanished.

They got their first serious lead five days after the body was found. It was a call from one of the provincial police stations up north of the capital, in the rich grasslands in the upper parts of the Bulgan *aimag*. One of the regional nomads had, in the course of reporting some trivial theft, mentioned—with a mild hint of xenophobia—that there were some unknown herdsmen in the area. The implication had been that, even if they were not directly responsible for the theft, they were nonetheless probably up to no good.

The policeman in question, although sceptical of the claims, had made a casual trip out to visit the camp, making enquiries about where the group had come from and to where it was travelling. It had been difficult, he said. The group clearly resented his presence and his questions, no doubt aware of what the locals might be saying about them. They had responded openly, but coolly, that they had travelled from the south looking for better pastureland, but that they expected only to stay a few days. The policeman had wondered about asking for their formal identity documents but could see no justification for a heavy-handed approach. There was no evidence of stolen property in the camp, and he had no grounds for suspecting the group of any crime.

It was only later, when he was re-reading through the various communiqués sent from headquarters during a quiet morning—of which there were many—that it occurred to him that this group might have been Mrs. Tuya's family. And finally, after a protracted series of calls around the capital's police network, the information had reached the Serious Crimes Team.

Doripalam had decided almost instantly to travel up here himself with Luvsan. But he had quickly begun to wonder whether they were wasting their time. They didn't even know for sure that Mrs. Tuya's family were in a position to tell them anything useful. If they had left, by arrangement, before her murder, then it was quite possible that they were unaware that she was dead, let alone in a position to shed any light on her killing. If that was the case, then Doripalam's role was little more than that of the junior sent to break the bad news. He doubted that the message would be any more palatable because it came from the senior officer.

And, of course, they didn't even know that this was Mrs. Tuya's family in the first place. Okay, they had come from outside the region, but then these people were, when all was said and done, nomads. Travel was what they did. Most of them tended to travel within relatively circumscribed boundaries, but it was far from unknown for them to travel further afield.

And, on top of all that, it now turned out that, by the time Doripalam and Luvsan reached the region, the camp had already moved on.

Looking round, Doripalam wondered quite why they had decided to do so. This was a beautiful place. From where they stood, the lush grassland stretched ahead of them, rising up into the gentle hills which formed the start of the Bürengiin Nuruu Mountains. In the morning sunlight, the colour of the grass was extraordinary, a shimmering gauze of emerald, shaded by the shifting patterns of the thin fluffy clouds above. Above them, snaking down the foothills, they could see the glittering twisted cable of a mountain stream, which widened into a narrow river and then a broad pool a hundred or so metres across the plain, before disappearing again, presumably back underground. Away across the hills, there were dark shadows of conifers, the first harbingers of the massive Siberian forests that lay beyond the nearby borders.

But, whatever the beauty of the surroundings, it was clear that the camp had indeed moved on. As Doripalam had pointed out, it was possible to discern the shadows and indentations that showed where the cluster of circular *gers* had been erected. There were some dark patches in the grass where the stoves had stood, and some cropped and scrubby areas of grass where horses or goats had been tethered. Judging from the marks, it looked as if the herdsmen had not been gone for long—perhaps a day, maybe two.

"So what now?" Luvsan said, lighting another cigarette. He had tossed his previous stub carelessly into the grass. Doripalam had watched its arc and landing with some distaste.

He shook his head. "We've come a long way," he said. "We can't go back now."

Luvsan nodded. "We'd look stupid," he said.

Doripalam smiled thinly. "We wouldn't be doing our jobs," he said.

"That too," Luvsan nodded. "So where do we go?"

"Back to Bulgan, I reckon," Doripalam said, referring to the regional capital. "The police there might be able to give us another lead." The suggestion sounded thin even to Doripalam, but anything seemed preferable to admitting defeat so quickly.

They drove back across the grasslands in silence, Luvsan maintaining his characteristic high speeds, occasionally allowing the rear wheels of the truck to slide gently across the rough ground as they took a corner. Doripalam closed his eyes and tried not to grip the sides of his seat too tightly. He had long since resigned himself to the prospect of writing off the new vehicle at some point before they returned to the capital. He could probably cope with that so long as he didn't live to face the consequences, he thought.

Bulgan itself was a small city—hardly even a town, but dignified by its status as the capital of the region or *aimag*. There was little to the place—just the Town Hall, the Government Building, a few functional and commercial buildings, a couple of hotels. There was a tourist *ger* camp to the north of the city, but otherwise surprisingly few examples of the characteristic round tents. In keeping with the surrounding woodland, the scattering of Soviet-style administrative and commercial buildings was complemented by clusters of comfortable log cabins.

Although still some way south of the Russian border, Bulgan looked like a true frontier town. The image was reinforced by the rows of horses tethered along the main streets and around the market. It was this sight, glimpsed as they had passed through the city on their journey north, that had prompted Luvsan's jocular references to the Lone Ranger. The city would not have looked out of place, Doripalam conceded, in the Hollywood Westerns that now found their way on to their televisions in the small hours of the morning.

Far from being a frontier town, Bulgan now gained much of its income from the groups of foreign tourists who used the city as an overnight stopping point on their way to the mountains and lakes of Khövsgöl Nuur in the far north. Because of this, it was a more cosmopolitan place than most of the country's smaller cities. People were accustomed to meeting travellers—locals and foreigners—and were relatively comfortable with the ceaseless traffic of visitors. The positive aspect of this was that the local police were very capable and responsive in dealing with any potential problems on their patch. The downside was that, whereas in most areas outside the capital newcomers would be a source of interest, gossip and possibly anxiety, here their presence would hardly be noticed. Even if Mrs. Tuya's family had passed through here, their presence might well have gone unremarked.

Still, it was never wise to underestimate the perspicacity of the local police, Doripalam thought. Although the initial report about the nomadic newcomers had been filed by a local policeman in one of the outlying villages, it had been transmitted rapidly and efficiently by the police in Bulgan down to the capital. It was possible that in the meantime they had gathered some other intelligence that might be worth investigating.

Luvsan turned into the town and passed by the tree-filled parkland around the Achuut Gol river, crossed the river itself, and then turned left into the main street. He was driving with some care, at least by his own unexacting standards. The street itself was relatively busy in the mid-afternoon—largely older people dressed in traditional robes making their way through to the market or simply enjoying the sunshine. As Doripalam and Luvsan approached the hotels at the far end of the street, they saw some clusters of tourists—one Western, one apparently Japanese—walking out to view the limited array of city attractions.

At the end of the main street, Luvsan turned right and drew the truck to a halt in front of the Government Building which, at its rear, housed the local police headquarters. As he turned off the engine, Luvsan lit another cigarette and sat back casually. "Are they expecting you, sir?" he said.

Doripalam nodded. "I called yesterday to warn them that we were coming on to their patch." This was always a wise move, in Doripalam's experience. However supposedly innocent or uncontroversial the mission, no local officer liked to discover that HQ was trampling over his patch without permission. "I said I'd probably call in on the way back, just to update them."

Luvsan nodded, blowing his smoke carefully through the half-opened window of the truck. "And to pick their brains."

"As it turns out, yes. Though whether there'll be anything worth picking is an open question."

Doripalam jumped out of the truck and strode along the pavement past the Government Building, then turned down behind it to the reception of the police offices. He didn't bother to look back to see if Luvsan was following. From past experience, he knew that Luvsan was smart enough to allow his boss to engage in any formal meetings alone, aware that his presence might cramp the senior officer's style. More importantly, Luvsan was also smart enough to make good use of his own time in these situations, putting his personable charms to use to extract whatever other information he could.

Doripalam guessed that, while he was comfortably settled with the senior officer, Luvsan would have casually ingratiated himself with the juniors in the squad room, most likely through the generous donation of the cigarettes that he seemed to carry in unlimited numbers. Doripalam was beginning to recognise that Luvsan was an officer with some potential, maybe even a possible successor in his own role. Doripalam could never claim that Luvsan resembled a younger version of himself—partly because Luvsan wasn't actually all that much younger, but mainly because his casual but streetwise sharpness was almost a diametric opposite of Doripalam's more cautious intelligence. But Doripalam was open-minded enough to recognise ability, even when it took a distinctly different form from his own.

As he turned into the gloomy concrete foyer of the police offices, he paused to gaze down the street. There were two or three more administrative and commercial buildings, then the street opened up to a line of smaller timber-built buildings—a few shops and then houses. Beyond that, there was the green parkland and then the gathering darkness of the trees, brilliant green in the descending afternoon sun. They still had several hours drive back to the capital, Doripalam thought. They would need to conclude their business soon if they were to have any chance even of starting the journey before nightfall.

He turned and made his way into the reception. The layout was familiar, a relic of the old days, with its heavily built reception desk, the official flags and emblems, the palpably unfriendly atmosphere. Designed to intimidate, rather than to encourage honest citizens to seek official help.

There was a young officer sitting behind a desk, apparently completing some form of official report, though Doripalam noticed, as he leant over the desk, that there was a pile of sports magazines tucked underneath. He had probably heard the door opening and adjusted his reading accordingly.

Doripalam held out his identity card. "I'm here to see your commanding officer," he said. "I spoke to him yesterday and said I'd call in this afternoon."

The young man took quick account of Doripalam's role and rank, and immediately sat up straighter. "I'll call him for you, sir." He picked up the phone and pressed an extension, spoke briefly in a whisper, then looked back up at Doripalam. "He's just finishing a meeting, sir. Five minutes at most."

Doripalam nodded. "Thanks. Is there somewhere I can wait?" He had already noticed an unprepossessing waiting room by the main entrance, presumably designed for potential wrongdoers and other members of the general public.

"You can sit upstairs," the young man said. "There's a small waiting area just outside the Chief's office."

Doripalam smiled and made his way slowly up the staircase that stretched from the centre of the lobby. There was indeed a much more comfortable waiting area, clearly designed for any official visitors, with a couple of armchairs, a low table and even—Doripalam noted with interest—a Western-style watercooler. This was something they hadn't yet managed to acquire in headquarters, though he noticed that the Ministry now had them in apparent abundance.

He lowered himself into one of the armchairs and sat back to wait. The chair gave a partial view of the lobby below, glimpsed through the stair rails. After a few moments, Doripalam saw Luvsan stride jauntily into the lobby and make his way over to the reception. There would, Doripalam presumed, very shortly be a proffering of both identity card and cigarettes.

"I'm so sorry to keep you waiting," a voice said from behind him. "I hope you've not been here long."

The local police chief was a short, squat man, though Doripalam guessed that his bulk was largely muscle rather than fat. His hair was cut sharp and his bright eyes darted up and down, appraising Doripalam's slim figure, clearly surprised by the senior officer's youth but equally clearly trying hard not to let this show.

"Not at all," Doripalam said. "I'm sorry I couldn't let you know more precisely when I was likely to arrive."

The Chief smiled. "I am Tsend."

"Doripalam. Thank you for taking the time to see me."

"It is a rare honour to meet the head of the Serious Crimes Team."

Doripalam shrugged. "Rare, I hope. Honour, I'm not so sure. People don't tend to welcome the implications of our presence," he said.

"But, fortunately, as I understand it, we are not this time dealing with a serious crime on our territory," Tsend said. "Which is a blessing for us, if not for you." He gestured Doripalam into his office, inviting him to take a seat at a small meeting table.

The office, on the other hand, was relatively palatial, and Tsend's heavy mahogany desk commanded an impressive view of the main street and the parkland beyond.

"A pleasant place to work," Doripalam commented.

"Well, we have little need to call on the services of your team," Tsend said. "Most of what we face here is trivial stuff. The odd theft, drunkenness. Some trouble with tourists, now and again. But nothing serious. Not like your Tuya case."

"You're aware of the case?" Doripalam said. They had discussed it only briefly during their telephone conversation the previous day.

"A little. I read the newspapers. A dreadful murder, I understand?"

"Dreadful and, to be honest, fairly baffling. From the little we know of Mrs. Tuya, there was little obvious motive for her killing."

"There is a missing son, I understand?"

"It appears so," Doripalam said. "Again, we've no idea why he might be missing. Or if he really is. We know he hadn't contacted his mother for some time before her death, but that's hardly an unusual characteristic of young men."

"But he'd have made contact once he learned of her death, surely?"

"You would assume so," Doripalam said. "Though it's difficult to be sure. Their relationship wasn't a strong one in recent years, I understand. And it's possible he's not even aware of her death, I suppose."

"Though it's been well covered in the media," Tsend said. "And you've made appeals for him to come forward?"

"Of course. But who knows where he is? There are still parts of this country where it's possible to escape the media." Doripalam's tone implied that this was an attractive characteristic.

"And you're trying to track down her remaining family, I understand?"

Doripalam nodded. "That's why we're here. As I told you, we had a report from one of your outstationed officers about some non-local nomads who had arrived in the area. From the description, it sounded like it might have been the group we're looking for."

"And was it?"

"I don't know. By the time we got there, they'd moved on and there was no obvious clue as to where they might have moved to. I was hoping you might be able to give me some more ideas."

Tsend shrugged. "I doubt it. Out there, they do tend to notice newcomers, if only because they're all competing for the best pastures. But it would only be reported to us if there was anything that required formal action."

"What about this particular group? I understand that one of your officers visited them?"

Tsend flipped open a manila file on the desk in front of him. There was a small pile of similar files next to it. "This is the report," he said. "It was just a routine visit. There'd been a spate of petty thefts and there were suggestions that this group of incomers might be responsible. People are always keen to blame strangers, though in my experience it's usually the local youngsters who are responsible. But I guess we thought we should check them out."

"But you found nothing?"

"According to the report, no. The officer just made a casual call, supposedly checking that they were all right. We have a social responsibility towards people as well, of course." He managed to imply that such considerations would be alien to the Serious Crimes Team.

"But there was no sign of anything wrong?"

"Not really. Though the report does suggest that they were behaving a little oddly. Most herdsmen are really just interested in finding the best pasture for their animals. They don't like to travel too far if they can help it, though of course they can't always control nature. But—judging from the report—this group just seemed to be travelling. They had some animals—some goats, horses—but not a great herd. And they seemed reluctant to talk about where they'd come from or where they were heading."

"They wouldn't say?" Doripalam leaned forward, growing more interested.

Tsend shrugged. "The officer didn't feel able to push them too hard, given that he was supposedly there on a friendly visit. But he asked a few casual questions and got deflected every time. As if they weren't keen to talk about it."

"He didn't ask for any ID?"

"Again, he didn't think it was appropriate. He had no grounds for suspicion. He had to nose around to see if there was anything to link them to the thefts, but there wasn't. And his overall impression was that they were more interested in moving on than in committing any kind of crime here."

Doripalam nodded, taking all this in. "If it's true that Mrs. Tuya's family did flee for some reason—and we're not at all sure about that—then it sounds as if this group could be them. And that they're still fleeing."

"You think they were responsible for her death?"

"It's possible," Doripalam said. "But it could also be that they're fleeing from whoever did kill her."

"But that's—" Tsend had clearly been about to say "ridiculous" or something similar, but then bit this back as an inappropriate response to a suggestion from a senior officer. "I mean, is that likely?"

"Anything's possible. That's the one thing I've learnt in this role." Doripalam's mind went back to the extraordinary spate of killings the previous year, the convoluted web of motives that had underpinned the murders. "But, no, it does seem farfetched." He paused. "We really do need to track down this group, though. Do you have any inkling where they might have moved to?"

Tsend shook his head. "I've been through all the reports from the last few days, just in case there was anything that might be relevant to you. I wasn't specifically looking for information on this group, but I didn't see anything in there that was likely to be of interest. And from where they were—well, they could have gone anywhere. Further north towards the mountains, maybe. If they were looking to hide, that might be the best bet. But other than that, all I can do is ask my people to keep their eyes and ears open and hope we pick up something. I presume you'll ask the same of the other neighbouring *aimags*?"

"Of course," Doripalam said mildly, biting back his irritation at being told how to do his job. Tsend was, he told himself, simply trying to be helpful. "And there's nothing else you can tell me?"

"I don't think so. As I say, I've looked through the files pretty carefully." He gestured to the pile on the desk. "But feel free to have a look for yourself if you want to." He said it as if challenging Doripalam, who briefly felt inclined to accept.

"No, I'm sure you've been through them thoroughly. But if anything comes up—anything you think might be remotely relevant—you'll contact us straightaway?" He could at least try to match Tsend in the egg-sucking tuition, he thought.

Tsend smiled. "Immediately."

He rose, clearly indicating that the interview was at an end, and led Doripalam towards the office door. "Thanks for your time," Doripalam said, as they stepped back out into the corridor. "I realise how busy you must be." In the silent building, it was difficult not to make the words sound ironic, but Tsend appeared to notice nothing.

"I am sorry we could not be more helpful," Tsend said. He gestured towards the stairs. "Forgive me, but I have another meeting I need to prepare for. You can find your own way out?"

"No problem." Doripalam gave no real credence either to this meeting or to the one that had supposedly delayed the start of their discussion, but he was happy to get out of Tsend's presence.

He made his way slowly down the stairs and smiled faintly at the sight of Luvsan, perched on the reception desk, chatting amiably to the officer behind it. Clearly, the intimidatory design had little impact on Luvsan.

As Doripalam reached the bottom of the stairs, Luvsan jumped to his feet, waving a cheery farewell to the reception officer. Doripalam noticed that a half-empty packet of cigarettes had been left casually on the desk.

Doripalam made his way back out into the bright sunshine. Luvsan trotted along a few feet behind him, whistling tunelessly.

As they reached the truck, Luvsan said: "Any luck, sir?"

Doripalam shook his head. "No. Willing to do anything to help us, apart from actually providing any useful information or support."

Luvsan smiled. "That's what you get for mixing with the top brass, if you don't mind me saying so, sir."

Doripalam paused, his hand on the truck doorhandle, looking at Luvsan across the bonnet. "You're going to tell me you got something more useful?"

Luvsan shrugged, still smiling. "It's all a matter of who you know, sir."

TEN

"I really don't know how you can drink that stuff," Nergui said, eyeing the foaming cappuccino as she raised it to her lips.

"I like it," Sarangarel said simply. She took a large mouthful. It was a testament to her elegance, Nergui reflected, that she could do so without ending up with a large foam moustache. "It's a comfort drink."

"I suppose so." Nergui glanced down at his own intense espresso. "I suppose comfort's usually the last thing I'm looking for in a drink."

She smiled. "I think you look for intensity in all things, Nergui."

"I'd begun to think you weren't coming," he said. "I could have understood why you wouldn't."

"Could you?" she said. It was a genuine question, he thought. It was as if she really had managed to put all those days behind her. "But, no, I'm sorry I'm late. Work, you know. Just a trivial case, but those are the ones that always run on. And you don't want to adjourn for the next day because it hardly seems worth it."

He nodded. It was difficult to imagine her behind the bench. Not because she lacked the ability or the presence for such a role, but simply because he had never seen her in that kind of formal setting. It was extraordinary to think that, if the Muunokhoi case had proceeded as planned, he would probably have attended the court as an observer and so would have encountered her, for the first time in years, in that context. If it had been a surprise when she turned up in his office, how much more astonishing would it have been to find her presiding over the trial of a man like Muunokhoi. Particularly given her background.

He had wondered, during their previous discussion, whether there was any perceived conflict of interest in her handling the Muunokhoi trial. But he supposed not. Apart from the fact that she could not be held responsible for her late husband's actions—and there was never any suggestion that she had any knowledge of what he was up to—the suspected links with Muunokhoi had never been identified, much less proved.

He contemplated again his motives for agreeing to this meeting. Of course, he liked her. He had always liked her, and there had certainly been a moment when the liking might have blossomed into something more substantive. But he was conscious that, after all these years, he found it difficult to approach any kind of relationship without at least half an eye on its potential implications, on the ways in which it might be used. Or, conversely, on the risks that it might potentially be used against him. He told himself that this was simply professional caution. As Sarangarel had said, he was used to keeping at least one step ahead.

But part of him recognised that, somewhere at the heart of this, there was also a defence mechanism, something that preserved his solitude, that kept him, not just a step ahead, but a step removed. He couldn't determine where professional caution stopped and emotional cowardice began, but he was smart enough to recognise that it was probably unwise to invite others to join him in the minefield.

But then, only a day or two later, she had phoned him. "I've done it all by the book now," she said. "I've reported the threats. They didn't seem very interested."

"I don't imagine you're the first judge to receive threats," Nergui pointed out. "And there's probably nothing in it. But at least you've put it all on record."

"Covered my back, you mean."

"Of course. It's an essential skill if you're to get on in public life."

"You speak as an expert?"

"None more so. But I've also done what I can at my end, though it's not much. We had no luck in tracing the calls, but I never thought we would, unless it was a real amateur. We've got your phone monitored and your flat under surveillance."

"A person could feel flattered by all this attention."

"You're getting priority treatment," Nergui agreed. "But that's mainly because you're a member of the judiciary."

"Mainly?" There was a teasing note in her voice.

"Mainly," he repeated, his voice giving nothing away. "We can't keep it up forever. Even for a member of the judiciary." He paused, and she had time to wonder whether the irony was playful or mocking. "But if there is any substance to the threat, we should find out soon enough."

"Try not to lay the reassurance on too thickly, won't you, Nergui?"

He laughed, finally. "I've told you. I don't do reassurance. I do realism."

"I suppose that'll have to do, then," she said. There was another, longer pause, as if both of them had run out of words.

Then she said: "I wondered if you fancied meeting for dinner. For old time's sake. Or I suppose we could convene it as a formal symposium between the Ministry and the judiciary, if that makes it easier."

"Only in that I could charge the cost to the Ministry, perhaps." He was laughing more easily now. "But, yes, that would be good. For old time's sake. And for the future, too." As he spoke the final words, there had been an ambiguity in his tone that she could not interpret.

They had agreed to meet in fashionable Millie's—probably because it was recognised by both as anonymous neutral ground. Everyone came here, even Nergui from time to time. It would give them time to chat, to reacquaint themselves with each other. And, if none of it worked, for whatever reason, it would give them time to bail out before they were committed to spending the evening together.

But so far it was going okay. The talk, for the moment, couldn't have got much smaller, which always made Nergui feel uncomfortable, but at least they were talking.

"It's busy," she said, looking round the crowded cafe. "Even at this time of the day."

"I'm told it's very fashionable," Nergui said. "I don't know about that. But they do a decent espresso. About the only place in the city that does."

"You have decadent Western tastes, these days," she said.

"I've always had decadent Western tastes," Nergui said. "It's because I spent too much time in the decadent West."

"Well, we're all slowly being corrupted." She sipped her foaming coffee. "I imagine I'll learn to live with it."

"I imagine you will," he said. "So—where shall we eat?" The question was out of his mouth almost before he could stop himself, as if his subconscious mind had decided to commit him to the evening before his conscious self could think about preventing it.

She shrugged. “I’m in your hands,” she said. “Where’s suitably decadent and Western?”

“The Western stuff is mainly pizzas,” he said. “There’s the Café de France. They do half-decent French stuff.”

“Fine by me,” she said. “Half-decent French stuff is probably more decadent than the best cuisine from anywhere else.”

She sat back, watching him closely while he used his mobile phone to make the reservation. It was difficult to tell whether Nergui had actually made an effort in getting ready for the evening. He was wearing his usual dark suit, offset by his trademark pastel shirt and tie, tonight in a pale mauve. He had dressed like this—though perhaps a shade more self-consciously—even when she had known him the first time. She had wondered then, as she continued to wonder now, quite what this was all about. He was, to say the least, very recognisable. The smart suit and distinctive trappings contrasted starkly with his dark, glowering, warrior-like features. He was hardly a public figure, though he had appeared in the media from time to time, but even in this café she could sense people glancing at him, wondering who he was, whether he was some celebrity they didn’t quite recognise.

“All sorted,” he said, ending the call. “Seven thirty.” He looked at his watch. “We’ve time for a drink if you’ve had enough toy coffee.”

They had, fortunately, managed to find overnight rooms at the Bulgan Hotel. The hotel itself was nothing special—typical of the larger hotels outside the capital—but the rooms were at least clean and had hot water. As Doripalam knew from bitter experience, this could not always be taken for granted.

And the Bulgan was situated in the park, with decent views of the scattering of timber houses before the dark encroachment of the forests. Sitting sipping beers in the sparse bar, he and Luvsan looked out over the parkland, the low evening sun scattering stark patterns between the trees. It was, Doripalam was forced to admit, almost pleasant.

"Okay," Doripalam said, "you've kept me in suspense long enough. What did you manage to find out?"

Luvsan paused, taking another slow drag on his cigarette. "I think it's worth investigating, anyway. It sounds like it's probably them."

"What sounds like it's probably who?" Doripalam said patiently. He knew that Luvsan liked to string this sort of thing out. Tonight, at least, they were in no particular hurry.

"Our band. The ones we're looking for. It sounds like it could well be them."

"What does?"

"Well—" Luvsan sat himself back in his chair, looking as if he was about to make a lengthy narrative of this. "There was some sort of disturbance, a couple of nights ago in one of the small villages five or six miles north of here."

"What sort of disturbance?"

"Something and nothing, apparently. A new bunch of herdsman had arrived, set up camp, put their animals—just a very scanty collection, apparently—out to pasture. But they chose an area that was already being used by the locals, so a bit of a dispute broke out. Then, later in the evening—after a few vodkas, reading between the lines—some of the locals set upon one of the incomers. There was a bit of a fracas, but it didn't last long. The newcomers just backed off, said they'd pack up and be out by morning. Didn't want any trouble, that kind of thing."

"The Superintendent didn't mention any of this."

Luvsan gave Doripalam a look that managed to convey,

with remarkable eloquence, his profoundly low expectations of any senior officer, Doripalam himself almost certainly included. "Well, he wouldn't have known, I imagine. By the time the police got there, it was all over. No one wanted to make any kind of fuss in the circumstances. So I don't imagine any kind of report was filed. I only picked it up because I was chatting with a bunch of the officers about any sightings of strangers in the area. As it happened, one of them had been talking to an outstationed officer on the phone that morning, and had picked up this story."

"But the group had moved on." Doripalam pointed out. "So we still don't know where they are."

Luvsan shook his head. "No, that's just it. I think I do know where they've gone. The police got there too late to deal with the disturbance, but one of the local officers was intrigued by the behaviour of the newcomers. Thought they seemed just a bit too concerned about making themselves scarce. So he decided to keep an eye on them. Let them get on a bit—they were mainly on horseback, though a couple of them had motorbikes and were apparently scouting ahead. Anyway, the officer noted the direction they went in, and then made a point of checking up an hour or so later in his truck. They'd only gone a few miles and then found a sheltered spot, on the edges of the forest, to settle in."

"But that was—what, the night before last? They could have moved on farther since then."

Luvsan shook his head. "Apparently not. The officer's been keeping a covert eye on them—he still thinks they might be up to no good and wants to keep them in sight. Anyway, he's checked them out again today and they're still there. It's a decent spot, he reckons—sheltered, sufficiently far from any villages not to be noticed, not treading on anyone else's toes."

"But do they know they're being watched? If they're trying to be inconspicuous, then the presence of some clumsy local officer might be just enough to send them scuttling for the shadows again."

Luvsan smiled. "I took the liberty of calling the outstationed officer direct while I was in the station, just to check up on the story. Seemed a sharp enough young guy. Wasted in the sticks like this. Anyway, he was adamant that he'd been subtle—if they were up to something, the last thing he wanted was to scare them off before he had any grounds to take formal action. So I told him we were interested—that we didn't want them to know they were being observed until we got there and to let us know straightaway if there was any sign of them moving."

Doripalam nodded. "All very professional. As I'd have expected. But there's still a risk they might decide to do an overnight departure. We should get over there this evening."

Luvsan sighed gently. "I thought you'd say that," he said. "The truck's all ready. I was just hoping we might get something to eat first."

Nergui had eaten better in Paris, but the food in the Café de France was good enough, at least by local standards. Sarangarel certainly seemed impressed.

"I didn't know you could get food like this here," she said, slicing neatly into the steak Roquefort.

"I'm not sure how they do it," Nergui said. "I don't know where the food comes from. I've never dared to enquire."

She smiled, unsure—as she recalled had always been the case with Nergui—whether he was being serious. "I don't normally get to eat in places like this."

"Even as a wealthy judge?" Nergui said. He cut carefully into his own rare fillet steak, watching the thin blood spill on to the crisp green of the salad.

She shook her head. "Wealthy? But, no, it's not so much that.

It's just that I don't often have cause to eat out. Or time, for that matter."

"So how do you spend your time? Outside work?" This was the closest that Nergui had so far come to enquiring about her personal circumstances.

"I don't seem to have much time outside work," she said. "I think I take it all too seriously."

"I'm not sure you can take that kind of work too seriously," Nergui said.

"Though from what I remember you wouldn't necessarily be the preferred source of advice on achieving balance in your life."

He smiled. "That's true. I've left far too many dead bodies in my wake."

"Literally and figuratively, no doubt," she said.

He nodded, noting that she had failed to give any kind of meaningful response to his question about how she spent her time. "No doubt," he said. "But I'm not sure where it gets you in the end."

She took a sip of the wine which, by some miracle, was not only genuinely French but even quite a decent Burgundy. "And where's it got you?" she said. "In the end."

"I hope it's not the end," Nergui said. He was watching her closely now, admiring the ease with which she'd evaded his questions and turned the focus of the conversation back on himself. "I'm not sure I want to spend the rest of my working life in the Ministry. And in any case the shelf life is probably fairly short. If the current Minister goes out of favour—which he will, because that's politics—I don't delude myself that his successor will necessarily be clamouring for my services."

"I never knew that false modesty was one of your vices."

"It isn't. But realism definitely is. Though you're right—there would be a demand for my services somewhere."

"And what are your services, these days?" she said. "I mean, what is it you're doing in the Ministry?"

Nergui's defences immediately rose. He disliked any direct question about his job. Not necessarily because he had anything to hide, though there were aspects of his role that were certainly not for general consumption. But simply because he was always suspicious of the motives of anyone who showed some interest. And, he was beginning to recognise, suspicion was the last thing he wanted to feel tonight.

"Enjoying myself," he said, finally, and with a slight shock realised that the statement was true. These days, he really was beginning to enjoy his position and everything that went with it—the challenges and responsibilities as well as the perquisites of power. "I didn't at first. I hated it. I mean, I'm a frontline person at heart. I like getting my hands dirty. So the last thing I wanted was to become a backroom pen pusher."

"So why did you take the job?"

"I don't think I had much of a choice. If a minister—well, certainly if this minister—wants you to do his dirty work, then it's not easy to say no."

"And is that what you do?" she said, watching him as she brushed back her dark hair. "His dirty work?"

Nergui smiled, his face as expressionless as ever. "No," he said, "not really. That's just my way of talking. I'm basically involved in running some of the larger scale security investigations—the kind of stuff that sits somewhere between the intelligence services and the police. A kind of coordination role, I suppose."

"Sounds fascinating," she said.

He shrugged. "Not really. Most of it is just pen pushing. A lot of bureaucracy. Making sure that everything's done by the book before it gets in front of people like you."

"You mean as wasn't done in the Muunokhoi case?"

His sharp blue eyes were unblinking. "I can't comment," he said. "It wasn't my case."

"No," she said. "Of course. You've moved on." She paused. "So why did I find you in the police headquarters?"

He carved another piece of rare steak and chewed it slowly, enjoying the taste of blood. "As I say, it's a liaison role. I spend a lot of time there. And elsewhere."

She shook her head. "I'm sorry," she said. "Too much shop. You can see what I mean when I say I'm not used to this kind of thing. It's not just the food. I'm not used to the socialising."

He nodded and smiled faintly. "You never did tell me how you *do* spend your time."

She placed her knife and fork neatly across the plate. "It's lovely food. But I think I need to leave a little room for dessert. The crème brûlée sounds excellent." She paused as Nergui allowed the silence to extend, continuing to chew slowly at his own steak. "The truth is," she said at last, "that there's nothing really to tell you. I work. That's it, really. I mean, it's a demanding job, though probably not as demanding as I make it. But I work long hours. I go home. I read a book. Maybe I try to watch TV. Then I go to sleep, get up early and go back to work. That's it."

It was difficult to challenge her words without sounding either patronising or rude. Nergui nodded, placing his own cutlery across his plate. "It sounds like your life might be even more unbalanced than mine." Though, really, he thought, her description sounded uncannily like his own typical evening.

"Well," she said, "it's not been an easy life."

"That's true," he said. "Though all that was a long time ago. You must have put it behind you."

She nodded. "I have. Really and truly behind me. It feels as if all that happened to a different person. Someone I met a few times and then lost touch with. Not me at all."

"It was a different life," Nergui said. "Everything's changed now. You've changed now."

This was certainly true. It was difficult to relate the elegant confident woman sitting opposite him to the scared figure he had first met that night—ten, eleven years before. Though it had hardly been surprising that she was scared, in the circumstances.

They had made the arrest in the small hours of the morning, in the coldest days of that bitterly cold winter. All of that had been deliberate—to take Gansukh by surprise and prevent him from destroying evidence or making contact with his associates.

There was thick snow on the ground, frozen into the hardest ice, and despite the best efforts of the snow-ploughs the city had been virtually at a standstill for the whole day. By the time the police were ready to make their assault, at around two in the morning, the temperature had dropped again, far below zero. They had positioned their trucks, with their snow chains, at the two ends of the narrow street containing Gansukh's apartment, blocking the exits. The arrest team, bundled up in heavy clothing against the rigours of the frozen night, had made their slow way down the icy street, firearms poised.

They had not known how dangerous Gansukh might prove to be. Forty-eight hours before, a routine customs search on a truck entering the country across the northern border with Russia had uncovered a consignment of classified drugs, including heroin, apparently of Afghan origin. The driver of the truck, who had initially denied all knowledge of his cargo, turned out to be a known associate of Gansukh, a small-time businessman who had been under Nergui's surveillance for some months. The driver had quickly named Gansukh as the instigator of the operation, pulling out the pitifully small handful of US dollars he had been paid up front for undertaking the assignment. An equivalent sum, he said, would be payable by Gansukh on delivery. He named an abandoned warehouse, on the south side of the capital, as the spot where he had been due to rendezvous with another named associate of Gansukh the following evening. The police had duly arrived at the warehouse at the appointed time and arrested the associate, who without prompting also immediately named Gansukh as the paymaster.

From that point, there was little time to waste. It was only a matter of time before Gansukh realised that the operation had not proceeded according to plan.

And so, there they were, at two a.m. in the depths of winter, making their way slowly down this narrow street, poised for the arrest. Nergui had half expected that Gansukh might have tried to make his escape. But he had overestimated Gansukh's perspicacity. As they stormed in through the shattered front door of his flat, Gansukh stumbled out to meet them, rubbing his eyes, dressing gown pulled around him, demanding in a sleepy voice to know just what the *fuck* was going on. Ten seconds later, he was pinned to the ground, his hands cuffed behind his back, still screaming obscenities.

It was at that point that Nergui had first met Sarangarel. They had discovered her, cowering in bed, like a child trying to hide from her nightmares. Even then, Nergui had been struck by her appearance. But it was impossible to relate that bunched, quaking figure with the poised woman now sitting opposite. He recalled her sitting slumped on the sofa in the small apartment, her head in her hands, staring at the floor, unable to comprehend what was happening.

Under questioning, Gansukh very rapidly admitted his involvement in the smuggling operation but—in what Nergui suspected was one of Gansukh's very rare acts of chivalry—he was insistent that his wife knew nothing of the scheme. Sarangarel herself had expressed only bewilderment. She had had no involvement in her husband's business schemes, no suspicion of any criminal activity.

Nergui would have believed her, even without her husband's insistent corroboration. Their apartment was modest—decently furnished, but with nothing to indicate any unexpected wealth. Nergui initially wondered whether Gansukh had smartly concealed his wealth elsewhere, but then recognised that Gansukh was exactly what he appeared to be—an unsuccessful businessman. It was just that his failed business was on the wrong side of the law.

Then, unexpectedly, the story became more interesting.

Although Gansukh had come clean about his own involvement very quickly, clearly recognising that he had little alternative, he insisted that the real instigator was elsewhere, a big fish, sufficiently removed from the action for his involvement to be deniable.

Nergui had no difficulty believing this, but it made little difference. Gansukh refused to give any more detail even in the face of repeated aggressive questioning and the threat of a lengthy prison sentence.

"You just don't know," Gansukh said, finally, "who you're dealing with."

There was something about the way he said the words that caught Nergui's attention.

"Muunokhoi," he said, quietly.

Gansukh tried hard to control his facial expression, but the sudden spark of fear in his eyes told Nergui everything he needed to know. He had Gansukh thrown back into custody and ordered a further inch-by-inch search of Gansukh's apartment and of a number of other commercial properties he was leasing.

Meanwhile, he and Tunjin—in those days, one of Nergui's protégés—conducted endless interviews with the nervous young man, trying to get him to acknowledge some link, to provide some evidence. They offered him the prospect of a plea bargain and access to the state's newly established witness protection programme. They talked and talked, and Gansukh sat, staring at the floor, saying nothing.

After several days of this, Nergui finally thought they were making progress. At heart, Gansukh was a loser. He had always been a loser, and now he was on the point of losing everything. But maybe, as he listened to Nergui talk, he had begun to think that, for once, he might just salvage something.

Late on the third night of interviewing, he dropped his head into his hands and, speaking through his fingers, he said. "Okay. Okay, maybe I can tell you something more. But I have to be sure—"

"Sure of what?" Nergui leaned back in his seat and watched the man across the desk.

"Sure it's worth it," Gansukh said. "You don't know—"

Nergui nodded, indicating that he knew only too well. "What would make it worth it?" he said.

"How would it benefit me?"

"There are no guarantees," Nergui said. "It's not in my power to guarantee, but it is in my power to influence. It will help you in two ways. First, it confirms you're not the lead player in this. And, second, your cooperation will be taken into account. With all that—and it being a first offence, even if a serious one—you should get a minimal sentence. Maybe even suspended." This was nonsense—regardless of the mitigation, the courts now took drug smuggling very seriously indeed—but it was what Gansukh wanted to hear. Gansukh nodded. "And what about protection?"

"We have a fully established programme now. Based on best practice from the West. If you go to prison, you'll get full protection there. And if you don't—or when you come out—we can organise an identity change, relocation, whatever it needs." Again, it was an exaggeration. Nergui had little confidence that he could offer any real protection against Muunokhoi's resources.

It was as if Gunsukh had read his thoughts. "I don't know what it needs," he said, his face pale. "I don't know that anything would be enough."

"We'll do whatever is humanly possible." Nergui paused, looking for the final lever that would unlock Gansukh's response. "And if this person is as fearsome as you say, who's to say you'll be safe even if you say nothing?"

Gansukh stared up at him. "What do you mean?"

"I mean," Nergui said, "that you've painted a picture of a very dangerous individual. Someone who makes you afraid even to open your mouth. To this person, you'll always be a risk. You *know.* You might decide not to speak today or tomorrow or ever, but he can't be sure." He leaned forward, staring at Gansukh through his hard blue eyes. "How safe are you?"

Gansukh shook his head. This was clearly a new thought to him. "I don't know," he said finally, in a voice scarcely more than a whisper.

"So if you don't speak, you go to prison, a long sentence, with no protection. Do you know how many violent deaths there have been in prison over the last year?" Nergui himself didn't know, but he thought he was unlikely to be required to provide a definitive figure. "Whereas if you tell us what you can, we give you full protection and support—in prison, if necessary, and outside." He allowed silence to fall across the conversation, almost able to read the thoughts that were rushing through Gansukh's head.

Finally, Gansukh looked up at him. "I need to think about it," he said. "I don't know—"

"It's late," Nergui said. "Think about it overnight. We can talk in the morning."

This was standard practice, allowing the interviewee to stew with his thoughts. But afterwards Nergui considered it the biggest mistake he had ever made.

He was woken in the small hours of the morning, the telephone in his silent apartment unnaturally shrill in the night. It was the duty officer at the station. There had been an incident. Gansukh was dead.

He had been found in his cell, hanging from the window bars, a bed-sheet twisted awkwardly round his neck. It looked an impossible way to commit suicide, though the pathologist claimed it was not unknown. Nergui bustled around, trying to find out how it had been allowed to happen. Gansukh had not been under any kind of suicide watch—there had been no reason to assume that this was necessary. His cell had been regularly patrolled but was not under continuous surveillance.

Nergui had to acknowledge that, with hindsight, suicide might have been a predictable response. Gansukh had been scared of the consequences whether he spoke out or not. This form of death might be a lot less unpleasant than anything Muunokhoi's people could inflict.

But something nagged at Nergui. He couldn't honestly say that Gansukh was not the suicidal type—how could you judge that?—but Nergui had never seen him that way. And the timing of Gansukh's death, so soon after he had indicated that he might be willing to speak, seemed too convenient.

But only he and Tunjin had been present when Gansukh had been speaking. Nergui quickly found Tunjin and asked him whether he had shared the contents of the interview with Gansukh with any of his colleagues. Tunjin, looking justifiably terrified of Nergui, nodded almost imperceptibly. "I'm sorry, sir.

I didn't realise—" It turned out that he had been transcribing the interview notes, and had chosen to share the contents with a number of colleagues. Quite possibly, by the time Gansukh had died, most of the officers on duty would have been aware of what he had said.

So did Nergui have any grounds to treat the death as suspicious? Only the most circumstantial ones. Gansukh had been under great pressure, was facing a lengthy prison sentence, might be at risk of reprisals. Suicide was hardly an outrageous verdict. This was how the pathologist saw it. After all, what did Gansukh have to live for?

Well, thought Nergui, there was the woman now sitting opposite him delicately eating her crème brûlée. Though by the time he died, he might well have lost her anyway. Certainly, when Nergui had visited her in her hotel room to break the news, she had been—well, upset, certainly, but perhaps also secretly relieved. She would not have to drag forward the legacy of that former life—the trial, her own role as a witness, the endless rounds of visiting Gansukh in prison, the slow and painful progress towards an inevitable divorce. Perhaps, Nergui thought, Gansukh's suicide—if that was what it had been—was less selfish than it might have appeared. Perhaps, after all, he had taken that final step to prove his love for his wife.

And, looking at her now, she had clearly taken full advantage of that freedom. She had made a life and a career for herself. She had a striking presence, a sense of hard-won but powerful authority. And he wondered precisely what it was she had lost, that frozen evening, when he had met her for the first time.

"I was expecting more sparkling conversation than this, if I'm honest," she said. "But as I don't get out much, perhaps my expectations are unrealistic."

He laughed. "I'm sorry," he said. "I was just thinking."

She raised an eyebrow. "I think that's been fairly obvious for some minutes. But about what?"

He shrugged. "I don't know. About the past, I suppose."

She nodded. "I don't do that. Far too dangerous. I think about the future. Like the rest of this evening, for example. And beyond."

He opened his mouth to speak, momentarily disconcerted by her tone. As he did so, he felt his mobile phone, tucked in the inside pocket of his jacket, vibrate twice. A text message.

"I'm sorry—" He pulled out the phone and waved it gently in front of her. "I'd better check. It might be urgent."

He thumbed the buttons on the phone and brought up the message on the screen. The number was familiar though it took him a moment to place it. The message simply said: "Call. Urgent."

Nergui stared at the phone for a moment, absorbing the message.

"Well?" Sarangarel said, spooning up the last of her dessert. "Was it urgent?"

Nergui looked back up at her. "I rather think it was," he said.

She nodded, amusement playing in her dark eyes. "Well, then," she said. "What a useful device."

The weather had grown more humid in the course of the evening, and now the first small spots of rain were beginning to fall on the windscreen. Luvsan cursed and switched on the wipers. "All we need," he said.

"I take it this won't affect your famed navigational skills," Doripalam said, gesturing towards the GPS system.

Luvsan shrugged. "The machine's fine. Whether I can make any sense of it in this darkness is another question entirely."

Doripalam sat back, knowing that in truth Luvsan was fully in control and enjoying every moment of this trip through the darkness. They were still on the main road at the moment, heading north out of Bulgan towards the mountains. There was no other traffic or signs of life, other than the vanishing glow of the small city's lights behind them. Doripalam watched the progress of their headlights across the road, the monotony almost hypnotic.

"How far do we think it is?" Doripalam said.

"Not far. Twenty kilometres or so. That's where we'll meet the local guy, and he'll take us on to where the camp is."

The local guy was the outstationed officer who had been keeping an eye on the camp. Luvsan had phoned him again from the hotel and asked for his help in tracking down the camp. He had agreed with alacrity, obviously excited at the prospect of working with the Serious Crimes Team. Doripalam could not help thinking that Luvsan had perhaps rather overstated the importance of their mission, but it had seemed to have the necessary effect.

Luvsan turned on the radio, and twisted the dial till he found one of the commercial stations playing Western-style pop music. He banged his palm on the steering wheel as they drove in time with the music, occasionally singing along with the choruses. It was irritating, but preferable to the endless silence of the night.

Twenty-five minutes later they saw the few scattered lights of a small village—nothing more than a handful of timber buildings, a couple of prefabricated official blocks, and a filling station with a single petrol pump.

"This is the place," Luvsan said, pulling to a halt. "There." He gestured out of the window towards one of the prefabricated concrete buildings, with the police symbol outside. As he spoke, the main door of the building opened and a figure stepped out into the glare of their headlights, waving to them. It was a young man, with thick dark hair. He was dressed in jeans and an anorak.

Luvsan lowered his window. "Yadamsuren?" he said.

"That's me," the young man said eagerly. "You're Doripalam?"

Luvsan smirked gently and gestured towards the passenger seat. "This is my boss. I'm Luvsan."

"Pleased to meet you both," Yadamsuren said. "And very pleased to be of assistance." He peered enthusiastically through the open window, the rain—falling more heavily now—dripping from his hair on to his forehead.

"You'd better jump in," Doripalam said. "You're getting soaked."

Yadamsuren looked almost overwhelmed at the generosity of the suggestion. He pulled open the rear door and climbed in behind them. "Thanks very much."

Doripalam twisted in his seat to look back at the young officer. "How far are we from the site?"

"Not far. A couple of kilometres, no more."

"They're still there?"

Yadamsuren nodded. "I checked again after you phoned."

"And you're sure they've no idea you've been observing them?"

"I was very careful. I parked some way away and then walked up there. I know that terrain very well, so I had no difficulty finding my way up there in the dark."

Luvsan peered gloomily out through the rain-spattered windscreen. "I hope we don't have to park too far away," he said.

"You can drive almost up to it. In this weather, you can probably get quite close before they'd hear the engine."

"Well done," Doripalam said to the young man. "We're very grateful."

Luvsan turned his head away, smiling faintly. He knew that

Doripalam was utterly sincere, but also that this was the most enthusiastic praise that was ever likely to issue from the chief's lips. In this case, though, it seemed to be more than sufficient. Yadamsuren looked almost overwhelmed at Doripalam's words.

"I hope these are the people you are seeking," Yadamsuren said. It sounded like a genuine expression of goodwill rather than any prompting for more information. Luvsan had given Yadamsuren no indication of why they were interested in these people, although, if Yadamsuren read the newspapers, he might easily have arrived at the answer for himself.

"I hope so, too," Doripalam said.

Luvsan started the engine and pulled back out on to the road. "This way?" he said, gesturing ahead.

Yadamsuren nodded. "Keep going up here a couple of kilometres," he said. "I'll tell you when to turn. The last part is over the grassland, but it should be solid enough even in this rain."

They drove on through the dark. To Luvsan, as he peered out between the sweep of the wipers into the glare of the headlights, the whole landscape looked identical. There was simply the endless passage of the road, clusters of conifers that thickened and then fell away.

Yadamsuren, though, was peering carefully through the window, clearly enumerating every turn in the road and every copse of trees they passed. "Here," he said at last. "Slow down. We're almost there."

Luvsan obeyed, slowing the truck down to a crawl, staring forward to try to find some discernible landmark.

"Just here," Yadamsuren said. "Before that clump of trees. Turn right there, and then drive up slowly past the trees. Take it gently. The ground's okay but a bit rough."

Yadamsuren's description seemed like an understatement as they slowly bounced their way across the uneven terrain up past the trees. "How far is it now?" Doripalam said.

"Just a few hundred metres," Yadamsuren said. "How close do you want to get in the truck?"

Doripalam shrugged. "I think in this weather we may as well go all the way. We'll still surprise them—so they won't have much time if they've anything to hide—and they're more likely to take us seriously if we turn up in a dirty great truck."

"I could turn on the sirens," Luvsan suggested. The truck had no police markings but carried a siren and lights for use in emergencies.

"I don't think so," Doripalam said. "I don't think we want to risk terrifying the life out of them. We don't know how they might react."

"Do you think they could be armed?" Yadamsuren said, nervously.

"It's possible," Doripalam said. "It's always possible. Bear that in mind. With this lot, we just don't know. Assuming it is the people we're looking for, all we know is that we want them as potential witnesses. But we don't know why they're hiding or what it is that they appear to be running from. So who knows?"

"This is connected with that woman?" Yadamsuren said. "The murder?" So he had been reading the newspapers, Luvsan thought. Smart boy.

Doripalam nodded. "This is her family. They travelled together. But they'd moved on before her body was found. We don't know why."

"You think they might have killed her?"

"They might. But they might also be running from whoever did. And maybe they'd left before she was killed. We don't know. That's why we don't know how they're likely to react."

They had reached the top of the incline now, and the ground fell away before them. In the headlights they could see the tops of a cluster of *gers*, pitched in a low hollow, surrounded on three sides by trees. It was a good hiding place, if that was indeed the intention. The tents were hidden by the trees, as well as by their low elevation in the hollow. They would not be visible from the surrounding terrain until they were right on top of them.

Doripalam saw the door of the closest *ger* swing partly open. It was impossible to disguise their presence any longer—the inhabitants of the camp would have heard the truck's engine, seen the glare of the headlights. Luvsan stopped the truck so that the headlights were shining down fully into the camp, and then killed the engine.

Almost simultaneously, before he had a chance to direct their next move, Doripalam felt his mobile vibrating in his pocket. He cursed, pulled it out and glanced at the screen. Headquarters.

"Just wait a moment," he said. "Keep an eye on what's happening down there. If you see any significant movement, we'd better get down."

He thumbed the phone and took the call. For a few moments, he listened, saying nothing, then said: "You've got people over there? Search the apartment. Minutely. Anything you can find. Anything that might be remotely relevant. We probably won't be able to get back till morning, but make sure you keep me posted."

He ended the call and turned back to Luvsan. "It's Tunjin," he said.

"Tunjin? I thought he was suspended."

"He is," Doripalam said, noting that, despite all their efforts at keeping this information under wraps, it was already common knowledge. "That's just it. There was some sort of disturbance outside his apartment block. Gunfire. His flat looked as if it had been ransacked. And Tunjin's gone missing."

"Gone missing? But how—?" Luvsan was about to make some joke about the difficulty of losing eighteen stones of solid fat, but he didn't finish the sentence.

It took them all by surprise. There had been no apparent movement from the camp below them. But then, suddenly, all at once, Doripalam caught the glare of gunfire, the sound of a shot, and the nerve-shattering explosion as their windscreen collapsed into countless tiny shards, brilliant in the glare of the headlights. And then there was screaming and the smell of blood and burning, and the sound of all hell breaking loose.

ELEVEN

He had his back to the wall and was watching intently, waiting for something to happen. Outside night had fallen and the darkness was thickening.

He needed to relax, he knew that. He couldn't keep up this pace, this intensity for long. He just wasn't built for it. And he knew, rationally, that as yet they could have no idea where he was. For the moment, at least, he was safe. The only question was for how long.

He breathed deeply, trying to calm himself down, trying not to think too hard about the implications of being found. He had bought himself some time, at least. Now he needed to make use of it. He needed to force himself to think, to work out what he was going to do next.

He looked about him, trying to rationalise his position, trying to think about what he needed to do. Okay, he thought, first things first. Work it all out, step by step. The position is straightforward. He had found himself a haven. As long as he stayed here, he was likely to be safe. The only problem was that he couldn't stay here for very long.

He was sitting in the corner of a storeroom in an abandoned shop on the south side of the city. It was one of the industrial areas that had been redeveloped with the emergence of capitalism, where dozens of supposedly entrepreneurial businesses had sprung up apparently overnight. As the grand old monolithic communist enterprises gradually ground to a halt, the westerners had been quick to tell them that this was where the future lay, in the energetic play of the free market. Let a thousand self-employed flowers bloom.

But of course it hadn't lasted. Tunjin had had friends and relations whose lives had collapsed during those fateful years, who had lost whatever security and savings they might have had. And he recalled the dreadful winters that had accompanied those years of depression, as if nature and the heavens had chosen to conspire with man's worst instincts.

The place was a wreck. The display window at the front had long been shattered, and large shards of glass still lay scattered across the tiled floor. Any remaining items of stock had been looted almost immediately, and all that was left now were a few broken shelves and display cabinets, faded printed notices advertising long-obsolete electronic goods.

Behind the shop itself was a small network of rooms—a living area with a small bed-sitting room, a kitchen and a lavatory, and then, behind that, the small storeroom where Tunjin was currently sitting.

There was no furniture in any of the rooms, other than a discarded broken table lamp and a few tattered remains of what had presumably once been blinds. The storeroom contained a few empty cardboard boxes, some scattered unidentifiable electrical components, and little else.

Tunjin had come to the storeroom simply because it represented the point furthest removed from the front of the shop and the outside world. He had come to the shop in the first place because—well, because he could think of nowhere else to go. His journey out of the city on the motorbike had been utterly terrifying, because he did not know how closely he was being pursued. The shots had faded behind him, but he did not know whether Muunokhoi's people would have other observers or pursuers stationed around the area. He half expected that, at any moment, another shot might bring him or the bike down, or that some car or truck would appear to block his route or sideswipe him.

But it didn't happen. He kept on, making his way through the ruined factories and warehouses, and then between the camps of semipermanent *gers* that surrounded the city, until finally he was away from the buildings and heading out on to the open steppe.

Finally, at that point, he felt able to stop and look back. Even if he were not being pursued, he was acutely aware of his potentially lethal ineptitude on the bike. In his younger days, he'd been a pretty skilled motorcyclist, having bought and maintained an old Russian bike when he was a teenager. He'd ridden that for years, around the city, out into the country, taking girls for dates on the back of it. It all seemed a very long time ago.

He'd even had a police bike for a while, and had received full professional training on how to ride it. So he should have known what he was doing. They said it was one of the things you never forgot. And that was probably the case, or he wouldn't have made it this far.

But the young man who had ridden that old Soviet bike as if it was a part of his own body was long gone, replaced by this overweight old slob. When he'd first set off on Agypar's bike, Tunjin's sheer bulk had been a problem—he could feel his weight wobbling around the bike's centre of gravity as he struggled to maintain his balance. But he'd eventually come to grips with that and felt much more comfortable. Even then, though, he was aware that his reactions were not what they once had been, and that the nerve and lack of fear that characterised his younger biking were long gone. Left to his own devices, he would have ridden as slowly as possible until his confidence returned. But there had been no question of that—he simply had to get out of there as quickly as possible.

And somehow he'd made it. He was out in the grassland, looking back at the city's jumble on the skyline. There was no evident sign of pursuit. It was a bright clear day, with only a few dark clouds clustering on the horizon. Everything looked beautiful and peaceful.

But out here, Tunjin felt exposed. Rationally he was safe. If anyone was pursuing him, he would see them from miles away. But, equally, they would see him. And perhaps someone was already watching him. Perhaps they had watched him the whole way, knew exactly where he was, but had not bothered to give chase. Perhaps they did not need to.

He looked up at the empty sky. Muunokhoi was a wealthy man. He would have access to aircraft, helicopters. He or his people could be out here in a matter of minutes if they so chose. Suddenly, the vast wasteland of the steppe seemed much less like a sanctuary.

It was that thinking that had led him back into the city, and back here. He had twisted the bike round and, taking a convoluted route back around the city, entered it again from the west side and made his way down here. He had used all his police skills and training to try to lose any possible pursuit, twisting and turning up and down alleyways, between and through abandoned buildings, jumping red lights, taking narrow passages so that pursuit by car was impossible. And finally he'd arrived here.

For the moment, then, he was safe. But he knew that this state could not last long. He would soon have to emerge to find some food and drink—he had managed a single stop on his way here to get some bread, fruit and bottles of water from one of the small new supermarkets, but hadn't dared to linger. And he was conscious that he already presented a conspicuous figure, with his heavy weight and dishevelled appearance. People would notice him, and he was sure that, sooner or later, the message would get back to Muunokhoi.

He wondered whether he'd made a mistake in coming back. Maybe he should have just carried on, maybe got a flight down into the Gobi or up into the north. Taken himself as far away as possible from the capital and from Muunokhoi, tried to make himself a new life somewhere else.

But he knew that this was impossible. Muunokhoi would track him down no matter how far he fled.

So what options did he have? Precious few, it seemed. Hide out here like a terrified rabbit for as long as possible, then emerge and take the consequences? It didn't seem much of a prospect.

Or he could try to take the initiative. He could at least try to use what few resources lay at his disposal. He could go down fighting.

It was his own fault, his own responsibility that he was in this mess. But there was one other factor that had contributed, one other person who was, at least peripherally, involved. One other person who had the same drive, the same motivation in this, as he did.

He looked at his watch. It was nearly nine. Outside, the sun had set and the deserted streets and alleyways were in darkness.

Tunjin reached into his pocket, pulled out the mobile phone he had not yet dared to use, and very carefully began to dial.

* * *

Doripalam was out of the truck and had pulled out his pistol almost in one movement, rolling across the wet grass until he was standing upright, facing down into the camp. He moved himself quickly back behind the truck's bulk, and stared out ahead of him.

There were four of them, standing in a row, all apparently holding rifles. They had all fired in sequence, round after round, the echoes still reverberating around the distant hillsides. It seemed, though, that only one bullet had found a target, shattering the windscreen of the truck.

Doripalam saw that Luvsan had followed his example, and was now moving back to join him.

"How's Yadamsuren?"

"Okay, I think," Luvsan said. "Bullet just grazed his shoulder. Fair bit of blood, and we need to get it bandaged, but it's not serious. Lucky, though. Could have got any one of us."

"Unlucky, I think," Doripalam countered. "I don't think they actually meant to hit us at all. That was just a stray shot."

"Oh, that's okay, then," Luvsan said. "When I get hold of those bastards, I'll make sure one of my boots strays into their teeth."

Doripalam carefully pulled open the back door of the truck, and lifted out a loud-hailer which he raised to his lips.

"Armed police. I repeat, armed police. Put down your weapons. Otherwise, we will open fire."

There was a long pause. The four figures below them, little more than black shadows in the truck's headlights, remained motionless. And then, like a soldier breaking ranks, the figure on the far left stepped forward and threw down his rifle. There was a further pause, and then, one by one, the others did the same.

Doripalam glanced at Luvsan. "I'll go down there," he said. "Cover me. If there's any sign at all of trouble, start firing."

Luvsan nodded. He had pulled a medium range rifle out of

the truck, and now set it down carefully across the roof, the sights trained on the figures below. "Good luck," he said.

Doripalam stepped out from behind the truck, holding his pistol out in front of him in both hands. The rain was still falling heavily, and the cold water ran down his arms, dripping off the steel of the gun.

The four men still stood motionless. Doripalam stopped and called out: "Put your hands on your heads. No other movements."

The men obeyed silently, watching his descent. He moved slowly, watching them carefully, alert for any movement.

He moved closer, reaching the point where the discarded rifles lay in the sodden grass. Moving carefully, his eyes still fixed on the four men, he kicked the rifles back to ensure they were out of the men's reach.

"Okay, you," he said to the man on the far left—the first to discard his weapon. "Take off your jacket—very slowly—and throw it on the ground. Then turn out your pockets. Slowly." The four men were all dressed in Western clothes, anoraks and jeans.

The man hesitated for a moment and then obeyed, throwing his anorak down on to the grass. He pulled out the pockets of his jeans—a wallet, a few coins, nothing else.

Doripalam repeated the process with the other three men, then beckoned Luvsan down to join him. Luvsan held his rifle trained on the men while Doripalam talked.

"I've an injured officer in the truck," he said. "Injured by one of you. I'm planning to arrest you all and charge you with assault, maybe even attempted murder. I'll go through all the formal procedure in a moment. In the meantime, any of you want to tell me what this is all about?"

Luvsan glanced across at him in mild surprise. But it was as clear as it could be that these men posed no serious threat. All four of them looked scared out of their wits, trembling not just with the rain and the cold, but also from the unwavering sight of Luvsan's firearm.

The men looked at each other in some confusion. Then, finally, the man on the left spoke. "I'm sorry," he said. "We have been very foolish. We did not realise you were police. We were terrified. We thought you were—" He stopped.

Doripalam waited a moment, but when it was clear that the man did not intend to continue, he said: "Who did you think we were?"

The man looked around at his companions, as if looking for support. "It's a long story," he said at last. "You said your companion was injured. Can we do anything for him?"

Doripalam hesitated, not wanting to lose control of the situation, but recognising that Yadamsuren did need attention. He looked at Luvsan. "He's right. There's a first aid kit in the truck. Go and get Yadamsuren bandaged up as best you can. I'll look after this bunch."

One of the men leaned forward. "I have some medical skills," he said. "I trained as a nurse. I can help."

The situation was, Doripalam thought, drifting towards the surreal. But he found it hard to believe that these cowering men constituted any kind of a threat. "Okay," he said to Luvsan. "Take him with you."

He turned to the man on the left of the group. "We're investigating a murder," he said. "In a nomadic camp close to the capital. Does that mean anything to you?"

"My sister," the man said. "We saw it in the newspapers a few days ago. It was not a surprise but it was—a shock. I did not really believe it."

"You didn't know she was dead?"

"Not for sure. Not until we saw the report. We thought she might have escaped somehow. But we did not really believe that she would."

"Escaped what? What's this all about?"

"It is a long story," the man repeated. "We do not even know the whole story."

Doripalam was becoming irritated with the cryptic responses. "You'll have plenty of time in custody to go through it all," he said. He began to intone the formal charges of attempted murder, following the prescribed procedure and wording, while the three men stared at him aghast.

"But we are not criminals," one of them said, as he finished.

"I would advise you not to say more until you're in custody," Doripalam said. "We can organise legal representation for you."

"We are not criminals," the man repeated.

"You have fired repeatedly on officers of the law, with no warning or provocation. You have injured a police officer. You have—and I mention this in passing—damaged a police vehicle. Whatever your motivations, these are serious crimes."

"But we did not intend—"

"That will be for the courts to decide. I can only work on the outcomes."

Doripalam sighed and pulled out his mobile phone. He was going to have to call backup from the local police to take these characters into custody in Bulgan. All this would take time, and the rain was continuing to fall.

"If you're prepared to cooperate, we can perhaps short-circuit some of the formalities. And I may be prepared to reconsider the charges, so long as my young companion does not wish to press charges." This, he thought, was all very unorthodox. Still, pouring rain in the middle of the steppe was not conducive to orthodoxy.

"Let's get inside and talk," he said, gesturing with his pistol towards the nearest *ger.*

The three men filed slowly into the tent. Doripalam followed them, still holding his gun at chest height, keeping them all carefully in view. It might be worth being unorthodox, but it certainly wasn't worth being reckless.

Inside, the *ger* was comfortable enough but very sparsely furnished, as if the men were travelling with the minimum of equipment. The first man gestured Doripalam to sit on one of the two wooden seats, while he and his companions crouched on the floor. The *ger* was lit dimly by two oil lanterns, but the tent was well enough illuminated for Doripalam to discern the anxiety on the men's faces. Doripalam held his gun casually, but kept it trained on the three men.

"Okay," he said at last, "so what's the story?"

"It's my sister," the first man said.

"Mrs. Tuya?"

The man nodded. "I'm Tseren." He gestured. "Damdin is also my brother. Kadyr is our cousin. Another cousin, Ravhjik, is assisting your colleagues."

Doripalam nodded. "Tell me about your sister," he said.

Tseren hesitated, as if unsure where to begin. "I suppose it starts with her husband," he said.

"The soldier?"

Tseren nodded. "Khenbish. The great war hero," he snorted, ironically. "Yes, with him."

"You did not have a high opinion of him?" Doripalam watched Tseren quizzically, wondering quite where this was going.

"He was a bad man," Tseren said, simply. "In every way. I have been amused reading the press coverage. The great war hero." He laughed, bitterly. He glanced at the other two men who looked back at him, stony-faced.

"What do you mean?" Doripalam said.

"You name it. He was a violent man. He drank too much."

"He was violent with your sister?"

Damdin began to speak but Tseren cut him off. "I think he was. She always denied it, but I have seen her with bruises. I am sure he was."

Doripalam looked at Damdin, wondering whether he was about to contradict his brother. Damdin shrugged. "I do not know," he said. "I do not like to condemn people without evidence. But I think Tseren is right."

"You are too generous," Tseren said. "Khenbish was a bad man. He was trouble for our sister. He was involved with bad people."

"What sort of bad people?" Doripalam looked between the three men. He had the impression that Tseren was keen to talk, but that the others were uneasy about saying too much.

Tseren looked at the others. "I cannot name names," he said.

"This is a murder enquiry," Doripalam said. "If you have information, it is your duty to give it to the police. If I think you're withholding evidence, we may once again need to revert to the formalities."

Tseren shook his head. "I am not trying to withhold evidence. I genuinely don't know the names of these people. I've no desire to know them."

Doripalam decided to let that one go for a moment. "So what kinds of people are we talking about?" he said.

Tseren shrugged. "Mostly small-time crooks, I think. Organised crime, though not on a grand scale—protection rackets, smuggling, robbery. Some pretty unsavoury types. I met them occasionally when I went to visit my sister. Some of them were ex-soldiers, which I guess is how Khenbish had got to know them."

Doripalam nodded. Once the USSR had withdrawn its support, the military, like most other parts of the economy, had collapsed. There were many soldiers who found themselves back out on the street, with no pension, no skills and few prospects. It was also common knowledge that a substantial proportion of the military armoury had found its way back on to the street with them.

"But I think there were other things he was involved in. Deals he got involved in during his time in Afghanistan—"

"You mean drugs?"

Tseren shrugged. "Well, he certainly had access to them for his own use. Openly boasted about it. So, yes, I think he was probably involved in some sort of operation."

"Drug smuggling?" It sounded far-fetched to Doripalam. Would it be possible for a soldier, even in those chaotic post-communist days, to be involved in smuggling drugs into the country?

"I don't know for sure," Tseren said. "I just know that he seemed to get himself caught up with some unpleasant people. I was frightened for what might happen to his family—"

"You met these people?"

"Sometimes. Again, when I went round there, he'd be engaged in what he described as business meetings, though he'd never tell us what kind of business was involved. But I got the impression that the meetings weren't always comfortable ones. If I know Khenbish, he'd have promised more than he could deliver. I don't know for sure, but there were a couple of occasions when I thought he was in serious trouble."

"He died in combat?"

Tseren laughed. "Is that what the records say?"

Doripalam shook his head. "I've not looked at the records myself," he said, "but that was what I understood."

"He was drunk," Tseren said, "and maybe more than drunk.

Fell into the path of a truck. They hushed it up, but that was the real story. The best way it could have ended, really. The family got an army pension—not a great deal but something—and were rid of him. That was when they moved back out to live with us."

"But what does this have to do with Mrs. Tuya's death?" Doripalam said. "He'd been dead for a long time by then."

"Gavaa idolised his father," Tseren said, as though changing the subject.

"Gavaa? The son? The one who went missing?" Doripalam said.

Tseren nodded. "Thought his father was marvellous. Well, I suppose every son has a right to do that, though not every father deserves it. Wanted to follow in his father's footsteps."

"As a soldier?"

"Yes. At first. But he wasn't cut out for it. But he saw his father as the great hero. Thought that everything he did was marvellous."

"What are you saying? That he followed his father—" For the first time, Doripalam lowered the gun and stared at Tseren.

"I don't know for sure what happened, but his mother thought he'd fallen in with a bad crowd in the city—"

"Mothers always think that," Doripalam pointed out. "Mine thought it when I joined the police."

"No, it was more than that," Tseren said. "She didn't say so to me, but I think she knew some of the people he'd got in touch with. I think he was trying to make contact with some of his father's business contacts."

"Mrs. Tuya said nothing about this when she came to us about his disappearance," Doripalam said.

"No, well, I don't think she wanted to believe it," Tseren said. "She didn't really have any concrete evidence—just hints he'd dropped on the few occasions when he'd spoken to her."

"I understand they didn't get on at the end," Doripalam said. "Surely that's the kind of thing that any teenager might say to bait his mother?"

"That's what she thought at first." Tseren paused. "It's certainly what I told her. It was only when he disappeared that she thought there might have been something more in what he'd said."

"And what had he said?"

"Something about job prospects. She was saying the usual stuff about wasting his life in some dead-end job, and he started telling her that he had real prospects. Stuff she couldn't even dream of."

"Doesn't sound very plausible," Doripalam said. "We've no evidence he did get another job. And his mother didn't mention it when she spoke to us."

"I don't think any of us took much notice of it, even when Gavaa went missing. We all thought it was just teenage bravado. To be honest, my concern was simply whether Gavaa could survive in the city. He had a high opinion of himself, but I'm not sure many other people shared it."

"Including you?"

"Including me. And, I think, even including his mother. He treated her badly—knew she hadn't really got on with his father and thought that was her fault. But he saw his father as a hero, whereas we all saw him as a drunken bully. But she was his mother. She loved him. I think that was why she was so worried when he vanished. Because she just thought that he wouldn't be able to cope."

"Did you take his disappearance seriously?"

Tseren shrugged. "Not at first. I don't imagine the police did, either. I was a bit embarrassed by the press coverage. But when we continued to hear nothing from him, I began to get more concerned."

"You'd have expected him to contact you?"

"If only to ask for money. He was always short. And then, when the men came—"

Doripalam looked up sharply and stared at Tseren across the dim expanse of the tent. "Men?"

"I wasn't there myself. We'd all made a trip into the city and left Bayarmaa—Mrs. Tuya—by herself looking after the animals."

"When was this?"

"I don't know. A couple of weeks before her murder, I suppose."

"And you never came forward—"

"No. We should have done that, I know. But we were afraid."

"Who were these men?"

"We don't know. They apparently arrived in a truck, two of them. Large, threatening men. The kinds of people that Bayarmaa's husband used to associate with, she told us. They were asking for Gavaa. Said he was in some serious trouble. They tried to give the impression that they wanted to help him, but Bayarmaa's impression was that if he was in trouble, they were probably the cause of it."

"But they didn't know where he was?"

"No, they were trying to track him down. They said it was some business deal that he'd been involved in but they wouldn't say more. They were clearly convinced that he was hiding out with his mother."

"She told them he wasn't?"

"Of course. But it wasn't clear that they believed her. From the way they spoke, it sounded as if they thought that, at the very least, she was in contact with him."

"Did they threaten her?"

"Not overtly, I don't think. She was a tough woman—I don't

think she was scared of them herself. But she was worried about Gavaa."

"And what about you? Were you worried?"

Tseren nodded, crouched down on the rugs that were spread across the floor of the tent. "Yes, I knew the kinds of people that Khenbish had associated with. If these were some of those people, then—well, yes, I had reason to be worried."

"And you thought they might be?"

Tseren shrugged. "I began to put two and two together. Remembered what Gavaa had said about having prospects. I thought he might well have approached some of his father's old associates and got sucked into something that was over his head."

Doripalam had lowered the gun. "I wanted to get out of there," Tseren continued. "Move on. I know these kinds of people. They don't take no for an answer. If they thought Gavaa was hiding with us, then they'd keep watching us. If they thought we knew where he was, then they'd take whatever steps they could to get the information out of us."

"So you moved on? Without Mrs. Tuya?" It was hard not to make the question sound accusatory.

Tseren shook his head. "Not immediately. I told myself I was just being paranoid, that there was no reason to be frightened. Then the following evening, I came out of the tent to see a truck parked some way away across the grassland. It was them. They were watching us. I could even see the binoculars. Worst of all, they weren't making any effort to hide themselves. They wanted us to know they were there. They didn't stay there long. But then a day or two later they were back again. Just watching. And that was when I knew that it would go on like that, that we really didn't have a choice, that we really should get away."

"So you did?"

"We did. The four of us left as quickly as we could to look for new pastures, somewhere far enough away that they wouldn't easily be able to find us."

"Why didn't you take Mrs. Tuya with you?"

"She wouldn't come. She thought there would be some news soon of Gavaa, and she didn't want not to be there. And there was a policeman coming to talk to her—"

"That was me," Doripalam said quietly.

"She thought you might have some news."

Doripalam shook his head. "I had nothing to tell her."

Tseren nodded. "I assumed that would be the case. I told her so. But she was desperate for any information."

Doripalam nodded, thinking back to how lightly he had treated Gavaa's disappearance. "And none of you stayed with her?"

Tseren dropped his head and stared at the floor. "We told ourselves that nothing would happen to her before we returned. She told us the same. And she said that the police were coming to visit her so the men wouldn't dare do anything. But I think we were just cowards."

"And you didn't go back?"

Tseren nodded. "We started to. We found a good pasture for the family. We left the rest of the family there—another cousin and her husband, their two boys—and then we went back for Mrs. Tuya and the rest of the equipment. But when we got within sight of the camp, we saw that it was surrounded by police vehicles."

Doripalam looked up and stared at Tseren. "So why didn't you come forward? Why didn't you tell us what you knew?"

"I don't know. We were scared. We didn't know what had happened. We thought—maybe that Bayarmaa had called you in or that she'd spoken to you about the men when you visited. But I think we knew from all the activity that—well, that

that wasn't really what had happened. So we panicked and fled. We've been running ever since."

Doripalam shook his head, watching the three cowering men in front of him. It was, he thought, a sight far removed from the Mongolian martial ideal. "You should have come forward," he said. "We would have protected you."

"You were not able to protect Bayarmaa," Tseren said. The statement was factual rather than accusatory. "You were not able to protect Gavaa."

Doripalam could hear the faint thudding of the rain on the roof. "We do not know that anything has happened to Gavaa," he said.

Tseren shook his head. "I do not believe we will see Gavaa again," he said. "I think he is dead."

TWELVE

Nergui, working his distinctive brand of bureaucratic magic, had managed to organise an official car to take them home. He had originally assumed, without making any definite plans, that they would go on somewhere after the restaurant. Maybe just to a bar for a nightcap or two. He imagined that both of them were getting a little old for nightclubs.

He had not thought what might happen beyond that. Quite probably nothing. He still wasn't sure about the nature of this relationship, or where it might lead. He was enjoying the companionship, and Sarangarel seemed to have enjoyed the evening, if only because she so rarely socialised. Nergui was reluctant to look any further forward than that. He couldn't imagine that romance was seriously on the cards for either of them, and he was still concerned about his own, possibly darker motives for reestablishing this relationship.

Even so, he found himself disappointed that the text message should have cut the meeting shorter than he intended.

The large black official car pulled to a stop outside her apartment block. Nergui was pleased to note that a police officer was positioned discreetly in the shadows, ensuring protection in case the threats should turn out to have any substance.

Rain had swept in from the north, falling in heavy windswept sheets down the dimly lit street. This was, he noted, one of the more upmarket parts of town, not far from his own apartment.

She peered out through the car window. "I'm going to have to make a run for it," she said. "I didn't expect this kind of weather tonight."

"It's cold, too," Nergui said. "Look, I'm really sorry I've had to bring you straight back. I was hoping we could have had another drink."

"Probably not the weather for it, anyway," she said. "But, yes, I'm sorry too. I've enjoyed the evening. It's a rare pleasure for me—eating out, someone else paying, and not even on official business. And I imagine that urgent phone messages are an occupational hazard for someone in your position." She paused, smiling. "Mind you, if it had come earlier in the evening, I would have assumed you were looking for an excuse to bail out."

He laughed. "On the contrary," he said, "I was trying to find an excuse not to bail out. But it really is urgent."

"Oh, well. I suppose that means I'm off to bed, while you're back off to work."

"Something like that," he said.

They made their goodbyes, even a polite European-style kiss on the cheeks, and then she was gone, out into the rain, holding her coat over her head. Nergui watched her run into the lobby of the apartment block, shaking off the rain and standing waiting for the lift.

The driver turned, blank faced. "Back to headquarters now, sir?"

Nergui hesitated. “No,” he said. “Take me home. I’ve got some calls to make but I can make them from there.”

Nergui’s own flat was only another ten or fifteen minutes away. He dismissed the driver, and then walked slowly across the pavement to the doors of the apartment block, perversely enjoying the slow drip of the rain through his hair and down his face. He was, he realised, delaying the moment when he would have to return home and start to deal with all of this. Even though he didn’t know yet what all this might actually turn out to be.

He shook the rain from his hair then hurried into the lobby of the apartment block, and made his way rapidly up the stairs to his first floor flat.

The flat was, as always, warm and comfortable, a haven that Nergui had created for himself away from the bustle of his daily business. He’d pulled strings to get some of the furniture, shipping heavy mahogany items in from Russia and the West. Unmarried, no dependents, with a high ranking government job, he could afford to spend money on this kind of thing. But there were times when it seemed a poor substitute for human company.

He poured himself a small glass of vodka and then sat down on one of the plush crimson armchairs. He pulled his mobile out of his pocket, thumbed the keys and looked again at the text message that had been sent earlier. The number had not been concealed, which might have been a mistake. Nergui had no idea how easy or difficult it might be to monitor mobile phone calls.

He hesitated for a moment longer, then dialled in the callback sequence. There was a long moment’s silence then the ringing tone. The ringing tone ran on, and at first Nergui thought that no one was going to answer. But, finally, just when he was on the point of giving up, the call was picked up.

“Yes?” The voice was hoarse, little more than a whisper.

"Tunjin?"

A pause. "It's you," Tunjin said, finally.

"Are you all right?" Nergui said. Tunjin's voice was faint, static ridden.

"For the moment, yes. But they're on to me—"

Nergui nodded, slowly. "It was inevitable," he said. "You should never have got caught up in this. Especially not the way you did." He cursed himself inwardly. There was no point in berating Tunjin about this now. Tunjin's intentions were good, but he'd done a stupid thing. He just hadn't realised what he was up against.

"Where are you—? No, don't tell me," Nergui said. "I don't know how secure this line is. Are you somewhere safe?"

"I think so," Tunjin said. "But I don't know how long I can stay here."

Nergui sat back in his chair, trying to decide on the best way forward. His own enquiries were going too slowly, making too little progress. He didn't have enough information to protect Tunjin. He still didn't know who was on the inside. But if they were after him, Tunjin was unlikely to have much breathing space.

"Can you get to the usual place?" Nergui said. "Just say yes or no."

There was another audible hesitation. "Yes."

"Can you be there in an hour? Again, just say yes or no."

"Yes."

"Well meet there," Nergui said. He looked at his watch. Ten thirty. "Eleven thirty. Don't say anything else. Just hang up."

As instructed, the line went dead and Nergui sat for a moment, listening to the silence. Maybe he was just being paranoid. He would certainly be wary of the phones in headquarters, and maybe even of those in his own office in the Ministry, even though those were regularly swept for listening devices. But he really didn't know what was possible with a mobile phone. He understood that digital phones were more secure, but didn't know what that really meant. And the one thing he had learnt from this whole sorry affair was not to underestimate the opposition. They had got on to Tunjin's schemes quickly enough, and then even more quickly had got on to Tunjin. They undoubtedly knew what Nergui was up to, even though his enquiry was supposedly confidential. Indeed, Nergui's logic had been that, since the chances of keeping his involvement quiet were effectively zero in any case, he might as well try to use his presence to try to smoke them out. But quite possibly they were too clever for that.

Nergui swallowed the last of his vodka. The next question was whether he could get to their designated rendezvous safely. The last thing he wanted was to draw Tunjin into an ambush. They had used the same spot as a meeting place for years—the legacy of a surveillance case they had been involved in years before. It had become almost a private joke between them, no need to spell it out. And Tunjin was even more streetwise than Nergui, so he would surely have spotted any pursuer. But there was always the risk that somewhere, somehow, they had been spotted.

Nergui poured a second vodka and strolled over to the window. He pulled back the heavy tapestry curtain and peered out into the night. The rain was still falling and the street below looked deserted. Nergui stared out into the pale slick of the streetlight spread across the rain-drenched street, trying to discern any sign of movement.

The meeting place was relatively close by—only a few minutes away by car, half an hour or so to walk. Probably best to drive, he thought. The car would be more conspicuous but would allow them the prospect of an immediate getaway if anything went wrong. In this situation, Nergui wanted to avoid vulnerability at all cost. He wanted to be in control. Or, at least, as in control as it was possible to be.

He walked into the bedroom and pulled out a drawer from the heavy dark wood dressing table by his bed. Then he crouched and reached into the drawer space. Concealed at the back was a built-in gun safe, which he had had installed following the kidnapping of the English policeman the year before. Prior to that, Nergui had never kept firearms in his apartment, believing that it was appropriate only to keep firearms in his official capacity where they could be safely stored. But the kidnapping had unnerved him and he had suddenly recognised the vulnerability of his own position. He had increased the security on his apartment, and had decided for the first time to store one of his licensed handguns at home.

He clicked open the safe and pulled out the pistol, feeling its cold weight in his palm. He knew he was unlikely to deploy it. Although he was fully trained in its use, all his instincts were against using a weapon in any context other than a formal police exercise. And this, he thought, was anything but.

He slipped the gun into his pocket, closed the safe and carefully replaced the drawer. Then he looked around him, as if he were being watched. The security on this place was as tight as it could be, but it was difficult to shake off the paranoia. There was no knowing who could be trusted here. He couldn't even have risked having his flat swept for bugging devices, because he wasn't sure he could trust those who would be doing the sweeping. He was prepared to take that risk in his office environment because he could manage the potential consequences. But he needed this place to be genuinely safe, a haven.

He shook his head. All this was getting to him. Maybe that was what had happened to Tunjin in the end. Maybe the paranoia had got to him, and that was what had forced him into that ridiculous plan. If so, who knew what state he might be in by now?

He looked at his watch. Just after eleven. Probably still slightly early to be setting out, but he was finding the waiting too much. He paced up and down again, and then made his way to the front door of the apartment. He paused for a moment and leaned forward to peer out through the tiny spyglass. The distorted image of the corridor showed it to be empty.

He hesitated for a moment, then turned and walked back into the kitchen. He picked up a loaf of bread, some pieces of fruit that were sitting in the bowl on the table, a couple of bottles of water. It wasn't much, but it was all he had easily available. Back in the hallway, he retrieved a canvas rucksack from under the coatrack and threw the items inside. Then he unlocked the door, pulled it open and stepped out into the empty corridor. Time to face the rain and the night, he thought, and whatever else might be waiting.

"You're sure you're okay?" Doripalam said, peering into the truck.

Yadamsuren nodded weakly. He looked pale and very shaken, curled up in the back seat of the truck.

"Serves you right for mixing with us city folk," Luvsan said. "We always bring trouble."

Yadamsuren smiled weakly. "Thanks for patching me up," he said. "It hurts like hell but at least it's not bleeding."

"I didn't do much," Luvsan said. "It was the old chap over there knew what he was about. Ten times more than my basic first aid." He gestured to where Ravhjik had now rejoined his cousins. It was still raining, but the four men were sitting outside the *gers,* the rain pouring onto them, as if they were performing some kind of penance.

"Do you want to press charges?" Doripalam said. He was also still standing out in the rain, his head peering in through the truck window, though he was well wrapped in a police-issue waterproof coat. "I'm very happy if you want to. I played softball with them in there to get them to talk, but I made it clear that it's your call. We're not normally too keen on allowing people to get away with shooting police officers." He had already outlined to Luvsan and Yadamsuren the content of his discussion with Tseren.

"From what you say, they were scared to death," Yadamsuren said. "I'm not hurt—well, not seriously anyway. Don't think we'd achieve very much by putting them through the legal mill."

"Increase your arrest tally," Luvsan said. "That always looks good."

"I don't think so," Yadamsuren said.

Doripalam nodded, mildly impressed by the young man's fortitude. "For what it's worth, I think you're right. But it's your decision."

Yadamsuren nodded. "I can live with the pain," he smiled.

"We'll take them in, anyway," Doripalam said. "I think they'll be happy to volunteer. We need them as witnesses—I don't want them getting away again. And we can offer them some protection." He looked at Yadamsuren. "How long do you think it will take your people to get here?"

"Twenty minutes. No more."

Doripalam looked at his watch. They should be here any minute then. "I'll go down and prepare our friends. They might want to bring a change of clothes with them."

He walked back across the sodden grassland to where the

four men were sitting crouched. There was an almost palpable sense of misery and shame hanging over the group, as if the reality of their relative's violent death had only now hit them. Tseren looked up as Doripalam approached.

"Truck should be here in a few minutes," Doripalam said. "Get yourselves a change of clothes if you can. You'll freeze to death otherwise. You'll be relieved to know that my colleague has very generously decided not to press charges. But we would like you to come into the local station with us."

"How long will you need to hold us?" Tseren said.

Doripalam shrugged. "I don't really want to hold you at all," he said. "I could arrest you and require you to assist with our enquiries, but I'd much rather you came voluntarily. We may need you as witnesses—you certainly have new information about Mrs. Tuya's death and possibly also about Gavaa's disappearance. More importantly, though, we want to ensure that you're safe."

"Do you think you can do that?"

"If you're not safe with us, you're not safe anywhere," Doripalam said, recognising that this didn't entirely answer their question. "We don't know if someone really is after you, but if they are you're safer with us than you are out here."

Tseren nodded and glanced at the others. "That sounds reasonable," he says. "I am very happy to come with you." The others nodded slightly in agreement, still crouched in the pouring rain.

"Thank you." Doripalam could see the lights of an approaching truck, some way distant across the plain. "They'll pick you up and take you to the local station," he said. "I've got other business now, but I'll send someone up in the morning to talk to you properly."

The truck pulled up a few minutes later. There were two local officers, bemused at this summons late in the night. Doripalam had explained the situation briefly to the senior officer, but it was not clear how much of this explanation had reached the officers now standing before him. The older of the two—a tall, skinny individual with an apparently permanent expression of disdain—emerged from the truck and stood in front of Doripalam.

"Who're we taking in?" he said.

Doripalam eyed him. "A 'sir' would be nice," he said. "This group. They're not under arrest. They've volunteered to come in to help us with our enquiries. And, in this case, that's not a euphemism. They want to help us, and I want them to be treated accordingly. Look after them. Give them a hot meal. Find them somewhere to sleep. I'll get one of my men up to talk to them in the morning. And I don't expect him to find that they've got anything to complain about in the way they've been treated. Is that clear?"

"Very clear. Sir." The officer looked down at him lazily. Doripalam recognised the all too familiar sight of the junior local officer determined not to be intimidated by the big boys from the city. But it didn't make him feel any less tempted to kick the gangling idiot's feet from under him.

"Good. One more thing. There's a possibility that these men might be in physical danger. I want them kept under close observation at all times. And, again, I'll be deeply unhappy if anything should happen to them while they're in your keeping. And you wouldn't want that, would you?"

"No. Sir." The officer turned and gestured to the four men to make their way to the back of the truck, studiously paying no more attention to Doripalam, who watched him with barely concealed amusement. His primary concern had been that, despite Yadamsuren's intention not to take the matter further, his colleagues might decide to take a little informal revenge once they got the four men back to the station. His confidence wasn't increased by having met this character, but he hoped that his warnings would be sufficiently authoritative to prevent any reprisals.

The two officers helped the men into the back of the truck. Yadamsuren was to join them in the front with the intention of taking him to the hospital in Bulgan so he could be given a full examination.

Yadamsuren paused as he was about to climb into the front of the truck, turning back towards Doripalam. "I am glad that your journey wasn't wasted," he said. "That these were the men you were seeking."

"So am I," Doripalam said, sincerely. "And I'm very grateful for your help. You did well in identifying these people. I'm sorry the night was more eventful than we expected."

Yadamsuren shrugged. "It could have been much worse."

It could indeed, Doripalam thought. He watched Yadamsuren climb slowly into the truck, clearly troubled by his injury. And it raised the question: What were the four men so afraid of that they were prepared to shoot indiscriminately simply because a truck turned up unexpectedly in the night? Was there something more they knew or suspected? Something they hadn't so far chosen to share with him?

He would have to make sure that whoever he sent up here was appropriately skilled in questioning, someone who could take whatever steps might be necessary to find out if there was something more, something that had not yet been said.

But now Doripalam had other matters to concern him. In all the excitement of the shooting and its aftermath, he had almost forgotten the call that he had received shortly beforehand. A disturbance at Tunjin's apartment building. Tunjin's flat ransacked. Tunjin apparently missing. What the hell was all that about?

He turned and made his way back across the grass to the

truck. Luvsan was standing by its side, working his way slowly through another packet of cigarettes.

"Back to the hotel?" Luvsan said.

Doripalam shook his head. "No. I'd thought we could stay up here to deal with whatever we found here—interview our four friends. But I need to get back."

"Tunjin?"

"Tunjin. It may be something and nothing. He's a strange character at the best of times. But given his current—status, I'm a little worried. I think we need to get back. Are we okay to drive in this thing?" Doripalam gestured to the shattered windscreen. Luvsan had punched out the shards of glass so the interior of the truck was now open to the air.

"No choice," Luvsan said. "Even if we were staying up here, I doubt we'd be able to get it repaired locally. It'll be cold, but if we wrap up warm we should be okay."

Doripalam nodded and thumbed a number into his mobile. He waited a moment for the call to be answered, then asked to be put through to the officer who had called earlier. "Sorry for the delay in getting back. We had a bit of an incident up here, but it's okay now. Anymore news on Tunjin?" He listened for a moment then said: "Well, keep us informed. We're heading back, but it'll be a few hours before we reach the city. If anything happens in the meantime, call us straightaway."

He ended the call and turned back to Luvsan. "Nothing. No sign of Tunjin. They're searching the flat. It's a mess—though they suspect that it was probably a mess anyway. Tunjin's domestic life seems to have been everything that you might have expected. But it also looks as if it's been searched pretty thoroughly already."

Luvsan pulled open the passenger door of the truck. "What would Tunjin have that would be worth searching for?"

Doripalam shrugged. "Who knows? But nothing would surprise me about Tunjin."

They climbed back into the truck. Luvsan turned it round, and slowly pulled back up on to the road and then turned left back towards the south. "Was there any sign of a struggle?" he said.

"What?" Luvsan was having to keep the truck's speed fairly low, but even so the continuous blast of cold air filled the truck with noise.

"At Tunjin's flat. Any sign of a struggle?" Luvsan shouted.

"Difficult to tell, apparently," Doripalam shouted back. "Whole place was turned over. No way of knowing if there'd been a struggle in the middle of it."

"So we don't know whether Tunjin's just gone to ground for some reason, or whether something's happened to him?"

Doripalam shook his head. "But as you were no doubt about to point out so politely earlier, someone like Tunjin doesn't go missing easily. He's a big person to lose."

THIRTEEN

The basement always made Nergui feel uneasy, though it was as secure as all other parts of the apartment block. This place mainly housed government officials, and, although Nergui had taken additional steps to address security in his own flat, the whole place was designed to offer substantial protection to a potentially vulnerable group. The concerns had been greater during the early days of democracy, when there seemed to be a permanent fear that some form of revolution, or perhaps counter-revolution, was brewing just around the bend. Now, things had calmed and most of those who lived here paid little heed to the security trappings that this place offered. But Nergui was grateful, now as much as ever, that the block offered at least some protection.

Even so, the basement felt more vulnerable. It was mainly just that the lights were dim and the place was riddled with shadowy corners, as well as the potential hiding places offered by the rows of residents' cars. It wouldn't be an easy place to penetrate, but if anyone did get in, there would be plenty of places for them to hide.

And tonight who knew what might be waiting? Nergui crossed the concrete floor cautiously, his hand resting on the steel of his pistol, his eyes watchful for any sign of movement. He knew he was being paranoid. But he also knew that, on a number of occasions, it was paranoia that had kept him alive.

His own Mitsubishi 4x4 was parked a little way along the row. He reached it without incident, unlocked it and climbed in, throwing the canvas bag into the rear seat. He started the engine, reversed out and turned back towards the entrance. Still no sign of anything.

As he approached the entrance, he lowered the window to wave the electronic tag near the monitor. There was a moment's pause and then the heavy metal gates that enclosed the entrance slowly drew back. He noted, in passing, that the slow movement of the gates might well allow an intruder on foot time to slip through once a car had departed. He had not thought about this before, and the revelation of this minor weakness in the block's security increased his unease.

And, he realised, his unease was feeding upon itself. The very fact that he was feeling so uncomfortable was unusual—the last time he had experienced this kind of sensation was when they had faced the series of brutal killings the previous winter. Then, as now, he had had the sense that his unconscious mind was telling him something that his conscious brain had not yet learned to interpret. That there was something more going on than he'd so far identified.

Nergui was smart enough and experienced enough to be able to assess realistically the risks involved in his journey tonight. As long as he was careful, they were likely to be minimal. But still something was nagging at him. There was still a sense that he was—not out of his depth, exactly. The waters would have to be very deep indeed before Nergui's limits were reached. But certainly that he was much closer to those limits than his rational mind might suggest.

And Nergui had learned to trust his instincts. Not as something supernatural or magical, but simply as the expression of all his years of experience. However slight the apparent risk, he would take no chances tonight.

He pulled out from the apartment block and turned into the main street. He hesitated just for a moment and then took a right, heading in the opposite direction from his intended destination, travelling west along Peace Avenue, out of the city. He continued for two or three miles, the long strip of the railway prominent on his right, the Onion Mountain visible on the left. At this hour, there was no other traffic and no sign that he was being followed.

As the road straightened out, he did a sharp U-turn and headed back, passing clustered *ger* encampments and then industrial areas until he once again entered the central area of the city. He passed no other vehicles. Driving at this time of night was a mixed blessing in terms of security. On the one hand, it would be difficult for any pursuer to remain concealed. On the other, Nergui's own car was highly conspicuous.

He drove back along Peace Avenue, and then turned right down towards Nairamdal Park. There were a few more people around here—drinkers tumbling out of the Khanbrau and East West Bars, a scattering of late-night pedestrians. Above to his left, he could see the clustering temples that formed the Monastery Museum of Choijin Lama. And then he was past that and the vast dark space of the parkland opened up beyond the road.

To his right, opposite the park, there was the squat tower of the Bayangol Hotel.

He turned into the hotel and parked his car inconspicuously alongside a row of others. Grabbing the bag from the rear seat and ensuring that the handgun was safely in his pocket, he jumped out of the car and crossed the road to the entrance to the park.

He looked around. There was no one in sight, and even the hotel lobby looked closed and deserted. The park gates were locked for the night but it was easy enough to climb over into the darkness beyond. He wondered quite how Tunjin would manage to negotiate the fence, but knew from experience that Tunjin would have identified his own entrance route.

He stepped away from the fence and walked a few metres into the shadow, listening hard for any sound of movement. The rain had long ceased, but he could hear the dripping of water from the trees as a faint breeze rippled through the foliage. Otherwise, there was nothing.

He began to walk slowly across the park, heading from memory in the direction of the lake. He had brought a flashlight, but wanted to avoid using it unless absolutely necessary.

There was no sign yet of Tunjin. In the near blackness, he could just make out the shapes of the aged Ferris wheel and other rides in the amusement area across the park.

He found the lake without difficulty, its dirty water giving a faintly luminous glow. The surrounding trees clattered quietly in the soft wind. He glanced at the luminous dial of his watch. Almost exactly eleven thirty. Perfect. The only question now was whether Tunjin would make the rendezvous.

The question was answered almost immediately. A larger patch of blackness suddenly emerged from the shadows further along the lake. Nergui walked forward and said, only just audibly, "It's me." He didn't give his name but knew that Tunjin—assuming that it was Tunjin—would recognise the voice. His hand slipped into his pocket, firmly gripping the pistol handle.

He glanced briefly around him, keeping his back towards the lake so there was no danger of being surprised from behind.

Within seconds, he had no doubt that it was Tunjin. The ungainly movement of his large body was unmistakable. Nergui relaxed slightly, suddenly aware that he had been holding his breath. But he continued to grasp the gun, conscious that, if they had been followed, it was at this moment of exposure that they were probably most vulnerable.

"You made it," Tunjin said, drawing up closer.

"It wasn't that difficult for me," Nergui said. "The more important thing is that you made it safely. You're sure no one spotted you?"

"As sure as I can be," Tunjin said. He glanced down at his heaving body. "You wouldn't think it to look at me, but I'm actually quite good at giving people the slip."

Nergui smiled, pleased at least that some signs of the old Tunjin were still in evidence. And the greatest miracle was that, as far as he could tell, there was no hint of alcohol on Tunjin's breath.

"What about you?" Tunjin said. "You're sure you weren't followed?"

"In any other circumstance," Nergui said, "I'd have you disciplined for impertinence."

"You can't," Tunjin pointed out. "I'm already suspended."

"So you are," Nergui said. "And your own bloody fault too."

"You're not the type to say 'I told you so,'" Tunjin said. "If you were, you'd be insufferable."

Nergui laughed, softly. "Glad to see that this mess hasn't entirely dampened your spirits."

"I haven't had time for my spirits to be dampened, other than by that bloody rain. Though I wasn't feeling too pleased with myself, holed up in the back of a semi-demolished shop."

"How are you?" Nergui said. "I mean, really."

Tunjin shrugged. "As well as can be expected. I've been suspended from the only job I've ever known, a year off retirement. I've been exposed as the thorn in the side of the most dangerous criminal psychopath in the city. And I'm on the run, with no obvious prospect of salvation. Under the circumstances, not so bad."

"At least it's got you off the drink."

"And where the bloody hell am I supposed to find booze? It's not for lack of wanting it, I can tell you."

"So what are we going to do?" Nergui said. "How are we going to get you out of this mess?"

"I was rather hoping that you might be able to tell me that."

"I don't think it's going to be easy," Nergui said. "The problem is knowing who to trust."

"That's been the problem throughout this whole bloody affair," Tunjin said. "Everywhere you turn, he's got people. I mean, I know I was bloody stupid and it was half-baked, but I'd never expected that it would leak like that. No one knew."

"Someone knew," Nergui said. "Assuming that you're not informing on yourself."

"At least that would have been simpler," Tunjin said. "Cut out the middleman and all that. No. Everywhere you turn there's someone. I'm not even sure about you, sometimes."

"To be honest," Nergui said, "I wasn't at all sure about you till you pulled this little stunt. And even now I'm wondering if it isn't some kind of double bluff."

"If you knew what I'd been through today, you wouldn't have any doubts. And I guess I know that, if you're not on the side of the angels, then the whole bloody police force might as well pack up and go home."

"It may come to that," Nergui said. "I'm getting nowhere in rooting out what really is going on there."

"What about Doripalam?" Tunjin said, "You think he's straight?"

Nergui hesitated. In any other circumstances he would be reluctant to express any views about a senior officer, particularly to the likes of Tunjin. But these were far from ordinary circumstances. "I'm pretty sure so," he said. "But that's the difficulty. All my instincts tell me he's straight. But even with him I can't be absolutely certain. And in any case there are too many others I don't trust. I've started to get together some pretty damning evidence on one or two characters, but in most cases there's just no way to be sure. We just don't know how far this goes."

"Further than you can imagine," Tunjin said.

"I thought about trying to organise you police protection," Nergui said. "But there's no way." He thought about what had happened to Sarangarel's husband, a decade before. The tentacles were in place already, even at that time. There was no way of knowing how far they might stretch by now.

"I'll happily decline," Tunjin said. "As things stand."

"It might be feasible to organise some sort of safe house through the Ministry," Nergui said. "But even there, even in the intelligence services—"

"You don't know for sure." It was a statement rather than a question.

"I don't know for sure," Nergui agreed. "It would be your risk."

Tunjin turned. "I'm tired," he said, in a tone that suggested that his weariness was more than merely physical. "Let's find somewhere to sit down." He began to trudge slowly across the silent park, Nergui following behind him, his senses alert for any other sign of movement. Ahead of them there were the floodlit facades of the Buddhist temples and then, beyond that, all the scattered lights of the city. By contrast, in the darkness, the park seemed inhospitable, a lifeless wasteland, its shadows containing who knew what kinds of threat.

They reached the play area. The rides were all firmly closed and locked, but there were benches where they could sit. The skeletal shape of the Ferris wheel towered above them, black bones against the cloudy night sky.

Tunjin slumped heavily onto one of the benches, the wood and metal creaking beneath his weight. Nergui sat carefully beside him.

"It's not a risk I want to take," Tunjin said, continuing their previous conversation.

"In your place, I'd feel the same," Nergui said. "It's one thing to be out here, keeping an eye out for yourself, however great the risk. It's another to hand yourself over to someone else's safe keeping, if you don't have confidence in them."

"And you're saying you wouldn't have confidence in the intelligence services?"

"I don't know. No. Not entirely."

"So, no, I don't think so."

"But what's the alternative?" Nergui said. "You can't stay on the run forever." He paused. "It's outrageous. After all these years. All my supposed authority. And I can't even provide adequate protection for a police officer in trouble."

"I'm still a police officer, then?" Tunjin said. "I wasn't sure."

"Of course you're still a police officer," Nergui said. "And as far as I'm concerned you'll stay a police officer till you retire."

"Assuming I live that long."

"Assuming you live that long. And, at the moment, I don't know how we ensure that. You can't keep running."

"I'm not exactly built for it," Tunjin agreed, looking down at his vast bulk.

"So what do we do?" Nergui said. "I can try to find you

somewhere to hide out. Somewhere only we know about. I'd take you back to my flat, but I can't believe that it's not at least under some kind of surveillance. That's why I was afraid of being followed tonight."

"I'm best where I am at the moment," Tunjin said. "It's not comfortable. But no one but me knows that I'm there. It'll buy me two or three days at least. But I can't stay there forever."

"I brought you some food and water," Nergui said, remembering the canvas bag he had slung over his shoulder. "Nothing much. I just grabbed what I had, but it'll keep you going for a while. If we arrange another meeting, I can get you some more."

"I could do with losing a pound or two, anyway," Tunjin laughed.

"But it doesn't solve the problem," Nergui said. "All we're doing is buying time. I'm out of ideas."

"As I see it," Tunjin said, "there's only one way forward."

Nergui looked across at the man sitting next to him. In the gloom, he could not make out his expression. "And that is?"

"I've got to finish what I started," Tunjin said. "Only this time I've got to make sure I do it properly."

There was a faint breeze rustling through the trees. For a moment, Nergui fancied that he could discern some other sound, maybe someone moving. He held his breath for a second, listening, but could make out nothing more.

"What do you mean?" he said, at last.

"What I say." Tunjin leaned back on the bench, which creaked alarmingly under them. "I need to finish what I started, but make less of a mess of it this time."

Nergui shook his head. "I don't know what you've got in mind," he said. "But you're hardly in the best position to start collating more evidence. And you presumably didn't find it all that easy last time, which is why you're in this mess."

Tunjin shrugged. "Maybe I was too complacent last time. I thought I'd covered all the angles, but I clearly hadn't. I didn't realise how far this thing went."

"I don't think any of us really did," Nergui said. "I was taken aback by what you tried to do, but I was even more startled that—with all your natural talents—you didn't manage to get away with it." He paused, as if wondering quite how many metaphorical cards to put on the table. "It scared the hell out me, actually. I mean, I always knew he had people on the inside. But then I also knew how smart you'd have been in trying to pull all that stuff off. And if you got caught out—well, it doesn't bear thinking about."

"That's the trouble," Tunjin said. "I tell you, nobody knew what I was up to. One or two would have had inklings, and I had some professional help with the forgeries, but there was no individual I confided in. And all the evidence was held confidentially, even within the team, because of its sensitivity. If they got to the bottom of that, well—anybody could be involved."

"Even Doripalam?" Nergui said.

Tunjin shrugged. "You can judge that better than me," he said. "But he was one of the few people with a real overview of all the evidence. If anyone was going to spot flaws or inconsistencies—well, he wasn't the only one, but there weren't many."

"I still don't think so," Nergui said. "I still think he's straight."

Tunjin made no response. After a pause, he said: "So maybe I'm in a better position to do something now than I was before. At least now there's nobody going to expose me. So maybe I can finish it off."

Nergui turned and stared at the grey silhouette of the large man beside him. "Finish it off?" he said. "What have you got in mind, exactly?"

"I don't know. But as long as he's there, he's going to want my blood."

"It's insane," Nergui said. "You know who we're talking about. We've never got close to him."

"No," Tunjin said, slowly. "But before we've all—even me, for the most part—have had to do it by the book. I don't have that constraint anymore."

"You're still a police officer," Nergui said.

"So you tell me. It doesn't feel like it. It didn't feel like it this afternoon." He paused. "Look, Nergui, all I know is I can't just sit here waiting for him to come to me. So I've got to go after him. If I decide to adopt methods that are—well, the kinds of things that might be unacceptable to you, I wouldn't dream of troubling your conscience by sharing them."

"I could arrest you now if I thought you were going to commit an illegal act," Nergui said.

"Yes, but you don't. And neither do I. But I do know that I haven't got much to lose. In fact, given what might happen to me if they catch up with me, I'm better off with the prospect of something quick and clean."

"It sounds like a fantasy to me," Nergui said.

"I'm in need of fantasies right now," Tunjin said. "I don't have much else."

Nergui looked around them. He was beginning to feel exposed, sitting motionless in this dark parkland. It was not a rational anxiety—if anyone was watching them, then they would just wait until Nergui was gone before tackling Tunjin. But there was something about the vast silence of this place that made him uneasy.

"We need to find a way out of this," he said finally.

"From where I'm sitting, I don't see too many options," Tunjin said. "You carry on with your investigations, but how much progress do you really expect to make?"

"I don't know," Nergui said. "Some. There are some I know are bent, some I know are on his payroll. I'll get them eventually. But whether I'll get them all—"

"There'll be no way of knowing, unless we take him down."

Nergui knew that he was right. There had been a time, even when he had started his enquiry, when he had thought that now finally he was in a position to deal with this properly. He had thought that Tunjin's actions and their fallout might have given him the opportunity and the ammunition he had been seeking for all those years. But he should have realised that Tunjin would not have messed up so easily. He should have realised quite how deeply ingrained the problem would be. He could catch a few bent officers—maybe even most of them—but unless he was confident he had identified them all, the problem would never be resolved.

Tunjin climbed slowly to his feet, hoisting the canvas bag over his shoulder. "Thanks for the food," he said. "I'll keep in touch. I don't want to use the mobile any more than I can avoid because I don't know how traceable it might be. And I want to save the battery for as long as possible. But if I want to make contact, I'll just send you a text—just 'Meet' and that'll mean—let's stick with the same time—that'll mean 11:30 p.m. here."

"I'll bring some better food next time," Nergui said. "If I've got a bit of notice."

"Glad to hear it. This selection's not very impressive."

"Tunjin," Nergui said, "I don't know what you've got in mind, but whatever it is, good luck."

Tunjin shrugged. "I don't know either," he said, "but thanks anyway."

He turned and began to trudge slowly back in the direction

of the lake. Nergui sat, unmoving, watching Tunjin's bulk disappear into the enveloping blackness, ready to draw his gun if there was any sign of trouble. But the sound of Tunjin's soft footsteps faded, lost in the faint rustle of the breeze, and there was no indication of any disturbance.

Nergui sat for a few moments, listening hard, wondering whether Tunjin had made his way out of the park safely. For a moment, he considered trying to follow him but he knew that this would be madness. There was little he could do to protect Tunjin, who could look after his own interests as well as anyone.

Finally, Nergui rose and made his way slowly back across the park, past the square block of the State Youth Theatre. He lifted himself back over the fence and out into the street. It was nearly half past midnight. The road was deserted, and even the Bayangol Hotel looked as if it was closed for the night. There were dim lights in the foyer, and the occasional bedroom light, but otherwise little sign of life.

Nergui's car was as he had left it. He unlocked it and climbed inside, mulling over his conversation with Tunjin. What about Doripalam? Could he be trusted? Nergui was as confident as he could be that Doripalam, of all people, was straight. But someone had betrayed Tunjin. Someone had realised what was going on, and had fingered Tunjin as the individual responsible. And there was no question that, as one of the most sensitive cases they had handled for years, the details of the Muunokhoi would have been available only to a selected few—certainly to none of those whom Nergui had so far identified as potentially corrupt.

So who was it?

Nergui jammed his car into reverse and pulled slowly back out of the parking space, and then drove forward out of the hotel car park. As he passed the entrance, his eye was caught by two figures, both wearing long raincoats and hats, standing in the shadows outside the lobby of the hotel.

Something about the figures struck him as incongruous, out of place in the scene. They didn't look like hotel staff. He pulled out into the street and up towards the junction with Peace Avenue, hoping that Tunjin had managed to get away safely.

FOURTEEN

It was already growing light by the time they reached the outskirts of the city. Doripalam was glad to complete the journey, after hours of the beating cold and noise from the open windscreen. Conversation, other than the occasional shouted exchange, had been virtually impossible. In the end, Doripalam had simply closed his eyes, though far from any possibility of sleep, and listened to the endless roar of the engine and the wind.

"Where to?" Luvsan shouted. "Back to HQ?"

"I think we have to," Doripalam said. "Get this thing in for repair, for one thing."

They came into town, driving with the river on their right and then, above them, the majestic Chinese-style temple of Gesar Süm, turned left past Liberty Square and the taxi stand, and then right down towards Sukh Bataar Square. The rain had long passed and it looked set to be a fine day, just a few wisps of cloud in the translucent sky.

They parked the truck behind Headquarters and Luvsan went

in to organise the repair of the windscreen. Doripalam stood for a moment by the front entrance, looking out across the Square, empty and silent in the early morning sunlight. He felt momentarily overwhelmed, struggling to come to grips with the responsibilities that were facing him. He understood his job as a police officer, as a detective. He knew what that was all about. Carrying out investigations, trying to get to the truth. That was—not exactly straightforward, but at least comprehensible. But now, in this job, he was never sure of his priorities. It was the political stuff that confused him—the constantly shifting balance of interests and demands. The kind of thing that Nergui had managed with his eyes closed.

And at the moment it was just one problem after another. The whole Muunokhoi debacle. All the publicity around Gavaa's disappearance. The horrific murder of his mother—so far, ironically, accorded less attention than the apparently much more mundane absence of her son. The possibility that she was being threatened—but by whom and why? And now, on top of everything, Tunjin going missing. It was as if a whole year's worth of serious cases had descended on him at once, with no clear rhyme or reason.

And then there was Nergui and his supposed enquiry. What was that all about? An attempt to use the Muunokhoi mess as an opportunity to root out whatever corruption there was in this squad? Doripalam knew that, if he had any dignity, he should have offered his resignation already in the face of Nergui's interference. But he also knew—because he knew Nergui—that there was likely to be more to this than was immediately apparent.

"Where now?"

Luvsan was standing behind him, holding two plastic cups of steaming coffee. For the first time, it occurred to Doripalam that he'd been up all night. And a pretty stressful night at that. The sense of tiredness swept over him like a wave, and he felt suddenly removed from everything around him.

He took the coffee from Luvsan. "Thanks. You must be exhausted. I know I am, and you did all the driving."

Luvsan took a sip of his own drink. "Can always manage without much sleep. One of my few talents."

Doripalam yawned. "Wish it was one I shared," he said. "I guess we should go and have a look at Tunjin's apartment. I take it there's no more news."

"Doesn't seem to be. I checked quickly with the duty officer. We've got the flat all cordoned off. Spoken to the neighbours and to those who witnessed the original disturbance, but it's not much clearer. We can get the full story once we're there, I guess."

Luvsan had procured them an alternative police vehicle, a marked car. Inevitably, he turned on the siren as they made their way through the centre of the city, even though it was still early morning and the streets were largely deserted. Doripalam regarded him with amused disapproval but said nothing.

Tunjin's flat was only a few minutes away and they were able to park without difficulty outside the apartment block. Even if Doripalam hadn't known the address, it would not have been difficult to identify the building. The glass fronted doors to the lobby had both been shattered, the doors now covered with temporary boarding.

"They told me on the phone that there'd been some shooting," Doripalam said. "It looks as if they were shooting their way in."

There was a uniformed officer stationed at the door, who recognised Doripalam without having to be shown any ID. "There's one of your people upstairs, sir," he said.

Doripalam gestured to the doors. "This was where the shots were fired?"

"Yes, sir. It looks as if the doors were locked or jammed in some way, and the intruders shot at the glass to make their entry."

Doripalam glanced at Luvsan. "The doors were locked or jammed? This was in the middle of the day?"

"Yes, sir. Late morning."

"That wouldn't have been normal, then? The doors being locked, I mean."

"No, sir. I mean, security here is normally pretty lax, apparently. Nothing to stop anybody entering the building during daylight hours."

Doripalam nodded. "Thanks. Who are you letting in at the moment?"

"Residents only, that's my orders. Not making ourselves very popular because we're not even allowing in residents' guests for the moment."

"Keep it that way. I don't want the press in here just yet. And I wouldn't put it past some of them to try to do a deal with some of the residents to talk their way in."

"That's what I thought, sir. We've been very rigorous."

"Glad to hear it. Keep it up." As always, Doripalam was uncomfortably aware that this commanding officer stuff was far from natural to him. The young officer didn't appear to notice anything, though, even if Luvsan looked mildly amused.

"Come on," Doripalam said. "Let's go and see the flat. First floor."

They made their way up the open, faux marble stairs to the first floor. It was far from a smart address. The lobby area had been full of junk, all of which, other than the scatterings of broken glass, presumably predated the disturbance. The whole place could do with a new coat of paint, he thought, looking around at the scuffed walls, the worn floor tiles, the chipped woodwork.

It was, again, not difficult to spot Tunjin's flat. A bored looking uniformed officer was sitting on a hard wooden chair outside, a folded newspaper in his hand. He looked up quizzically as the two men approached.

"Doripalam." He flicked open his ID and waved it in front of the seated officer. "Serious Crimes Team. I understand one of my people's inside."

It took the uniformed officer a moment to take all this in. Then he jumped to his feet, scattering the newspaper untidily to the floor. "Yes, sir. Please go in."

Doripalam smiled and pushed open the door. His smile faded almost immediately. Partly it was the smell. Not an overwhelmingly unpleasant smell—Doripalam had had all too frequent cause to enter rooms containing corpses, and this was nothing like that. But it was there, nonetheless. A scent of decay, of organic matter left too long in the spring warm, a smell of sour milk and rotting vegetation, underpinned with a strong smell of alcohol.

The appearance of the apartment matched the smell. It was clear that, however much the flat might have been ransacked by the intruders, it had hardly been a model of organised living beforehand. There were plates of half-eaten food scattered on every surface, buzzing with flies. There were several empty or nearly empty vodka bottles. Clothes—presumably dirty—were scattered about the floor.

But, on top of all that, the room had been systematically turned over. Drawers from the cabinets lay emptied across the floor and sofa. Pictures had been pulled from the walls. A cupboard stood with its doors agape and its contents tossed, apparently casually, to the ground.

In the middle of all this, a young officer stood, a clipboard in his hand, apparently making an inventory. He looked up as Doripalam and Luvsan entered. "Good morning," he said. "Sorry it's not more homely."

Doripalam carefully made his way through the scattered debris towards the young officer. "Good morning, Batzorig. You pulled this one, then?"

"Looks like it," Batzorig said. "Not quite sure what I did to deserve it."

"Something pretty bad, clearly," Doripalam said. "So this is how Tunjin lived, then?"

"Well, not entirely, to be fair," Batzorig said. "He can take responsibility for the food and the booze, but probably not for the emptying of the drawers and cupboards."

"No." Doripalam looked around carefully. "It's been ransacked pretty thoroughly. So they were after something. Do we have any idea what?"

Batzorig shook his head. "It's difficult to know what Tunjin might have had that they would have been interested in," he said.

"Unless it was something he'd taken from HQ," Luvsan said, from behind.

Doripalam turned. "Like what?"

Luvsan shrugged. "No idea. Files, paperwork? Who knows?"

"The last time I saw Tunjin," Doripalam said, "he didn't give me the impression he was intending to follow up assiduously on his paperwork." He turned back to Batzorig. "And we've no idea what might have happened to Tunjin?"

"None at all," Batzorig said. "He's just vanished."

"With the intruders?"

"We don't think so."

"So what's the story?" Doripalam said. "Walk me through it."

"It's an odd one," Batzorig said. "From what we've been able to piece together from talking to neighbours and passersby, there was some sort of disturbance yesterday. One of the residents of this block—coming back from the market, I think—discovered she couldn't get in the front entrance. It's normally left unlocked during the day. She tried to unlock it with her own key, but the door was jammed. She asked a passerby for some assistance, but he couldn't do anything. It looked as if, as well as locking the doors, someone had jammed a broomstick into the handles."

"To stop it being opened from outside?"

"Exactly. Anyway, a bit of a crowd started to gather. The general consensus was that it was kids—you know, youth of today, all that stuff. Then, in the middle of all that, with this small group milling about outside the doorway, two men came up, dressed in dark glasses, baseball caps, leather jackets, you know the kind of uniform—?"

Doripalam looked up at him. He knew the uniform. The hard men, the hired help, all over the seamier side of the city.

"These two guys came up, gestured for the crowd to move aside, and then pulled out a handgun each and shot out the glass in the doors. I think the crowd dispersed pretty quickly."

"And no one thought to call us?" Luvsan said from behind.

"Well, yes, they did eventually. But I think they were all a bit shocked. Anyway, from what we can tell, the two men cleared and opened the doors, made their way up here, kicked down Tunjin's door and got in here. We don't know quite what happened after that because no one was getting too close to find out. But we assumed they didn't find Tunjin and they went through the flat pretty quickly—probably only a few minutes. We've got some witnesses who then saw the two men exit the front of the block, probably five minutes or so later. There was no one with them so we presume they didn't find Tunjin. The two men then ran down to the far end of the block. There was the sound of more gunfire, and somebody reported the sound of a motorbike speeding away. Nothing more after that. It looks as if the two men had a car parked somewhere, but nobody seems to have seen them leave. We've got one witness down in the end block who thinks he may have seen something."

"So we think Tunjin might have made an escape on a motorbike?" Luvsan said, incredulously. He was clearly struggling to picture the image.

"Who knows? The motorbike might have just been a coincidence. But it certainly looks as if—well, either he escaped or he wasn't here in the first place."

"The gunshots at the far end of the blocks suggest that they were trying to stop someone," Doripalam pointed out. "Has anyone had a look down there yet?"

Batzorig nodded. "Yes. There's a patch of waste ground out there. And an encampment—one of the permanent ones. We found an old man—" He stopped to glance at his notebook. "Agypar, apparently. Lives in the end block and happened to be down in the utility room in the basement at the time. Said he heard some gunshots and peered out. Saw two men, one of them apparently injured. Looked as if he'd been shot in the knee."

"Tunjin?"

Batzorig shook his head. "Definitely not. I think Tunjin's build would have been unmistakeable. This man was nothing like that. More likely to have been one of our two intruders. The old man thought he was wearing a leather jacket, but he was too far away to see anything for sure. When the old man realised it really was gunfire, he made himself scarce."

"What about the motorbike?"

"Knew nothing about it," he said. "Said he didn't see or hear anything of that kind. There were a few bikes chained up there, but most of them looked as if they'd been standing there a long time. There were some tyre tracks, but it was difficult to be sure how recent they were."

"Any sign of blood?" Doripalam said.

"We found a few traces on the ground. We've sent a sample to be analysed, see if it matches Tunjin's records."

"If the old man's right, it sounds as if Tunjin might have been doing the injuring, rather than the other way round." That wouldn't have been particularly surprising, Doripalam thought. For all Tunjin's failings, he knew how to look after himself.

He looked round the room. "I take it the scene of crime people have done their stuff?" he said.

"Pretty much so," Batzorig said. "The only clear prints we can find match Tunjin's, but there are smeared prints that would indicate the intruders were wearing gloves. Not much else. No evidence of any kind of struggle—not easy to be sure given the state of the place, but there's nothing to contradict the assumption that Tunjin wasn't here when they arrived."

"I guess in that case," Doripalam said, "we can do Tunjin a favour and get the place cleaned up. Don't suppose he'll object if we get someone to do his washing up for him."

"I still wasn't sure if it was an excuse," she said. "I mean, as I said, it seemed a little late in the evening for a bail out call, but I suppose that depends on what it was you thought you might be bailing out of."

He put down his espresso and looked at her. "I don't think I'm even going to try to follow that," he said. "I had a late night last night, and I'm not at my sharpest."

Sarangarel laughed. "Well, so long as you really were working, I won't be too offended. But thanks for the offer of lunch anyway."

Nergui nodded, wondering what it was that had prompted him to make the call that morning. Partly just straightforward guilt. He had felt genuinely bad about terminating their date the previous evening, even if he hadn't been entirely clear what it was he was terminating. Also, he thought—and this was another distant echo of the less admirable part of his character—there was still some curiosity, reignited by his midnight conversation with Tunjin. It was strange, almost a little too strange, that these ghosts from his past should have reemerged now.

That icy midnight raid. Sarangarel terrified and confused. The small hours phone call that told him that Gansukh was dead. The sense, following that call, that a prize that had been almost within his grasp had suddenly vanished, like some cheap conjuring trick. And the realisation that, if Gansukh's death had really not been an accident, then Nergui's team was more corrupt, had been infiltrated further, than he had ever imagined possible.

Gansukh's death had marked the start of what Nergui now felt to be the longest sustained period of failure in his career. This was not to say that Nergui had carried out his role badly. The Serious Crimes Team had gone from strength to strength, and—certainly by comparison with other parts of the civilian police—developed an enviable reputation for both integrity and effectiveness. Nergui had been promoted to the Ministry simply because he was one of the few senior police officers who was respected and trusted by all parts of the political establishment.

But Nergui himself felt that this was all a sham. As the years went by, he increasingly felt as if he was operating with one hand tied behind his back. It was as if he had been given a licence to operate so long as certain unspecified boundaries weren't transgressed. Ordinary crime was fair game, organised crime was off-limits. And whenever he got close to the boundaries, whenever he might have the makings of a case against Muunokhoi or one of his wealthy cronies, somehow things fell apart. Evidence went missing. Confidential information suddenly appeared on the front pages of the newspapers. Witnesses disappeared or refused to speak. Every time, he somehow found himself standing on quicksand.

For Nergui, who had been accustomed to playing by his own rules even in the dark days of communism, this was a shock. But he was a pragmatist. All he could do was fight the battle, make whatever inroads he could, bide his time until an opportunity presented itself.

Others, he suspected, had been less stoic. He could never be sure, but he suspected that Tunjin's personal and professional decline had started with his unintentional mistake over Gansukh. Though he had never said so, Nergui believed that Tunjin had blamed himself for Gansukh's death. Though he had always been a very capable officer, he had never seemed the same, never displayed the same commitment and focus as in those days. For years, Nergui had never been sure whether Tunjin's guilt was that of the perpetrator or the victim—that is, whether Tunjin himself had already been corrupted. Over the years, he had investigated Tunjin repeatedly but—although his increasing drinking and dissolute behaviour might have made him a natural blackmail victim—there had never been any evidence, substantive or even circumstantial, that he was bent. But it was only with the recent debacle over Muunokhoi's trial that Nergui had finally been convinced that Tunjin had been waging his own quiet vendetta over the years. And maybe now when Nergui finally trusted Tunjin fully, it was all too late.

And that brought him back here, full circle, with the woman who had been here at the start of all this and who had been there, incredibly, as the trial judge when it all came to a head. Who said that ghosts didn't exist?

And now they were sipping coffee and eating American-style club sandwiches in the Casablanca café, only yards from where he had met Tunjin the previous night.

She finished her caffè latte and smiled at him over the table. "You keep doing this," she said. "You take me out and then you sit staring moodily into space. It's company of a kind but it's not particularly flattering."

He shook his head. "Sorry. I've a lot on my mind. I should stay indoors until I provide better company."

"Is this about your call last night? It must have been a late night for you."

He shrugged. "I've had a lot worse. And, yes, it's partly about that. But it's about a whole stack of things actually." He paused, wondering whether to go on. "But mainly about Muunokhoi."

She put down her glass slowly and stared at him. "Muunokhoi? What about him?"

"I'm not entirely sure about the ethics of this," he said, "given your professional role."

"I don't see an issue," she said, "unless you're going to draw my attention to some misadministration of the trial, in which case this isn't the appropriate forum, I don't think. But, otherwise, the trial is over. If there's any subsequent trial, I won't be involved. So I don't think there's a problem."

He nodded, as if thinking this over. "It's nothing to do with the trial," he said. "Well, not directly. It's broader than that. It's—well, in part, it's about Muunokhoi and Gansukh."

"Gansukh?" But she spoke the name without surprise, almost as if she had been waiting for the subject to arise. Perhaps waiting for a long time.

Nergui swallowed the last of his espresso. "Maybe we should go for a walk," he said.

FIFTEEN

After the previous day's rain, the new day dawned bright and chilly. Tunjin pulled his coat more tightly around him and hunched himself into the corner of the desolate room.

The cold of the night and the unyielding hardness of the floor had kept him from sleep. Instead, he had propped himself against the wall, his eyes fixed on the empty doorway, his ears straining for any sound of movement.

Someone had been watching Nergui and himself in the park, he was convinced of it. He was not really surprised. Nergui's flat would be under surveillance by these people—they would be trying to keep tabs on his enquiry as best they could, though Tunjin knew that Nergui would make this very difficult. Nergui would have done his very effective best to ensure that he was not being followed to the park, but it would not have been very difficult to keep track of a solitary car travelling through the city at that time of night. Tunjin was unsure what kinds of resources

Muunokhoi would have access to, but he knew they would be plentiful.

It was fortunate, therefore, that no action had been taken against them in the park. They would not have known, initially, that Nergui's rendezvous was with Tunjin, and their priority was probably simply to keep Nergui under observation rather than confirm his suspicions that he was being followed. So if—or, more likely, when—they had recognised Tunjin, they would not have wanted to take action until the two men had parted.

And that was where Tunjin had been too sharp for them. He had banked on the fact that the observers would not be particularly close at hand, since they would not have wanted to risk being spotted. On leaving Nergui, Tunjin had moved with surprising agility and light-footedness to hide himself in the thick bushes surrounding the play area. He had watched Nergui as he sat waiting—clearly wondering whether he himself should follow Tunjin, which thankfully he had not chosen to do—and then as he had slowly left across the park. Nergui's hesitation had been helpful, buying Tunjin some time before the pursuers were able to step into the open.

They had appeared a few minutes later. Two men, dressed in leather jackets, one carrying a mobile phone, the other carrying what Tunjin assumed to be a gun. The two men had stopped and looked around, obviously concluding that Tunjin had departed and unsure which direction he had taken. Tunjin had wondered, nervously, whether the two men might be armed with night sights or infrared gear but it appeared not. People always tended to underestimate Tunjin's abilities, and not for the first time he was profoundly grateful for this.

One of his great qualities was his patience, and this once again proved his saviour. He remained concealed in the bushes, scarcely breathing, for long minutes, as the two men looked around, spoke on the mobile and then departed, taking what they thought to have been Tunjin's path.

He was tempted to emerge then, but he knew that could prove suicidal. When the men failed to find him further out across the park, they might well return. So, instead, he remained concealed in the bushes, watching carefully, remaining as motionless as he could. As expected, after ten or fifteen minutes, the men reappeared, talking to each other in a whisper, seeming mildly agitated. They paused, looked around, then set off in the opposite direction. Tunjin waited another thirty minutes or so, having lowered himself to the earth, and then, when he was sure that they were not returning, he eventually emerged. He made his exit from the park, and walking silently though the city streets, his senses alert for any sign of pursuit, he had made his way back here.

The experience had confirmed his view that he couldn't stay here for much longer. Apart from the sheer physical discomfort, he did not know for how long this place would be secure. Sooner or later, someone would stumble across him—maybe a police patrolman making a routine examination of this rundown area. And at that point he would no longer be confident of remaining undetected.

No, as he had told Nergui the night before, the only way forward was to take some positive action, to take the initiative. He still had no idea what he meant by this, but he needed to do something. Even if he failed at least he would feel in control, at least he would feel that he was making the running.

He dragged himself slowly to his feet, looking down at his stained and grubby clothing. How long was it since he had had a drink? It seemed like an eternity. It was difficult to tell whether he felt better as a result. His life was in so much of a mess that any kind of oblivion seemed attractive as an alternative.

But he had to be positive. He opened the canvas bag that Nergui had given him, and took a large gulp of the water. He began to chew slowly on the end of slightly stale bread. Access to food—even food as primitive as this—began to make him feel slightly more human. Outside, the day was brightening, sunlight beginning to stream in through the doors and windows. There was no sound other than an occasional rustling, presumably of mice or rats.

Okay, he thought. Another day. Maybe his last day on earth. But surely, surely there was something he could do, some positive action he could take.

All he had to do was think of it.

By day, the park looked more welcoming. It had seen better days, certainly, and even in the bright spring sunlight its facilities were clearly worn and run-down. But at least it looked like a place that had been designed for pleasure, rather than the vast black wasteland it had seemed the previous night.

They had entered the park by the entrance opposite the Bayangol Hotel, and had walked slowly across to the play area. Neither had spoken for some minutes, Nergui unsure where to begin and Sarangarel sufficiently patient to wait until he had found the words.

Nergui led them across to the row of benches by the play area, and they both sat down. It was not, he thought, the bench where he had sat with Tunjin the night before, but maybe two or three along.

"I'm not sure I know where to begin," Nergui said.

"I think I'd guessed that," she said, "from the fact that you hadn't done so."

"I suppose I need to begin with Gansukh."

She nodded. "I thought you might. I've put all that behind me. It's a different life. A different person."

"I know it is, and the last thing I want to do is drag you back there—"

"But you're going to."

"I suppose I am," he said. "I don't know if you remember, but—well, when we were questioning Gansukh, I asked you some questions about any relations he might have with Muunokhoi."

"I remember," she said. "I thought you were insane."

He nodded, looking up at the slowly turning Ferris wheel. He had been up there only once, a long time ago, enduring the agonisingly slow elevation, seeing the breadth of the city slowly opening out before him, the texture of the streets and buildings, the untidy sprawl of the *ger* camps, the vast expanse of the steppes and mountains beyond. "I know you did," he said. "Do you still think that?"

There was a long pause. So long, in fact, that Nergui became convinced that she was not going to respond. Above them, the Ferris wheel continued its silent motion.

"No," she said at last. "No, I don't."

He looked at her. "You think he was working for Muunokhoi?"

"I know he was."

It was Nergui's turn to be silent. There were some young children, scarcely more than toddlers, playing on the swings and roundabout off to their left. The sound of their high-pitched voices carried faintly across the grass. Behind them, there was the deep blue of the lake, glittering in the midday sun. "How do you know?" he said at last.

"I know," she said. "I don't mean just—oh, you know, women's intuition, that sort of thing. I mean evidence. Of a sort, anyway."

"You should have told us, if you knew. You might have helped save his life." The words were out of his mouth before he could stop them.

She laughed. "Do you think that would have been an incentive? At the time, that was the last thing I wanted. But, no, in any case, I didn't know then. But I do know now."

"How do you know?"

"As far as I'm concerned," she said, as though embarking on a different narrative, "I'm not that person anymore. I'm not the person who married Gansukh. I don't think I would be anyway, even if—all that hadn't happened. Our marriage wouldn't have survived. When you arrested him, I realised that I wasn't surprised and that—other than worrying about what might become of me—I wasn't that sorry."

Nergui nodded, wondering where all this was leading.

"But, of course," she went on, "that's not quite how the world out there sees it. I'm still Gansukh's widow. I haven't remarried. We're still—in some people's eyes—a couple." She paused. The breeze ruffled her dark hair, toying with the folds of the long silk dress she was wearing. "He had a cousin who died recently, down in the Gobi. Someone I'd met—well, only once or twice, as far as I can remember, years ago. But he'd left some possessions—originally intended for Gansukh. But when Gansukh died, he apparently changed his will and left them to me. So, a couple of months ago, I received an unexpected parcel through the post."

Nergui was watching her closely now, struck by the intensity with which she was recounting the story.

"The parcel contained a stack of different things. Some petty trinkets that, for some reason, he'd decided to leave to Gansukh and then to me. A small amount of money—there were few other living relatives, apparently. And, with all of that, a stack of papers and documentation."

"What sort of papers?"

"These were, as far as I could tell, things that Gansukh had deposited with his cousin, years ago, presumably for safekeeping. Do you remember that, not long after Gansukh's death, our apartment was burgled?"

This was news to him. "Burgled? I never knew that. You must have reported it?"

"Of course. But this was—what?—two or three months after Gansukh had died. I'd started to move on. I didn't associate the burglary with Gansukh's death—just put it down to another instance of the bad luck that seemed to be following me around. So I just reported it to my local station. They took down all the details, but told me it was probably just an opportunist robbery. Not much chance of catching the perpetrators, they said."

"No wonder the general public has such faith in us policemen," Nergui said. Inwardly, though, he was cursing. The robbery had never been reported to him. Probably just oversight—no one had thought to link this incident with the arrest weeks before. And he was all too aware that, given any opportunity, the local forces were often only too keen to withhold information from the arrogant bunch in headquarters. Or maybe, once again, there was a more sinister explanation.

"I didn't take it too seriously," she continued. "They ransacked the place but by then there was very little worth stealing. Bit of old jewellery, a few dollars in cash. Not much more."

"But you think they were looking for something else?"

"I don't know," she said. "But what I do know is that, before he died—before he was arrested—Gansukh had made a point of packaging up a stack of formal documents and sending them, in a sealed package, to a cousin he'd scarcely met."

Nergui nodded. If you were looking to hide something, then an unknown cousin, across the other side of the country, might well be a better bet than any conventional safe deposit box. Particularly if you were looking to hide it from someone like Muunokhoi.

"I'm not sure why he did it," she said. "I think it was some sort of insurance policy—but it's typical of Gansukh that he wouldn't really have thought it through."

"What kind of papers are we talking about?" Nergui said.

"Well, it's not really a smoking gun," she said. "At least not in the sense that it provides any definitive evidence of Gansukh's dealings with Muunokhoi. But, as far as I can understand it, there are copies of notes and paperwork that do at least show there were commercial dealings between Gansukh's businesses and Muunokhoi."

"Legitimate dealings?" Nergui stretched out his legs and leaned back on the bench. Today, his characteristic dark suit was offset by pale blue socks.

"It's difficult to be sure," Sarangarel said. "I mean, yes, in the sense that the paperwork includes—you know, invoice copies, payment details, that kind of thing, relating to what look like legitimate transactions. Import–export business, mainly, as far as I can see. But it's all relating to goods that Gansukh had no involvement in, as far as I know."

Nergui straightened up in his seat and looked at her. "How do you mean?"

"Well, for example, there are invoices relating to the import of various foodstuffs. That was never a business that Gansukh got involved in—too difficult, all that perishable stuff. He was always very clear about that—liked to get things that had a decent shelf life. Not surprising, given how useless he was at selling it." She smiled.

"So you think the paperwork was a cover for something else?"

She shrugged. "That sort of thing's more your line. But it doesn't make much sense as it stands. So, yes, I think there's something of that sort. I think he needed some sort of cover to justify the money that was being paid over, and that was it."

"It doesn't prove much in itself," Nergui said.

"Not in the legal sense, no," she said. "I don't think I'd be very impressed by it if it was presented as evidence in a case I was presiding over. But I went through it very carefully and did a little checking. There were various companies involved and all of them were either directly owned by or closely associated with Muunokhoi. There's little doubt in my mind that he commissioned many of Gansukh's shady operations."

Nergui nodded. "It's probably more than we've been able to get on Muunokhoi before, even if it's not exactly definitive. I wonder why he was so lax in dealing with Gansukh."

"I don't think he was, particularly. I imagine that he'd have had dealings of this kind with countless suppliers. All this material was well presented and would have just got lost in the records of most companies. You wouldn't notice anything odd about it. I think Muunokhoi made the same mistake that everyone did in dealing with Gansukh."

"Which was?"

"He overestimated him. Gansukh was brilliant at the front, at the bluff. People were only too ready to believe that he was a world-class businessman, a big operator. But he wasn't at all."

"Muunokhoi would have had him checked out."

"Of course, and that's probably why he only got some limited, pretty risky business. Probably the stuff that no one else was keen to touch. But even so, I'm willing to bet that Muunokhoi thought that Gansukh had more substance than he really did. I think Gansukh's dealings with Muunokhoi's companies would have been noticeable simply because there wouldn't have been a lot else. But I also think that, as always, Gansukh was just trying to be a bit too clever. He'd have known that Muunokhoi wasn't one for leaving any traces, so he gathered up all the relevant paperwork and hid it—sent it off to this cousin. Then he had some kind of insurance policy if things went wrong."

"As they did. So why didn't he use it?"

She shrugged. "Maybe he was just about to. I suspect it was intended as a last resort, for when he was really in trouble. This was his way of trying to shift the responsibility—he was always very good at that—of having at least some evidence that he wasn't the big noise behind all this."

"So that would have been part of the deal he would have offered us?"

"I think so. But he didn't get the chance."

"No." Nergui looked out across the sunlit park. There were children on the playground. A group of old men in traditional robes—looking far too hot for the warm spring day—were sitting smoking on one of the benches, apparently content simply to enjoy each other's company in silence. It all seemed a world away from these machinations.

"Do you think Muunokhoi knows that this paperwork exists?"

"He knows that something exists." She spoke with a calm certainty that startled him.

"What do you mean?"

She didn't answer immediately. Instead, she climbed slowly to her feet, the bright silk dress shaking softly in the breeze. "Let's walk down to the lake," she said.

Nergui rose and followed her without speaking, assuming that she would begin to talk in her own time. She said nothing until they reached the edge of the grey water. "It needs cleaning," she said.

Nergui came to stand beside her in silence. The water rippled gently in the sunshine, scattering glittering reflections of the midday sun.

"You're as sharp as ever, aren't you? You knew there was something."

It was only as she spoke that Nergui realised that she was

right. He had known that there was something. That was part of the reason—though only part—why he had been keen to spend time with her again. That was, he thought, why all these ghosts kept rising unbidden into his mind.

"I suppose you're right," he said. "I did know that there was something. But I don't know what it is."

"I was lying, earlier," she said. "When I claimed that I was a different person, that I'd put all of that behind me. Of course, it's true in some ways. But in other ways—probably more important ways—it's not true at all. I'm still the same person I was that night when you came barging into our flat."

Nergui said nothing. There was very little he could say about that, after all this time, all these years.

"And I suppose," she went on, "the other thing that I haven't wanted to admit to myself is that—despite everything—I loved Gansukh. I mean, I know he was a crook—a small-time petty crook, at that. And what he did—well, at the time it felt as if it had destroyed my life. Though in the end the opposite was probably true. But because of that I spent a long time trying to persuade myself—and probably everyone else—that I really didn't care for Gansukh at all."

Nergui looked across at her, standing at the edge of the lake. She suddenly looked, he thought, much more like the woman he had met ten years before—vulnerable, confused, lost.

"But I did. There was a lot about him to like—he was good company, lively. And I think he genuinely cared for me. Part of what drove him to do the things he did was to try to make a better life for the two of us. So I did care about him. And I did care that he died." She paused. "And most of all I did care that he was killed."

"He killed himself," Nergui said. "That was the verdict."

She turned and looked at him. "You didn't believe that, even then," she said. "You certainly don't believe it now."

Nergui shrugged. "I've no evidence," he said. "But, no, his death was always too convenient." He wondered, in the light of what she had just said, whether his words sounded unduly callous.

"Muunokhoi had him killed," she said, simply. "And it was one of your men that killed him."

Nergui nodded. The logic was inescapable, as it always had been. If it was true that Muunokhoi was responsible for the death, then it had indeed been one of Nergui's men who had betrayed and killed him.

"It's been eating away at me," she said. "For years. That knowledge. I thought I'd managed to put it behind me, but then when I came face to face with Muunokhoi in court, it all rose up again—it all rose up again, as potent as ever."

"Surely it wasn't appropriate for you to be the presiding judge in Muunokhoi's case?" Nergui said.

"Of course it wasn't. But nobody but me—not even Muunokhoi himself—had made the connection. Why would they? It was a long time ago. I don't look like the same person. My name is different."

"You should have declared an interest." It was, he realised, a fatuous thing to say. But if you're a policeman, you try to uphold the law.

"Of course I should have. But I didn't want to. I wanted—not revenge, but justice. I wanted to make sure that justice was done."

"But it wasn't."

"No. That was the worst point of all. To be so close, and then to have it all snatched away by what—incompetence? There I was, having to play the impartial judge, acknowledging Muunokhoi's case, badgering the poor man from the Prosecutor's Office who was clearly trying to defend the indefensible—and, well, in the end there was no choice. The trial had to be abandoned. You can't imagine how I felt."

Nergui nodded. "I think, in a way at least, that I can. I've been trying to bring this man to justice for nearly two decades."

"I told myself that it was probably just as well," she said. "I'd put myself in an impossible position. It was insane. I mean, there was nothing wrong in principle with my presiding over the trial, given that there's no proven link between Muunokhoi and Gansukh. But in any case I don't think I'm entirely rational about all this."

There was something about the way she spoke the final words that caught Nergui's attention. "And what about since then?" he said. "When you received these papers?"

There was a long pause. She stared out across the lake, watching the movement of the trees in the wind. "I was—I don't know, thrown by the outcome of the trial. It had come so close and then—nothing. Back where we started and no way forward. And then, just a couple of weeks later, I received that package in the mail. It was as if all my unspoken prayers had been answered. I recognised that it wasn't hard evidence, but I began to think that it might provide some leverage—"

"What did you do?" Nergui asked quietly.

"I don't know what I was trying to do," she said. "I told you, I'm not rational about this. I'd received this material, but didn't know what to do with it. So I wrote, anonymously, to Muunokhoi—just addressed to him as Chief Executive of one of his companies—and told him I had some material linking him to Gansukh's death—"

There was a long silence. Nergui watched a flock of birds launch itself, with impressive synchronisation, from one of the trees at the far end of the park. "You're sure he couldn't have traced the letter back to you?" he said.

"I don't see how. I mean, it was just a word-processed letter. I sent it from somewhere across town."

"Why did you send it?" Nergui asked. "I mean, what did you think you might achieve?"

"I don't know. I suppose I was just trying to provoke some sort of reaction. Make something happen. I didn't know how to make use of the information I had. I thought about taking it to the police, but I didn't think you'd take it seriously. I mean, there's no real substance to it."

"You're probably right," Nergui said. "Though if you'd brought it to me, I'd have taken it seriously."

"I thought about that afterwards. It was one reason why I turned up on what I thought was your doorstep. But I'm getting ahead of myself. The reason I sent the letter to Muunokhoi? Well, I didn't know how else to use the material. I suppose I thought it might shock him, jolt him out of his complacency. At least make him aware that there was someone out there who *knew.*"

"I don't think Muunokhoi's likely to be too jolted by a single anonymous letter," Nergui said.

"No, well, neither did I. That was why I followed it up."

He looked at her. "Followed it up?"

"I know. But I sent—well, three letters in all. Including some photocopies of what I felt were likely to be the most suspicious of the materials I had, but hinting that this was just the tip of the iceberg. That it was only a matter of time before everything was exposed—"

Nergui whistled softly. "And you were still confident that he couldn't track the letters back to you."

"I don't know. I didn't think so, but I've only just begun to realise quite how much influence he has. And it's possible he'd made the link between me and Gansukh. I mean, between

Judge Radnaa and Gansukh." She paused. "And I suppose that might really have rattled him. He might have realised that, for all his power, he could actually be vulnerable." She paused, as if reluctant to follow through the logic of her own words. "It was shortly after that that I received the first of those threats I told you about. It might have just been coincidence. I can't prove that there was any link with Muunokhoi—"

"But it was a coincidence," Nergui said. "Another one. Always another coincidence." He paused. "That would be Muunokhoi. One step ahead." He looked around, realising that even in the bright spring morning he was feeling nervous, wondering if someone might be watching them. "And if it's true, that's a serious matter. You need protection. Real protection. Not just a uniformed officer standing outside your apartment."

She nodded. "That's why I came to see you originally. I mean, all that stuff about looking for the police station. That was all nonsense. I was looking for you. Didn't realise you'd moved on. You were one of the few people I thought I could trust."

That, he thought, was perhaps even more true than she realised. "So why didn't you tell me?"

She shook her head. "I don't know. I was embarrassed. I'd behaved stupidly. Maybe even compromised my position." She hesitated. "And I suppose, knowing you, I thought you'd work it out for yourself. As you seem to have done."

"I'm not sure about that," he said. "But we've got there in the end, between us. And maybe you're right about him being rattled." He thought about Tunjin, living who knew where, on the run from the same Muunokhoi. And he thought about Muunokhoi, engaging in apparently pointless vendettas with those who had tried and failed to bring him to justice, perhaps risking more than he knew.

"We need to take care of you," he said, finally. "We need to keep you safe. Where are the papers?"

"I think they're safe," she said. "I took them to my lawyer first, made sure everything was recorded, and then I lodged them in my bank, in a safe deposit box. Even if Muunokhoi somehow knows where they are, he won't be able to get at them without my cooperation."

Nergui looked at her. "Don't underestimate Muunokhoi's influence. I don't welcome the idea of him trying to secure your cooperation. Look, let's get you back to police headquarters. I'll speak to my contacts in the Ministry, try to find you a safe house where you can stay." He didn't add that he could not trust the police to provide her with an uncompromised guard.

He began to lead her back from the lake, over towards the park entrance opposite the Hotel Bayangol where his car was parked. He felt genuinely nervous, aware of the possibility that they were being observed. Inwardly, he cursed her for not being open about this before, as he realised for the first time quite how vulnerable she had been for the preceding days.

They reached the gates in silence and hurried out into the street. Nergui's car was parked in the hotel car park, over the road. The street itself was deserted. He looked around then gently bundled her in front of him across to the hotel entrance, his hands already closing on the keys in his pocket.

The car came from nowhere. It had been parked parallel to Nergui's own, facing forwards, just a few yards closer to the car park entrance. Its engine started suddenly, and the car was thrown forward as if the handbrake had just been released. Its front wing hit Nergui a glancing blow and he was thrown across the car park, landing roughly on the concrete. At the same moment, the rear door of the car opened, the car slowed momentarily, and two hands grabbed Sarangarel, who was standing transfixed by the unexpected drama. Without a sound, she was dragged into the back of the car, the rear door slammed shut, and with a loud screech of tyres, the car spun round and back out into the street.

Nergui lay on the ground, semiconscious, an agonising pain in his left leg, his brain scarcely working but his aching head telling him, over and over again, that it was too late, that it was all over, that he had failed.

SIXTEEN

Doripalam was at home when the message came through, but he would rather have been almost anywhere else. It was unusual for him to take a day's leave in the week, and he had known right from the start that it was a mistake. But it was hardly as if he had a choice.

"I mean," Solongo had said, "they can surely manage without you for one day. It's not as if you don't put in the hours."

He had wondered, momentarily, about pointing out the inconsistency in her position. It was Solongo, after all, who was always suggesting that his job was under threat, that everyone around him was waiting only for the opportunity to see him fail. It was Solongo who, without ever quite uttering a word on the subject, had persuaded him that he needed to be in the office every waking hour—and possibly some sleeping ones too—in order to demonstrate his indispensability.

But that, of course, was when she wanted him out of the

house so that she could get on with living her own life. Today, she needed him in the house for the same reason.

Doripalam had known it would be excruciating from the moment she had first raised the idea. As it turned out, it was even worse than he had envisaged. And now, here he was, at four o'clock in the afternoon, sipping weak coffee while listening to what was quite possibly the most boring lecture he had ever been compelled to endure. Even the worst rigours of university and police training had not prepared him for this. And, more to the point, Solongo had certainly not prepared him for it.

In advance, she had made it sound almost interesting. As part of her continuing quest for social advancement—or, perhaps more accurately, her quest to combat the almost inevitable social decline she associated with Doripalam's chosen profession—Solongo had accepted an invitation to become a trustee of one of the city's major museums. It was an honour, as Doripalam was happy to acknowledge, and it carried certain responsibilities. One of which, apparently, was to play occasional host to the trustees' bimonthly committee meetings which rotated between the members' homes.

Doripalam had been willing to go along with the idea for Solongo's sake, and had been quite happy to throw his home open to any number of his wife's cultural associates. But he had failed to take account of her expectation that he should be present for the occasion.

As soon as they had begun to arrive that afternoon, Doripalam had recognised the type. They were precisely those who, twenty years before, would have been senior Party apparatchiks, and who had somehow made a seamless transition into the new order. Doripalam had nothing in common with these people. Except of course that, in his elevated role, he was now on the verge of becoming one of them.

He found himself, on his second glass of vodka, standing talking to Solongo and a tall, middle-aged man who was apparently some bigwig in one of the former state energy companies.

"Solongo tells me you're a policeman," the man said, with a clear implication that Doripalam should really be out patrolling the streets.

"Sort of," Doripalam said.

"Doripalam is Head of the Serious Crimes Team," Solongo said. Doripalam was quite sure that she would have provided this information already, possibly several times, but for once he felt no qualms about her reaffirming his status.

The man nodded slowly, sipping his vodka. "Were you the bunch behind the Muunokhoi debacle?"

Doripalam bit back his immediate response. "We were involved in the arrest, yes. Those kind of charges fall under our jurisdiction."

"He was only doing his job," Solongo said. Doripalam glanced at her, slightly annoyed at her unnecessary defensiveness. On the other hand, in the circumstances, there was probably some need to be defensive.

"It's a scandal," the man said. "The whole thing was politically motivated."

Doripalam raised an eyebrow, and took a deep swallow of his vodka. "You think so?"

"Of course. It's the same as the way Putin's been behaving in Russia. You can't control the likes of Muunokhoi, so you persecute them."

"I've persecuted nobody," Doripalam said, trying to subdue his irritation.

"I don't mean you personally," the man said, in a tone which indicated that Doripalam himself was below any kind of serious consideration. "You're just an agent. But there are forces in the government that would want to bring Muunokhoi down, I'm sure."

Doripalam shrugged. Perhaps the man was right, but it wasn't his own impression. From what he'd seen—and from what he'd heard from Nergui—the government largely just kowtowed to money and power, regardless of its source. Yes, the Justice Minister had tried to gain some political capital out of Muunokhoi's arrest, but that was only because the Minister had assumed that Muunokhoi's power was on the wane. Doripalam could easily imagine the Minister's subsequent flailing to regain the ground he had lost.

"If that was the case," Doripalam said, "they weren't very successful."

"Just as well," the man said. "It's people like Muunokhoi who are the future of this country. He's smart, he's a step ahead." He smiled, jabbing a finger towards Doripalam. "And, as we all know, he's got people like you in his pocket." The man rubbed his thumb and finger together in an unambiguous gesture.

Just for a moment, Doripalam gave serious consideration to the potential consequences of a senior police officer punching one of the great and the good on the nose. Even accepting those consequences, the idea was a tempting one.

He opened his mouth to respond—if only to point out the inconsistency of the man's arguments—but Solongo was clearly one step ahead of him and was already steering the man off towards another group. She glared back at Doripalam, daring him to speak. Doripalam nodded and then smiled at her, suddenly recognising that she hated all this nonsense almost as much as he did.

It was a moment of unexpected warmth between them, not quite dissipated as she moved to engage in another tiresome conversation. It had struck him for the first time quite how hard she was working on his behalf. For a moment, he was tempted to break into her conversation, to make some acknowledgement of how much he appreciated, if not the effect, at least the good intentions behind what she was doing.

But as he moved forward he felt his mobile phone vibrate in his jacket pocket. He pulled it out, thumbed the keyboard and glanced at the message, feeling a chill down his spine as he did so.

When he did break into Solongo's conversation, his words were very different from those he had planned only moments before.

"I'm sorry," he said. "I've got to go. It's Nergui. He's been in an accident." He turned away quickly before she could respond.

Minutes later, he was making his hurried way out of the flat and down the stairs. It would probably be a while, he thought, before he and Solongo would be able to recapture that brief moment of mutual warmth and support. For that matter, it would probably be a while before she was prepared to speak to him again.

The house wasn't quite what Tunjin had expected. It was an impressive enough place, but he had expected—well, something more grandiose, more impressive. Something in keeping with Muunokhoi's status. This was, admittedly, only one of several residences Muunokhoi possessed, although, from Tunjin's recollection of the files, this was the place he was most likely to call home.

There had been something in the files, too, about the history of the place. As far as Tunjin could recollect, the house had originally belonged to one of the bigwigs in the Party, in the days when communist grandees lived in places like this. It was, Tunjin supposed, a summer house, a dacha, located a few miles outside the heat and fumes of the city centre, but close enough to allow the occupier to continue working in the city.

It was a wooden construction, a chalet design, with long sweeping rooflines, tucked away amongst the trees, designed to be cool and shaded through the warmth of the summer. Tunjin had taken the Vincent motorbike around the house, keeping his distance, ending up on the undulant hillside and woodland that overlooked the house from the rear. From here, he could gain a good vantage point of the layout of the building and its surroundings.

Tunjin wished he had binoculars so that he could get a better view of the estate. As far as he could see, there was no obvious security, though he was under no illusions about how well protected the house and gardens would be. The garden itself was not particularly large and mostly laid to grass, scattered thickly with fir trees. A curving drive swept from the imposing front gates to the house itself.

There was no sign of life. There was a single car—a large black Mercedes—parked to one side of the building, but Tunjin had seen no one enter or leave. He didn't even know for sure that Muunokhoi was staying here at present. The files had indicated that he had another house up in the north of the country, in the picturesque Khövsghöl Nuur region, as well as a flat in the city centre. But Tunjin's impression had been that the second house was used largely for holidays—or possibly for more clandestine meetings—while the apartment was used as a place to bunk down when Muunokhoi was engaged in his characteristic long working days. He might not be back here tonight, but he typically spent only one or two nights a week in the apartment.

And even if Muunokhoi wasn't here, it was likely that the house was staffed with both domestic and security people. Someone would be down there.

Tunjin had sounded confident enough, in his conversation with Nergui, talking about the need to take Muunokhoi out of the picture. And there was no question that, in principle, he was right. If he wanted to regain his own security, his own peace of mind—no, forget that, if he wanted to live—then that was the only option.

But he didn't have a clue about how he might bring it about.

What was it that he had had in mind? Was he planning to break into Muunokhoi's house and perhaps steal some incriminating documents, some perfect piece of substantive evidence which Muunokhoi happened to have left handily lying about on his dining room table? He would probably have a better chance of success if he just tried to talk Muunokhoi out of killing him.

No, like everything else Tunjin had attempted in respect of Muunokhoi, this was worse than half-baked. He didn't even have a clue what the ingredients might be, let alone how to start cooking up anything. He had no equipment, no support, no resources and—above all—no ideas. Perhaps he should just walk up to the front door, hand himself over, and invite Muunokhoi to do his worst.

Tunjin slowly lifted himself off the bike, kicking down the stand as he did so. He was positioned near the top of the low hill, up amongst the thickening fir trees, where he hoped that he was invisible to any observers below. There was always a risk that the chrome on the motorbike might reflect the sun, but as far as Tunjin knew this was open land so it would not be unusual to find walkers, and perhaps even the occasional biker, up here.

It was another beautiful spring day, only a few wisps of cloud in the sky. From the hillside, the grassland fell away, a patchwork of emerald green and darker shadows, down to the house and garden below, then across to the road. Beyond that, there was more grassland, a few houses, and nothing but the open steppe until the distant blue haze of the city.

Tunjin slumped down on to the ground and took stock of his position. All he could do was to keep watching, in the vague hope that inspiration would strike. He scrutinised the layout of Muunokhoi's house carefully. From here, he was at a diagonal angle to the house and could see both its front and rear elevations, though not its far side. It looked to be a fairly simple layout. At the rear he could see large double patio windows, which opened out onto a paved area arranged with an array of tables, chairs and other garden furniture. There was another window to the left of that, which Tunjin assumed was probably a kitchen. Above were lines of windows on the first and second floors, presumably bedrooms, with the occasional frosted window indicating a bathroom.

The front was similar. There was an imposing double door as the main entrance, with a substantial pine-built porchway over it, studded with lamps. And then lines of large windows, presumably of bedrooms and reception rooms.

Tunjin was surprised that, other than what looked like a standard domestic burglar alarm, there were no obvious security measures. He guessed that, somewhere around, there would be CCTV cameras, though he could see no sign of them from up here. He'd also presumed that some of Muunokhoi's security staff would be located on site, but again he had so far seen nothing.

Tunjin might be aware of the true nature of Muunokhoi's operations, but to the world at large he was simply a very successful businessman. People would expect him to have some security in place, but would not expect to see his domestic residence swarming with hired hitmen. Muunokhoi had an image to sustain.

But none of this was helping Tunjin. He needed some idea,

some spark of thought that would give him a way forward. Anything.

And, as if in answer to this plea, there was finally some movement in the panorama spread out below.

Tunjin heard it before he spotted it. A car engine, distant, but unmistakeable in this silent landscape. He looked up and scanned the scene in front of him, and finally made out the rapid movement of a car, still miles away, heading away from the hazy fog of the city out in this direction.

He watched the car's progress, fully expecting that it would bypass the house and head on out north into the steppes. As it came closer, he saw it was a large black vehicle—a saloon car rather than a 4x4, probably Western. A Mercedes, maybe, or a BMW, but it was too distant to be sure.

To his mild surprise, as it approached the house, the car slowed. In almost perfect synchronisation, the large wrought iron gates at the end of the drive began slowly to open, clearly operated by someone from inside the house. The car turned into the entrance and made its way, at a much slower speed now, up the driveway towards the house.

At the same time, Tunjin noticed that the large double doors at the front of the house had been opened, and two men—both dressed in the standard leather jacket and dark glasses that seemed to be the uniform for Muunokhoi's hired help—stepped out into the sunlight. Both were holding something. In one case, this seemed to be a mobile phone, as the man was holding it close to his ear. In the second case, Tunjin caught the glint of sunlight on the metal. A handgun of some sort.

Tunjin watched in some fascination as the car pulled to a halt. The two men stepped down to greet it, as the two front doors of the car opened. Two further men, dressed in identical fashion to the first, emerged and conversed briefly with their colleagues. Finally, one of them opened the rear door of the car, reached inside and, with assistance from his colleague, he pulled out what Tunjin at first took to be some kind of bundle—a parcel or a roll of cloth.

Then Tunjin realised that it was a body—a woman. She had dark hair, and was wearing a brightly coloured silk dress which fluttered gently in the breeze as the two men lifted her carefully towards the door of the house.

The other two men watched him for a moment. Then the one holding the gun slipped it back into his pocket, said something to the other, and they followed their colleagues and the woman into the house.

Tunjin watched for a few more moments, trying to take all this in, wondering whether anything else would happen. But the house remained as silent as before, the scene unchanged except for the addition of the new car parked on the drive.

Finally, Tunjin slumped backwards and lay on his back on the damp grass, watching the slow movement of the scattered clouds across the empty blue of the sky.

Okay, so something was happening here. Something that perhaps required some response, some action. Tunjin still had no idea what he was going to do. But at least now he had a positive motive for trying to do it.

"You don't believe in a quiet life, do you?"

"I don't recall it being part of the job description—" He hardly knew what he was saying. He was engaging in badinage on automatic pilot. It was like being in a dream, or perhaps just waking from a dream, except that he was unsure whether he was awake or still sleeping.

"Not of yours, certainly." The volume of the voice faded in

and out, so that he was still unsure whether or not he was really hearing it or whether it was just imagined. His dreams were so vivid. Sarangarel. The car. The abduction.

Nergui opened his eyes suddenly. "Where is she?"

"Where's who?" The response was soothing, as though patronising a child or someone mentally ill.

Nergui sat up in the bed. "Where is she?"

It was Doripalam sitting by the bed, anxiety etched into his features. "Who? Who are you talking about?"

Nergui shook his head, trying to clear his fogged brain. "Her, Sarangarel. Where is she?"

Doripalam stared at him. "Who's Sarangarel?"

"She's—she's the judge. Judge Radnaa. Where is she?"

Doripalam was looking at Nergui as if, finally, after all these years, he really had lost his reason. "You've been injured," he said at last. "Concussion. You really need to rest."

Nergui's eyes were wide now. He was beginning to distinguish between dream and reality. He was beginning to work out where he was. "No," he said. "It's true. She's been kidnapped. She's in danger." He paused, taking in the implications of this statement. "No. Really. In real danger. Muunokhoi." Even saying the name seemed to exhaust him.

Doripalam blinked. "Muunokhoi? What do you mean?"

Nergui leaned forward, forcing himself to think clearly, trying to sort fact from—whatever else was clouding his brain. "She was with me. When the car—whatever it did—when it hit me. She was with me. And they took her into the car. They kidnapped her—" He stopped, feeling exhausted by the explanation.

"We don't know what happened to you," Doripalam said. "We don't know how you were injured. We don't know what the story is."

This was finally making sense to Nergui, though he was not

yet in a state to work out the implications. "I was attacked," he said. He paused, trying to get the narrative straight in his mind. "It was like this. I was having lunch with her. With Sarangarel. Judge Radnaa. She's a judge—" he added, perhaps unnecessarily, but knowing that the narrative would be making little sense to Doripalam. And then there was the question—which his damaged, sleep-raddled mind hadn't begun to come to terms with—of whether it was wise for him to make sense to Doripalam in the first place. "We went for a walk in the park," he went on, "and then came back to the hotel car park. I was going to give her a lift because—" What should he say? What version of the truth was it appropriate to share with Doripalam? How far—because this is what it came down to—could he be trusted?

Nergui paused, partly to regain his breath, partly to work out how much he should say. But his mind was still confused. He could not come to grips with the idea of not trusting Doripalam. "We were having lunch together," he repeated, finally. "We went back to the hotel car park. The Bayangol. And then this car—it came from nowhere. It was parked. Drove out. Hit me. But—no, this is the point. The back door of the car opened and—they grabbed her—"

"Who? They grabbed who?"

Nergui knew that Doripalam was an intelligent man. He seemed to be being almost wilfully obtuse. "Sarangarel," he repeated patiently. "Judge Radnaa. They kidnapped her."

"They kidnapped a judge?"

Nergui breathed out, like a runner who had finally reached his destination. "Yes. Exactly. They've kidnapped a judge. Judge Radnaa."

Doripalam was staring at him. "You said Muunokhoi. What did you mean?"

It was Nergui's turn to stare, all his doubts returning. "I don't know," he said. "What did I say?"

Doripalam sat back, looking at his former boss, sitting propped up in the hospital bed. "I think I'd better tell you what I know. How we found you." He paused. "All we know is that you were found in the Hotel Bayangol car park. One of the hotel staff found you. You were bleeding from the head and he assumed—rightly, as far as we can tell—that you were hit by a car. An accident—"

"It wasn't an accident."

"No, well, that wouldn't be a surprise. Anyway, he called for medical help. You were brought in here. And they found your Ministry ID and so contacted us."

"I wasn't alone," Nergui insisted. "When I was hit by the car."

"Yes, well, I'm beginning to understand that. You were with Judge—"

"Radnaa. She's been kidnapped."

"Judge Radnaa. Why do I—?"

"She was the judge in the Muunokhoi case. The aborted case."

"Is that why you think—?"

"It's a long story," Nergui said. "But, yes, I think she's been kidnapped by Muunokhoi's people."

There was a long silence. Finally, Doripalam said: "You do know what you're saying? I mean, you were concussed."

Nergui was sitting bolt upright in bed now. "I know exactly what I'm saying. The only question in my mind is whether I ought to be saying it to you."

The silence was even longer this time.

"What do you mean?" Doripalam said at last.

Nergui shook his head. He realised, only now, that his head was aching, very intensely, a dull numbing ache that still seemed to cloud his reason. His normally razor sharp instincts seemed blunted, and he felt unable to trust his judgement. "This is a very long story," he said. "How badly hurt am I?"

"Hardly at all," Doripalam said. "I've always suspected you

were indestructible and this proves it. Not many people get into an argument with a car and walk away."

"I didn't exactly walk away," Nergui pointed out, "and it wasn't really an argument. More like a very brief exchange of views. And it doesn't really feel like I'm hardly hurt at all." As his senses had slowly returned, Nergui was becoming increasingly aware that some parts of his body—his hip, one of his arms—were in considerable pain.

"Even so," Doripalam said, "I checked with the doctor. You suffered some bruising—some of it very painful but not serious. You hit your head, but they've done a scan and there's no lasting damage. Not that I could have deduced that from the way you've been talking."

"No," Nergui said. "So when can I leave?"

"I think they'll sign you out as soon as you think you're ready," Doripalam said.

"I think I'm ready. I think I'm more than ready." Nergui twisted himself across the bed with some difficulty and sat up on the edge. He was wearing a hospital issue gown. "Where are my clothes?"

"I really don't think you ought to—"

Nergui looked up at the younger man. His dark face was as impassive as ever but his blue eyes were blazing with an emotion which Doripalam could not read. "Listen, Doripalam. There isn't time. Sarangarel's been taken by Muunokhoi's people. We don't know where. We don't know what might happen to her. But we have to assume the worst."

"But you don't know for sure—"

"That Muunokhoi's behind this. I do know. But, no, I can't prove it. And if Muunokhoi is true to form, he'll make sure that he's a long way away from whatever might happen. Although—" He stopped and stared at Doripalam, as though trying to fathom some intricate puzzle.

"What?"

"It doesn't feel right for Muunokhoi, all this. All these years of caution. All this time we've never been able to lay a finger on him. And now—"

Doripalam was watching Nergui, clearly wondering whether the concussion had been more serious than he had originally imagined.

"Now," Nergui went on, "he seems rattled. He seems almost to be panicking. It's—" He stopped, still perched on the edge of the bed, and looked back up at Doripalam. "I need to know," he said. "I need to know whether I can trust you."

Doripalam opened his mouth to speak, but no words emerged. Finally, he said: "What are you talking about?"

"Find me my clothes," Nergui said. "We need to get out of here. We need to talk."

SEVENTEEN

It was nearly dark outside.

Tsend's main office window faced north and the setting sun was already invisible, lost behind the endless forests and low hills, the last crimson rays draining from the sky. He could almost see the movement of the night's shadows spreading across the rolling grassland.

The call would come soon, he knew. The second call since the young man from the city had been here. Doripalam. So confident and cocksure. So patronising. And so much further out of his depth than he could ever have imagined.

Tsend smiled, standing by the window, staring out at the darkening landscape. It was amusing, he thought. Ironic. Left to himself, he would have never made the connection, never realised who the four men were. He had been following, with some detached amusement, the news stories of the missing son and then the murder of the mother. And he had noted, with no real interest, the official request that any new arrivals in the area should be reported back to headquarters.

But he had not taken the request seriously. And he had certainly not registered its deeper significance to his own position.

So it was thanks only to some overenthusiastic local rookie that the men had been spotted. And—even more amusingly—it was thanks only to Doripalam's own assiduousness that the four men had been positively identified and then brought back here. Into Tsend's safekeeping.

It was only then that Tsend finally learned who the men were. And who else was interested in them. And just how much that interest might enhance his own standing. For the first time, he had the opportunity to prove himself, to show that he was more than just another local hick on the take.

The only question now was what happened next. The first call had simply told him to keep hold of the men, ensure they were kept safe. Someone would be coming up from the city to question them, but that was okay. That was all in hand.

But once that was out of the way, the matter would have to be finished off. Tidied up. Tsend should await further instructions.

He was still gazing fixedly out of the window when the mobile phone vibrated in his pocket. He pulled it out and thumbed the call button. "Yes?" Use only this phone, they had said. Never give your name.

"Someone will be coming up from the city tomorrow morning," the voice said. Tsend thought the speaker sounded familiar, but immediately put the idea from his mind. He didn't want to know. "Make them welcome. They will question the men. You should cooperate. That's all under control."

Tsend had never doubted it. "And then—?" he breathed.

"Then the men should be released," the voice said.

"But I was told to keep—"

"The men should be released," the voice repeated, as if Tsend had not spoken. "They should be sent back to their camp. They should be told that there is nothing to worry about. That they are safe and under your protection. You will keep them under observation until we contact you again."

"And then—"

"Then, with your assistance, we will take care of things," the voice said, evenly. "We will take care of everything."

"This is outrageous," he said. "I've never been treated like this." The words were automatic. She hardly knew what she was saying, her mind still struggling through the fog of semiconsciousness. But already she was recognising the need to assert her will, to try to gain some control of the situation.

The man sitting opposite her merely nodded and shrugged. He was watching her closely, but it was clear that he had no intention of engaging in any kind of conversation or offering any kind of response.

"How long are you intending to keep me here?"

The man shrugged again, this time smiling faintly. His impervious calm was almost the most infuriating aspect of the situation in which she found herself.

She was still half-asleep, her mouth was dry and her head was aching. She was lying uncomfortably on an overstuffed sofa, a blanket draped decorously across her, although she was still fully clothed. She had no idea how long she had been unconscious, but her stomach felt empty and nauseous, as if she hadn't eaten for days. She pulled herself upright and looked around her.

In other circumstances, this would have seemed a very comfortable environment. It was a large, well-appointed living room, clearly the property of someone possessing both good taste and the wealth needed to express it. The furniture was expensive and well-chosen—mahogany woodwork, plush upholstery, delicate splashings of gold and silver here and there. At the far end of the room was something she had never seen before—a large, flat-screen television. There were shelves of books—all leather bound, apparently unopened.

Through the window beyond the television, she could see a large expanse of grass, dotted with some pots of apparently exotic flowers. The garden was bounded, at the far end, by a large fence, fronted by rows of dense fir trees.

There was no way of knowing where she was. As soon as she had been pulled into the car, she had been blindfolded and moments later she had felt the prick of a syringe in her arm. She had fought hard against the blankness that began to overwhelm her, trying to maintain consciousness. Her last recollection had been a brief exchange of words that had told her there were two men in the front seats, and then she had remembered nothing until waking up in this room.

How long had she been unconscious? She had no watch and no idea of the time. But the sunlight streaming through the windows was low, and something about the quality of the light suggested that it was morning rather than evening. Was it possible that she had been unconscious overnight?

"Won't you at least give me an idea what this is all about?" she said. "I mean, is it some kind of joke?"

It was a ridiculous question. What sort of joke could this be? What sort of joke would involve seizing a member of the judiciary, while apparently in the process also running over a senior officer from the Ministry of Security?

The last question sent her thoughts back to Nergui. Could he possibly be all right? The sound of the car hitting his body had been indescribably awful—all the more dreadful for its softness. She had seen him—only for a moment before she was dragged into the car—fall backwards, his head thudding against the concrete of the hotel car park. It was possible, she supposed, that he was badly injured or even dead, though she rapidly pushed the thought to the back of her mind.

She looked back at the blank-faced man sitting opposite her. They were seated like prospective diners or perhaps chess players, facing one another across the polished mahogany table.

She rose slowly from her seat and made her way towards the rear window. The man watched her movement with no apparent interest.

As she had expected, the view from the window told her nothing more. There was a well-tended garden at the rear of the house, largely laid to grass, scattered with conifers and potted plants. The concept of a garden was not widely appreciated in this land of vast open plains and desert, and she could only assume that the owner of the property had spent some time in the West—or, she supposed, in Japan, although the style of the garden was essentially European. She wondered quite how expensive it would be to maintain this kind of garden in this extreme continental climate, with its subzero winters and dry summers.

The rear boundary of the garden was marked by a high solid fence lined with tall conifers. She could see nothing beyond—no sign of the mountains or forests, no clue as to where this house might be located.

She moved away from the window, and wandered back across the room, pausing to glance at the glass-fronted bookshelves that lined the adjacent wall. The books were all antiquarian, leather bound, virtually all of them—other than an ornate edition of *The Secret History of the Mongols*—with titles she did not recognise. The library looked like the kind of anonymous collection that might be held by any rich man as an investment or perhaps simply as an indicator of his wealth. There was no sign that any of the books had been read. There was also no clue even to the personality, let alone the identity, of the owner of the house.

She turned back from the bookshelf as the door opened and a figure stepped quietly inside. For all the absence of evidence, she had been assuming—on the basis of her discussion with Nergui—that she had been brought here at Muunokhoi's behest. She had similarly assumed that Muunokhoi would appear to greet her and carry out whatever purpose had been behind her apparent abduction.

But, she realised, this was naïve. Muunokhoi had not revealed his hand so far, and there was no reason to assume he would start now. She could not even assume that this was Muunokhoi's house—it was far more likely that he would find some anonymous location to take whatever action he had in mind, rather than have her taken to his home. Not that there was anything obviously anonymous about this place.

Certainly, the man who now entered the room was not Muunokhoi, and did not look like one of his henchmen. He was a short, relatively young man—probably in his early thirties—dressed in a smart dark suit. His hair was trimmed short, and he wore angular black framed glasses which Sarangarel presumed were some kind of fashion statement rather than simply an optical aid. In his hands, he carried a small silver tray, with a plate of bread and cold meats and a jug of water.

He moved softly across the room and placed the tray carefully on the table. Then he sat down opposite the first man, who nodded and left the room.

The young man gestured Sarangarel to take the vacated seat. "Mrs. Radnaa," he said. "Will you join me?" It was a voice which carried no expectation of a negative response.

She nodded to him and walked slowly back across the room,

but made no move to sit down. "I presume you're going to tell me what this is all about?"

He smiled. "Please sit down, Mrs. Radnaa. It is very awkward holding this conversation with you standing up. If it's any reassurance, I think that even sitting down you are likely to be taller than I am."

She watched him for a moment, then nodded and sat down on the chair. "So, Mr.—"

He smiled. "I don't think that the name is important," he said.

"That rather depends," she said, "on what you have in mind. I don't think it's unreasonable to want to know the name of my abductor."

"'Abductor' is rather a strong term," he said. "I'd rather think of myself as your host."

She stared at him for a moment. "Well," she said at last, "I think you leave me speechless." She paused. "So this place is yours?"

He shrugged. "I live here," he said.

She nodded. "I see. So this belongs to someone else. Who presumably shares your eccentric view that dragging someone involuntarily into the back of a car doesn't constitute abduction."

He smiled. "You're a lawyer," he said. "I am sure you know best. But—however you arrived—you are here as our guest. You will not be treated badly." He gestured towards the tray. "You must be hungry."

For a moment, she contemplated refusing the food, but realised that her hunger was too great. She pulled the tray towards her and took a slice of bread and meat, trying not to appear too eager. As she ate, the man poured her a glass of water.

After a few moments the food and water dispelled the worst

of her nausea. Her mind was still fogged, but she felt more in control. "Guests are normally free to leave when they wish," she pointed out. "I take it that is not the case here."

"Not at present, no," he admitted. "But I hope that we can conclude our business relatively quickly."

She sat back in her chair and regarded him. "And that business would be?"

He hesitated for a moment, as though seeking the most appropriate words. "We believe," he said, "that you are in possession of some material, some—paperwork, that rightly belongs to us."

"I don't think so," she said. "Though of course it's difficult to be sure without knowing who you are."

"I don't think there is much point in playing games, Mrs. Radnaa," he said, calmly. "We know more than you can imagine."

"I'm sure you know things I couldn't begin to imagine," she said. "But I am not sure where that gets us. I am not playing games. I really don't know what you're talking about."

The man leaned forward across the table, staring at Sarangarel. "I have told you," he said. "We know. We know about your husband. We know that you recently—and unexpectedly—received a legacy indirectly from your husband."

If Sarangarel was surprised by this announcement, she did not allow it to show. She smiled faintly. "You're very well informed," she said. "But I fail to understand why this information should be of interest to anyone but myself."

The man gazed at her for a moment, as though—against his expectations—it was he who had been surprised by her words. "We know about your husband," he repeated.

"What do you know about my husband?" she said. "You know that he was a businessman? Not a very successful one, I should say." She looked around as though seeing the room for the first time. "Much less successful than you, if you really are the owner of this place. And what else do you know? You know that he was arrested, supposedly for smuggling, but that he was never brought to trial? You know that he died in police custody?" She paused. "I'm not sure what else there is for you to know. I can tell you his shoe size and probably several more intimate facts about him, but then you're probably ahead of me there as well."

The man looked down at the table, as though Sarangarel's attempts to embarrass him had succeeded.

"But," she went on, "all of this is public knowledge. Perhaps you thought it would cause me difficulties, as a member of the judiciary, but, no, I've been able to put all that history well behind me. So, you see, I really don't know what it is you're talking about."

The man made no immediate response and at first it seemed as though he had no response to give. If it was the case that he was acting on Muunokhoi's behalf, then he was really now facing something of a dilemma. He had clearly hoped to intimidate her into handing over the papers immediately. Instead, all he had succeeded in doing was confirming that there was—or at least he thought there was—something significant in the papers. And if he were to say anything more, he would at the very least confirm that fact and might risk revealing something more. Even the issue of her husband's identity had no significance unless it really was the case that he was somehow linked with Muunokhoi.

Finally, the man looked back at her, his dark eyes revealing nothing. "All I can say to you, Mrs. Radnaa, is that while we do not, for the moment at least, intend you any harm, you cannot be released until you give us what we seek."

"In that case," she looked around her, "I am glad that you have provided me with such a comfortable prison."

* * *

Even at the time, Tunjin had no idea how it happened. But that was the story of his life.

He had stayed on the hillside all night, initially with some half-idea that he might try to break into the house under cover of darkness. But he didn't fool himself that the security would be any less tight at night, and he still had no idea how he could gain entry. Eventually, he had wrapped himself in an old blanket he had found in the pannier of the motorbike, and settled down to try to get some rest. He had expected that sleep would be elusive, but in fact he had succumbed very quickly, cushioned by the soft grass and exhausted by the travails of the previous days.

When he awoke, the sun was already rising over the hills to the east. It was another fine spring day. He was cold and hungry, but beginning to recognise what sobriety felt like. It was years since he had felt this alert on first waking. He dragged himself to his feet, and dug out the last remnants of the bread and water that Nergui had given him. As he ate, Tunjin made his way back along the hill, trying to gain a good vantage point over the house, wanting to get as clear an understanding as he could of its layout, likely security protection, and anything else that might assist him in the—as yet unknown—activity in which he was about to engage.

He moved slowly, his eyes fixed on the estate below. Before him, the slope dropped gently away, a smooth contour of grassland which became progressively steeper as it swept down towards tall blank fences that surrounded the house. The wind rippled gently through the grass, a brilliant green in the spring sunshine, and some way off before the trees a cloud of butterflies scattered into the shadows.

It was, perhaps, the butterflies that distracted Tunjin, though he had thought his attention was entirely fixed on the house. He stepped on—what was it? A loose stone, a more slippery area of grass? He wasn't sure. He knew only that, suddenly, his feet went from under him and his considerable weight toppled him, at first slowly then with increasing speed, down the hillside. His feet skidded on the grass, still wet from the morning dew. The next moment, he was, quite literally, rolling, his hands flailing to try to obtain some purchase. He saw the darkness of the trees, the brilliance of the clear blue sky, the dazzling sunshine, strobing through his vision as he fell, completely out of control now, spinning down towards the wooden fence.

His tumbling body hit the steeper part of the hill and bounced into the air, knocking the breath from his large body, and then he was rolling again, spinning faster, his flesh bruised and scraped despite the softness of the ground.

The end came suddenly and brutally, as his body slammed into the brown wooden fence. All the breath was expelled from his body and he lay on his back, gasping, assuming that at any moment his heart would give out and relieve him from the agonising pain that coursed through his limbs.

It took him some minutes to register that, despite the pain, he did not appear to be seriously injured. His breathing slowed, and he lay on his back, staring at the blue of the sky, watching the slow drift of the white clouds above him. He could move his limbs. He stretched out his arms, feeling the ache of the bruises, but grateful that nothing seemed to be broken.

He was lying pressed against the wooden fence, still lacking the energy to move. He had struck the fence with a deafening crash. So much for his idea of approaching the place surreptitiously.

Finally, he pulled himself up to a sitting position. He looked back up behind him. At the top of the hill he could see the sun glinting on the Vincent motorcycle. Was there nothing he could do right? He hadn't even managed to conceal his transport.

But then he realised that his fall had actually achieved something. The impact of Tunjin's weight against the wood had cracked several of the slats, leaving a gaping opening. The fence was, Tunjin now realised, rather less substantial than it appeared. He sat forward, gasping slightly, and pulled gently at the wood.

The first slat came away very easily, and Tunjin tossed it away on to the grass. Behind it, he could see dark undergrowth, thick trees and, beyond that, more grass. He climbed up on to his knees, and began to pull at the wood. Two, then three more slats were pulled back, and thrown on to the grass. Very shortly, Tunjin had cleared a space large enough for even his body to squeeze through.

He kneeled in front of the hole, hesitating, wondering what kind of security protection might lie beyond it. There was no way of knowing. It was likely that there would be some kind of camera arrangement, perhaps even alarms. But what were the options? He could turn and climb away—not that the prospect of climbing the hill was particularly attractive—or he could continue.

He pushed himself forward through the hole, squeezing with some difficulty through the limited space. On the far side he found himself in shady undergrowth, thick conifers towering above him. The sun barely reached here, shaded by the trees and the fence itself. Through the undergrowth he could see an expanse of grass and a network of paths.

Once through the fence, he climbed slowly to his feet, still feeling the bruises across his body. The garden was silent, apart from the faint whisper of the wind through the trees.

Tunjin pushed forward, feeling the thick conifers brushing against his face. Across the grass, he could see the solid wooden bulk of the house. He still didn't even have the beginnings of a plan, had no idea what he might be about to do now that he had managed to enter this place.

There was no sight or sound of any alarm, though that didn't necessarily mean that strident sirens weren't sounding within the house.

Finally, Tunjin emerged on to the path, feeling an unaccountable sense of release as he entered the open light and air. He paused on the path, wondering precisely where he should proceed next.

But, almost immediately, the choice was taken from him. As he straightened up, he heard a voice behind him.

"Well, I suppose it cuts both ways. You're fat enough to break through the perimeter. But you're not hard to track down."

Tunjin turned slowly. A man was standing on the path behind him, having apparently appeared from nowhere. But all Tunjin really saw was the shining black barrel of a gun, pointing steadily towards his chest.

EIGHTEEN

Earlier in the day, in the brightness of the spring afternoon, the place would have been heaving with people, locals and tourists alike, perhaps looking for a dose of spirituality or simply seeing the extraordinary sights. Now, though, as the afternoon came to an end, the grounds had emptied and provided a perfect backdrop to the uneasy conversation between Nergui and Doripalam.

"Are you all right?" Doripalam said solicitously as they made their way slowly up the steep hill.

Nergui nodded, though the honest answer would have been negative. He was not entirely all right, either physically or mentally. Perhaps not even spiritually, he thought, in which case they had at least come to the right place.

"I used to come here a lot," Nergui said, looking around as they reached the summit of the hill. He was breathing heavily, his limbs still aching from the cuts and bruises. "But not for a while. Perhaps it's been too long."

Nergui was not a religious man. Or at least not religious in a way that any conventional faith would appreciate. But he had always found that the Monastery of Choijin Lama, with its clustering of ornate temples, provided some kind of sustenance, something which, he supposed, could be described as spiritual. Perhaps it was the history. Perhaps it was the way that this faith, these rituals, had managed to survive through all the days of suppression. Or perhaps it was simply the rituals themselves, the sights, the sounds, the sonorous music, all redolent of something greater than anything merely human.

Even now, as they strolled among the gaudily coloured buildings, scattering pigeons as they walked, they could hear the clattering of the dazzling prayer wheels, the repetitive chanting of the monks faintly discernible from inside. Beneath the brilliant blue of the sky, it was as if they were somehow connected with a world with more significance than anything found in the hazy shadows of the city spread out below them.

Not that this improved the connection between the two men themselves. They had barely spoken as they made their slow way up the hillside. Doripalam had insisted that Nergui's departure from the hospital should be handled by the book, and Nergui had reluctantly acceded. They had had to wait until the doctor in charge had appeared and then had to spend further time persuading him to release Nergui. He was initially reluctant. He acknowledged that there was nothing seriously wrong with Nergui, but felt that he needed more rest. It was only as it became increasingly obvious that, inside or outside the hospital, rest was the last thing on Nergui's mind that the doctor finally agreed to his departure.

They stopped at the top of the hill, the temple behind them, and looked down at the sprawl of the city.

"So," Doripalam said finally, "are you going to tell me what this is all about?"

"I'm not sure I can tell you what it's *all* about," Nergui said, still staring down at the streets and buildings beneath them.

"And are you sure now that you should?" Doripalam said. "These things are difficult for me to understand, given that I don't normally move in your exalted circles."

Nergui turned and stared at the young man, and then burst out laughing. "Is that what you think this is all about?" he said. "My overinflated sense of my own importance?"

Doripalam shrugged. "As I say, it's difficult for me to judge."

Nergui turned his back on the view below. "Doripalam. I want to talk about Muunokhoi."

"I know all about Muunokhoi," Doripalam said. "He almost cost me my job."

Nergui laughed again. "And you accuse me of having an overinflated sense of my own importance?"

"You put those words in my mouth," Doripalam pointed out. "I didn't say it."

Nergui smiled. "But how much do you really know about Muunokhoi? What do you know of the history?"

"I know you were after him. I know you've been after him for a long time."

"It was that obvious, then?" Nergui said. "Yes, I suppose it was. I've been after him for—what, the best part of two decades. Probably not particularly rational. Except that he's one of the biggest crooks this country's produced."

"Do you know that? I mean," Doripalam said, "are you sure? We've never laid a finger on him. You've never laid a finger on him. He's one of our more respectable citizens. You admit you've not been entirely rational about this."

Nergui was watching a flock of pigeons sweeping softly across the sky, attracted by the scatterings of bread crumbs left by tourists in the heart of the temple. "There's a history to it, of course. Of course there is. And for Tunjin as well."

"Tunjin? What do you know about Tunjin?" Doripalam looked at him sharply.

"It's a long story. But there's history there, too. Tunjin's been after Muunokhoi as long as I have."

"So is that why he pulled that stupid stroke?"

"Trying to forge the evidence against Muunokhoi? Yes, of course. He was getting near the end of his career, running out of chances. He thought it was worth a try."

"That was how he explained it to me," Doripalam said. "I thought he was mad."

"He probably was," Nergui said, smiling faintly. "Or, at least, not entirely rational."

"But you're sure it's true? You're sure that there's a case against Muunokhoi?"

Nergui regarded the young man closely. "You keep asking me that. Have you some reason to question it?"

"You trained me. You'd expect me to challenge you on this. He's one of our more respectable citizens."

"And respectability never goes with criminality?"

Doripalam laughed. "You should know. You're the one who mixes with politicians."

"That's better," Nergui said. "You're finally beginning to sound like the Doripalam I know. You know—" He stopped.

"What?"

"I even thought it might have been you. Just for a moment. I really thought even you might have been one of them."

"One of who?"

Nergui paused and then carried on slowly. "The reason why we have never managed to lay a finger on Muunokhoi is because he has people—I don't know how many people—on the inside."

Doripalam stared at him. "You're the second person today who's implied I'm on Muunokhoi's payroll. I nearly punched the first one."

Nergui shrugged. "He seems to know everything. Why do you think Tunjin's plan failed? Not because it was half-baked. I don't condone what Tunjin did but I have to concede that he did it well. His forgeries were simple but good enough to do the job. He pitched it just right. It should have worked. But it didn't. And the reason it didn't work was that Muunokhoi found out what was going on. Almost immediately."

"And you really think that I—?"

Nergui shook his head. "No. No, of course not. Not really. But we're talking about someone—maybe more than one—who has access to the most sensitive information. When I started the enquiry—"

"So that's what it was all about, the enquiry. Not just cleaning out the stables. You wanted to know how Muunokhoi knew what Tunjin was up to." He paused. "Does that mean you knew about Tunjin's scheme?"

Nergui nodded. "I suppose I can't be too offended about that question, given what I've just said. But, no. I didn't. If I had, I'd have stopped it. But once the whole thing collapsed, it was obvious to me that Muunokhoi knew."

"So you persuaded the Minister to let you head the enquiry to find out how?"

" 'Persuaded' is perhaps a bit strong. But, yes, I did."

Doripalam paused, staring out over the city. There were a few fluffy clouds in the sky now, drifting slowly out towards the rich green of the steppes. "And you investigated me?"

Nergui shrugged. "I investigated everyone. Including you."

"And found nothing, I trust?"

"If you really had been on Muunokhoi's payroll, I'd have found nothing anyway. But, no, I found nothing."

"So why don't you think I am? On Muunokhoi's payroll, I mean."

Nergui shrugged. "I'm a policeman," he said. "I trust my instincts. Don't you?"

"Not as much as I should, probably," Doripalam said. "But, okay, you trust me, and I suppose I should be flattered, though I'm not sure that's exactly how I feel at the moment. But where does that get us? What's this all about?"

"It gets us into an almighty mess," Nergui said. "We've still got nothing on Muunokhoi. Sarangarel—Judge Radnaa—has been abducted. Tunjin is missing. And we don't have a clue how any of this fits together."

"And Mrs. Tuya was brutally murdered," Doripalam said. "And her family are terrified."

Nergui had been watching the slow movement of a freight train through the centre of the city. Now he turned back to look at Doripalam. "What do you mean?" he said. "What does that have to do with Muunokhoi?"

"I don't know. Possibly nothing. But I somehow made the link in my mind as you were talking. Maybe I'm finally trusting my instinct. Anyway, you remember the story. Gavaa had moved to the city. Boasted he'd got some impressive job, but nobody knew what. Then he went missing. And then we found his mother's body—"

"And you think this might somehow be connected with Muunokhoi?" They had turned back towards the temple now, and were walking back down towards the cluster of buildings. A line of orange-clad monks emerged from the temple and walked slowly ahead of them. The rows of prayer wheels glittered and clattered in the early evening sunshine.

Doripalam shrugged. "It wasn't a connection I'd made till just now. I had a sudden image in my mind of the mother's mutilated body." He paused. "I've heard all the stories about Muunokhoi and what he's capable of. Those four terrified men up in the mountains—"

Nergui nodded. "Did you get anything out of them?"

"I sent someone up there, but they clammed up, apparently. Nothing at all. Nothing to add to what they told me."

Nergui nodded. "It may depend on who you sent."

Doripalam turned and looked at him. "Did your enquiry give you any idea who we can trust? Or who we can't?"

"No. I've identified one or two junior officers who I'm pretty sure are on the take, but even there it's hard to find real evidence. But among the senior officers—no. I wouldn't even want to guess."

Doripalam stopped walking. They were looking out over Nairamdal Park, where Nergui had held his midnight meeting with Tunjin. "You really think it's that serious?" Doripalam said. "You really think we've been infiltrated that deeply?"

"I'm sure of it," Nergui said. "Muunokhoi does what he likes." He paused. "But there's something else happening here. We've never got close to Muunokhoi before, never got anywhere near to laying a finger on him, other than Tunjin's doomed effort. And Muunokhoi's never needed to get his hands dirty. And yet now—"

"What?"

"Now we have Tunjin missing, on the run from Muunokhoi—"

"How do you know he's on the run?" Doripalam was watching the older man closely, realising that as always he was several steps ahead in his thinking, already playing with thoughts that Doripalam had not yet begun to conceive.

"He called me," Nergui said. "I met him. Here." He gestured out towards the green sweep of the parkland, the distant blue sliver of the lake. "The night before last."

"But why didn't you say? Why didn't you do something?"

Nergui looked back at Doripalam. "What should I have done? I did not—do not—know who to trust. I could not even offer Tunjin the protection of the police. Think of that."

"But he's safe?"

"For the moment. Tunjin is no fool, despite appearances. He can look after himself."

"I hope so," Doripalam said. "I wouldn't wish to be on the wrong side of Muunokhoi."

They had resumed walking, making their way down from the Monastery grounds out towards the park. "But why is this happening?" Nergui said. "Why is Muunokhoi risking playing his hand? Why is he bothering to pursue Tunjin? Why has he had Sarangarel abducted?"

"You don't know for sure that he has," Doripalam said. "I mean, you don't know for sure that Muunokhoi is behind this."

"I know," Nergui said. His voice, as always, carried an absolute authority. "And I think you're right. That he was also behind the murder of Mrs. Tuya. And quite possibly behind the disappearance of her son. But why are these things happening? This is not Muunokhoi. This is not his way of working."

"Maybe it's not Muunokhoi," Doripalam suggested. "Maybe it's—I don't know—maybe someone in his organisation. Some loose cannon. Taking things into his own hands."

"I don't think so," Nergui said. "That wouldn't be Muunokhoi's way of working either. It might happen once—perhaps an overenthusiastic servant. But it would not happen twice." He paused. "There is something wrong here. We need to find Sarangarel. Quickly."

"That won't be easy," Doripalam said. "Even assuming you're right, and Muunokhoi is behind this—" He raised his hand to cut off the older man's objections. "I'm not disagreeing with you. But we have no evidence. Muunokhoi is an important man. We can't simply have him arrested. We can't even go and search his property, unless we have a far more substantive reason than anything that's emerged so far."

"There are things we can do—"

"I know, and I've already set them in motion while you were negotiating your way out of the hospital. I've got surveillance on all of Muunokhoi's houses and business premises. I've got Muunokhoi himself under surveillance. And of course I've set all the standard processes in place to try to find Mrs. Radnaa. The kidnapping of a judge would still be a serious offence even if she wasn't a friend of yours."

Nergui nodded, accepting the mild rebuke as justified. "Of course," he said. "You know your job."

"But you're worried."

"I'm worried. And if you've set all this in motion, then Muunokhoi will already know we're after him."

Doripalam shrugged. "There was no way of avoiding that," he said, "if your suspicions about infiltration are correct."

"And it may not be a bad thing. There is something happening here. Perhaps Muunokhoi will feel the pressure."

"Perhaps," Doripalam said, "but I do not think we should place much faith in that possibility."

They had entered the park now, the children's play area ahead of them. In the late afternoon the park was crowded with families, teenagers eating ice cream, old men in traditional robes talking the day away.

Nergui stopped walking and looked at Doripalam as though a thought had just struck him. "What happened to Mrs. Tuya's family?"

Doripalam looked at him. "What do you mean?"

"You spoke about the four men. Up in the mountains. Afraid they were being chased. What happened to them?"

"They—" Doripalam stopped, his mind suddenly pursuing the train of thought that Nergui had presumably already followed. "I left them up there. Told the local police to keep them under surveillance. Give them any necessary protection. But I didn't really think—"

"That they needed it?"

Doripalam hesitated. "No. I mean, they were clearly afraid. But I couldn't see why anyone would want to pursue them. Even given Mrs. Tuya's murder. They had nothing that anyone might want—"

"Except that we don't know that," Nergui said. "We don't know anything."

"And if you're right," Doripalam said, "by offering them police protection, I might have sentenced them to death."

Nergui shook his head. "We don't know that," he said. "But we can't take anything for granted." He stood silently for a moment, watching the carefree crowds spreading out across the green of the park. "We can't trust anyone."

Doripalam nodded and took out his mobile phone. He flicked through the saved numbers and dialled the direct line for Tsend, the police chief up in Bulgan. He found himself redirected through to a secretary.

"I'm sorry," she said. "He's tied up in meetings all day. I can take a message."

"Tell him it's Doripalam of the Serious Crimes Team. Ask him to call me back urgently." The tone was more peremptory than usual for Doripalam, but he had little expectation that Tsend would return his call quickly.

He ended the call, looked at Nergui and shrugged. "I'm not sure how far I'm going to get through official channels," he said. "Tsend was hardly cooperative when I was up there before. I assumed it was the usual cynicism about visitors from the capital, but who knows?" He began to flick through the saved numbers again. "There's one other route I can try."

He dialled the number for the local station where Yadamsuren, the outstationed officer, was located and, after a few moments, succeeded in being put through.

"It's Doripalam," he said. "From the Serious Crimes Team. You remember?"

"I'm not likely to forget quickly," Yadamsuren said. "My shoulder's still sore."

"I've been trying to get through to the main station in Bulgan," Doripalam said, "but I can't raise anyone who might be able to give me any information. I just wanted to know what happened to our four nomads. They're still around, I take it?"

There was a long silence at the other end of the line, so that Doripalam began to think that the signal had been lost.

"I don't really know," Yadamsuren said, finally. "I've not really had any contact since it all happened."

There was something in Yadamsuren's voice that made Doripalam uneasy. "What about their *gers?*" he said. "Have they been back there?"

There was another pause, less extended, but somehow more freighted with meaning than the previous one. "No," Yadamsuren said. "I've not seen them here. The *gers* are still there—" There was a hesitation. "Some of the officers from Bulgan came out," he said. "They conducted some sort of search through the tents."

"A search?" Doripalam said, looking up at Nergui. "For what?" He had, he thought, made it very clear that this was a Serious Crimes case. The local brief was simply to provide protection, not to get involved in any kind of investigation.

"I don't know," Yadamsuren said. "They didn't give me any kind of explanation. Well, there was no reason why they should. I mean, I assumed—well, I assumed that it was your people behind it."

"What did they say?"

"Well, not much. They told me that I should just keep an eye on the *gers* until they were dismantled. And to find someone to look after the animals, temporarily."

"When the nomads returned, you mean?"

"Well, that wasn't very clear. I had the impression it would be the police who would do it. Presumably just to keep the tents safe. I assumed that the nomads were under protection of some sort."

"They are," Doripalam said, deciding that there was no point in raising Yadamsuren's interest further. There was no reason to suspect Yadamsuren, but any information could potentially get back to those who were perhaps less trustworthy. "Just seems to be a bit of confusion, that's all. That's why I've been trying to find out what's going on. Thanks for your help."

He ended the call. Nergui was watching him closely, having apparently followed the gist of the conversation.

"I think we need a trip to the mountains," Nergui said.

Doripalam nodded. "I'll go," he said. "You need to be here. In case there are any developments on the kidnapping."

Nergui shrugged. "There is nothing I can do here except worry. It is better that I'm taking some action." He paused, still scrutinising Doripalam closely. For a moment, Doripalam wondered whether Nergui really did trust him, or whether he was reluctant to allow the younger man to make the trip on his own. But he also knew that Nergui, ever the pragmatist, was right. There was little they could do here for the moment, except make sure that the usual investigatory processes were in place.

"And if you're right," Nergui went on, displaying his usual uncanny ability apparently to follow Doripalam's train of thought, "if there is some link between Muunokhoi and the Tuya murder, then perhaps this is another thread we can begin to pull. Let us hope that something of this begins to unravel before it's too late."

NINETEEN

"Well," the voice said, "it's always pleasing to welcome an unexpected visitor."

The tone was surprisingly relaxed in the circumstances. After all, even Tunjin had to acknowledge that he did not, just at the moment, present the most prepossessing sight. His usual shambling overweight figure was clad in a T-shirt and trousers which were quite clearly showing the impact of his brief period of living rough. His always-greasy hair was matted down on his head. And, on top of all that, he was covered in grass and bruises from his tumble down the hill.

He might have expected a rather less calm response from the man facing him. On the other hand, he also had to recognise that the man in question was holding a handgun, pointed unerringly at Tunjin's heart. Perhaps the man could afford to be relaxed.

Tunjin looked behind him at the broken fence, wondering precisely what kind of explanation he might offer for his presence. "Um, I'm sorry," he said. "I slipped." It didn't sound particularly appropriate.

The man was dressed in a plain dark suit, with a pale grey tie. He was Mongolian, but otherwise had few obviously distinguishing features. His hair was slicked back and he wore a pair of mirrored sun glasses, providing Tunjin with a disconcerting convex view of his own disarray. Tunjin noted irrelevantly that the effect of the curved mirrors did little to flatter his already obese figure.

The man, unsurprisingly, ignored Tunjin's offer of an explanation, and instead gestured with the barrel of the gun. "I think you had better come this way," he said. "So that we can welcome you properly."

Tunjin walked forward in the direction indicated by the gun barrel. The house was ahead of them, a rear door open in the spring sunshine. Tunjin hesitated, wondering if he should enter.

"Keep going," the man said. "Inside."

Tunjin nodded, noting that the man's voice had become less welcoming. Tunjin found this oddly reassuring. At least, that was closer to what he understood.

He followed the path towards the door, glancing momentarily around at the tidiness of the garden. The grass was well-trimmed, the conifers neatly pruned. It hardly looked organic, he thought. It was as if someone had sculpted it from stone or wax. Even the colours seemed too bright.

"Inside," the man said, again. His tone was definitely less friendly now, almost aggressive. Tunjin obeyed, and stepped through the doorway into the gloomy interior.

He wasn't sure what to expect beyond the door. Perhaps a hallway, or a kitchen. Instead, though, he found himself in a blank, empty room, probably originally intended as a scullery or cloakroom. Tunjin stopped, hearing the footsteps of the man with the gun behind him.

"Turn round," the man said.

Tunjin turned, taking the opportunity to look around the room. There was little to see. The room was painted grey, with a floor of heavy stone tiles. There was no window, and the only light came through the door by which they had entered. There was a another door at the far end of the room, a solid-looking wooden edifice which appeared to be closed and, perhaps, locked. There was no furniture, and no decoration on the walls. Even as an entrance hall, the room looked bizarrely bleak and inhospitable.

The man reached behind him and pressed the light switch. Tunjin glanced up. There was a single bare lightbulb, which gave a harsh glare that served only to expose the asceticism of the room. The man smiled thinly, and then reached behind him to pull closed the outer door. It was a duplicate of the interior door—just as solid, just as impenetrable. It slammed shut with a dull thud, and the man carefully turned a large key in the lock. Still smiling, he slipped the key into his trouser pocket.

"There," he said, "now we're secure." He was still smiling, but there was no warmth to the smile. It was as if the expression was a mask, painted on his face.

He walked forward slowly, still holding the gun pointed steadily at Tunjin's chest. For the first time—as though, up to that point, he had somehow managed to resist the evidence of his own eyes—Tunjin realised that his predicament was serious. He was in trouble. Deep trouble. And he had walked—or, more accurately, fallen—into it entirely of his own volition.

The sun was setting behind them, staining the western sky a deep crimson. Blood, Nergui thought. It does really look like blood. It was as if a tide of blood was pouring down on the city. As if chaos really had arrived. As if all control was lost.

"I'm getting old," he said to Doripalam, sitting beside him. "I'm getting melodramatic. Sentimental."

Doripalam laughed. He was leaning forward, concentrating on the road. He wondered whether they should have brought another officer, someone who could at least have done the driving. Luvsan, for example. He loved this kind of trip. Loved the buzz of driving these new 4x4s up onto the steppe. But Nergui had insisted they make this trip alone.

"I look forward to the day when you're sentimental," he said. He paused, wondering whether to point out that, to take just one instance, Nergui had preferred to make this trip to the mountains rather than to stay in the city and wait for news of Sarangarel. It was a rational decision—of course it was, there was little that Nergui could do in the city—but it was not one that many men would have taken in the circumstances. But perhaps that thought was better kept to himself. "Melodramatic," he went on, "perhaps, yes, I can see that. But you've always been that. It's nothing to do with growing old."

Nergui grunted, although it was unclear whether this sound represented assent. "It's as if," he said, after an extended pause, "as if we lost control a long time ago, but didn't know it. As if everything had spiralled out of our grip, and now we're flailing around trying to hold on to something—"

"Yes, melodramatic," Doripalam nodded, his hands gripping the steering wheel. The empty road stretched ahead of them. In the distance, they could see the mountains, a dark strip against the translucent mauve of the evening sky. "That's definitely the right word." The truck hummed beneath them, echoing the repetitive pounding of the road. "It's strange, though, isn't it?" Doripalam went on. "Okay, if you're right, things have been out of our control for a long time. Or, at least, we've had nothing like as much control as we thought. But maybe that didn't matter too much—"

Nergui snorted—a sound which somehow managed with absolute eloquence to express his disgust. "How can you say that?" he said, staring out of the passenger window at the hypnotic passing of the landscape. "You see why I was suspicious of you?"

Doripalam sighed. "You understand my point," he said, "even if you choose to misinterpret it. If Muunokhoi really had infiltrated the police to the extent you suggest—"

Nergui turned his head slowly towards Doripalam. "There is no question," he said. "Muunokhoi had—has—infiltrated the police to the extent I suggest. If not more."

"But my point is," Doripalam said, "that even if that is true—I'm sorry, yes, I accept it, I know that it is true—Muunokhoi was simply protecting his own interests. He may have constrained our work—or, at least, made sure that we didn't constrain his work too much—but he wasn't concerned to disrupt our work generally. We were able to police serious crime—"

"So long as it was serious crime not perpetrated by Muunokhoi," Nergui pointed out.

"I'm not trying to excuse or justify it," Doripalam said. "I'm not—I'll keep repeating this till I'm absolutely sure you believe me—I'm not on Muunokhoi's payroll. I'm saying only that—well, it was a controlled situation. It was an explicable situation. It might even—I shouldn't say this—it might even have been a manageable situation." He paused, still watching the curves of the road. "But now things have changed."

Nergui looked across at him, nodding slowly. He smiled faintly. "You're right," he said. "Of course you're right. You're always right."

"I thought that was your prerogative," Doripalam said, barely able to contain the edge of smugness in his voice. It was strange how, even now, after all this time, and despite his own seniority, their relationship remained that of master and pupil.

Nergui smiled. "Not now," he said. "Not at all now. I think I have not been right for a long time. Not in this matter. But, yes, on this occasion, you are certainly right. Things have changed. But I don't know why."

Doripalam clutched the wheel. "That's the point, isn't it?" he said. "Whatever the situation before, it was rational. It was possible for us to respond to it. We could handle it."

"And now we don't know what's happening," Nergui said. "We have a brutal murder—perhaps, though let us hope not, more then one. We have kidnapping—certainly one, perhaps more. We don't know about Gavaa. We don't even know now about Tunjin." He paused. "They may have caught up with him," he said, finally.

Tunjin had been expecting it, at least in theory. Nevertheless, when the blow came, it took him by surprise. The man moved suddenly, an unexpected jerking motion, the gun barrel abruptly raised, then thrust across his face.

The metal barrel was cold and hard against his flesh. Tunjin fell backward, gasping for breath, startled less by the pain than by the suddenness of the action. The pain was slow in coming, but when it came it was sharp and agonising. He staggered backwards, trying to suppress a scream, and then his own substantial weight dragged him off his feet, and he fell backwards on to the floor.

He floundered for a moment, rolling around on the cold stone like a turtle toppled on to its shell. The man moved forward, the harsh light of the bare light-bulb glittering on the mirrored lenses of his sunglasses. He drew back his foot and kicked savagely out at Tunjin's ribs. Tunjin rolled, avoiding the worst of the blow, which glanced across his shoulders. The man struck out again, forcing Tunjin back against the wall, this time absorbing the kick painfully against his stomach.

Tunjin gasped for breath, cowering back in expectation of the next blow. But the man paused, holding the gun barrel steadily towards Tunjin. "Now," he said, "perhaps you will tell me the truth. I have to confess that, after your unexpected disappearance, we were not expecting to encounter you again so soon."

Tunjin rolled over, still cowering against the wall, and stared at the man. It was difficult not to imagine that Muunokhoi had some powers that were more than merely human. He had managed—through who knew what kind of inside information—to see through Tunjin's half-baked attempt to frame him. He had managed to identify Tunjin as the perpetrator of this idiotic scheme, almost before he'd had time to admit his guilt to Doripalam. And, now, when Tunjin had harboured vain hopes of taking him at least momentarily by surprise, this operative had recognised him almost straightaway. How was that possible? If the explanation was not supernatural, he could assume only that his picture—the policeman who had dared to threaten Muunokhoi with prison—was hanging up as a dire warning all around Muunokhoi's properties. The thought was not comforting.

"You look surprised," the man said, echoing Tunjin's own thoughts. "You should not be. We have a very good memory in this organisation. And good communications. It is helpful of you to have made yourself available so readily, but you would not have escaped us for long."

The man smiled, the smile all the more terrifying for the blankness of his mirrored gaze. "Though I confess I do not understand why you have chosen to come here. You are clearly more accommodating than we imagined."

Tunjin said nothing, staring up at the towering figure of the man. Even if he had wanted to, he did not think that he could have provided any coherent explanation. Like so much of his life, it had seemed a good idea at the time.

The only question now was what would happen to him. He

could not believe that Muunokhoi's people had in mind to furnish him with a simple clean death. There would be more to come.

Again, with almost telepathic precision, the man echoed his thoughts. "So," he said, "what are we going to do with you? There is nothing complicated about this. You know what you've done. You know what is likely to happen to you." He paused, the smile, like the gun barrel, unwavering. "For my part, I am curious to know what prompted you to come here. I am not sure whether to admire your courage or despise your stupidity. Quite possibly both, I suspect."

Tunjin couldn't really argue with this judgement, which largely replicated his own. In any case, he was hardly in a position, or a state, to offer any kind of meaningful response. There was a part of him that hoped that, if he just kept still—if, for once, he just kept his mouth shut—he might still be allowed out of all this.

"You don't seem to have a lot to say," the man observed. "Perhaps I should offer some encouragement." He stepped forward, and aimed another kick at Tunjin. Tunjin wrapped his arms around himself, pressed into the corner of the room, awaiting the blow.

Even so, its ferocity took him by surprise. He rolled just in time, taking the force of the impact on his arm. The blow was agonising. It felt as though his arm was broken. It was fortunate that the kick had not hit him in a more vulnerable part of his body, though for the moment that seemed little consolation.

"Now, do you feel encouraged?" the man said. "Would you like to be a little more talkative?"

In truth, Tunjin felt precisely the opposite, though he suspected that this would not be a welcome response. He gasped, trying to grunt out some kind of answer, some words that might at least momentarily stay any further violence.

"I'm sorry," the man said. "I'm having difficulty following you. Perhaps you need a little more prompting."

He stepped back, lifting his foot, preparing to aim another kick at Tunjin. Tunjin twisted awkwardly, feeling the agonising pain from his arm, the underlying pattern of bruising from the previous assaults and from his tumble down the hillside. This, he realised, was simply going to continue. Blow after blow. Kick after kick. Pain following pain, until he could bear it no longer. With any luck unconsciousness would follow, but he imagined the man would keep him awake for as long as he could. And then at that point he might introduce some more imaginative form of torture.

Afterwards, he remembered seeing the man raise his foot. He remembered tensing, his body poised for the impact. And he remembered somehow twisting suddenly, his body moving purely through instinct, his legs moving with an agility unexpected for someone of his bulk.

It was as if, up to that point, Tunjin's streetwise skills—the instincts that had enabled him to survive through thirty years of hard policing—had deserted him, as if he had suddenly become a victim. And then, just as unexpectedly, all those instincts, all that unconscious savvy, suddenly returned.

His movement clearly took the man by surprise. Tunjin spun over, ignoring the agonising pains coursing through his body, and hooked his foot behind the man's leg. The man had been in the process of kicking, one foot raised, the other anchored to the floor. Tunjin dragged his foot around the latter, pulling the man off balance. Caught by surprise, the man staggered, toppling backwards. Tunjin took his momentary advantage and kicked out with his other foot, hitting the man at the top of his thigh. Then he kicked again, savagely, as the man fell, aiming for the groin.

The effect was better than he might have dared hope. The

man fell, his arms flailing, his pistol clattering into the far corner of the room. He staggered backwards, trying desperately to regain his balance, slipping on the smooth flagstones, and then finally fell, his head hitting the solid stone floor with an appalling thud.

There was a long silence. Tunjin lay, gasping for breath, waiting for the man to sit up, to resume or increase his assault. But nothing happened. The man lay motionless, apparently unconscious.

Tunjin sat up, wondering what to do next. He clambered on to his hands and knees, his breath still coming in agonising bursts.

There was blood spreading from the man's head, seeping out from beneath the splayed skull. The stain, crimson as the spring sunset across the steppe, expanded slowly across the grey stone, stark against the unrelenting flags.

TWENTY

It was like another world, Nergui thought. Like an alien planet.

He always felt like this, away from the city. He was an urban creature, a creature of the twenty-first century. For all its faults, for all its shortcomings, the capital was part of the modern world, part of everything he associated with the West.

Nergui was hardly typical of his countrymen. Indeed, he was probably close to unique here. He had travelled widely in the West. He had lived in the US. He had lived in Europe. He was able to compare all this—everything his fellow citizens took for granted—with something different.

Not necessarily something better. He was no apologist for the West. He recognised, and was happy to acknowledge, its shortcomings. It was a godless place, he thought, a faithless place, with an emptiness at its heart. It was—ironically, given the nomadic culture of this place—a rootless civilisation. Here, for all the privations and suppression of the communist era, something spiritual had survived, some sense of contact with the land, the past, community and family.

But, out here, out in these rural spaces, it was difficult to feel that. They had driven through mile after mile of empty grassland, the rolling plains abolishing all sense of distance, as though this landscape might simply continue forever. In the clear spring evening, they saw no other vehicles, no other sign of life. Ahead, there was the dark shadow of the mountains, sharp against the crystalline sky. And before that they could see the black shading of the forests, though the shapes of the trees were too far away to discern.

Eventually, they saw the small scattering of hazy lights that revealed the presence of Bulgan in the distance. From here, it looked like a solitary beacon in the fading light, a single indication that human life had not abandoned this landscape.

It was another forty minutes or so before they reached the outskirts of the town. The woodland had thickened around them as they drove, and they began to see a scattering of log cabins and other buildings.

"Where's the place we're looking for?" Nergui said.

Doripalam turned. "The camp. Just a few miles north of Bulgan. I hope I can find it again."

"Assuming that the *gers* are still there."

"Yadamsuren said the tents were still there yesterday. He's obeyed his orders and not gone near them, but he's been keeping an eye on them from a distance."

"Assiduous of him," Nergui commented.

"He's a good officer," Doripalam said. "We could use more like him in the team. He's wasted up here. Perhaps worse than wasted."

Doripalam had wondered whether to make another effort to contact Tsend, to see whether he could glean anything more about what had happened to Mrs. Tuya's family. But, despite the supposed urgency of the message Doripalam had left, Tsend had not so far returned his call. In the circumstances, they had to proceed with caution. If Tsend's behaviour was suspect, there was little point in giving him any further warning that they were heading up here.

"You should make him an offer," Nergui said. "See if you can tempt him into the big bad city."

"I don't know whether he'd want to go."

Nergui looked out of the truck window. They were passing through the centre of Bulgan. Even though it was the *aimag* capital, in the evening it looked like a ghost town. The streets were largely deserted, other than the occasional knot of bored-looking teenagers drifting aimlessly through the central square. There were a few parked cars, but little traffic. "If I was in his position," Nergui said, "I'd go tomorrow."

"With respect," Doripalam said, "I'm not sure your views are representative."

They passed through the town, and the buildings began to thin out again as they headed north into the forests. Once the city was behind them, Doripalam slowed, keeping alert for the turnoff to where the *gers* were situated. It was dark now, and there was little to distinguish any part of the tree-lined road in the sweeping glare of their headlights.

At first, he thought he had missed it. Then, finally, when he was convinced they had gone too far, he spotted the angled track leading off the metalled road up towards the trees.

He slowed right down. "There it is."

"I'm impressed," Nergui said. "It looks just the same as the last four or five miles of forest to me."

Doripalam turned the truck so that the headlight beams shone up through the trees, illuminating the rough track. "No, that's it, I'm sure."

"Where was the camp?"

"Over the hill. There's a kind of hollow beyond that. The tents are well concealed. You can see nothing at all from the road. You wouldn't know they were there unless you went looking for them."

"Or unless someone had told you they were there," Nergui said.

Doripalam nodded grimly. "That's what worries me," he said.

The two men emerged from the truck and stood for a moment breathing in the clear woodland air. It had been a warm day and the evening air was still temperate, rich with the scent of the pine trees. Other than the occasional rustling of the trees, the silence was complete.

Doripalam flicked on his flashlight and shone it up the path. "This way," he said. "It's not far."

He began to walk slowly up the incline, mindful of his last visit here—the pouring rain, the unexpected gunshots, the fear in the eyes of the four men. In the soft warmth of the night, it was hard to believe this was the same place.

They reached the top of the hill and stared down into the hollow beyond. There were no lights other than the flickering beam of the flashlight and for a moment Doripalam thought that the *gers* had gone. Then he shone the beam a little farther back and found the grey shape of the foremost tent.

"There they are," he said. "Still there."

Nergui moved beside him and nodded. "No sign of life, though," he said.

"I hope that's all it is, though," Doripalam said. "An absence of life rather than the presence of death."

Nergui glanced at him, seeing the silhouette of Doripalam's face. "You're getting philosophical," he said. "Maybe you've been on the job too long."

Doripalam said nothing, but began to make his way slowly down into the hollow, approaching the door of the first *ger.* He shone the flashlight carefully along the wall of the tent. The two other *gers* stood behind, as silent and dark as the first.

Doripalam reached out and pulled open the ornate wooden door. It was not locked and swung open easily to his touch. Beyond the door, there was only blackness. Doripalam stepped forward and shone his light into the interior, recalling the similar search he had conducted with Luvsan in Mrs. Tuya's *ger.*

It was immediately clear that the tent was empty. The interior had a slightly stale smell, with an undertone of soured milk—maybe someone had spilt some *airag*. But there was nothing more unpleasant than that. Doripalam shone the flashlight around the enclosed space.

"Looks as if they conducted a pretty thorough search," he commented. All the cupboards were pulled open, clothes and personal goods scattered across the floors. The bed had been pulled out, and the coverings torn from it. Drawers lay upended on the floor. Various containers—jars, tins, bottles—that had contained dried foodstuffs had been emptied with no concern for their contents.

"They were policemen," Nergui said. "Professionals. What would you expect?"

"The question is," Doripalam said, "did they find what they were looking for?"

"If they did," Nergui said, "they clearly didn't find it quickly. Let's have a look in the other *gers.*"

They stepped back out into the night. The sky was clear above them, studded with stars. There was a yellow moon rising over the horizon, enormous and swollen. They made their way around to the remaining two gers and systematically entered each one, looking carefully around at the contents. All of the *gers* were in the same state, clearly resulting from a painstaking search of their interiors.

"They've made no attempt to clear them up," Nergui said. "Just left them as they were."

"Which is a serious dereliction of their duty," Doripalam smiled grimly. "But more importantly—"

"Suggests that they didn't have a high expectation that the owners would be returning to the tents anytime soon."

"So what's happened to them?"

"Perhaps we do now need a conversation with your friend, Tsend," Nergui said. "It will be interesting at least to hear what story he comes up with."

Doripalam nodded and pulled out his mobile. He dialled the number of the station in Bulgan. After a couple of rings, the call was answered, clearly by a desk officer on night duty.

"I need to speak to your Chief," Doripalam said. "Yes, I do know what time it is. I wasn't aware the police up here ran an office-hours only service. No, it is urgent. This is Doripalam, Head of the Serious Crimes Team in Ulan Baatar. I'm up here in your territory. I left an urgent message for your Chief earlier this afternoon, but he hasn't deigned to call me back. Now, I'm standing out in the night at what may be a crime scene and I need to speak to him. Immediately. And, no, I don't care what your orders are. I'm standing here with Nergui, representing the Ministry of Security, and I don't think either of us will be very pleased if we don't receive a response in the next—well, shall we say the next two minutes? Yes, you do that."

He ended the call and looked back at Nergui. "Tsend will call back immediately."

Nergui raised an eyebrow. "Let us hope so. We Ministry types do not like to be kept waiting."

As if in response to his sardonic comment, the mobile rang

immediately. Doripalam smiled faintly and answered the call. "Very good of you to call back," he said. "No, I wouldn't dream of it. But I think you may very well be risking wasting ours." He went on, his voice rising, clearly overriding whatever Tsend was saying at the other end of the phone. "No—frankly, I don't care what you think about my behaviour. You can complain to whoever you like. I'm sure my colleague from the Ministry will be only too pleased to expedite your complaint. In the meantime, I'd like to know why my orders have been disregarded."

There was a moment's silence, which clearly extended also to Tsend at the other end of the phone.

"I left four men in your custody," Doripalam went on. "Potential material witnesses in a murder case. In need of police protection, which I asked you to provide. I also made it very clear that this was a Serious Crimes case which fell outside your local jurisdiction." He paused, waiting to see if Tsend made any response, but the silence at the far end of the line continued. "I'm now standing at the site of the men's camp. And I discover that their tents have been thoroughly searched, apparently by your men. I would be very interested to know why. I am also concerned to know where the men are now."

Again, there was no response. Doripalam had almost begun to wonder if Tsend had hung up, though he thought he could hear the other man's breathing. He stopped speaking himself, determined to offer no further prompt.

Finally, Tsend spoke, sounding almost out of breath. "The men left," he said. "We couldn't hold them. They were not under arrest, you made that very clear. We could not hold them against their will."

"And why were they suddenly so keen to leave?" Doripalam said. "They were desperate for protection."

"I do not know." There was another prolonged pause. "We had organised some accommodation for them. A safe house. I was about to contact you to seek further orders—" There was an implied reproach in Tsend's tone which Doripalam knew was at least partially justified. He had not followed up the men's situation as he should have done. Things had moved too quickly since then, but that was no excuse. "But then, overnight, they vanished. I do not know why. That was why I sent my men out to check their camp. To see if the tents had been removed. To see if there was any clue where they might have gone." There was another slight hesitation and then Tsend continued, more confident now. "I thought that you would want me to have all the facts before I advised you of the situation."

It sounded plausible enough, if you accepted the suggestion that the four men had simply disappeared. It would not have been surprising if this local police chief had wanted to be pretty sure of his ground before he reported back on the situation. Maybe that was why he had taken so long to return Doripalam's call. On the other hand, this still did not explain why the men had suddenly chosen to leave.

"And you've no idea why they left? Or where?"

"None at all," Tsend said. "But then I had little knowledge about the significance of these individuals in the first place. This was, of course, a Serious Crimes matter." He was sounding much more confident now, Doripalam thought, having negotiated his way successfully through this discussion. It was even possible that Tsend's role in this was entirely innocent. If the nomads had felt under threat from within the police service—or, even worse, if anything had actually happened to them—then the culprits might well sit at more junior levels. And maybe this was all just paranoia, another Muunokhoi-inspired ghost.

"As you say," Doripalam acknowledged. "But these people are important witnesses—even more important now, perhaps, than we originally thought. We need to have them found. I want to put as much resource as you can on this."

There was only the briefest grudging pause before Tsend said, "Yes, of course. My men are already on to it. But I will treat it as a priority."

"I would be very grateful," Doripalam said, trying hard to keep any edge of irony out of his voice. "I'm sorry for disturbing your evening."

"No problem. As I said, I am always pleased to assist the Serious Crimes Team." Tsend made less effort to moderate his tone. "Goodnight."

Doripalam stood for a moment, looking at the silent phone. He looked up at Nergui through the darkness and repeated the gist of the conversation.

Nergui shrugged. "As you say, it sounds convincing enough. But it does not explain why the men suddenly decided that police protection was not for them."

"We have to assume that they did not feel sufficiently protected."

"Either that," Nergui said, "or they learned that from experience."

Doripalam nodded grimly. "Let us hope not," he said. "Let us hope that their departure was voluntary."

Nergui took some steps forward into the thickening darkness and peered at the cluster of *gers*. "Do you think there is anything more for us to learn here?"

"Probably not," Doripalam said. "If there was anything here, I'm sure the locals would have found it. They searched the place pretty thoroughly."

"All the same," Nergui said, "I'm reluctant to leave the hunt for our friends solely to the local force."

"I'm not sure we have much option," Doripalam said. "We've little chance of making progress here on our own."

As if not listening, Nergui switched on his own flashlight and began to walk slowly around the *gers*, his eyes fixed on the ground as if searching for some discarded item. Through the trees, the moon had risen higher, casting pale light across the steppe.

"Nergui," Doripalam said. "I don't think—"

Nergui raised his hand, as if silencing Doripalam. He was little more than a silhouette against the paler star-filled sky, the torchlight jumping in his hand. For a moment, Doripalam lost sight of him as he disappeared behind the *gers*. He reappeared unexpectedly, shining the torch directly at Doripalam. "There is something," he said, his voice little more than a whisper, "something not quite right here."

"What do you mean?" Doripalam said.

"If the local police really are looking for these men," Nergui said, "surely they would have kept this place under observation. If the men really are missing, surely there is a good chance they will return, if only to collect their possessions."

"Maybe not. There are lots of possibilities. If they're as scared as we think, then they might well think it's not worth coming back here, regardless of what they've left behind." Doripalam paused. "And of course it's possible that they're not simply missing. That they're in no position to return anywhere. And, on top of all that, you're assuming that Tsend was telling the truth about having started looking for them."

"You're right, of course," Nergui said. "But I think he would have—at least to the extent of staking out this place. It doesn't make any sense that he would have sent his people out to search the place and then just left it."

"Unless he knew that they were never going to return."

"Of course, but—even if we assume that Tsend is involved in all this—unless we assume the whole force is corrupt, he'd want to go through the motions if only so it would look convincing to you."

Doripalam nodded, unsure of the logic of all this. "But in any case," he said, "how do you know the place isn't being staked out?" He looked around uncomfortably. "We could be being watched."

"We could," Nergui said. "But if he saw two men hanging around here, wouldn't he have called for backup by now? And either backup would be on its way or—if he managed to get hold of Tsend—he'd know who we are and come out to introduce himself." Doripalam could just make out Nergui's dark face in the moonlight. He seemed to be smiling. As so often with Nergui, Doripalam was wondering both how seriously to take all this and—at the same time—quite where it might all be leading.

"I don't know," Doripalam admitted. "I'm not sure I have quite your faith in the rationality of other people's thought processes."

"The thing is," Nergui said, "I know that the place was being staked out. Until quite recently."

Doripalam looked up sharply at Nergui. "What do you mean?"

"I'm sorry," Nergui said. "I have just been trying to work out the logic in my own mind."

"What logic?"

Nergui had begun to wander back around the tents, gesturing Doripalam to follow him into the dark shadow of the trees.

"The logic," Nergui said, "of precisely who this is and how he came to be here."

He shone his torch, with a vaguely melodramatic action, into the darkness. But there was no need for any further melodrama. Lying on the rough grass, his head twisted awkwardly towards the sky, blank eyes glittering in the thin moonlight, was a dead man. And not just any dead man, but a police officer, his uniform dark with his own recently shed blood.

* * *

Sarangarel was staring out of the window. There had been some commotion out in the garden, just a few minutes before, but she had been unclear about its significance. Someone—one of the staff, she assumed, one of the heavies—had run across the pristine lawn, a startled expression on his face. She had seen that, as he ran, he had been pulling out a handgun, so she assumed that this interlude, whatever it might be, had not been planned.

But, sadly, she had lost sight of him after that. He had run briefly past the window, a determined expression on his face, his eyes lost behind mirrored sunglasses that momentarily caught the glare of the late evening sun. Then he was gone, and she was left to wonder what had happened and what this might portend for her position here.

She was unclear precisely what that might be. But she was at least clear that the short man, the man who had questioned her, had been unhappy with her responses. It was clear that she had not given him what he wanted, what he had expected. It was clear that these people, whoever they might be, thought she had something, some information. And perhaps she did. Perhaps she knew something, but did not know that she knew it.

Something connected to the papers she had received and to her husband, that was for sure. Well, of course, what else would be interesting about her life? Even though she was a member of the judiciary, even though she held a senior legal position, it was obvious that she couldn't leave all that behind. She had thought she had turned into someone different. She had thought that it was possible to recreate herself, to forget everything that had gone before. But of course that was not possible. She was, underneath it all, the same person who had entered into that marriage all those years ago. She was the same person who had lived with the consequences. And she was—and this was the really unnerving part—the same person who was living with those consequences now.

She stood for some more moments, staring out at the silent empty garden, watching the play of the setting sunshine on the treetops, crimson against the brilliant green of the leaves. Then she turned back to look at the luxurious room behind her. Her original guardian had returned and was sitting as he had before, motionless, apparently uninterested in her presence. He looked across the room at nothing in particular, his expression blank.

"How long will this go on?" she said.

He turned his head to look at her, as if seeing her for the first time, but did not respond.

"This is ridiculous," she said. "It's quite clear that I can't answer any of your questions. It's equally clear that you can't keep me indefinitely." She paused, wondering about that. They could keep her here as long as they chose. It depended on what they were willing to do. "It would be much simpler if you let me go now. It's clear that there's been some misunderstanding. Of course, I appreciate that. I know how these things happen. But it would be simplest if you were just to let me go. Take me back." She was babbling, she thought, keeping only just this side of desperation.

The man said nothing, but continued to stare at her, as if she was speaking some foreign language. Perhaps she was, she thought. This man looked like a local, but perhaps he wasn't. Or perhaps he was deaf. Or perhaps . . .

She shook her head. This was ridiculous. These were just mind games that they were playing with her. Toying with her. Keeping her waiting. Leaving her with this man who seemed incapable of responding to her in any way. They were hoping that, if she did know something—if she did know whatever it was they wanted to hear—that eventually she would break down and tell them. And very probably they were right. She would be only too happy to talk right now. If only she knew what it was they wanted.

She was about to try again with the guard—not because she expected any response but simply to keep her mind alert—when the door of the drawing room opened. She was expecting to see the short man again, but instead there were two men, both dressed in dark suits and wearing similar mirrored glasses to those she had seen on the man outside. Clearly, this was some sort of uniform in this household. It was possible that one of these men was the figure she had seen through the window, but she thought not. Although they all looked similar—Mongolians, with slicked back dark hair, with their identical dark suits—she was fairly sure that these men were different from the individual she had seen previously.

The two men stood silently in the doorway for a moment, watching her. Then one of them gestured to her to follow. "This way," he said, in a quietly spoken but authoritative tone.

She hesitated for a moment, wondering where all this might be leading. The man at the table had remained motionless, hardly acknowledging the presence of the two figures at the door.

"I'm not sure I—" she said, unsure quite how she was intending to finish the sentence.

In the event, she had no need to. One of the men walked forward and seized her roughly by the arm. He dragged her across the floor and over to the door. She opened her mouth to protest and then, seeing the expression on his face, thought better of it.

She was pulled violently out of the room and into the hallway beyond. She barely had time to glimpse the vast size of the hallway before she was pulled through another doorway.

Beyond the doorway, at first there was only darkness. Then, just in time, her eyes grew accustomed to the gloom and she realised that, at the end of a short landing, a set of stone stairs fell away into deeper darkness. The man on her left pulled at her arm and dragged her forward, virtually dragging her onto the stairway. She tried to protest but the words jammed in her dry throat. And then she was being pulled down the stairs, her feet in their high heels stumbling on the hard stone risers. At one point, she almost fell but was dragged back to her feet by the two men.

Within seconds, they were at the bottom of the stairs. Immediately, the room was filled with an eyeball-burning glare. She blinked, unable to see for a moment, then slowly her vision cleared.

They were in some kind of cellar, she supposed. It was an empty space, the opposite of the well-appointed room she had occupied upstairs, with a blank stone floor and bare brick walls. There was no furniture, other than some functional metal-framed chairs and a line of benches along the wall, and no other sign of occupancy. There were no obvious windows or doors other than the stairway by which they had entered.

The men waited a moment, then, suddenly and unexpectedly, one of them pushed her. She stumbled and fell, grazing one of her knees on the hard stone floor, tearing her tights, feeling her silk dress ripping slightly. She landed awkwardly on her side, momentarily breathless.

Then, her spirit not quite yet destroyed by her predicament, she rolled out and began to shout expletives at the two men, with a sudden outburst of the anger that had been building in her since she had first been dragged into the car.

There was no response. The two men turned on their heels and began to climb the stairs. She staggered to her feet to try to follow them, but it was too late. They reached the top of the stairs and pushed open the door. Then, as a final act, one of the men reached out and turned out the lights, throwing the cellar back into pitch darkness. Sarangarel stood, not daring to move, her mind as blank as the darkness around her. From somewhere above, she heard the click of a key turning in the lock.

Tunjin was still lying half on his side, scarcely able to recover his breath. The man who had brought him here, the man with the mirrored sunglasses, was motionless. Tunjin could see the blood seeping from the man's skull and thought that it looked as if the man might well never move again.

Finally, still gasping, Tunjin dragged himself to his knees and looked at the figure sprawled on the stone floor. He reached out and gingerly took the man's wrist, alert for any sign of sudden movement or response. The figure lay, inert, while Tunjin tried to see if there was any pulse.

There was none. It was difficult to be absolutely certain—these were hardly ideal circumstances for a medical examination—but Tunjin was sure that he was dead. In the circumstances, he found it hard to be too regretful.

So where did this leave things? Did anyone else know he was here? Had the man been responding to orders, or had he contacted others in the household to let them know what he had found? It seemed likely. How else would the man have known who Tunjin was? Perhaps Tunjin had simply been unlucky and stumbled upon someone who happened to recognise him. But it seemed more likely that Tunjin had been spotted on some closed-circuit television screen and a collective identification had been made.

Still, even if that was the case, Tunjin had at least managed to buy himself some time. Even if others knew he was here, they now presumably thought he was safely under lock and key. They would not know the truth until his captor was missed. Which, Tunjin was forced to acknowledge, might not take very long.

He crawled across to the wall, and pulled himself slowly to

his feet. As so often, he wished that he was fitter, or at least less completely corpulent. Still, the way things were going, he might be destined to leave his corporeal self fairly definitively behind before too long, so there was no point in fretting too much. If he ever got out of this, he thought, he would lose some weight. He would give up drinking. All that. And how often had he made those promises?

He looked about him, taking in the blank empty room. Which way should he go? He could head back outside, which felt safer. But was it really? They had spotted him quickly in the garden. And, more to the point, what could he achieve outside?

If he penetrated further indoors—well, there was every chance that they would apprehend him quickly, but then that was true outside as well. And at least he might have a chance of finding out what was going on here, perhaps identify the woman he had seen being brought into the building.

It sounded pretty thin, even to the ever-optimistic Tunjin. But, still, here he was, one of Muunokhoi's heavies lying dead at his feet. There was no obvious way of going back. All he could do was go forward, wherever that might lead.

At least half-convinced, he stepped forward, his heart beating heavily, and began to turn the handle on the door that led into the house.

"He's dead," Doripalam said, dropping the wrist in which he had been trying to detect a pulse.

Nergui nodded. "Thanks for your perseverance," he said. "Though I think you are only confirming what I had assumed."

Doripalam shrugged. "I'm nothing if not scrupulous. If it adds anything, he's not been dead for long. There is still some warmth in the body. It is not a cold evening, but—well, who knows? Maybe two or three hours."

"Our pathologists would not be more precise," Nergui conceded. "Recent, anyway."

"Recent," Doripalam agreed. He rose from his crouching position and looked around at the surrounding trees, their dark shadows visible only against the pale moonlight. "And shot. Which means that he could have been shot from some distance away."

"Which means," Nergui said, "that we could also be targets."

"I always like to be cautious," Doripalam said, switching off his flashlight.

Nergui followed suit. "I suppose you're right," he said, "though it does little to alleviate my feeling of vulnerability. The prospect of a sniper is never an attractive one."

Doripalam nodded. This was ridiculous, he thought. There's a killer out here. We don't know who he is or why he's killed. All we know is that, so far, his one victim is a policeman. We should get out of here, come back in daylight. On the other hand, this was the only lead they had.

His cogitations were cut short by the sudden, shattering sound of a gunshot. Nergui dropped instantly, and for a moment Doripalam thought he had been hit, but then he saw him roll over and throw himself against a tree. At the same moment, he saw the silver glimmer of a handgun in Nergui's hand. Not for the first time, Doripalam was left wondering how a man twenty years his senior could move so rapidly. Almost as an afterthought, he dropped himself, reaching for his gun, wondering what the hell was happening.

He lay pressed against the cold damp grass, looking feverishly around, trying to spot their assailant, but there was no sign of movement. He looked across at Nergui.

And then they heard the voice calling, thin and tremulous in the chilly night air. "Please don't move," it said. "Please stay still." There was a pause, and they could almost hear the nervous intake of breath. "I don't want to have to kill you too."

TWENTY-ONE

For long minutes she stood in the darkness, wondering what the hell was going to happen now. The blackness seemed complete, and there was no sound that she could detect, once the tiny echoes of the locking door had died away.

She dared not move. As far as she could recall, the room had been empty of furniture so there was no real risk in walking through the darkness till she reached the walls. On the other hand, there was little point, either. She sighed and slowly lowered herself to the cold stone floor, feeling the sharp pain from her bruised knee.

She realised that her optimism—never more than halfhearted in the first place—had been entirely without foundation. Having brought her here, in search of whatever arcane piece of information, there was no way that they were simply going to let her go. What had she imagined? That they might just acknowledge that they had made a mistake, that she would simply shrug it off as a misunderstanding?

No. Having embarked on this route, there was no obvious

way they could turn back. And she had no choice but to go with them all the way. Wherever that might lead.

She sat back on the cold floor, feeling the despair sweeping over her. There was no way out of this, she thought. Wherever this might be leading, it was nowhere she wanted to go. This darkness might as well go on forever.

But, of course, it didn't. Even in the midst of that thought, the light suddenly came flooding back, blinding her with its unexpected brilliance. She sat motionless on the stone floor, feeling its unyielding pressure on her back and buttocks, wondering what might happen next.

"Mrs. Radnaa," the voice said. "Or, rather Judge Radnaa."

She blinked, still unable to see, wondering who was speaking, thinking that she had heard the voice before.

"I'm sorry," the voice said. "I had not intended that things would reach this point."

She continued blinking, not able to see, not really trying to see, unsure whether she wanted to face whatever might meet her gaze. The light seemed too bright, as if she might never be able to see again.

"But here we both are," the voice said. "There is nothing we can do. We have to live with it."

She dropped her head into her hands, still trying to see, noting that way that the speaker, whoever it might be, had somehow managed to implicate her in the situation, as if she was partly responsible for this.

Finally, as she rubbed her eyes, her vision began to clear. She could see the blank emptiness of the room, the bare brick walls, the stone floor. And then, there at the far end of the room, a solitary wooden chair. And on the chair a figure.

She recognised him, she thought. She knew him from somewhere. But her mind was barely working, was barely able to compute any information.

"Good afternoon, Mrs. Radnaa," the voice said. "I'm sorry I was unable to greet you earlier."

The figure was relaxed, slumped on the hard wooden chair. He was dressed in an expensive-looking striped shirt, open at the neck, and blue denim jeans. He was shaven headed, an earring dangling from his left earlobe. And he was smiling.

She sat up, conscious of her undignified position sprawled on the hard stone floor. Rather different from the last time they had met. "It is you then?" she said, conscious of how ridiculous her words sounded, echoing round the empty room.

"Well, of course," Muunokhoi said. "Though you never really doubted that, did you?"

"I suppose not," she acknowledged. She paused. "Though I have no idea what it is you want." She stumbled to her feet, trying hard not to show any sign of weakness, though her efforts were hardly convincing.

He nodded, his limbs sprawled relaxedly. "I appreciate the difficulty of talking about these things." He hesitated. "I'm sorry," he said. "I am hardly being a gentleman. You will want to sit down." He gestured beside him. There was a second chair, a few yards from his own. "Please."

For the first time it occurred to her to wonder where these chairs, not to mention Muunokhoi himself, had come from. Still half-dazzled by the glare, she looked around her. The room looked as blank and empty as ever. There was no obvious entrance other than the steps down which she had been brought. Muunokhoi had, it seemed, come from nowhere.

But all of that was nothing more than showmanship, designed to disconcert her. It didn't really matter where Muunokhoi had come from. He was not a ghost. He was a solid, living man. He had come from somewhere. There was some other way in, some other concealed entrance.

She was surprised how difficult it was to convince herself of this.

"I cannot talk to you like this," Muunokhoi went on. "Please, Mrs. Radnaa, I ask you to sit down."

She stumbled forward, still not entirely steady on her feet. She had wondered vaguely whether she might gain some sort of psychological advantage by remaining standing. But she realised now that this was not a serious option. She could barely manage to stay upright.

She took three steps forward and slumped onto the hard wooden chair, looking up at Muunokhoi. "Okay," she said, trying to sound uncowed. "Talk to me now. Tell me what this is all about."

Muunokhoi shrugged and paused, as if not knowing how to begin. "It is a long story," he said.

"I don't doubt it," she said, gathering some courage. "But I'd expected better of you, Muunokkoi. I wasn't brought here to listen to fairy stories."

He smiled faintly. "You are right," he said. "I should not be subjecting you to stories that begin 'once upon a time.' We Mongolians are always storytellers."

"I hear plenty of Mongolian tall tales in court," she said. "I'm not sure I want to hear yours."

He nodded, as though seriously taking account of this comment. "I do not wish to bore you," he said. "But my story is an interesting one. Especially to you, I imagine."

She shrugged, tired already of this interchange, suddenly feeling the sharp pain in her knees and all the weary aching of her body. "Tell me," she said. "You clearly intend to."

He looked at her, no longer smiling, and paused as though now, at this point, he was suddenly unsure whether he really did want to share his story. Then he said: "Okay. Indulge my storytelling. This is not quite, 'once upon a time,' but it begins fifteen years ago—"

She nodded, determined to strip any shreds of melodrama from his story. "When else?"

He shrugged, smiling again. "You are clearly ahead of me," he said. "Perhaps I should ask you to tell the story. But, no, you claim not to know all the details. That is the point. Fifteen years is, after all, a long time."

"At the moment," she said, pointedly, "five minutes is beginning to seem like a long time. If you have something to tell me, please get to the point."

His smile was unwavering, his eyes fixed on hers, their dark pupils glittering in the brilliant cellar light. "I had not intended to try your patience. But I have to start fifteen years ago. You were, I believe, married then?"

She stared at him, refusing to give any acknowledgment of his question. He knew full well that she had been married then, and to whom, just as he presumably knew equally well that she was not married now.

Nevertheless, Muunokhoi nodded as if she had responded to his question. "Your husband, as you have probably surmised, worked for me." He paused. "He was not one of my more effective associates. But then, I imagine that is also not a surprise to you." Again, he paused, as though expecting some sort of response. This is, Sarangarel thought, a man used to playing to an appreciative audience.

"Your husband was a fool in many ways, Mrs. Radnaa. Let me enumerate some of them for you." He smiled faintly, watching her closely. It was all an act, she thought. Every word, every gesture. This was no more the real Muunokhoi than the silent figure who had sat opposite her in court. His eyes were blazing, staring at her unblinking, but there was nothing behind them, no sense of life or personality.

"Some would say," he went on, "that your husband's first foolish act was accepting my offer of work in the first place. But he did not know that the offer was mine, any more than I knew, initially at least, that it had been made. It was simply an offer of a commercial contract from one of my companies for the handling of some import work. The terms were generous, as they always are with my suppliers. I think loyalty is always worth buying, don't you?" He smiled and waited a moment, as though seriously expecting her to answer the question. "As you can imagine, I had no personal awareness of your husband at that point. He was recommended to us by some mutual contact. We were told that he was already running a successful import and export business."

It was Sarangarel's turn to offer a thin smile. "I hope that your sources are better informed today." She paused, wondering how far to take this. "But perhaps not, given that you've brought me here in the hope of obtaining some information."

Muunokhoi ignored her comment. "You are right, of course. We had been misled. Though I believe that your husband was always skilled at creating the illusion of success."

"One of his few talents," she said. "A fatal one, as it turned out."

"We realised very quickly that your husband's business was less prosperous than he might have led us to believe. That did not necessarily worry us unduly so long as he was capable of fulfilling our contract—which did not initially appear to be a problem. After a trial, we offered him more work which he carried out to our satisfaction, and he became a regular supplier to us. More than that, he introduced us to some of his own contacts—notably, Khenbish, the soldier, who was able to offer us some useful, ah, overseas relationships. We were very pleased with your husband at first. His contacts opened up some useful seams of business for us. Some profitable areas."

"I never met Khenbish," Sarangarel said. "He had served in Afghanistan, I understand," She paused, regarding Muunokhoi closely, trying to read his expression. There was nothing to read.

She remembered this period of their marriage, shortly before Gansukh's arrest and death. Gansukh had finally thought that things were coming right for him. There was the prospect of ongoing work, money was coming in. For the first time, the business was something more than merely hand to mouth. He told her little about the nature of these new contracts, and she had not wanted to enquire too closely. She hadn't really believed a word of it; Gansukh had always been full of pipe dreams—an apposite description given the kind of business he was probably involved in. She knew he had, at that moment, been making some good money, but she had assumed it would just fizzle out like all his previous schemes.

Even now, she was not entirely sure what Muunokhoi was talking about, but she could easily envisage the nature of these illicit imports best handled by some disposable third party. Probably, despite what Muunokhoi now said, they had selected Gansukh precisely because his business was struggling. He would have done anything for these people, and he was the kind of small fry who could be dropped at a moment's notice if anything went wrong. As, of course, it had.

As though reading her thoughts, Muunokhoi went on: "But it was then that your husband began to demonstrate quite how foolish he could be. First, we discovered that he was handling other, similar consignments alongside our own. Not necessarily a problem in itself. We do not demand exclusivity from our suppliers—that would not be realistic—but we do expect that they exercise some discretion and care. We have our own interests to protect. And it soon became clear to us that your husband was less discreet and careful than we might have liked." He paused.

"So we began to pay a little more attention to him. And we discovered that his foolishness was really quite considerable. Not only was he handling other consignments alongside ours, but it appeared that, on occasions, he was substituting inferior product for ours." He stopped again, as though allowing Sarangerel an opportunity to appreciate the enormity of this behaviour. "In other words," he continued, "there were occasions when our customers received goods inferior from those they had expected. Whereas presumably your husband was selling our products on to his own customers. Not good for our business reputation."

Sarangarel was beginning to find the circumlocution very wearying. "What are we talking about here?" she said. "Drugs?"

Muunokhoi smiled at her. "We supply a wide range of import needs," he said. He sounded as if he was giving evidence to a government committee.

"So why didn't you do something about Gansukh at that stage?" she said. "I'm sure you have means of dealing with those who don't meet your exacting commercial standards."

He nodded. "We would have taken some action. Some disciplines are needed in business. But it was rendered unnecessary by your husband's own continuing foolishness."

"He was arrested," she said. She hesitated as another thought struck her. "Were you behind that?" After all, she thought, there was really no need for Muunokhoi to engage in strong-arm tactics. A quiet word in the right quarters would presumably be sufficient.

"I run a very efficient business, Mrs. Radnaa. I have good contacts. I maintain high commercial standards. If someone—one of our suppliers—was behaving inappropriately, I would certainly consider drawing this to the attention of the appropriate authorities. But in this case it was not necessary. Your husband was not only dishonest. He was also incompetent."

Sarangarel wondered whether Muunokhoi thought that all

these disparaging references to Gansukh were likely to have an impact on her. If so, he knew little about either her or her marriage.

"We have a range of operating procedures. We have developed these over years as the most effective and secure methods of handling our business. We asked your husband to follow these procedures. He chose not to. He was arrested. No action was needed on our part."

It was easy to believe, she thought. Gansukh had been capable of making many enemies, but none worse than himself.

"I'm sorry," she said. "I still don't understand why you're telling me all this. It was all a very long time ago. I knew nothing of it. I still know nothing of it."

"I understand that," he said. "But this was only the beginning of your husband's foolishness. As I say, we do look for a little discretion from our suppliers, particularly if things go wrong. That is partly why we pay them so well. We organise things very carefully so that the nature of our business relationships does not become too explicit."

I bet you do, she thought. "You mean so that no one can link you to the poor bastards who do your dirty work," she said.

"Not quite the words I would use," Muunokhoi said. "But, yes, a reasonable summary."

"But you must have contracts? Written arrangements of some kind?"

He nodded. "But the nature of the contracts—the companies involved—do not always fully reflect the nature of the business transacted."

Sarangarel wondered where Muunokhoi had picked up this kind of Western business speak. Was this how all the gangsters talked these days? Concealing the reality of their activities under this shell of meaningless verbiage. Another triumph of Western capitalism. "So how do you make sure your—suppliers adhere to your real terms?" she said, despising herself for adopting the same kind of euphemistic language.

He shrugged. "Most of our contracts are verbal," he said. "It does not matter. Our suppliers—and our customers—fully understand the implications if they fail to adhere to our terms. It is a matter of honour."

She almost laughed out loud. Did Muunokhoi really believe all this? Had he become so lost in the tangle of his own commercial transactions that he no longer recognised what he was really involved with? It was quite possible, she thought. And arguably this was no different from any other business—just a difference in scale, perhaps. Those at the top didn't allow themselves to reflect on the realities of their activities. "And I take it Gansukh was not so honourable?" she said. For the first time, she almost began to feel a trace of admiration for her late husband.

"You might say that. I think he had tried to take out some insurance. He knew he was playing a dangerous game, but I'm afraid that greed got the better of him."

Muunokhoi was shameless, she had to give him that, lecturing others on the perils of greed.

"So he tried to preempt what we might do. He had recorded some of the conversations he had had with my people—both telephone and face to face. Probably not good quality, but enough to be potentially incriminating. And then there was Khenbish. We built up a rather more substantial relationship with Khenbish than we did with your husband, as he was able to put my companies in contact with some lucrative overseas opportunities. Our relationship was a little more—formal. We hadn't realised—at least, not initially—that Khenbish was also working closely with your husband and was involved in some of his petty scams. A pity. Khenbish could have worked very successfully with us without getting involved in that kind of sordid enterprise, if only he'd played straight."

In her professional life, Sarangarel never ceased to be astonished at the subtle gradations of criminal morality. In other circumstances, she would have been blackly amused at Muunokhoi's contempt for those engaged in less successful criminality than his own.

"We hadn't realised—not until a little later—that Khenbish had shared some of these formal arrangements with your husband. We don't know precisely what was disclosed, but we have reason to believe that your husband copied at least some of the material."

To her own surprise, she found that this time she did laugh out loud. For the first time, Muunokhoi showed some reaction, opening his blank eyes wider in surprise. "You find something amusing in this?" he said.

"You've gone to great lengths to illustrate how foolish my late husband was—which, I have to tell you, was scarcely news to me. But it seems to me that he was probably smarter than you gave him credit for."

Muunokhoi nodded. "There was a degree of—street cunning there, I admit," he said. "He was a different creature from those we were used to dealing with."

"Anyway," she went on, looking to press home some sort of psychological advantage, even though she was still unsure where this discussion was heading, "how do you know he tried to take out this—insurance? Did he try to—make a claim?" This euphemistic nonsense was disturbingly catching, she thought.

"He did not have a chance," Muunokhoi said.

"That was why you had him killed," she said simply, watching for his reaction.

He threw up his hands and laughed. "Mrs. Radnaa, I am not a murderer. I cannot deny that your husband's suicide was convenient for me, in that it removed a risk. But it required no intervention from me. He had nowhere else to go."

She stared at him, trying to detect some sign of emotion, some revelation in his expression, but there was nothing.

"So why do you think he had this material?" she repeated.

Muunokhoi shrugged. "Some of it we learned from Khenbish, who was rather more cooperative once he realised what we knew about his dealings with your husband."

"I bet he was," she said. "I hope that you looked after him well in return."

"Sadly, we did not have the opportunity."

"You killed him as well."

"Mrs. Radnaa, you really do have a low opinion of me, don't you?"

"You've no idea," she said.

"He was a soldier. He died in action. Or, at least, on duty."

"You really are an unfortunate man, Muunokhoi. People are dying all around you."

He smiled icily. "Then you should be concerned at being in my presence, Mrs. Radnaa. Especially as I believe that some of your husband's insurance policy is now in your possession."

"You think I have materials that might incriminate you?"

"I don't know what the content of these materials is," Muunokhoi said, "but I believe that your husband thought they might offer him some protection."

"And that was why he sent them off for safekeeping with some cousin on the other side of the country?" she said. "If so, it was another smart move. So he was one step ahead of you there as well." She recalled the break-in at her flat, shortly after Gansukh's death, when her world was still in turmoil. She had had few possessions of any value, and nothing had been stolen other than a small amount of loose cash. But the apartment had been left in a mess, presumably—or so the police had suggested—because the intruders had tried to find something else worth stealing. Now, though, she was sure that

Muunokhoi's men had been behind this, hunting for these mysterious documents.

Muunokhoi nodded his head. "Smarter than we thought, certainly. It is a pity that he never had the opportunity to exploit such intelligence. A pity also—for him, that is—that he never had the chance to use the insurance policy he had so carefully arranged."

"The police thought he was about to make a deal," she said. "Just before his death. It seems a strange time for him to have committed suicide."

"Who can fathom the workings of the disturbed mind?" Muunokhoi said piously.

"I'm certainly having great difficulty just at the moment," she said. She leaned forward. She was still feeling deeply anxious, trapped here in this bare room with a very dangerous individual, but somehow she had been able, for the moment at least, to push her fears to the back of her mind. The only way out of this was to reason her way out, somehow persuade Muunokhoi that it was not in his interests to harm her. It was the longest of long shots, but she saw little alternative. No one else knew she was here. Quite probably no one other than Nergui knew that she had been kidnapped, and she had no idea what kind of state Nergui was in. If he was safe and unharmed, then he would probably assume that Muunokhoi was behind her kidnapping, but she did not fool herself that mounting a search of Muunokhoi's properties would be a straightforward task, even for Nergui. In the meantime, the only option she could see was to keep probing, in the hope that she might uncover some means of justifying her release.

"What I don't understand," she went on, "is what you're really worried about. Even if Gansukh did somehow manage to cobble together some potentially incriminating papers—and, even if he turned out to be smarter than you expected, you shouldn't overestimate his abilities—surely the threat went away once he was . . . after his death."

Muunokhoi nodded, as though absorbing new information. "We thought that was probably so," he said. "But we couldn't be sure. If your husband really was smart, he would have wanted some bargaining counter in place in case he was threatened. He would need some means of releasing the incriminating material even if he were incapacitated or dead. Otherwise—and I speak only of what might have gone on inside your husband's fevered mind, you understand—the material would only have increased his vulnerability to threat."

"So why wasn't the material released after his death, then?" she said. This all sounded far-fetched to her. She couldn't imagine Gansukh having the wit or the energy to engage in anything so sophisticated.

Muunokhoi shrugged. "I suspect that your husband didn't have his plans in place in time. He was concerned about what we might do to him. He wasn't expecting to be arrested. That probably took him by surprise."

That sounded plausible enough. The story of Gansukh's life. Even if he had been foresighted enough to arrange this supposed insurance, it was almost inevitable that his plans would come to nothing. "But he'd already got rid of the documents."

"I suspect he would have done that at the earliest opportunity, just so there was no evidence against him if we should become suspicious. Probably just sent them to his cousin—perhaps without much explanation—saying he'd come to sort out the materials shortly. But he didn't get the opportunity to do it. Or to find anyone who might be prepared to release the documents if anything happened to him."

"I can see why that wouldn't be an attractive role," she said.

"Which may be why you refused to do it?" Muunokhoi said.

She looked up and him. "You think he asked me?"

"Who else could be trust?"

"Probably nobody," she said. "But, by the same token, he wouldn't have trusted me either. Not with that. He never shared any of his—business dealings with me. He knew what I thought of them."

"But you were happy to turn a blind eye and live off the proceeds?" Muunokhoi said, with a trace of amusement.

"I earned my own living," she said. "Not a great deal in those days, but then Gansukh was hardly rolling in money either. It sounds stupid now but I was in love with Gansukh. I didn't approve of what he did, and I told him so, but I didn't take much advantage of it either." She didn't know why she felt any need to justify herself to Muunokhoi, except that perhaps she recognised that, even allowing for her youthful lack of judgement, there was some truth in his comment. "But I would be the last person he'd have trusted with something like that."

"So perhaps he had difficulty in finding anyone," Muunokhoi said. "Which is why the material remained unused."

"Did it ever occur to you that Khenbish might have just exaggerated things to ingratiate himself with you and maybe try to shift your attention on to Gansukh?"

"I'm sure he did," Muunokhoi said. "But I'm equally sure that the documents existed. And that they still exist."

"I still don't see how I can help you, or why you felt it necessary to bring me here against my will. So I've received some material that used to belong to Gansukh, which for some reason he deposited with his cousin. And some of that material undoubtedly relates to his business dealings. But I've been through it all. I didn't see anything that might incriminate you. And I've no doubt that if you had just wanted to get hold of those papers, you could have found a means of taking them." She paused, her mind working. "After all, someone must have informed you that

I'd received them in the first place." She shook her head, marvelling at her own naivety. She had thought she was being smart, registering the papers with her lawyer, keen as always to ensure that anything associated with Gansukh should be handled as formally and transparently as possible, so that her own professional position could not be compromised.

"It was important to keep a close eye on you, Mrs. Radnaa. Even after all this time. Just in case."

So it looked as if Nergui had been right. Muunokhoi had indeed infiltrated everywhere. Whichever way you turned, his associates were there, passing on information. No wonder that Gansukh had been unable to trust anyone with the papers.

She shrugged. "It doesn't seem right that we should both be paying for my lawyer's services. I must ask for a refund. But then surely all this is unnecessary. If my lawyer's on your payroll, the papers—or copies of them—must already be in your possession."

Muunokhoi nodded. "And you are also right that there is nothing incriminating in the papers. Nothing significant, anyway. One or two things that might potentially cause me a little commercial embarrassment—or might have done at the time, anyway. But nothing major."

"So why am I here, then?" she said. Maybe this whole situation was less rational than she had thought. Perhaps Muunokhoi wasn't simply after the documents. Perhaps there was something else. For the first time, she began to wonder about Muunokhoi's state of mind. She had seen him as a calculating businessman—not an attractive figure, but amenable to rational negotiation. Now she was less sure.

"I think you know more than you are saying, Mrs. Radnaa. I think that you knew that you might be under observation. I think you found something more in those documents which you chose not to deposit with your lawyer."

"Why would I do that?" she said. "I don't want anything to do with all this. Apart from anything else, I've my own professional position to maintain. That's why I placed all Gansukh's materials with my lawyer in the first place, so no one could ever accuse me of hiding anything. If I'd found anything important in those papers, I'd have handed it over to the police."

Muunokhoi smiled faintly, sitting back in his chair. "Ah, but would you, Mrs. Radnaa? Would you have even trusted the police with this material? You are an intelligent woman, and I think you would have recognised that there might have been risks in handing over such material. Even to the police."

She stared at him, astonished at the calmness with which he was confirming Nergui's worst suspicions.

Again, it was as if he were reading her thoughts. "And, interestingly, Mrs. Radnaa, we now know who was with you when we—picked you up. One of my people recognised him but couldn't initially put a name to his face. When he told me, my first thought was that this was a very intriguing companion for you. Nergui and I go back a long way. He is one of the senior officers whom you could certainly trust."

"Nergui is a friend," she said. "We also go back a long way, as you no doubt recall."

He nodded, smiling now. "It is always good to reinvigorate an old friendship. But don't take me for a fool, Mrs. Radnaa."

She was, finally, beginning to feel angry now, her rising fury driving out her gnawing anxiety. "I'm not sure what to take you for," she said. "I suspect you're insane. Pursuing some decade-old—well, I'm not even sure what. A vendetta? Because, for all your ruthlessness, my husband managed to make more of a fool of you than you'd care to admit? Is that it? For once, someone was a step ahead of you, and you didn't manage to tie up every last loose end?"

She was aware that her temper was getting the better of her, that she might be losing whatever chance she might have had of talking her way out of this. But the words kept tumbling out of her mouth as she struggled to make some sense of her absurd predicament. "I don't know what Gansukh did," she said, "and after all this time I don't much care. Maybe for once he was smart. Maybe he did really have something on you. All I do know is that there was no sign of it in the papers I received." She paused, recovering her breath and trying to recover her composure. "You're chasing ghosts, Muunokhoi. I think the truth is that you are going to end up in jail. But not because of anything that Gansukh might have had on you. Just because you're running out of time. You're not the man you were. Someday, somehow, someone's going to catch up with you."

Muunokhoi seemed untroubled by her diatribe. "Your friend, Nergui, has been chasing me for twenty years and never got close. I don't think he's going to catch me now." He paused, the empty smile playing again across his pale face. "But we are really wasting time, Mrs. Radnaa. I admit that, in your current position, you perhaps have plenty of time to waste. But I do not. I want to know what else was in those papers you received."

She stared at him, unable to come to grips with what appeared to be little more than monomania. "I've told you, there was nothing else. Everything was placed in the hands of my lawyer. And so, it appears, was handed directly over to you."

"I have told you, Mrs. Radnaa, do not take me for a fool. You're an intelligent woman. You would not have trusted your lawyer. You would not have trusted the police. You would have disposed of the materials in some other way. If you've handed them over to Nergui then I will need to arrange for their recovery."

"Recovery?"

His smile grew wider, somehow emphasising the emptiness of his eyes. "Ah, I see. You are concerned about Nergui's safety.

Quite understandable, given the views you have expressed about my own morality. But you will not be placing Nergui in any greater danger by acknowledging that he now has the relevant material. You will merely be simplifying matters."

"Don't you understand?" she said. "I've nothing to tell you. I've handed nothing to Nergui."

He shook his head slowly. "Everything would be so much easier if you were to cooperate. But I can see that that would be difficult for you. You accused me of conducting a vendetta. But it seems to me that it is you—and, over the years, Nergui—who have been conducting the vendetta. Nergui has his own reasons for wanting me behind bars—not least, I think, because he sees me as the symbol of everything he has failed to achieve in his professional career. He is an honourable man and I've no doubt he has the best interests of our nation at heart, but he is a man out of time. He has been unable to hold back the tide of Westernisation, and every day he sees our country embracing more and more of those corrupt decadent ways. It is a tragedy, no doubt, but it is not my tragedy." He paused, as though daring her to interrupt. "As for your motives, Mrs. Radnaa, well—I don't know. A mixture, I imagine. In part, you hold me responsible for the death of your husband."

"If you think—"

"And, in part," he went on, overriding her, "it is no doubt a matter of professional pride to you. You had to oversee a trial which was—well, frankly, a fiasco. Not through any fault of yours, I understand. But it must have been deeply frustrating to see a figure of my supposed criminal stature slip through your fingers in that way."

"You really don't understand anything, do you?" she said, feeling her anger rising again at the presumption of this man. "You've no understanding of my feelings—or my lack of feelings—for Gansukh. And you don't even understand that my role as a judge is to ensure a fair trial, not to indulge some ancient, nonexistent vendetta."

"Even when faced with a conflict of interest as great as this? Believe me, even if the prosecutor's office had not messed things up so spectacularly, I would have ensured that your own position in the trial would have come under close scrutiny." His smile now looked as if it were painted on his face.

"What position? What conflict? I've told you, I didn't even know that Gansukh worked for you. Can't you understand? I don't care about you or what you might have done. I've no interest."

Even as she spoke, she knew that the words were untrue. There was an obsession there, still, somewhere buried deep in her mind. That was why she had behaved so irrationally after the trial. That was why she sent the anonymous letters to Muunokhoi, trying to provoke some response, not suspecting that, by then, he had already learned of the existence of the legacy. Not suspecting that all she was doing was reinforcing a paranoia that had been building for more than a decade.

But this was what she had been seeking. This confrontation. This opportunity to challenge, face to face, the man who had killed her husband, who had thrown her life into chaos. A chance, after all these years, for some kind of resolution, some kind of closure. Some kind of ending to that part of her life.

And so here she was. But, of course, the closure would be Muunokhoi's alone. Her actions had simply led her straight into his hands, allowing him finally to tie up the one loose end that had always trailed behind his apparently unstoppable ascent.

Still, though, he showed no reaction. His mouth was twisted in an expression which would have resembled a smile only if his eyes had been concealed. The eyes themselves were as blank as ever, as if all expression, all emotion, had been stripped from them.

"I am sorry, then," he said, at last. "Your cooperation would have made things much more straightforward. For me. For you. And for Nergui." He shrugged. "But so be it. I cannot waste more time talking to you. I will leave you to think. Perhaps you will have a change of heart. But, if so, I fear that by then it will be too late."

He climbed slowly to his feet, as though wearied by their conversation. Sarangarel wondered whether he was going to exit as mysteriously as he had entered—she could imagine that he would enjoy the showmanship—but instead he simply walked past her across the room towards the stairs.

She wondered, briefly, whether she could take some action. Perhaps try to use one of the chairs as a weapon. But both chairs, she realised then, were tightly bolted to the concrete floor. It was, she reflected, probably not the first time that Muunokhoi had used this bleak venue for this kind of purpose.

There were no other weapons at hand, and in any case Muunokhoi had already reached the bottom of the stairs. She contemplated running after him, but it was too late. He began to climb, pausing halfway up to turn and look down at her. "Think about it," he said. "I do not know how long I may leave you down here. Or what I will do when I return. But there is no way now that you can help Nergui. It may be too late to help yourself. But you may still be able to cooperate."

It sounded like an invitation and she wondered whether she might be able to buy herself some time by offering her cooperation, even though she had nothing to tell him. She half opened her mouth to speak, but then Muunokhoi turned and, as if someone had responded to a signal, the heavy door opened to let him out.

The slamming of the door behind him had a terrifying finality. She'd blown it, she thought. She was smart and articulate. She should have been able to talk her way out of this somehow, or at least bought herself some time. Maybe Muunokhoi really was out of his mind, but she should have been able to handle that. Instead, she'd just tried to argue rationally and then, when that hadn't worked, she'd allowed him to goad her into losing her temper.

And she was still trapped in this featureless room, with no knowledge how long she would be left here, and no idea of what might be facing her at the end of that time. For the first time, she allowed herself to face the reality of her position. Muunokhoi was never going to allow her to leave this place alive. She was going to die. The only questions were when and how. From what she had heard and seen of Muunokhoi, it could not be assumed that her death would be either quick or humane.

And, on top of all that, there was something else—something, she realised, that terrified her almost as much as her own impending death. Somewhere out there, Muunokhoi and his people were waiting for Nergui. The way Muunokhoi had spoken at least gave her some hope that Nergui had at least survived the impact of the car, though it was quite possible he was lying injured or incapacitated, a helpless potential victim. And, she thought, whatever his current position, his well-being was likely to be substantially worsened in the very near future.

TWENTY-TWO

Doripalam lay, as motionless as he could, on the cold earth, holding his breath, trying to detect some movement in the darkness around them.

He knew that Nergui was lying similarly, his handgun poised, a few metres to his left, although in the blackness he could no longer see him.

After the tremulous voice had died away, he had heard nothing. No footsteps or movement, nothing that revealed any human presence. The only sound was the faint whisper of the breeze through the firs. The moon was higher now, skimming the trees, scattering pale silver across the woodland and steppe. But Doripalam could see nothing but a filigree of grey and shadow, with no solid shapes other than the triangular silhouettes of the *gers*. He could conjure up all kinds of ghosts in this near darkness, but he had no idea about the location of the sniper.

He looked across, trying to locate Nergui, but the grass between the trees was empty. Nergui had already changed his position, though his movements must have been as silent as the breeze. Doripalam glanced around, trying to spot Nergui among the trees, but could still see nothing.

He twisted around, positioning his back against a tree to minimise the chances of the sniper catching him from behind. He could still see and hear nothing.

And then, suddenly, he saw a movement, little more than a shifting shadow against the trees, a momentary blackness against the glimmer of moonlight. He eased out his own pistol and waited, holding his breath, watching the spot. Was it the sniper, or was it Nergui circling round the *gers*?

The silence extended, and then, somewhere farther round the clearing from where he had detected the movement, there was a noise. It was little more than a faint rustling, possibly no more than some wild animal making its way through the trees and undergrowth, but Doripalam tensed, watching for any further sign of life.

Then there was a much more distinctive sound. First, a thud of footsteps across the grass, a clattering as if something had been dropped, and a sudden sharp cry, immediately stifled.

Doripalam rose, pressed himself behind the tree, peering out into the dark, trying to work out what was happening. There was definitely movement now, a bundling of shadows beneath the faintly moonlit trees, then suddenly a whisper of voices and the movements ceased.

Doripalam raised his gun, poised to fire as soon as there was some positive indication of a possible target.

"I think you'd better hold fire," he heard Nergui's voice say. "It would take some explaining if you were to hit me by mistake. You can switch your flashlight back on now, though."

Doripalam fumbled in his pocket for the torch which he had extinguished as soon as the shot had sounded. He pointed it in the direction of Nergui's voice, flooding the woodland with sudden light.

Nergui was lying on the ground, his arm clutched firmly round the neck of a young man, his pistol pointing unwaveringly at the man's head. The young man himself looked terrified, his eyes blinking frantically as he tried to take in the scene. His own handgun lay on the grass, several metres away, presumably where he had dropped it as Nergui had launched himself at him.

"If you've got your handcuffs with you, that would probably be helpful," Nergui said. "I'd rather talk to this individual in a standing position."

Recovering his composure, Doripalam pulled his handcuffs from his pocket and crouched down to snap them on the young man's wrists. There was no attempt at resistance. Looking at the young man's frightened expression, Doripalam suspected that he would have been compliant even if there had been no cuffs on his arms or gun pointed at his temple.

Doripalam dragged the young man to his feet and thrust him against the side of the nearest *ger.* He quickly searched the man's pockets for any sign of a further weapon, but there was nothing. Behind them, Nergui climbed slowly to his feet, brushing the dew from his clothes. "This suit's going to need cleaning," he said. "Another strike against this young man."

"Along with the murder of a police officer, you mean?" Doripalam said, still holding his own gun against the man's back.

"Alongside that, yes," Nergui said, his expression strangely casual. Doripalam glanced at him. In the normal run of things, there were few crimes more serious than the murder of a serving officer.

Doripalam pulled the young man round to face him. He should begin the formalities, arresting the man on suspicion of the murder of the officer they had found in the woods. Not to mention, he thought, the possible attempted murder of himself and Nergui.

He opened his mouth to speak, shining the torch up at the young man's face, and then he stopped. He turned slowly to Nergui. "We've already met," he said. "You were one of the four men here when we came before. One of Tseren's cousins." He stopped, searching for the name.

"Kadyr," the man stuttered. "Yes." He paused as though seeking some adequate form of words. "I'm sorry," he said, at last.

"Sorry?" Doripalam stared at him. "You—or one of your kinsmen—injured one of my colleagues before. Tonight, you've completed the job on another officer. And, quite frankly, I've had my fill of you taking potshots at me."

"I'm sorry," Kadyr said again. "It's not—" He stopped. "It's not how it looks."

"How else can it be?" Doripalam said. "There's an officer dead. Another injured."

"I know," Kadyr stammered, "but—" He stopped, clearly at a loss now, looking as if he were trying to offer some sort of coherent explanation but lacking the language.

Doripalam was about to respond, but Nergui cut in from behind him, speaking with his usual calm authority. "He's right," he said. "It's not how it looks. But then we know that. I think you can put the gun away, Doripalam. Kadyr's not going anywhere, not as long as we're here, anyway. There's no one else he can trust. Not anymore."

Doripalam turned to look at the older man, trying to work out—as so often—what precisely was going through his mind.

"We should get back to the truck," Nergui said. "There'll be others out here soon. 'We need to get away from here while we've still got time."

"Others? You mean—"

"More police. More of Tsend's people."

"But—"

"And if they find us here I think we may find that the local force has little respect for intruders from the big city, even if they're as senior as we are. Let's get moving. We've got a lot to talk about with—what did you call yourself?—with Kadyr here."

There was something about the way that Nergui uttered the last sentence. He knows something, Doripalam thought. It's the same as ever. He's a step or two ahead, working out something that I'm only just beginning to grasp. It was clear that, for whatever reason, Kadyr thought so too. He was staring at Nergui with an aghast expression, his terror clearly even greater than before.

"Come on," Nergui said, with greater urgency. "We need to move."

He grabbed Kadyr's arm, and began to drag the young man back down the slope towards their truck. The moon was higher above them now, casting its cool light down along the path, exaggerating the shadows and potholes in the ground. Nergui began to move faster, almost running, as if he had suddenly noticed some change in the landscape. "Come on," he said again.

And then Doripalam, following a few steps behind, heard it. The sound of a car engine, still distant but approaching rapidly. Despite Nergui's urgency, Doripalam paused momentarily, trying to locate the vehicle. Finally he saw it, two dim lights coming closer across the undulating steppe, obscured partly by the distance and partly by the fact that, despite the darkness, the vehicle was using only its side-lights. The driver had obviously hoped to delay being spotted for as long as possible, knowing that full headlights would carry for miles across the empty landscape.

Doripalam began to hurry down the slope behind Nergui

and Kadyr, trying to calculate how far away the vehicle might be. Two or three kilometres, probably. And it would take them four or five minutes to reach their own truck, even running. Even if they reached the truck, there was no guarantee that they could get away easily, assuming that the new arrivals were as dangerous as Nergui was assuming.

Nergui was virtually dragging Kadyr now. It was as if the young man had finally given way, as if all the energy had drained out of him. Doripalam tried to hurry forward so he could assist the older man, but, even supporting Kadyr's weight, Nergui was moving too quickly. Doripalam considered himself reasonably fit, but he was already becoming breathless and could barely keep up with the pace.

By now, the slope had taken them below the level of the trees and Doripalam could no longer see the lights of the approaching vehicle. He had no idea how much time they had, or what might happen when they reached their own truck. There was something irrational, almost superstitious about their running, as if Nergui believed that if they reached the truck, everything would be all right.

And perhaps it would have been. They were never to find out since, just as they came within sight of their own truck parked by the roadside, the dim lights of the second vehicle appeared ahead of them. Nergui staggered to a halt, still clutching the young man as if he might otherwise float away. Doripalam followed behind, scarcely able to breathe.

The approaching vehicle—another off-road vehicle, Doripalam thought—slammed on its brakes and skidded to a stop, angled across the road. Its headlights came on, blazing on full beam, and for a moment Doripalam could see nothing for the glare. He stumbled on down the slope, catching up finally with Nergui and Kadyr. Kadyr by now looked little more than semiconscious, his eyes staring blankly into the dazzling light.

Slowly, Doripalam was able to make out two figures emerging from the vehicle. The first figure stepped into the light, and Doripalam let out his breath in relief, realising that Nergui's assumptions had for once been wrong. There shouldn't have been any doubt, he thought, given that unique approach to stopping a car.

"Luvsan," he called out, "thank—"

And then he stopped. The second figure had stepped forward, and, suddenly, like a camera coming into focus, the whole picture became clear in Doripalam's mind. Nergui was staring down into the light, as if he had known this all along.

Luvsan was smiling up at them, a powerful handgun clutched in his hand. Not police issue, Doripalam noted irrelevantly, his brain still trying to make the connections. Behind him, holding an assault rifle, was Tsend, the local police chief.

"Good evening. Sir." Luvsan nodded slowly to Doripalam and then to Nergui. "Though I imagine we can dispense with the hierarchical conventions in the circumstances."

"I find myself in illustrious company," Tsend said from behind him. "But then I have always been happy to cooperate with requests from headquarters." He glanced, still smiling, at Luvsan. "As your colleague here will be only too pleased to confirm, I am sure."

"And I hope," Luvsan said, "that you will find it equally easy to cooperate with our requests." He gestured with his gun. "It would be most disrespectful of me to have to use this on a senior officer or indeed—" He bowed slightly towards Nergui. "—on a Ministry official."

"This way, gentlemen," Tsend said. "We have an appointment to keep."

Tunjin had begun to open the inner door, but then he stopped, walked back across to the man on the floor. There was no doubt now that he was dead, his head lying crushed in a rapidly darkening pool of blood. Tunjin had seen plenty of dead bodies in his career, but had never previously been personally responsible for the death. It was an odd sensation. He knew that he wasn't to blame—his action had been legitimate self-defence, and the death itself had been an accident. Moreover, from what he knew of Muunokhoi's heavies, the death was unlikely to be a major loss to society.

Even so, as he leaned over the body, Tunjin felt a shudder of—what? Guilt? Disgust? Both of those, he thought, along with a quite understandable tremor of fear. He didn't imagine that those who killed Muunokhoi's henchmen normally survived for very long themselves. On the other hand, given his broader predicament, he couldn't imagine that this would have significantly worsened his life expectancy. He contemplated briefly whether it would be possible to conceal the body in some way, but decided that it was impossible. There was nowhere to hide the body in this room. He could perhaps drag it outside and hope to hide it among the trees, at least to delay its discovery, but the risk of being spotted on the security cameras would outweigh any possible benefits.

Tunjin looked around and saw the man's pistol lying in the corner of the room. It was the thought of this that had made him hesitate at the door. He had suddenly realised that his own handgun, the one that Agypar had given him, was no longer in his pocket. He couldn't recall if he had left it up on the hillside with Agypar's motorcycle, or whether it had tumbled from his pocket during his fall down the slope. Either way, he had just been about to enter Muunokhoi's house unarmed. Probably not the smartest of moves, but typical of his approach so far.

He picked up the gun, weighed it gently in his hand, and checked that it was loaded. He had to do everything carefully from here on. Think it through. Not just go blundering in his usual manner.

His resolve in this respect lasted only slightly beyond his cautious opening of the inner door into the house. He peered carefully out, and saw that the door opened into a long passageway, its ornate wallpaper and thick carpeting contrasting starkly with the bare room he had just left. He stepped out into the hallway and let the door close behind him, hearing it shut with a solid click. He realised, just too late, that it had locked itself. He gently tried the door and discovered that it could not be opened without a key. Brilliant. His one known exit route and he'd just managed to seal it. At least it reduced his options. He was hardly spoiled for choice.

He began to make his way slowly down the hallway, feeling desperately exposed. There were a couple of doors opening off each side of the passageway, but it would be too risky to explore at this stage—there was no way of knowing who or what lay on the other side of them. He had to try to get an understanding of the layout of the place.

At the end of the hallway, the passage opened out into a broader area. Tunjin cautiously peered around the corner, where the thick carpeting gave way to a polished light wood floor. An entrance hall with, some metres away, what Tunjin took to be the main front door of the house. To the right, an imposing stairway rose to the upper floors.

Across the hallway, another door stood half-open and Tunjin could hear voices coming from inside. He took another step or two forward to glimpse the interior of the room, and then he froze. He could see, in side view, a figure he recognised instantly.

Muunokhoi. There was no doubt about it. The short, stocky but somehow imposing figure. The shaved head. And, though the face was currently turned away from him, Tunjin had no doubt about the dark, empty eyes. He made a movement backwards, praying that those eyes would not be turned in his direction.

So Muunokhoi was here. And presumably his presence was in some way connected with the woman whom Tunjin had seen being led into the building earlier in the day.

Tunjin took a further step forward, keeping out of the line of sight of the door, hoping desperately that no one would decide to emerge. He tried to hear what might be being discussed, but could make out no clear words. Muunokhoi's authoritative tones sounded anything but happy.

Tunjin looked down at the gun in his hand. It would be easy, he thought. He could just walk in there now and, without a word, gun down Muunokhoi. He would be shot himself almost immediately by Muunokhoi's henchmen, but that would be a small price to pay. Tunjin was not a man with any future. He could at least make sure that the same was true of Muunokhoi. Few people—maybe only Nergui and a handful more—would recognise the worth of what he had done, but the nation and society would be immeasurably improved. Nevertheless, whatever its potential merits, the prospect of cold-blooded murder did not come easily, especially to one who, for all his personal peccadilloes, had devoted his life to upholding the law.

But, before he could think any further, Tunjin heard another sound that, momentarily, made his heart freeze. It was the sound of a key turning in the lock of the massive front door. He realised that, while he had been straining to hear the conversation going on in the opposite room, his mind had somehow filtered out the sound of a car arriving outside, although now the sound of the running engine was all too clear.

Tunjin backed away rapidly down the hallway. Whatever the morality of taking Muunokhoi out, there was no merit in being caught at this point. Hearing the key turning, he looked frantically behind him for some point of concealment.

The only options were the various doors lining the passageway. The majority of these looked like the doors to internal reception rooms which might harbour any kind of peril. But one, at the far end of the corridor next to that through which he had entered, looked different. Like the neighbouring door, it had a substantial lock which suggested that it might lead outside the house. Unlike the lock in the neighbouring door, however, this one still contained a key.

There was no time to hesitate as the front door was already opening. Tunjin leapt two or three steps backwards, his agility again belying his impressive bulk. In one movement, he turned the key, opened the door and stepped inside, pulling the door to behind him but leaving a small gap so that he could see out. He glanced behind him, trying to ensure that he had not simply stepped into further peril.

It looked safe enough. He appeared to be in the entrance to some sort of cellar. A set of stone steps descended away from the landing on which he stood. There was a light, but he could see only a few metres beyond the bottom of the steps. Still, it was safe to assume that no one was down here, since there had been no reaction to his entry.

Secure for the moment, he pressed his eye to the narrow gap he had left between the door and the frame, and peered out at the group entering the hallway. For a second his breath died in his throat and he could scarcely believe what he was seeing. The first two men were unknown to him. There was a young man who looked terrified—not an unreasonable reaction for someone entering Muunokhoi's residence, Tunjin thought, especially if the entry was not entirely voluntary. Behind him, there was a heavily built middle-aged man who, on second glance, appeared vaguely familiar though Tunjin could not think where he might have encountered him.

It was the remainder of the group, though, that had left Tunjin breathless. There was Nergui, his dark face as impassive as ever. Close behind him was Doripalam, his face also for once unreadable. And then, behind the two senior officers, was the supposed high flyer, Luvsan, the one everyone thought of as Doripalam's protégé.

So was that it then? Had Muunokhoi's influence penetrated much further than anyone had dared to believe? If even Nergui was on his payroll, then there really was no hope. It didn't matter whether Tunjin, or any police officer, lived or died, whether they did their duty or not. Whatever happened, Muunokhoi was in control.

Despair almost swept over Tunjin at that point. He had, he realised, given up on his own life, his own future, long before. From the moment that his half-baked scheme against Muunokhoi had collapsed, he had known that the death sentence had been pronounced, that he was effectively dead. He could flee. He could try to fight back. And maybe, somewhere, somehow, he might have some success, but it was difficult to see how all this would end other than in his own killing.

But his faint hope, the smallest glimmer that had kept him going through all this, was that, just maybe, he might succeed in taking Muunokhoi with him. It was true that if Muunokhoi was out of the picture, others would eventually come along to take his place. But there was no one—not yet, not in this country—like him. There was no one with the same power, the same network, the same wealth, the same influence—or, most important, the same ruthlessness. There would be pretenders, but it would be a long while before anyone else occupied the throne with equivalent authority.

And then the hope briefly came back, as he watched the group file across the hallway. Muunokhoi's henchmen were holding pistols, pointed firmly at the backs of Nergui, Doripalam and the young man. They weren't Muunokhoi's guests. They were his prisoners. For a moment, the position seemed almost reassuring. These senior officers—these few men he had been sure he could trust—were not corrupt. There was still some sanity left in the world.

But his relief was short-lived. Nergui and Doripalam might be straight, but they had somehow fallen into Muunokhoi's power. And Tunjin had no illusions as to how wide-ranging that power might be. If Muunokhoi had brought them here, he would not be allowing them to leave. Worse still, he realised, as the group moved past, not all the police officers were prisoners. Luvsan had been one of those holding a gun.

But none of that, he thought, invalidated the simple plan he had formulated while standing in the hallway. Here he was, undetected in the heart of Muunokhoi's house, a loaded gun in his pocket. There would never be another opportunity like this. All he had to do was move swiftly and silently out there and make sure that he acted before anyone could stop him. He could gun down Muunokhoi and then—well, take the chance to shoot anyone else he could before he was finally stopped. If all those people were on Muunokhoi's payroll, then, as far as Tunjin was concerned, they were legitimate targets. He should feel no compunction—even about Luvsan.

He peered out into the hallway again. The group had disappeared into the room where Muunokhoi had been waiting. He could hear the sound of voices—largely Muunokhoi's, he suspected, though it was difficult to be sure—carrying down the hallway.

Tunjin took the opportunity to reach out and remove the key, ensuring that he would not find himself accidentally locked in the cellar, then stepped back and allowed the door to close fully, while he thought through his actions. He needed to move quickly, he thought, while the group was still together in that room. If he allowed them to separate, or if any of Muunokhoi's heavies stumbled across the dead body, his task would become impossible.

He straightened up and took a deep breath. It was a long time since he had had any kind of a drink. There would have been a time—a very recent time, he realised with a shock—when he would have thought that an impossible achievement, the pinnacle of his ambition. Now, it seemed irrelevant. Not that the craving for alcohol had vanished. On the contrary, he would have given almost anything for a drink just at the moment.

He reached out to open the door. And then there was another heart-stopping moment, as he heard a clear footstep on the concrete floor of the cellar behind him. He spun round, cursing himself for not having checked properly that the cellar was empty.

As he turned, a voice, softer than he would have expected said, "So you've come for me, then? At last."

TWENTY-THREE

"It has been a long time," Muunokhoi said. "I presumed that even your persistence had its limits."

Nergui shrugged. "I take the long view," he said. "But I rarely give up."

Muunokhoi nodded, his mouth smiling, his eyes as dead as ever. "As you say. Though I think your investigations have always proved fruitless. I have considered bringing a formal complaint before now. But I understand that you and your colleagues—" He nodded vaguely towards Doripalam, "—have a job to do."

"We do our best," Nergui said. His gaze rested, just for a moment, on Luvsan. Then he looked back at Muunokhoi. "Now," he said, "perhaps you will tell us what this is all about."

"I think you know what it's all about, Nergui," Muunokhoi said, quietly.

Nergui nodded, as though giving serious consideration to this assertion. He looked around the plush reception room.

It looked, at the moment, like some bizarre house party. He and Doripalam had been seated on a large, overstuffed sofa, with Kadyr hunched beside them, his face knotted into an expression of pure fear. Muunokhoi sat opposite, in a comfortable looking armchair. Luvsan and Tsend, along with what were presumably a couple of Muunokhoi's security staff, were seated on hard chairs around a mahogany table, watching the interchange.

"I know what some of it's about," Nergui said at last. "But by no means all. I suspect that I know rather less than you think I do." He paused, his gaze fixed on Muunokhoi. "Though, in some respects, perhaps also rather more."

"Opaque as ever, Nergui," Muunokhoi said, with a touch of harshness in his tone. "But I'm sure we will be dazzled by your insights."

"I have limited skills," Nergui said. "I used them as best I can. Shall I tell you what I think I know?"

Muunokhoi sat back in his chair. "I am keen to hear."

"I know quite a few things," Nergui said. "It is really a question of where to start. I know, for example, that yours is the most destructive, corrupt regime that has ever gained any kind of power in this country. Which is quite an achievement, when you consider the kinds of power that have been wielded here over the centuries. I know that despite that—or, to be frank, because of that—you exercise enormous influence in all aspects of our daily lives, both through your legitimate business dealings and through the more—sordid aspects of your activities. I know that more people are in your pocket than I could begin to conceive—" He gestured elegantly towards Luvsan at the table. "Though I am not sure that you always pick your servants wisely. Luvsan's taste for fast cars—for expensive fast cars—had already made him a prime candidate in my investigations."

"Though too late as always, I note," Muunokhoi said. "Your

views on my business influence are most interesting, but I am not sure that they are entirely pertinent."

"They are no doubt entirely impertinent," Nergui said. "But they are sincerely held and, I think, very relevant to our—presence here today." He paused, his face as expressionless as ever, his eyes firmly fixed on Muunokhoi's blank gaze. "We are here because, for the first time in twenty years, you feel vulnerable. You think your regime is under threat."

Muunokhoi laughed suddenly, though there was no humour in his expression. "Really? And yet I think it is you who are here, at my behest, betrayed by one of your own officers."

Nergui shrugged. "That seems to be the case. But the question is why you brought us here in the first place. And why you kidnapped Mrs. Radnaa. And, for that matter, why you had Mrs. Tuya killed."

For the first time, Muunokhoi looked at Nergui with something approaching interest. "Who is Mrs. Tuya?"

It was Nergui's turn to laugh, and he seemed genuinely amused. Doripalam glanced across at him, as astonished by his apparent good humour as by what he was saying. Sometimes he wondered quite what it would take to shake Nergui's confidence.

Nergui turned, still smiling, to the young man sitting cowering next to them on the voluminous sofa. "Mrs. Tuya," he said, "is this young man's mother." He paused, enjoying the silence while those around absorbed this information. "And this young man," he said, turning back to Muunokhoi, "is of course your son."

The silence was even more protracted this time. Doripalam stared at Nergui, wondering just what kind of complex game he was playing. Kadyr was looking more terrified than ever, his body twisted as though he hoped that the bulk of the sofa might swallow him up.

"I'd heard you were smart, Nergui," Muunokhoi said at last. "But I never knew you had such an imagination."

"Perhaps I am simply making a fool of myself," Nergui said, still smiling. "But since you are not planning to allow to us leave here alive, I think that is a fairly minor consideration."

Muunokhoi looked between Nergui and Doripalam. "We can reach some accommodation," he said. "Things are not so absolute."

Nergui shook his head. "I don't really see what accommodation is possible. We know the truth about you, or at least something approaching the truth. And you have already committed a serious offence simply by bringing us here. I don't see that you can let us go."

"I'm sure we can reach some accommodation," Muunokhoi repeated. "Once things have been resolved."

"I don't think so." He glanced across at Luvsan. "Not everybody has a price."

He's right, Doripalam thought. We're dead. If we were different people, Muunokhoi might be able to walk away from this. We might be able to walk away from this. But Nergui would never do that. And, Doripalam realised, neither would he.

Muunokhoi stared at Doripalam, as though expecting him to disagree with Nergui. But Doripalam simply shook his head. "He's right," he said. "There's no accommodation."

Muunokhoi shook his head. "Perhaps you are right," he said. "In which case, I am sorry. I simply want what is mine."

"Nothing is yours," Nergui said. "Everything you have is stolen. Or corrupt."

"You know nothing. You have been pursuing a vendetta for twenty years. You see me as a symbol of all that you think is wrong in this country. But you have never been able to lay a finger on me. You know nothing."

Nergui smiled. "You've always been a step ahead. Perhaps

you still are. You will walk away from this and we will not. But it's not true that I know nothing. I don't know everything. But I know a lot."

Muunokhoi stared at him, his eyes as blank as ever. "Go ahead," he said. "What do you know?"

"Your story," Nergui said. "Which begins a long time ago. Sixteen, seventeen years ago, I guess. It is difficult for us to remember now. You have been so good at building your own mythology. But you were not quite then the power you are today. You were small time."

For the first time, Doripalam thought that Nergui might have got under Muunokhoi's skin. "I was bigger than you'll ever be, Nergui. What were you in those days? A secret policeman?"

"Something like that, I suppose. But you were—what? A small-time crook with a lot of ambition. Protection rackets. Smuggling from Russia and China. Small-scale drug dealing. Prostitution. Illegal gambling. Anything where you could turn a quick buck." He paused. "We could have had you then, but we didn't take you seriously enough."

"Not usually one of your failings, Nergui."

"We had other things on our minds," Nergui smiled. "The state was more concerned with what was happening in the Soviet Union than with petty criminals. Except that, for exactly that reason, you weren't going to be petty much longer. All those changes across the border would start to open doors for you. And then you made what probably seemed to others a pretty dumb business decision. You went into partnership with Gansukh."

Muunokhoi raised his eyebrows, as though about to challenge this assessment of his business acumen, but he remained silent.

"Perhaps I'm giving you too much credit," Nergui went on, "but I don't think you were taken in by Gansukh's bravado. You saw him for what he was. Small-time, no brains, a risk-taker.

Gansukh was dispensable. But he had one thing that you didn't. He—or at least his associate Khenbish—had good contacts in the drugs trade. I'm not entirely sure how he acquired them even now—I don't imagine, even in those confused days, that it was easy to develop those kinds of networks as a soldier in Afghanistan. But Khenbish *was* smart. He *was* like you. If you'd let him live, he might be sitting in your place today."

"You've no idea what you're talking about, Nergui. I'm not the only one skilled at mythmaking."

Nergui leaned forward in his seat, staring at Muunokhoi. "I got close to the story at the time, but not close enough to pin you down. You brought Gansukh and Khenbish on board. They didn't have the resources or expertise to take advantage of their contacts, but you did. You tried to muscle in, but Khenbish was too smart for that. He insisted on a deal." Nergui paused. "And for the first and probably last time in your business career, you were forced into the open. You knew how important this was. You knew the opportunity that was out there. And you knew it couldn't be left to intermediaries. This had to be face to face, with them and with their contacts."

Nergui's voice was hypnotic in the silent room. Doripalam watched him in something close to awe. Muunokhoi was a charismatic figure, capable of dominating a room without obviously trying. But Nergui was matching him easily.

"And it was worth the risk," Nergui said. "You established a dominance in the drugs field just at the right time. The iron curtain was crumbling, the borders were opening and chaos was spreading across eastern Europe. By the time the game might have been open to other players, you had it sewn up. It's been the foundation of your empire ever since, the base on which everything else—the energy interests, the media empire, everything—has been built." He paused. "But it's also your one area of vulnerability."

"I should simply kill you now, Nergui," Muunokhoi said,

dismissively. "It would save us from listening to this nonsense." But there was something in his tone that belied the words, as if, finally, he wanted the story to be told.

"You exposed yourself too much," Nergui said. "Gansukh and Khenbish weren't to be trusted. I imagine they tried to blackmail you, tried to squeeze out a better deal. Even then, you had a lot more to lose than they did. You were building a public profile, making friends in the right places, developing the networks that have served you ever since. You needed Gansukh and Khenbish, or at least you needed what they could bring you, but you couldn't afford to be held to ransom by two small-time crooks." Nergui hesitated, as though he were just at that moment working out the final details of his story. "So you had Khenbish killed. Not difficult. He was a serving soldier. He drank heavily. He'd made enemies in the army and outside. And, before he was killed, you tried to make him tell you what information he had. But Khenbish, being the smart one, tried to buy his own life by laying the blame on Gansukh—it was him behind the blackmail attempt, he had the incriminating material, all that. It didn't matter whether you believed him or not. When you couldn't get anything else from him, you had him killed anyway. Then you went after Gansukh."

"It was your people who went after Gansukh, if you remember," Muunokhoi said.

Nergui nodded. "Gansukh's usual inept sense of timing. You were coming to get him, but instead he managed to get himself arrested. And then, like Khenbish, he tried to talk his way out of trouble by claiming that he had useful things to tell us." Nergui stopped again, and then continued almost wistfully. "And maybe he had. I really thought, just for a moment, that I might have had you then."

"So where does this leave you, Nergui? All this nostalgia for two decades ago, and the vendetta you've waged against me ever since?"

Nergui smiled. "I don't know where it leaves me. But it left you, Muunokhoi, in a very interesting place. There's one part of the story we haven't touched on yet. Your affair with Khenbish's wife. Mrs. Tuya. A very attractive woman in those days, I imagine, though I don't know if that's what you were interested in. If I'm not drifting too far into the realms of psychology, maybe it was a power issue. You'd given a lot of ground to Khenbish. Perhaps you wanted to get some back. And, traditionalist that you are, you did it in the way that would have most impact on an old-fashioned Mongolian male. Possibly you even took steps to ensure that he knew, or at least suspected. And one side effect, if you'll excuse me—" Nergui gestured apologetically towards the cowering young man, "—is this poor individual, who was introduced to us as Kadyr, one of Mrs. Tuya's cousins, but who is, of course, Gavaa, her son. Who has spent the last few weeks on the run from you. No wonder he looks terrified."

"He's no son of mine," Muunokhoi said.

Nergui shrugged. "I don't see any strong resemblance at the moment. But you believed he was. And it suited you to allow his mother to think so."

Muunokhoi shook his head. "You're rambling, Nergui."

Nergui continued as though Muunokhoi hadn't spoken. "Gansukh and Khenbish were both dead. But you still didn't know whether there was anything incriminating out there. You searched Gansukh's flat. I imagine you did the same with Khenbish's. But you found nothing. For a while, you lived with the fear that they might somehow have arranged for the material to be released posthumously. But it didn't happen. And you'd put in place an insurance policy of your own. You encouraged Mrs. Tuya to believe that Gavaa was your son, and you offered to pay her a very generous continuing allowance. If she had the materials, or if she knew where they were, there was a strong incentive for her not to use them. And, over time, nothing happened, and you allowed yourself to relax a little, assuming that now nothing ever would."

Muunokhoi smiled. "So tell me why, eighteen years down the road, I should suddenly take an interest in all this?"

"Well, that is the question, isn't it?" Nergui said. "As I see it, a combination of things all happened at once. The most important one, I'm sure, is that young Gavaa here found himself on the brink of adulthood. His mother realised that, before long, the allowance was going to cease. So she made one last request. Or was it a demand? She asked you to take him into the family business."

Gavaa sat forward, looking as if he had suddenly returned to life. "She didn't do that. It was nothing to do with her. I made the contact. She always thought she had to do everything. But it was me. I wasn't going to be stuck out there forever, herding sheep. I wanted to be—"

"Like your father?"

The young man nodded, his face reddening. "I suppose so. He'd talked to people—to my uncles and others—years ago about how he was working with Muunokhoi—this was when Muunokhoi was just beginning to become a public figure—about how he had Muunokhoi just where he wanted because he had evidence that would bring him down. Nobody believed him. They thought it was just the drink talking. And, years later, when Muunokhoi became really famous, my uncles used to tell the stories, laughing at what my father had claimed, making a fool of him—"

"But you thought he had been telling the truth?"

"I knew he'd been telling the truth. He was a clever man and a brave one." He stopped and looked at Muunokhoi. "Worth ten of this—"

"So you approached Muunokhoi?"

"Yes. I made contact. It wasn't easy. But when he realised

who I was he agreed to see me. I didn't threaten him or anything—"

Muunokhoi laughed harshly. The words sounded absurd coming from the mouth of the trembling teenager, but Nergui seemed to be taking him seriously.

"Of course you didn't," Nergui said. "You just talked about your father and how he'd worked with Muunokhoi. And you asked whether Muunokhoi would be prepared to give you a job."

"That's what happened," Gavaa said, miserably. "I just thought that—well, that he must have respected my father. That he'd want to help."

"You didn't know that he'd been paying an allowance to your mother all your life? That he might be your father?"

"He's not my father," the boy said indignantly. "But, no, I didn't know any of that. I was just using my initiative. Following up my father's networks. And it worked. He took me on. Said he wanted me to be his—"

"Protégé?" Nergui prompted.

"Something like that. He wanted to honour my father's memory—"

Nergui turned to Muunokhoi. "It was just another lever for you. Another insurance policy. Make sure he was with you, implicated in everything you did. Even if his mother did have any dirt on you, she couldn't use it."

Muunokhoi opened his mouth to say something but the boy interrupted before he could speak.

"That's exactly it," he said. "Exactly what he did. I thought he was going to involve me in the business but he didn't. He put me with his heavies, his—security team—" He stopped, almost sobbing now, then continued, barely in control. "We killed someone. The second day I was there." His eyes were wide, staring at the ground, but it wasn't clear what he was actually seeing. "They called it discipline," he said. "Someone who'd—I don't know—but they were going to punish him. I had to go, they said, so I'd understand how things were done. I thought—I thought they were just going to burn the car. I thought it must be his car—the person they were punishing." He paused, hardly able to continue. "But he was inside, locked in the boot. They told me later, but I already knew. And they said it should be a lesson to me if I ever did anything—"

Muunokhoi shook his head and climbed slowly to his feet. "Enough of these stories," he said. "Why do you think I am interested? Why do you think I brought you here?"

Nergui shrugged. "I presume for the same reason you brought Mrs. Radnaa here. Or wherever you've taken her."

Muunokhoi laughed. In other circumstances, Doripalam thought, it would have been fascinating to watch this clash of egos. Muunokhoi was standing, looking as if it was he who was out of his familiar element, trying to regain some ground.

"You're right, of course, Nergui," Muunokhoi said. "I wanted you here initially because of Mrs. Radnaa. I thought she might have given you—whatever she had." For a moment, he looked confused as if suddenly even he was unsure where all this was heading. "But that is unimportant now. If you and your colleague—" He glanced down at Doripalam. "If you and your colleague are out of the picture, then I no longer need to have any concerns about what incriminating material might be out there."

"What makes you think that?" Doripalam said, speaking for the first time. "Nergui and I are just two small parts of the machine. If there is something out there to incriminate you, it will see the light eventually."

"Do you really believe that?" Muunokhoi said. "You're even more naïve than you look. Do you really understand the nature of the team you supposedly lead? I think Nergui knows better."

"You don't own everyone," Nergui said. "Not every officer is in your pocket."

"Of course not. I would not be so presumptuous. But I own, as you put it, most of those who matter. Yourselves excluded, of course." He glanced across at Luvsan, who avoided his gaze. "Luvsan is one of my most loyal and proactive servants, but he is by no means the only one. I think that now I can be reasonably confident that, even if some material does emerge, it will be handled with—discretion."

"So what are you planning to do with us?" Doripalam said. "Even you wouldn't dare to kill two senior government officials."

Muunokhoi smiled. "You really don't understand this, do you? You really don't understand me. I can do anything. I'm the power in this country now. Me and people like me."

There was a moment's silence. Then Nergui said, his face as expressionless as ever: "I haven't finished telling the story yet. Perhaps I should."

"There's no need, Nergui," Muunokhoi said. "I think we all know how the story is going to end."

"Go on, then. You may as well get on with it," she said.

Tunjin stared down at the woman, wondering what she was talking about. "I don't—"

"Are you the best they could find?" she said. "Still, I don't imagine they expected much resistance. Maybe I should try to prove them wrong."

She looked vaguely familiar, he thought. A very elegant middle-aged woman, now slightly dishevelled. Perhaps she was one of Muunokhoi's girlfriends, maybe a celebrity of some kind. But, if so, what was she doing in the cellar? Perhaps she'd just been down here for some reason and had assumed him to be—what? A burglar? It was as if she had been expecting him.

Tunjin held up his hands, realising too late that he was holding a gun in one of them. "I'm sorry," he said. "I'm not going to hurt you."

Her eyes opened in surprise. "You aren't? Then why are you here? I told Muunokhoi, I don't have anything. I can't harm him. He's made a mistake." She paused, thinking that it was worth one last effort. "He can let me go. I mean, I'm not pleased about any of this. But I'm not going to make an issue of it. Not if he just lets me go."

Tunjin blinked at her, trying to work this out. "Muunokhoi is holding you against your will?"

"Well, of course he is." She looked around the empty cellar. "Did you think I was enticed by the comfortable environment?"

"No, but—" He was finally beginning to work out the misunderstanding here. "I don't work for Muunokhoi." He smiled, finally, with the recognition that he and this woman might be potential allies. "I'm a stranger here myself," he said. "That is, I'm an intruder. I broke into the house."

"A brave intruder, then," she said, trying to understand this. "I don't imagine many people choose to break in here."

"It's a long story," he said. "But I'm not a thief. I'm a policeman." He paused. "Or at least I was."

She nodded, trying to behave as if this was the most natural conversation to have while locked in an empty cellar. Or rather, she thought suddenly, reflecting on Tunjin's presence, now apparently not locked in a cellar. "Well, that's obviously destiny," she said, "because I'm a judge."

"A judge?" He stared at her for a moment, as his brain made connections. So that was why she'd looked familiar. She'd been pointed out to him—before everything fell apart—as the judge in Muunokhoi's aborted trial. "Is that why you're here?"

She shook her head. "Not exactly. It's another long story. And one I'm not sure I understand myself." She looked behind him at the stone stairs rising up to the cellar entrance, conscious that at any moment they might receive another, less welcome visitor. "Look, I don't know why you're here," she said. "But can you get us out of here? The cellar, I mean."

Tunjin produced the heavy key from his pocket. "From the cellar, yes. But I don't know that we'll be able to get out of the house. It's very secure. Cameras. Guards. You name it. They'd stop us before we'd got five metres."

"What about you?" she said. "How were you planning to get out?"

He shrugged. "I wasn't, really. I'd resigned myself to the fact that I wasn't going to."

She stared at him. "What do you mean? What were you going to do?"

"I was going to kill Muunokhoi," he said, simply. "I thought it would be a public service. If I don't, he'll kill me anyway. So I might as well try to get a two-way deal. But—" He paused, as if a new thought had struck him. "I don't know what will happen to the rest of them."

"The rest of them?"

"You're not the only captive here. Muunokhoi has more upstairs." He stopped. "He's gone mad. He really must be insane."

"What captives? Who?"

He shook his head. "Police officers. Senior officers. Ministry officials. He's insane."

She was staring at him aghast. "Ministry officials? Who do you mean?"

"It's unbelievable," he said. "You know Nergui? Used to be our chief. And Doripalam. He's our chief now. They're both there."

"Nergui?" she said, with a look more despairing than he

might have expected. "That must be because of me. That's my fault. He warned me. Muunokhoi warned me. But I never imagined he could do it so quickly."

"I think none of us know what Muunokhoi is capable of," he said. "Some of us thought we knew. But we've always fallen short. He's always been one step ahead." He looked at the elegant Mrs. Radnaa, wondering how it could be that Nergui's imprisonment here could be her fault.

"We have to do it," she said. "You're right. Nergui wouldn't want us to hesitate. If we don't do it, they're dead anyway. We're all dead anyway."

He nodded. There was no question really. The only issue was whether, talking like this, they had now left it too long, missed their opportunity.

And that question was answered almost immediately by the sound of the cellar door opening above them.

"I think it is time," Muunokhoi said, "for you to be reunited with Mrs. Radnaa. It will be very touching."

Nergui said nothing, and his face gave nothing away. His pale blue eyes were blazing but there was no way of reading his emotions. Doripalam, a step or two behind, tried to emulate the older man's apparent lack of emotion, but feared that he was far from successful. Perhaps Nergui had some plan up his sleeve, but it was difficult to conceive what it might be. There could be no way out of this. He glanced back at Luvsan, who was standing holding his gun, apparently casual, but careful not to catch Doripalam's gaze. I hope he feels it's worth whatever he's getting for this, Doripalam thought.

They were standing outside the door of the cellar. Muunokhoi reached forward and then stopped, looking quizzically around at his henchmen. "Who's got the key? I left it here."

There was a moment's silence. Muunokhoi turned the handle, clearly not expecting the door to open. He stepped back in surprise as it swung back easily. "Who's been in here?" he said. He looked at each of them in turn. "One of you idiots forgot to lock it."

Again, there was no response. Doripalam looked around at the group. It wasn't difficult to gauge what they were thinking. It was Muunokhoi who had come out of that door last. It was Muunokhoi who had failed to lock it behind him. It was Muunokhoi—they were thinking but dared not say—who was losing it.

"She can't have got out, anyway," Muunokhoi said, as if to reassure himself. "Just be more careful next time, whoever it was."

He pulled open the door and then stared down the stairway. At the bottom, just visible, Mrs. Radnaa was standing. He could see little more than a silhouette. She stood, apparently calmly, as though awaiting an expected visitor.

Muunokhoi stepped aside and gestured Nergui, Doripalam and Gavaa to step forward onto the top landing. Doripalam hesitated on the threshold, recognising that there was likely to be no way back from this point, wondering how it might be possible to resist.

There was, it turned out, no opportunity. Seeing Doripalam's hesitation, Muunokhoi gestured to Luvsan, who stepped forward and, raising his gun, slammed it hard against his former chief's head. Doripalam collapsed forward, staggering onto the top of the steps, and then fell halfway down the stone flight, hitting his head against the wall. He lay, sprawled and motionless, his body twisted. There was no way of telling whether he was still alive.

There was a moment's pause, as if everyone had stopped breathing in sympathy. Then, moving with extraordinary speed,

Nergui grabbed Luvsan's gun arm and twisted it painfully. Somehow managing to remove the gun in the process, he turned and threw Luvsan past Doripalam's prone body down the stairs. Luvsan hit the concrete floor with a sickening thump and lay still. This time, there seemed little doubt about his mortality.

Nergui turned, grabbed Gavaa and pulled him behind him, trying to keep the boy safe. There was confusion as Muunokhoi's henchmen struggled to pull out their guns. Nergui shot one before he could move and the man fell back, pumping blood thickly onto Muunokhoi's thick carpet. The second had his gun out but Nergui was close enough to slam Luvsan's pistol hard down on the man's arm. He screamed, dropped the gun, and let out a painful, half-swallowed shout as Nergui thrust the pistol hard against his head. The man reeled back, tripped over his colleague, and fell in a heap on the floor, barely conscious.

For a second, there was no sound. Nergui looked back at Muunokhoi, expecting to find that Muunokhoi's weapon was pointed firmly at his own head or heart.

But it wasn't. Instead, Muunokhoi was staring down into the cellar, his gun pointed towards Sarangarel. He began to walk slowly down the steps. "Don't try anything, Nergui. I'm too quick for you. If you shoot me, Mrs. Radnaa will be dead before I am. You would not want that on your conscience."

Nergui hesitated, unsure whether Muunokhoi was capable of carrying out this threat. But he knew from bitter experience the risks of underestimating Muunokhoi's capability in any field.

Muunokhoi moved slowly and smoothly down the steps until he was a metre or so from Sarangarel. "Kill him," she said, calmly. "It doesn't matter what he does to me. It's worth it."

Nergui raised his gun, but could do nothing, his finger frozen on the trigger. "Nergui," she called out, "if you don't, he'll kill me anyway. He'll use me as a hostage as long as it suits him. He'll get away again. So kill him now. It doesn't matter about me."

She was right, of course. He knew she was right. But Muunokhoi, one step ahead as always, had judged that this was the one thing that Nergui would not be able to do. The one thing he could not have on his conscience.

Muunokhoi stepped behind Sarangarel, raising the gun barrel towards her head.

She was right, of course. Of course she was. In any moment, the last chance would have gone and they would be back to playing Muunokhoi's game.

In the final moment before Muunokhoi raised his gun to Sarangarel's temple, Nergui finally lifted his own gun. And a shot echoed round the empty cellar.

TWENTY-FOUR

The prayer wheels were spinning somewhere behind them and they could hear the sonorous chanting of the monks. It was a hypnotic sound, at one with the breath of the wind and the cries of the children from the park below. The pure blue sky seemed endless, echoing the eternal sweep of the green steppe beyond the city.

"I could get used to this," Doripalam said. "So long as you were doing the pushing."

"You do realise quite how vulnerable you are up here?" Nergui said, taking the wheelchair to the edge of the slope down to the park. "I could simply let go and you'd roll all the way down till you hit something."

"Solongo's already pointed that out," Doripalam said. "Quite forcibly, in fact. I think it's her way of expressing her affection for me." Her reaction had been a characteristic mixture of concern for his condition and disapproval of the fact that he had allowed it to happen. He was hoping that, for the moment at least, the concern would remain paramount.

Nergui nodded, watching the flight of some bird of prey across the empty sky. The weather was finally warming up. It would be summer soon. "You'd better keep on the right side of her, then," he said. "We need you back at work as soon as possible. Now especially. The Minister isn't happy at losing my services while I cover for you."

"There's no one else, though, is there? No one we can trust, I mean."

"There are some I think we can. But nobody with enough experience to cover for you while we start to clean things up."

"And we don't know who's straight and who isn't. We don't know how much Muunokhoi was exaggerating."

Nergui shrugged. "Muunokhoi had countless faults. But he had no need to exaggerate his influence. It's a hard one. I've got some clues from the enquiries I was already conducting. And it should be easier now, with Muunokhoi out of the picture. There's no one to protect them."

"But there's also nothing to protect. With Muunokhoi gone—well, they're not corrupt cops any more. Not active ones, anyhow. There may be nothing to find."

"If they've been corrupt once, they'll be corrupt again. Integrity's like virginity. You can't get it back."

"Very philosophical," Doripalam said, wondering if this was an apposite moment to ask about Mrs. Radnaa.

Nergui had described those final moments in the cellar, but even now Doripalam could barely imagine what it must have felt like. When, at the sound of the single gunshot, Mrs. Radnaa had fallen, leaving Muunokhoi standing over her. Nergui had stared at his own hand, certain that he had not yet fired, but certain also that Muunokhoi had not shot Sarangarel, that the bullet had come from somewhere else. He glanced behind him, but there was no sign of movement from the two henchmen.

And then, just as the horror was rising in Nergui's throat, Muunokhoi had finally staggered forwards, his body twisting, and Nergui had seen the blood pouring from his back. It was as if, in those few seconds, Muunokhoi had been focusing every last ounce of will in a desperate effort to deny the inevitability of his own death. But then there was a second shot and Muunokhoi's head had exploded as his body crashed down onto the stone floor. By then, mercifully, Sarangarel was already unconscious.

As so often, it was as if Nergui had read Doripalam's thoughts. "I saw her—Mrs. Radnaa—this morning. She's recovering well. There was no serious physical hurt. Her collapse was mainly shock."

Was it corruption, Doripalam wondered, to bury the disciplinary charges against Tunjin? The shooting of Muunokhoi had been unavoidable, but Tunjin had been a long way from following any established procedures. And there was also the indisputable fact that, at the time of the killing, Tunjin had still been formally suspended from duty.

But Nergui had had no concerns about these niceties, and had applied his ministerial authority accordingly. Tunjin had saved their lives. Tunjin was unquestionably straight, one of the few about whom they could be certain. He was the kind of man they needed in the force. Tunjin himself—or so Doripalam had been told—had celebrated his return to duty by downing a bottle of vodka. Or possibly two.

"You never did finish the story," Doripalam said.

"I never did, did I? But you will have worked it out for yourself."

"Humour me," Doripalam said.

Nergui smiled. "So what did we have? We had Muunokhoi

trying to terrify the life out of poor Gavaa. Who, to do him credit, didn't go along with all the things that Muunokhoi was showing him, but made his exit as soon as possible. And did the only thing that an eighteen-year-old boy can do in those circumstances."

Doripalam raised an eyebrow. "Which is?"

"Go home to his mother. Whatever's gone on between them, his mother will always take him back in. He tells her the whole story, and she's scared out of her wits. She knows Muunokhoi. She knows what he's capable of. She knows how paranoid and vindictive he is and that he's not going to let the boy out of his clutches. So she hides Gavaa, hoping that she'll be able to look after him till Muunokhoi's wrath subsides. And she even makes a lot of fuss about going to the press and the police about her poor missing boy, just so that Muunokhoi will never think that the boy's being hidden as part of her family." Nergui stops and smiles. "She was a resourceful woman, gives nothing away even when Muunokhoi's heavies turn up. But then, maybe inevitably, one day Muunokhoi himself arrives. Maybe he tries to remind her of old times, tells her again that Gavaa is probably his son. Maybe he threatens all kinds of things." He paused.

Nergui began to push the wheelchair back up the slope towards the temple. "But she's smart. When she sees the way the conversation is going, she starts to intimate that maybe she's got some evidence that Muunokhoi wouldn't like to see the light of day. She threatens Muunokhoi with exposure if he doesn't forget about her son. And Muunokhoi's response is—"

"To murder her in cold blood."

"Indeed. But not, as we know, before he also subjected her to some dreadful abuse, trying to force her to reveal her son's whereabouts. Which, of course, being a mother she did not."

"An interesting way to treat your ex-lover. And the supposed mother of your son. And Gavaa himself had already gone off with the rest of the family, pretending to be a cousin."

"Exactly. Which is why they were so terrified about anybody—that is, Muunokhoi—catching up with them. Which, with a little help from our friend in the north, he eventually did." They had still not managed to track down the bodies of Gavaa's three relatives. Gavaa had told them how a team of police officers, apparently from Tsend's team, had arrived in the camp in the middle of the night, dragging out the three men. Gavaa himself had been hidden away from the main camp, just in case of such an eventuality. He had heard the cries of the men being dragged away, supposedly under arrest, and had hidden himself further into the woods, emerging only once the team had gone leaving behind a solitary sentinel in case Gavaa should return. But it was the guard himself who had been taken by surprise as Gavaa had obtained at least some small revenge.

Tsend had been arrested and was being questioned, but to date had denied all knowledge of the men's supposed arrest, as had all other officers in the Bulgan force. Maybe they would find the bodies one day, Doripalam thought, though Tsend was likely to have covered his tracks well.

Doripalam looked up at the line of monks crossing the path, still chanting. "But what about this supposed evidence? Do you think Mrs. Tuya really had it?"

Nergui shrugged. "Who knows? Maybe it never existed. Gansukh and Khenbish were quite capable of living in a fantasy world and helping others to do the same. I can easily imagine that, having tried to gather meaningful stuff, Gansukh just faked some more serious evidence to keep Muunokhoi at bay. Maybe they really were just a bit too smart for Muunokhoi. And a bit too smart for their own good."

"So all this was for nothing?"

"I fear so. But I think Muunokhoi had hit the paranoid stage long before this. He saw everything as a threat. All of this must have seemed—well, preordained. Muunokhoi found himself sitting in court for the first time in his life. A court overseen by the wife of the man he killed. I imagine he would have been scarcely able to believe it. Even though the trial collapsed, it might have been enough—with all of this going on—to tip him over the edge."

"You think he went mad?"

"I think his world was much less stable and secure than he had imagined. I think he saw some cracks beginning to show. There was probably some justification to his paranoia. But, yes, in the end, I think he went mad."

They had stopped at the edge of the temple ground, looking out over the windy spaces of Nairamdal Park. Below, the weathered amusement rides glittered faintly in the early afternoon sun. Children were racing across the grass, shouting and playing games. Clusters of old men smoked and talked, wrapped in their unseasonable *dels*. Beyond the park, there was the endless grassland, the distant mountains, the land without boundaries. Life continuing.

"So what now?" Doripalam said.

"We have a job to do," Nergui said. "Muunokhoi is gone. Most people won't know why or how. A lot of people will mourn him." No one had challenged Nergui's account of events—people did not tend to challenge Nergui on such matters—but there had been no desire, from the Minister upwards, to make the circumstances of Muunokhoi's death public knowledge. He had, it appeared, died unexpectedly of natural causes after a short illness. Which, Doripalam acknowledged, was at least a version of the truth.

"And there will be other Muunokhois coming to fill the vacuum. It's the way of things. Our world here is changing. We can't stop that. We can even welcome it. But we have to hold a line, make sure we retain control." They listened to the distant sound of the monks enacting their ancient rituals in the ornate buildings behind them. "We have a job to do," he said again.